Heart of a Pirate

A Novel of Anne Bonny

Pamela Johnson

Stone Harbour Press
Berkeley, California • Ocho Rios, Jamaica

Stone Harbour Press

This is a work of fiction. Names, characters, places, and incidents are the products of the author's imagination or are used fictitiously. Any resemblance to actual events, locales, or persons, living or dead, is entirely coincidental.

Copyright © 2009 by Pamela Johnson. All rights reserved.

No part of this book may be used or reproduced in any manner whatsoever without written permission. For information contact Stone Harbour Press.

First edition.

ISBN 978-0-615-27560-4

Published in the United States by Stone Harbour Press
P.O. Box 186
Oregon House, California 95962

www.stoneharbourpress.com

For Erik

Whose love made this work possible

Acknowledgements

As in any endeavor, a finished product never belongs to any one person. With a full heart, I must gratefully acknowledge and offer thanks to the many who helped bring this work to fruition.

Primary among those is Donald Ellis, publisher, whose unwavering encouragement, guidance, expertise, and unequivocal friendship was the force behind this publication. Words cannot express my gratitude for his generosity of time and spirit.

To the manuscript readers and editors, who took the time to make this a better work with insightful and critical feedback, especially, Wendy Pearl for her initial encouragement, Phyllis Partain, Katherine Czesak, Cynthia Josayma, Patrice Robson, David Cour, Neil Robson, Daniel David, Timothy Scully, Ann Einhorn, Paul Smith, Kelsey Magness, and Erin Thomas, and in Jamaica, Carla Dunlop, David Mais, Anthony Pasmore, and Annie Paul. To Kathleen Caswell for suggesting the title of the book. To Patti Buckley for kindly forwarding a picture of the author. Special, eternal thanks to Wendy Lee in Jamaica for her final, brilliant copy editing of the novel.

To Paul Samuelson, editor, for his several readings and professional suggestions, who saw the possibilities of the novel and actively promoted the book.

To Wayne Pope for his typesetting and cover design, and Randy Gallegos for his conception of Anne in the original art of the cover. Their assistance in style and art made this book a more interesting work to read.

To the pirates of Taft Federal Institution for their careful reading, chapter by chapter, for their patience and courage, and for their knowledge and understanding of the themes of the story. You know who you are.

For the writers of the Backroom Writing Group, who generously read the Prologue more than once and offered many helpful suggestions.

To Dr. Marcus Rediker of the University of Pittsburg who found time in his busy schedule to read the Writer's Preface, corrected my historical research, and who graciously allowed me the use of many of his insightful and innovative ideas on 18th century capitalism.

To the librarians of the National Library, Kingston Jamaica, for their assistance in primary text research.

To Erin, Owen, and Adam, who spent many a day watching Mum write and wondering where it would all lead, but whose love has given me courage and carried me through indecision. For Sophie and Danielle who love these sons of mine, and who have been daughters to me.

For Nicolas, pirate *extraordinaire,* who writes his own stories of Anne Bonny, and for Liam, and Emery, who also give meaning to my life.

Finally and foremost to Erik, my husband, who was not only the inspiration for the story, but who has stood by me through months of writing and rewriting, offering helpful suggestions and support of every kind. For him my love and gratitude knows no bounds.

. . . damn ye, you are a sneaking Puppy, and so are all those who will submit to be governed by Laws which rich men have made for their own Security, for the cowardly Whelps have not the Courage otherwise to defend what they got by their knavery; but damn ye altogether: Damn them for a Pack of crafty Rascals, and you, who serve them, for a Parcel of Hen-hearted Numskuls. They vilify us, the Scoundrels do, when there is only this Difference, they rob the Poor under Cover of Law, forsooth, and we plunder the Rich under the protection of our own Courage.

Charles Bellamy, pirate, lecturing a captured captain

The law locks up the man or woman
Who steals the goose from off the common
But leaves the greater villain loose
Who steals the common from off the goose.

The law demands that we atone
When we take things we do not own
But leaves the lords and ladies fine
Who take things that are yours or mine.

Anonymous
On the Enclosure Movement
18th Century

Author's Forward

At the height of the Golden Age of Piracy, 1716-1726, around four thousand pirates—from Spain, Portugal, the Netherlands, France, England, and Africa—plied their trade from the western coast of Africa to the Caribbean and north to the bays and inlets of the Atlantic Coast, wreaking havoc and plundering merchant ships at a time when trade was a vibrant source of new wealth for European capitalists.

These desperate men were generally in their late twenties and had known war most of their lives. 'Bred to the sea' as young boys, they would have been part of the War of the League of Augsburg, 1689 to 1697, then resumed fighting in the War of Spanish Succession, 1702 to 1713. When that war ended, the British Royal Navy plunged from 49,860 men in 1714 to 13,475 by 1716, leaving many of the unemployed to 'straggle and beg' across Europe, while others chose the only life they had ever known, the taking of enemy ships.

On merchant and naval vessels, sailors would have endured the absolute authority of the captain, overcrowded quarters, poor food and drink, hard work, brutal discipline, low wages, and disease, disabling accidents, and premature death. In contrast, the early eighteenth century pirate ship was an anomaly in a world dictated by rank and privilege. In this alternative society, multi-cultural-national-racial, the Articles of Brotherhood established a new system of justice that limited the authority of the captain, and included reparation for loss of limb, division of the spoils, and democratically elected officers.

The beginning of the eighteenth century also saw massive worldwide migrations. In the Americas hundreds of thousands of Native Americans had died from warfare and disease, while many thousands more had relocated to the interior of the continent. Africa had already given up 2.5 million of its people, sold for transport to the New World and Europe. The Enclosure Movement of England and in other parts of Europe, would dispossess thousands, eventually forcing men, women, and children to take jobs as meager wage earners in factory, army, or navy. Hundreds of thousands more embarked for colonial plantations as laborers, some indentured.

In Ireland, by 1700, two-thirds of ancestral domains had been given to Protestant mercenaries who had accompanied Cromwell in conquering that land, the estates conferred on them by the Act of Settlement of 1662 and the Act of Explanation, 1664. The Irish, subjected to plague, starvation, warfare, and perpetual poverty, and smoldering from the injustice, waged an ongoing subversive war. Looking for support in the return of Catholic lands, an underground resistance made overtures to Spain for financing a rebellion to bring back James, the son of the executed Charles I, to the throne of England. Only then, with a Catholic king, would the old gentry reclaim their lost dominions. The British Crown, worried that a back door to England might be opened through the efforts of these Jacobites, continued its brutal suppression of the Irish people.

Against this background of war on the seas and in Europe, of international relocation, of rebellion in Ireland and the battle between Catholic and Protestant, our story begins. In the city of Cork, Ireland, William Cormac and Peg Brennen, are forced to flee to Charles Town in the Carolinas with their infant daughter, Anne, a child who would one day grow to become the center of legend and a byword for freedom.

The events in this telling are, for the most part, as true to fact as we know. The interpretation is my own.

Prologue

Jamaica

October, 1720

The *William* slid though the sea, guided by pirates still rum drunk, the sun hard on their eyes, the shoreline a distant, green outline of trees and mountains. After the morning's rain, the day had turned as fine as any Anne could remember. A wind blew strong from the east, filling the sails and leaving a frothy wake that encouraged pelicans to dive into the sea. She stood balanced at the aft rail absently watching the birds and looking back over the water. Only when she noticed shadows lengthening on deck, did she think to rest easy, for they were now leagues away from the cave where she had hidden the small chest with its treasure.

"The deed's done," Mary murmured quietly, coming to stand beside her. "No sense in trying to reclaim the past."

"Aye. The deed's done. And Jack'll be fierce angry when he discovers the coin and jewels missing."

"But that's not what troubles you, is it?"

Anne shook her head and cried quietly, "It's all wrong, Mary! God knows that we are in danger. What can Jack be thinking?"

"Cap'n 'll come round," Mary tried reassuring her. "We just need to leave these waters. A few days more 'e's said. No sense running into the last o' the hurricanes."

"There's more," Anne added, her voice lowered, "after yesterday's acts, I think we should remain dressed as men for the time. Keep to the pants, shirt, and jacket. Best not to remind anyone of our sex."

On the day before, there had been an incident that had unnerved both women. Anne and Jack had argued over the offense and a fight had ensued, the first ever contest between them, their swords ringing amidst the cheers of the men.

Looking full into Mary's eyes, she asked softly, "Should I have fought Jack true?"

"Best the Cap'n? Would ye be ready to take control of the ship and crew? Anne, 'tis a hard pass we've come to. Maybe 'tis time for me to find the inn I've wanted."

Anne nodded and covered Mary's hand with her own, "Or possibly a piece of land. For the children we carry."

By late day they had rounded the western end of the island and dropped anchor. Bloody Bay they called this bit of water off the coastline of Jamaica. Here the whalers took shelter and carved their great catch, rendering the fat. With sails stowed and evening soon to come, the men began to think to the accordion and the fiddle and the rum in the hold. On shore were turtle fisherman, and the crew cried for them to come aboard and share in the rum punch and make merry. Even before the sun started to set, they were done, passed out on deck and below, a few drunken voices rising from the hold.

Anne stood at the watch with Mary, absently wrapping her hair in a scarf, the sky deep gold and the red sun quickly descending. A sigh, and she breathed in the full measure of the beauty before her.

Suddenly she froze, and looked intently across the water, wondering if she saw true. She raised a hand to her eyes to shield the glare, the better to be sure.

"The glass!" she cried to Mary, her body no longer accepting the peace of the evening, but hard and ready to move, a flush raising the hairs on her arms. "Give it to me! Oh, God's blood! Pray I am mistaken!"

Lifting the spyglass to the horizon, her heart leapt.

"A sloop! A sail hidden in the sun. On the king's errand as sure as I draw breath! Get Jack up here! Christ, they make straight for us! And quick! They've picked up the wind off the point!"

"By all that's holy, you're right, Anne! Dear God, what're we t' do?"

From below Jack heard their shouts and climbed to the wooden planking, ambling unsteadily across the deck, while Fetherston, his mate, followed in his wake, wavering and just as off course.

"Ah," Jack mumbled, squinting into the fading light. "Mr. Fetherston, my glass."

He lifted lazy eyes to the west, peered, and slurred, "Why, you may be right, Anne. I believe 'tis the gov'nor's ship." He straightened his hat more comfortably upon his head, the long red plume dancing. "Hoist the black flag and show 'em our colors."

"Jack Rackham!" Anne screamed. "'Tis no game! The brig has us if we don't weigh anchor and put on cloth!"

Reeling back and forth on his toes, Jack threw back his head and laughed, for he had looked around the deck at men dead to the world from their drink, considered those out cold below, and knew there was no going anywhere.

Furious, throwing Jack murderous looks as he lifted a bottle and brought it to his lips, Anne primed her pistols and turned to Mary.

"What say ye?" she asked, her eyes wide with uncertainty.

"There's only one thing that can be done," Mary answered taking up a cutlass. "We'll do what we can to protect the other."

"Ahoy, the ship," a voice carried over the water. "Who is your captain?"

"That would be me," Jack shouted in return. "John Rackham of Cuba!"

"I am Captain Jonathan Barnett on the king's mission. I've a warrant for your arrest, Captain Rackham. Surrender peaceably and I will give you quarter."

"The fool gives his own name!" Mary muttered, moving away, thinking to roust the crew. "Curse all the bloody rum in this world! Surely t'was made t' make men stupid!"

"They have us if we do not fight!" Anne cried. "I will not go back to prison, Jack! I swore long ago that I would rather die!"

With grim determination, pistols and cutlass at the ready, Mary pushed and kicked the drunkards where they lay on deck, shouting that they up and make ready.

"You worthless sons of whores!" she screamed when she could get no response. "Do ye want t' die?"

Not until the sloop of Captain Barnett was almost upon them, did Jack's vision clear, and with a rude awakening, realize he stood with drawn sword in one hand and bottle in the other.

"For the love of God," he muttered, "what am I about?"

Tossing the bottle overboard, he rushed to the swivel gun that stood on deck, for there was no time for maneuvering the ship, no time to consider a broadside or rouse the men. Indeed, they were out of time. A roar, and the small cannon he aimed fired, the shot falling short of the on-coming sloop. Those below who could still move, heard the hostilities, and several staggered up top to see what the noise was about.

Barnett was prepared, and without warning, let off a round from his ship's starboard cannon that took part of the rigging of the *William,* yardarm and halyards crashing to the deck, sending the men who had just come up hastening back to safety below.

"On deck!" Anne screamed, rushing to the hold to look down, pistol cocked and ready to fire if they did not obey. "Come back and fight, ye contemptible cowards! Come up and fight like the men ye think yourselves to be! For God's sake, think to your lives!"

"It's no use, Anne!" Jack called to her. "Grappling hooks are at the ready and they'll soon board. We haven't a chance. Not with this lot. I must ask for quarter!"

"You can ask all you want," Anne returned fiercely, reloading from the shot she had fired, "but I'll not be surrenderin'!"

"Nor I!" cried Mary, for both women thought to the children they carried and refused to give birth in a prison.

At that moment the ships touched and the jolt of the meeting was hard, black smoke obscuring sight, debris from the downed rigging still floating through air. Anne whirled on Jack from where they crouched behind the wheel, the better to avoid the musket balls raining down on deck.

"If you give in, you'll only live a few days more," she pleaded. "Blackbeard knew the truth of it. When his end came he chose death on deck to hangin'! Fight, I say! Fight, damn you!"

Jack grabbed her arm and shook her, none too gently, the better to make his point.

"Listen, lass, the Royal Navy hung his head in the ship's riggin'. I'll not have that happen to you. If I surrender at least we have a trial and who knows what might happen."

More sorrowful now than angry, she turned from him, for Barnett's men had come over the side and must be met. Reaching for the pistols in her belt, she aimed and pulled, firing directly into the charge, then drew the sword at her side. Raising it, she stepped forward to meet the first of the attackers.

With startling clarity she made vague note of the man's ruddy face, his determination and clenched teeth. The blow he lay upon her came from a heavy arm, the shudder of impact ringing through her bones, the blade turned too close to her neck. Without thinking, she pivoted and brought her own sword up and across his chest, screaming as she made contact, hacking a long, deep cut that caused the man to howl in pain and stumble among the downed rigging, his fingers red and gripping his wound.

Before she could gather breath, another sword forced her back, the man young, wiry, stabbing in furious, angry retaliation, swinging down to split her skull. Her legs buckled even as she lifted her sword hand, so sudden and fast she had no time to think or see, only enough sense to keep the blade at arm's length and use one of Jack's tricks. Moving with the blow, she unbalanced her attacker, a twist away from the strength of his body, a dagger from her boot, and the sailor would forever carry a scar across his cheek. His blood sprayed hot on her knife hand, its pungency mixing with the odor of cannon smoke and burning canvas and the acrid scent of her own sweat and fear. For a terrible moment her stomach heaved from the confusion of shouts and uncertainty and the possibility of death for herself and the child.

Turning quickly, she found she stood before a half dozen more attackers . . . and faltered . . . for dear God, the cause was hopeless, no help from her crewmates, and she could not win. Digging deep for courage, she swung, sword in one hand, dagger in the other, moving toward where Mary slashed, the two fighting for their lives and the lives of the crew. As she moved, her eyes searched for the place where Jack might be.

At last she spied him, and with no small amount of shock, watched as he hesitated in his struggle, glanced toward her, then lay down his weapon, immediately surrounded. So devastated was she at the sight, that she slackened her grip on the sword in hand and had it struck from her, the weapon flying away. Arms empty except for the dagger, she held it before her, turning left and right, desperately trapped. Blades to her body, she could do nothing but stand, while Mary soon met the same fate, completely surrounded and facing sure death if she did not surrender.

Voice shaking with emotion, Mary cried, "'Tis not for me that I give up my cutlass!"

Captain Barnett came aboard and observed the crew of the *William* slowly brought up on deck, some still so drunk they were just realizing what had happened, the turtle fishermen mixed with the lot, then regarded the two men who had fought when all was lost.

"Take them," he told his lieutenant. "That one. With the knife. See to it."

"Put it down, mate, or you'll not live to see the next hour. That's it . . ." the words were spoken calmly, the seaman moving stealthily, hoping the man would lower his weapon before more harm was done.

In the next instant, three marines were upon Anne, brutally wrenching the knife from her fingers, and in the scuffle and scrapping, Anne's shirt was so pulled from her shoulder, that a white breast showed.

"How now?" gasped one of the sailors, stepping back, gaping in amazement.

"They're no men that ye look upon," Jack called to him. "Those hellcats are women, to be sure. And I'll be havin' you treat them with respect."

"Aye," Anne told him, covering herself. Standing

shoulder to shoulder with Mary, she removed her scarf to let down her hair, running a hand through it. "'Tis women we are."

"And if ye've a mind t' mess with us, I'll have your gizzard," Mary spat, voice trembling in fear and fury.

"I daresay," Barnett said to no one in particular, his eyes filled with interest, "this bit of news will go down well in the governor's mansion. Your names?"

"Anne Bonny . . . and this is Mary Read. We've a mind to know your intentions."

"Why, Mistress Bonny and Mistress Read, I have in mind to invite you aboard my ship . . . as prisoners. As for Captain Rackham, put him in irons."

"Beggin' your pardon, sir," the mate answered, "but the women . . . I worry they will start up trouble. Fought like demons, they did. While the men hid below, they met us hand to hand."

"I'm afraid you're right, Mr. Andrews," he agreed with no small amount of disdain. "Put them in irons as well. But separate them from the men."

A single heartbeat passed, and Anne crumbled quickly into the sickness of complete despair, the world dissolving around her, a nightmare finally fulfilled – her escape from the drawing rooms of Charles Town, estrangement from her father, the alleyways and taverns and work on ship, the men she had known in New Providence, those hung and gone, the prison she had once been forced to endure, the death of loved ones – all the trials of her short existence, all leading to this one feared moment. An hour ago she'd had all the freedom of the seas, could make any choice, move with abandon and decide her own fate. Now, everything in her existence would depend on the whim of her captors. If only she could go back, even one hour. If only she had known. But . . . she had known. Why else hide the treasure? Why fight with Jack to sail north?

Jack. With devastating finality she knew she could no longer take him in her arms. As they brought her to the railing, she cast one last look in his direction and saw that he watched her, knew they might never see each other again. Their eyes locked and Anne shivered. In the depths of his gaze was the love and light that had pierced her soul from their first moment of meeting. She smiled to tell him she understood, memorized his face.

In the passing at the ship's rail, she whispered to the mate, Fetherston, "Tell Jack the treasure is gone. I took it this morning while you were . . ." and felt herself rudely pushed toward a small cabin on the sloop, the room where shackles awaited.

The cabin was small, dark, and tight. Night had fully descended and only a whisper of light pierced the door seams from the lanterns on deck. She and Mary clung to each other knowing they were doomed, their emotions floating about them as easily as seaweed on the surface of the sea, tangible, washing against them in a high swell, themselves helpless in the grip of a power over which they had no control.

"How has it come to this?" Mary whispered, her lips pressed against Anne's neck, her breath warm, her eyes dry, too sorrowful to cry. "What shall we do?"

Anne closed her eyes and with emotions she rarely permitted, sank into the mist of remembrance. She was all of twenty years old, a woman grown, but she yearned for her mother.

"Oh, my dear," she murmured, taking Mary's hands in her own. "I have come to this place because once, my own beginnings were born of defiance."

Part 1

Cork, Ireland

1699

Peg Brennen

Chapter One

The blanket of an Irish winter covered the city of Cork, and even though it was only mid-afternoon, daylight had started to fade. Dampness from cold and rain penetrated the stone building on St. Patrick's Street. In his office, William Cormac stooped before the hearth to place another log on the fire, the better to bring comfort to his guests. His old friend, Ambrose Worthington, had arrived not more than three days ago from the Caribbean with a new business partner, Philip O'Conner. Now the three men looked past the cold and gray towards the fireplace, reveling in the cheer it brought to the room.

"I understand the island of Jamaica is warm, even at this time of year," William said over his shoulder as he knelt before the grate. "How is it ye are managing this terrible weather, Mr. O'Conner?"

"I daresay, Mr. Cormac," Philip O'Conner answered, giving a startled shiver at the thought, "if I had to live in this climate, every winter would seem colder than the last. And the darkness! However do you manage? Why, were we in Jamaica now, the sky would be blazing with color and our windows open to the breeze, and in the night, fireflies would sparkle, their own fairy selves aglow."

"Bless my soul, sir, if you aren't a poet. Like all us Irish," William told him, smiling and stirring coals. "A fine thing too. Might I ask how you coped with a sea journey in winter?"

"Dreadful!" O'Conner cried. "If not for Ambrose, I don't know how I would have fared. 'Tis true enough we have our winds, Mr. Cormac, but I have never seen seas like the ones we encountered. Squalls with forty foot waves and skies the color of slate. We pitched and tossed so I thought the ship would surely roll. Thank God I will not have to return until spring. But then, I've much to accomplish while I'm here."

Ambrose Worthington leaned his husky bulk comfortably back into a red-cushioned chair. "There, Will, give the log a jab with the poker. That's it. Brings the heat out. And I'll try a glass of your good Irish whiskey, if you don't mind. The very remembrance of that journey puts a chill into my bones."

"Well, I'm more than glad you've arrived safely," William told him honestly, standing and moving toward a table with its bottles and glasses, the wooden floor creaking where he stepped. "Cork has missed you, Ambrose. As have I."

"My thanks," Worthington told him, accepting a glass. "We've come to see to some contracts for O'Conner's sugar interests. He's just come into his majority, you see, and takes his inheritance. I've my own interests, I might add. I've bought land near Kingston Harbour, and I've a foreman already planting cane."

William raised an eyebrow. "And who's doin' the plantin', if I might ask?"

"Oh, Will, do not begin your lecture on slave labor. Have to, man. It's the climate, you see. And the blacks are used to it."

"Ambrose, there are already slaves on the island, to be sure, but at the docks I hear of more ships making for the Indies with human cargo. Why not find another method of labor before you are completely dependent on stolen Africans?"

"Why, Mr. Cormac," O'Conner interrupted, sitting abruptly upright in the chair, "how else do you expect the cane to be planted? No white man can manage that heat. You must come and see the truth of it for yourself. I tell you sugar is the future. There is a fortune to be made if a man has vision."

"I thank you for the invitation," William answered, shaking his head. "But I've grown used to the comfort of my own home, to pubs, and this . . ." he held up his glass. "And to the theatre, the one good thing the English have encouraged. No, it will take an act of God, some great natural disaster, to move me out of County Cork."

"For myself," O'Conner countered, "I am a rum man, sir. Another good reason for cane production. I'll have a bottle sent round. Perhaps then you can see the efficacy of our system. Slaves, sir, will be the foundation of our wealth."

"Wealth based on human misery," William insisted. "No good will come of it, Mr. O'Conner."

"But . . . but . . ." O'Conner puffed, eyes bulged, quite beside himself, "the social order, sir, the social order. Think upon it. Our natural superiority . . . our God-given responsibility to guide and govern . . ."

"I'm afraid, Mr. O'Conner, you are too removed from the politics of Ireland. If you were not, you would know that is exactly what the English say to us Irish as they continue to take every item of value we own, including our self-respect."

"Will," Worthington shifted, suddenly uneasy, reminded. "Will, I've heard . . . that is to say . . . there's a rumor going round that you took on a criminal case. True?"

"Indeed. A charity case actually. But if ye've heard of my court appearances, then you probably know my efforts did not go well."

"Allow me to ask, then, what possessed you to take time from a lucrative practice to see to a thief? And to defend the man to the admonishment of the judge? Why, word is you were almost arrested for contempt!"

"What's this?" O'Conner asked, leaning forward and nervously tapping his cane.

"The man you call a thief has a name. Sean Brennen. He is of old family and a Catholic . . ." William answered, unable to keep the bitterness from his voice, ". . . cheated of his land and title by a Protestant Parliament and condemned for his poverty by a Protestant judge. And like many Irish filling the prisons, left to the lash, branding, and hangman's noose." Then with more than a little sarcasm, added, "But the man was fortunate. Because of my arguments, his fate was merely transport to the colonies to work as a slave. What say ye, gentlemen? Shall we raise our glasses to Cromwell and his

Act of Settlement? Damn, but it stinks to have to pay for our own defeat."

"But, almost arrested?" O'Conner cried, looking from one man to the other, dark eyes wide, his broad, pale face puzzled.

"Merely threatened, Philip," Worthington told him, trying to calm his distress.

"Do ye not understand the results of the Act of Settlement, Mr. O'Conner? It's been fifty years since Oliver Cromwell landed in Ireland to deal with the Irish *rebellion.* And no rebellion it was. Only decent Irishmen supporting good King Charles. But Cromwell murdered the King, and then the old devil brought his practices here. Brutal he was. He had it in mind to break the power of the landed class to make sure there was no support for the return of a Stuart king."

"Will speaks true, Philip," Worthington agreed, "and a nasty business it was. Hundreds with royalist leanings were gaoled or hung. Ships transported thousands to the colonies."

"Aye, and their lands confiscated and given to the mercenaries who fought with Cromwell. Do ye not see? They took ancestral land and beggared the families. And therein lies the problem. There's many an Irishman who wants his land back. Sean Brennen among them. And the English are just that sure he will not have it."

"Gentlemen, I am well acquainted with the details," O'Conner told them, somewhat impatiently, waving a hand as if to dismiss a matter. "My own grandfather was amongst those who left Ireland for the Indies. Fortunately, he had a bit put away, you see, and once in Jamaica, he bought land, and then more, as his fortunes increased. But, forgive me, Mr. Cormac, what has this to do with your court case? The courts are the authority, and surely, we must have order and law. If not, why," and here he puffed his chest again, "why, we face anarchy. Surely, if you are threatened with gaol, this is a serious matter. And for a common thief?"

"Can ye not understand?" William told him, whiskey and indignation going to his head. "The theft was not for the man's own pocket, Mr. O'Conner, but for a purse to support the return of King James. A Catholic prince, aye? From Ireland it is an easy jump to England, where other Jacobites are waiting. Without James a Catholic will never have any power in Ireland!"

Worthington shook his head and held up a hand to stop him from saying more. "Will, Will, do be careful. Here you are among friends. But this kind of speech, spoken in the wrong quarter, well, I do not have to tell you. Some would name it treason. My dear man, and you ask why I've moved my holdings to Jamaica. A body can make a fortune there away from the influence of sectarian bickering."

"Mr. Cormac," O'Conner insisted, trying to clarify his own misgivings, "you are not involved in this . . . this rebellion?"

William cast his eyes in O'Conner's direction, hard enough so that the man winced and sat back in his chair. Taking his public measure, he surmised the wealth he should have noted earlier—white wig, dark greatcoat of some style and worth, diamond in the lapel, stockings silk and gartered, good wool breeches.

Rebellion? By all that's holy, William thought, *an Irishman who's the king's man. And as long as he remains the king's man, he keeps his fortune.*

William leaned over his desk and lowered his voice. "It is not rebellion if you consider James the rightful king, Mr. O'Conner."

Sight of O'Conner's red face caused him to sigh deeply, and he thought to reassure the man, for, in truth, he needed his business. With the murmurings about the trial of Sean Brennen, his client list had fallen off of late.

"But have no fear. I am not involved in the . . . issues. Nor does the Crown believe the crime anything more than common theft. I simply had some sympathy for the young man who was charged and had no advocate . . ."

Except his sister, William thought, the memory of soft whiteness, of thigh and breast, causing another low exhalation of breath. She had come to him quietly one evening, and in the darkened room had opened her blouse and made her bargain. Easy enough. But he had not expected to be so enchanted with the girl, nor feel such empathy for the man and his politics.

". . . no, do not fear. The incident is past and I am returned to wills and torts and contracts."

"Well, it's our good fortune you are back to business, I say," O'Conner told him firmly. "Our good fortune, indeed, that you are back to proper business. Ambrose says you are the best at what you do."

Worthington cleared his throat and held his glass toward the whisky bottle on the side table. "Believe I'll have a spot more, if you will do the honors."

"Now," and William held up his own glass, "here's to warmer days. To fireflies and island breezes. And to a profitable future."

"Indeed," O'Conner added, tapping his cane once more. "To the high price of sugar."

Night had fully descended when William turned the key in the lock of his rain-swollen office door. The steps were icy and he gingerly reached out to the handrail, for the drink of the afternoon had left him unsteady on his feet. No moon graced the sky, or stars, and the canopy overhead was dark and cloud covered. The road ahead was poorly lit, in some places, dark enough to hide a man. Still, he decided a brisk walk home would serve to clear his head, and rather than hail a carriage, began to manage the street. With some small irony, he reminded himself that Sean Brennen, the man he had saved from the gallows, had stood among these very shadows to rob men of their purses.

On the cobblestones he faded into the gloom in his dark jacket, his wig alone picking up a taste of lamplight. The wind was biting, enough to rouse him. With one hand he clutched his coat tight across his chest, its heavy wool a comfort, with the other, he held his hat tight to his head. Certainly there were those on the street tonight whose coats were threadbare and who suffered. Damn, but he hated injustice and the poverty it created, and more, he hated his own impotence, for nothing could be done.

Only William's profession had given him both the power to use the law and a sizeable income, for he *was* good at his practice. But it was a slippery slope he climbed. Sean's trial had cast eyes his way, and just as he warily traveled the darkened streets of the town, he must now cautiously tread through the legal system.

"My dear, at last," Amy cried, moving forward hurriedly to close the door against the chill brought in with him. "I was beginning to grow worried."

"Now, Amy, we've been through this before," William answered, rubbing together his cold-reddened hands. "You know I carry sword and pistol."

"Yes, yes, dear. So you have said."

"Many times," he added more gently, removing his coat and passing it to his wife.

"How is Ambrose? Is he well?"

"Very well. He has bought land in Jamaica and plans to grow sugarcane. Would that we were in the tropics now," he told her, for his hands ached as they thawed and he continued to work his fingers. "Amy, pour me a drink, will you? I am froze through. That's a good girl."

"And," she asked quietly, moving to the table where he kept his bottles, her voice pitched low so the servants would not hear, "did . . . did he mention . . . the case?"

"The case? Why, what an excellent way to put it," he teased with some amusement, unbuckling his sword and placing it across the arms of a chair near the fireplace. *"The* case. In fact, he did. Seems I'm something of a celebrity. Damn, but it's too bad my fame is based on notoriety, eh?"

"Oh, William," she cried, handing him the glass of spirits,

"whatever shall we do?"

"Do? Do ye not understand?" he replied without thinking, all humor fled. "The man has been flogged and branded before transport to the Colonies. My dear, Amy, I have done all that I can."

At sight of her stricken face, he made a short apologetic bow. "I beg your pardon. I have forgotten myself. I should not have mentioned so distasteful a situation," for he grasped of a sudden that they spoke of different things. "You are concerned for our place in society, are ye not?"

Amy regarded him, tall, straight, proud, his light brown eyes reflecting an unexpected grief, and was suddenly alarmed that she could neither understand his sadness, nor he, the importance of their standing in the community.

"No . . . no, my dear," she murmured, shaking her head. "You are right. Of course, you have done all you can."

For a brief moment he thought to explain, to give her some awareness of the truth, but with a rush of further insight, knew understanding was beyond her ability.

"Amy . . ." he began, but the awkwardness of the moment was resolved by a knock on the parlor door.

"Supper is ready, mistress," the maid's voice called.

William held out an arm to her, but Amy paused, and with no little embarrassment whispered, "We dine alone this evening. And then later I thought . . . perhaps . . . well, I've had a fire laid in our room . . ."

With some tenderness, well aware how much she wanted a child, he raised her hand to his lips and smiled as she blushed crimson, her eyes unable to meet his.

"Come, my dear," and he led her to her place in the dining room where the light of candles and fireplace logs cast a ruddy glow, the corners of the room darkened into shadows.

At the sideboard the kitchen maid stood ready to serve, herself softened in the dimmed light. She held her hands folded over a starched white linen apron, eyes on the ground as the master of the house took his place at the head of the table.

"Soup, sir?" Peg asked quietly, placing the tureen near his bowl.

She watched his brief nod and saw that he glanced up for only the blink of an eye, but it was enough. The look she had returned from under dark lashes had caused an almost imperceptible tremor in his hand as he reached for the soup-spoon. Leaning to retrieve his fallen serviette, her cap tumbled to the floor, one glorious blue-black curl released from bondage to fall beguilingly down her white neck. She made the most of leaning over, the swell of her breasts clearly evident atop her gown.

"Your serviette, sir," she murmured.

A dangerous game Peg played, William knew. How could Amy not feel, not *smell* the overripe lust between them? What shook him more was that this was no common seduction, the lines over where it had begun blurred beyond recognition. At first he had satisfied his guilt by telling himself that all men had affairs at one time or other with their serving maids. But Peg had gone beyond the timid lass who quietly worked in the kitchen and who had come to him when Amy was away to lay bare her breasts and plead for the life of her brother Sean. When she looked at him as she did now, he saw more than her body and the heat between her legs. No, he saw a promise of something further in this life. In her gaze was the hint of distant shores he had never traveled, and the promise of adventure created a humor that stirred his blood and rendered him powerless to say no.

At the end of the meal, he sat alone with Amy, the last of the apple tart on the table, and gazed into the expectant face of his wife. The look he gave her was so appraising she could not hold his eyes, but blushed to her shoulders, praying he liked what he saw, that the simple brown of her hair was not so plain, or her lips too thin, that her heart, her devotion, her very *goodness,* would raise his desire.

"Well, then, William, I believe I shall retire," she spoke softly and with some allure. "I'll light the fire. The room will be warm."

Standing and turning to the door, she cast a single look over her shoulder, her eyes bright, almost like the first time she had accepted him on their wedding night. After a blessing from the priest, he had come to her, whiskey on his breath, to bed the virgin he had always wanted. For the briefest of moments William was torn.

"I'll just have my pipe," he told her, rising as well and reaching for the long-stemmed clay pipe he kept above the mantle. "I'll be right along."

A tiny hesitation, and she smiled graciously. With a nod, she turned toward the hallway and the stairs, a single candle lit to lead the way.

William listened until the sound of the creaking stairs was quieted, heard the soft pacing above. Then quickly, he made for the kitchen stairs and the hallway below, his footsteps careful, his way lighted by candle stubs set in sconces and still lit, for the dinner table needed clearing.

Peg must have expected him although they'd had no plan, for she was out of the kitchen ere he could draw breath, calling over her shoulder to Agatha, the cook, "I'll get the table."

Before he could recover from her nearness, she had pushed him into the pantry, closed the door, and stepped back and away from him, the greater to arouse his anticipation.

In the flickering candlelight she quickly removed her cap, a sense of urgency fueling her motions. Hands trembling, she pulled the pins from her hair, dark curls falling to her waist. Without taking her eyes from his, she licked her lips, all the while untying the ribbons of her bodice, releasing nipples large and brown. A soft smile, and she lifted her arms above her head, swaying her hips. William gasped and pulled the stays of his breaches, his member ready, felt he might burst before touching her. The flour was stacked and the sacks available, and he turned her, pushing her over the pile, raising her skirt, spreading her legs with his knees, heavy breasts falling into his hands, entering into smooth liquid fire, faster and faster until his semen flooded her and he felt the convulsions of her sucking him and all his fluid into her body. Even before the pulsations died, he brought her face to his, and kissed her mouth, hard. Suddenly, both knew. This affair was a thing apart. One more dangerous because what was felt was more than the lust of the body mingled with the spice of political intrigue.

From the door of the kitchen, William could hear Cook calling impatiently for the dishes.

Opening the cupboard door, Peg called, "Coming, Miss Agatha. I needed something from the pantry."

She remained a moment longer, retying her bodice ribbons and asking with her eyes what they would now do.

"I go to the country house for the holidays," he whispered hoarsely. "You and I shall go ahead to prepare."

She nodded, twisting up her hair, then picked up the tray, and without another word, left the closet.

Upstairs the fire was neat and warm in the room, the only light from the flames. Amy wore a sheer white linen nightgown, and when she stepped from the bed to the table to pour him a glass of whisky, he could make out the lines of her body, darkened beneath the thin fabric. But there was no temptation other than the drink, no dance, not even a glance. Amy's desire was to have a child raised in the sight of God, rather than a child produced of their love.

William threw the drink back, removed his clothes, and scrabbled into a nightshirt, while Amy covered her head with the bedcovers in that winter room. Then he poured another glass and thought of Peg, her breasts swinging, full and ripe, and again felt his sex aroused.

Without a word he climbed atop Amy and she timidly accepted him. In minutes it was over, and while Amy delicately placed a linen handkerchief between her legs, he closed his eyes thinking of the trip to the country and imagined running his hands over Peg's naked body.

Chapter Two

The horse's breath was white frost, its hooves digging into mud and ice on the road. William rode next to the heavy wagon carrying supplies for Christmas week, while the driver cracked a whip above the heads of the team, encouraging them to struggle up the hill. Beside the driver the serving girl rode, quiet and stoic in the cold, wrapped in a cloak, a blanket across her legs.

"But, sir," cook had exclaimed nervously, suspiciously, "I need Peg 'ere in the kitchen. Why, I've the bakin', cookies and cakes and breads, all t' be prepared. Then there's the marketin'. And I've need of her help in closin' the house. The furniture covers are just that heavy, and mind you, I canna' be askin' Mistress Amy to help, not after her bein' sick an' all. Why, and then there's the Mistress's personal needs. The girl helps her t' dress and does up her hair, as well."

"Well, Mistress Amy will have you to do all those things, Agatha. And I have need of Peg." He lowered his voice to a whisper, and leaned his head forward. "I've special surprises of the Yuletide for your mistress. Now don't worry. I know you can manage and we shall expect you by week's end. The coach'll be here on Friday morning."

"But, beggin' your pardon, sir," Agatha simpered, her thick fingers grasping at her apron, "the wags . . . oh, it's not me, but . . ."

At the top of the stairs leading to the kitchen, Amy had just started to descend, her mother's recipe for Christmas pudding in hand. The tone of cook's impassioned plea caused her pause, stopped by a premonition she had tried to push from her thoughts.

"They'll say what they wish to say," William interrupted.

"You know you can't stop those who wish to gossip from making mischief. Poor bored souls with nothing better to do than speak ill of others. Peg comes. And it may do you some good to remember the notion of Christian charity."

Amy sucked in her breath and quietly backed up the stairs.

"I . . . I'm sorry, sir," Agatha stuttered, admonished and red-faced, curtseying. "You're right. It's not my place."

Now it was an odd mixture of jealousy and pride that coursed through William as he watched Jonathan, the driver. The man had first regarded Peg with a sharp, involuntary intake of breath. Her beauty could not be hid beneath a cap and hood, nor could anyone miss the delicate features of her face, large dark eyes, skin white and unflawed, her full, ripe mouth. On the road he had tried to make conversation with the girl, but Peg had answered his questions with brevity, then remained silent, and Jonathan had been forced to turn his attention to the team.

Ahead William could see the gate of the property and the road leading to the house, a thick hedge of green, and beyond, dormant lawn leading to gardens that were a prize in summer. In the cold, the flower beds sat bare and empty, bulbs covered with straw, the last brown dregs of old stems fallen haphazardly, and border plants cut back to the nub. The sky overhead was gray, and the air at this late hour was freezing and keen with the smell of coming storm.

"I believe we'll get snow tonight, Mr. Cormac," Jonathan called, watching the departing sun. "The horses'll appreciate the stables."

"I'm glad for their comfort," he answered, for William loved his horses. "Bring the wagon up to the front door, Jonathan."

"It'll be easier to unload round back at the kitchen, Mr. Cormac."

"Indeed, and so ye shall. Drop Mistress Brennen at the front door."

"The front door, sir? But the kitchen . . ."

"At the front door, Jonathan."

Suddenly the man cast a sharp, sideways glance at Peg, the dawning understanding leaving him abashed and searching for words.

William tied his horse to the back of the wagon and held up his arms. Without a word Peg turned her back to the driver and smiled as she floated through air, her feet softly put to ground.

"Come," William murmured, as the wagon rolled away. "I'll have you see the house."

He lifted her and carried her over the threshold of the great wooden door, her eyes close to his, her mouth already tempting him. But no, he'd enough stolen kisses and secret embraces, enough closets and darkened hallways. Instead, he would show her the rooms, leading her to the bedroom last, and there he would make love to her with the shades up and a fire in the hearth, and he would see her just as God had made her.

"My dear, dear love," she said softly, as he placed her gently on the carpet in the hallway, "do ye know what ye do? What ye defy? I would not ruin you, Will."

"Too late, for surely, I am totally and completely ruined."

"But, the cost. I heard the words Mistress Agatha spoke before we left. She's right. People are talking, and not kindly either."

"I cannot live without you, Peg. Whatever the cost. And your brother . . ."

"Hush, you did what you could. And truly, transport for Sean is better than hanging."

"But I could not save him from the lashes and the branding," he returned with frustration. "I spoke too rashly by far! They will have it all, you know, not just the land stolen, but our souls as well. And they will support their theft with laws created by a Parliament where no Catholic can sit. Rather than your brother coming into his estate, he is condemned by the very men who took it from him."

"Will, he is alive because of you."

"That old man stared down at me from his bench with red eyes and spoke his judgment with spittle flying. Sean was sentenced to be branded to show me . . . *me* . . . dear God, I failed you!"

"If it were truly known why he stole, you and I both know they would have tortured him 'til he'd named every man he'd ever known. At least this way, God willing, I may yet see him again someday."

"But . . . the injustice!"

Shaking her head, Peg smiled. "Surely now, ye aren't surprised. Are not most men who are tried sentenced unjustly? A matter of politics? Think ye of all the reasons why a man stands before a judge."

He gently framed her head in his hands, looking deeply into her eyes. "What else is locked within your thoughts, my dear one?"

"Is that not part of the mystery of love?" she whispered, desire rising. "I pray you spend many hours unlocking the secrets of my heart."

The bedroom was small and snug. Together they removed the coverings for bureau, chair, and bed, and William prepared the fire and poured the whiskey, just as he'd imagined. He had thought of how it would feel to be with her entirely, but was unprepared for the raw emotions that coursed through him while he helped her undress piece by piece, stomacher, bodice, petticoat, corset, until finally she stood fully naked before the fire and slowly parted her legs. For this moment William had risked much, and now he basked in the joy of his choice, his eyes leaving hers to travel across her perfect face, her shoulders and breasts, rounded stomach, firm hips, the curling fur over the entrance to her doorway of pleasure. But . . . there was something about her body that was . . . special . . . something he innately sensed. The glow of her face, nipples large and red, her breasts fuller than he remembered . . . something . . .

"Yes," she whispered, "I am with child."

Already she had made plans to return to the north with

a claim of widowhood that would fool no one.

For a long moment William stopped breathing, realizing the life he had known until this moment was over. He closed his eyes. Then a soft breath escaped his lips.

"You and the babe will always have my love . . . and my protection."

Suddenly she was weeping, and in the next instant he was upon her, his mouth on hers, drawing from her lungs what solitary life she had left. Gasping with desire, he lifted her to the bed to experience all the pleasure openly denied them until now.

In the afterglow, her head lay upon the pillow while he caressed her breasts, their legs entwined, the room warm, soft firelight dancing against the walls.

"Peg, I *will* have you."

Too content to laugh aloud, she simply murmured, "If I didn't know you were married, I'd swear that sounded like a proposal. Tell me the same in the morning." But a glance into his face and she found herself surprised to see resolve. "Will, the good priest will never allow you the blessings of the Church. You would be outcast, excommunicated. There would be no accepting the Body of Our Savior, no burial in consecrated ground."

"And what about you? What of your immortal soul? Do ye think our love sin?"

"No," she sighed, "love cannot be a sin. But, hurting the mistress . . . that can be sin, as surely as you and I love."

In the morning they rose with the sun, even though they had talked half the night. Peg built the fire up in the kitchen hearth, hung the kettle for tea, and sliced crusty bread and salted ham brought from town. For once she worked without uniform or apron, only in her nightdress, her hair a mass of falling curls, disheveled, glorious. William stood to the side and watched her beauty, hardly able to believe she could be his and carried his child.

After breakfast, they dressed and walked the graveled

road to the river swollen with rain. Its roar preceded them, and the smell of trees and earth was pungent and rich. With unspoken promises, they took hands above the waterfall. The wild beauty of the land matched the stark passion that possessed them, and the river carrying debris downstream carried their old lives with it. Rugged cold and rising mist burned their faces and seeped through their clothes. Snow began to fall in soft flurries.

"Come," William said into her ear over the din of the water. "A fire awaits."

As they moved away from the chasm and its cold breath, nature became still, quiet. Walking arm in arm, he leaned close. "Why me, Peg? Why did ye come to me?"

"Shall I tell you truly?" And at his nod, said, "We had hoped for my brother's release. To have him arrested was a double blow. First to have him taken from us, then the money for the weapons lost. Although Spain makes overtures for funding a revolution, we have seen precious little of it."

"There will be support in England, you know. Too many decry William and Mary and wish to bring James back to the throne. But that does not answer my question. Why me?"

"Your name was suggested," she told him forthrightly, "because you have a reputation for drink and a certain foolishness with women. They thought you could not resist my offer."

"An honest appraisal," he answered, although she heard well enough the ire in his admission.

"That is not the sum of it. You know your work and were kind to me. A man of his word. I thought I might be used, as is oft the case with men of influence. But with each passing day you held true to your promise, and I came to love you more, as surely as one breath follows another."

"What will ye do now, Peg? Oh, not about the child, for the babe is mine as well as yours, and I will care for you both. But the rebellion. If you are arrested for sedition, I tremble to think what might happen to you and the babe in prison."

"I will continue to support the cause in any way I can. I must. What will I offer my child without a birthright? If the Catholics come back into power, we will take back our family estates."

"Our child will have the birthright I give it," William told her firmly. "Is it not enough? Can ye not be thinkin' to the wellbein' of the babe before all else?"

Somewhat startled, she answered with equal candor, "I have taken willingly to your bed these last six months, and I love you more than the world. But I must think to what is real. You've a wife and life apart. In truth, how do I know your feelings will not change? That circumstances will alter what you can or cannot do? I must make preparations for I've only meself. My brother is gone and I am alone."

"Peg, I swear to you, here and now and for all time, that you are mine and I will not let you go," he promised passionately, his famous temper stirring. "But I will insist. I will not have you embark on anything that will jeopardize your health or that of the child."

"And do ye think I would consciously do so? Have ye so little faith in my judgment?"

Unused to being challenged, William answered tightly. "The world is a large place and there are dangers that you can only imagine."

"And so you will tell me how to think and act?" came the quick, terse reply in response to the anger she heard. "Perhaps ye've a drop of the English in your blood."

Shocked, hurt, and truly taken aback, he stopped walking to take her by the arms, snowflakes gathering on his shoulders and in her hair. "Will ye fight me, then? This is about keeping you and the babe safe."

At his wounded face, Peg shook her head, ashamed of her own quick temper. "No. No my love. Forgive me. I will heed what you say, mindful of your concern, and I will be careful. But you and I . . . we will decide things together, aye?"

"You've a will to be sure, girl," he nodded. "And truth be

told, I'm glad for it," for he'd enough acquiescence in his marriage and found it tiresome. "All right, together then."

"Do you mean it, Will? For I will only have a true partnership."

"Aye," he nodded, rising to the challenge. "My promise on it."

Cold, he glanced up at the sky and saw only gray, snow falling in larger flakes. "It looks to get worse. What say we spend the rest of the afternoon watching this snowfall from our bed?"

"As you wish, sir," and Peg laughed, "for I am your servant."

"Ah, that's just the point, isn't it? You were never anyone's servant."

Again, the afternoon drifted away into evening, into candlelight and fire glow, the smell of their bodies thick in the room. Peg lay naked atop the covers, William's hand traveling softly over her back and bottom as she told him the story of her journey and arrival in Cork. He wanted to know everything about her, every thought, every wish for the future, a part of him already fighting the hours, for time ran away with the day.

"I do not know how I can bear for this week to end," he whispered, running his lips across the back of her neck.

"Will, we must talk." She sighed as his lips moved down her back, her skin tingling to his caress, his hands searching gently between her legs. "Mistress Amy accepted me into her house and was kind to me . . . ah . . . yes, my love, just there . . ."

As if speaking a name could conjure the devil, William heard the front door open, the sound of rushing voices, laughter, the stomp of many feet.

"William!" Amy cried from the bottom of the staircase. "William, I'm here!"

With a gasp, Peg bounded up and out of bed, the sheet covering her body, her face whiter than chalk, eyes round with apprehension.

"Stay here," he murmured, pulling on his breaches. "How damned inconvenient."

"Will, this is more than inconvenient. What shall we do?"

"Just wait here."

He left the room pulling on a shirt to cover himself. At the top of the stairs he looked down to see, not only Amy, but Margaret Cormac, his mother, looking grim and sour, Agatha, the cook, and the Hutchinsons, friends from church and town.

"Amy, what on earth possessed you to come out here tonight? In this weather? You weren't due until Friday. Nothing's ready. Mother, have you no sense than to bring Amy out? You know she has not been well."

"Oh, William," Amy cried, "what a greeting! And it only started snowing as we approached. Agatha said you were planning surprises for me, some decorations. But William, a week apart is too long. Mother thought it would be so much more fun if we helped. In the spirit of the season!"

She started up the stairs.

"Wait, Amy," he called, glancing at the crowd in the hallway, "give me a minute and I'll be down. I had thought to go to bed early."

"All right, we'll be in the dining room. We've brought supper. Has Peg taken care of you?"

"Oh, yes, quite nicely."

Mrs. Cormac's eyes narrowed, her glance piercing, and without a word to her son, turned to lead the Hutchinsons into the next room. Cook followed, pretending to be absorbed in the baskets she carried, unable to meet William's fierce gaze.

The whole scene played out before him in the instant. While he had made his plans, Agatha had gossiped, that same gossip she feared would come to haunt her, and word had reached his mother by way of back kitchens. This early journey was Mrs. Cormac's idea, she who encouraged her daughter-in-law to take possession of her husband and home.

William returned to the bedroom, the sound of the closing door grating in a room where only moments before the world had been at perfect peace. Peg was dressed and backed against the wall, her eyes still wide with fear.

"It's not that I mind anyone knowing," she whispered, "or losing my position. That will go soon anyway, for I've already grown large enough. It's the row, Will, the moment of everyone knowing. Is it the window then? I could have been out at the stables. I can manage the roof and drop. I've looked."

"I will tell her, Peg. As sure as I love you."

Peg shook her head. "I have said it. I will not have you ruined."

"And I've told you . . . too late," and he smiled.

Chapter Three

Morning brought a fine, rare winter day, gray evaporated, blue sky covering the land, the sun brilliant on snow. Jonathan had just returned from the nearest village where he had hired a return carriage for the guests who had unexpectedly arrived the night before. Amy, pale and silent, sat in the darkened parlor away from the light, while Margaret Cormac took a seat to her left, straight-backed, her mouth a thin, angry line, fan furiously speaking her sentiments. On another brocade-covered chair, a disconcerted and hesitant Mrs. Hutchinson, wringing her hands, tried making conversation. Casting imploring glances at her husband for support, the woman stammered while Mr. Hutchinson refused to meet her eye, instead, he stood gazing from the window, back to the emotion of the room, outnumbered and unnerved.

With as much speed as possible, the carriage was loaded and lap blankets readied. William handed his silent and stiff wife up into the carriage, then his mother, who murmured one last, "For the love of God, think upon what you do."

Margaret looked into the eyes of her only living son and felt the fool, furious she had lost this gambit and brought upon herself and the family all she had tried to avoid. Mrs. Hutchinson would tell and retell this story to all they knew. The only solution was to place the blame where it belonged—on the girl. Eventually, William would see reason. Public penance, gifts for Amy, and all would once again be well.

"Good-by, Mother, take care of Amy," was all he said.

The sound of the carriage still carried over the fields when William made for the small stone room beside the stables.

"They've gone," he said to Peg.

"Will, Will, what 'tis it ye've done?'

"I've secured my future. Mine and that of my family. You and the babe. And the week we asked for . . . now, 'tis a lifetime."

Shortly after the first of the year of 1700 arrived, William and Peg returned to town and a scandalous outcry from society, church, and more importantly, from William's clients. Refusing to be intimidated, he looked for rooms, not an easy task under the circumstances, finally settling on a small two-room apartment with sparse furniture. But he and Peg barely noticed, so great was their joy in simply being together . . . until the afternoon William returned early, his hands clasped behind his back as he walked the length of the room.

"You're home early," Peg said, stirring the stew that would be the evening's meal.

"There was not much on my desk today," he told her, taking in the growing round curve of her belly. "Love, I have been thinking . . ."

"Something has happened."

With somber face, he turned to her. "Yes. Something to do with spoons."

"Spoons? Whatever do you mean?"

"Spoons, Peg. Apparently there was some discrepancy over the number that were supposed to be in the drawer. I believe Amy is suggesting that you tried to make away with some of the silver before making away with me."

"Why, that . . . that is absurd! I never . . . never even thought . . ."

"She's claiming you were having an affair with a man in town whilst she was visiting for some days with my mother. A tanner. And that the both of you stole three silver spoons, my back being turned. Playing me false. You see, I am to doubt you."

"But, surely, this is nonsense!"

"The man was questioned," he continued, "and confessed

to having made your acquaintance. But fearing you had accused him, told the constable that you probably stole the spoons with the intention of placing the blame on him. The house was searched and the spoons were found between the sheets of your bed. I . . . I have had a rather emotional exchange with Amy. You see, she has pressed charges."

"Charges?" Then as if fully comprehending, "Why, I do not believe Mistress Cormac would succumb to such an injustice."

"I'm afraid she feels the injustice is done to her. Peg, I'm sorry. I've talked to the constable, but it seems you are to be gaoled until the case comes to trial," his eyes held a mixture of fury and despair, "and there is nothing I can do except push the court date as far to the front of the calendar as I can. But I am out of favor, you see . . ."

"Oh, Will, am I to go prison?"

"I made arrangements to deliver you myself," he told her quietly, "so that the constable would not carry you through the streets in manacles."

Almost two months passed and William raged desperate, terrified his child be born in the filth and cold of the gaol, knowing all the evidence lay with Amy and that she held his life in her hands. As surely as Peg went, so did he. Never so acutely did he realize that when a man or woman was sentenced, the terms actually fell on the family, on those who loved.

At last he devised a plan, praying God it would facilitate the situation and bring things to some resolution. Because he was forbidden entry to his house, he entreated Amy to visit his office, telling her he had something of consequence to share. Finally, she agreed. On a day late in February, accompanied by his mother, she knocked at his door.

"Mother, please." He guided Margaret Cormac to a chair. "Do make yourself comfortable. Are you quite well?" for her face was pallid and pinched.

"Well enough under the circumstances," she answered testily.

"My dear," he held a second chair for Amy, and she gratefully accepted, a long shawl wrapped tightly around her body.

Without waiting for small conversation, he began anxiously, "You know Peg is with child."

"Indeed," Amy nodded stiffly, "we only just learned in the last months. After the arrest."

"I would not have her delivered in gaol," William said plainly. "Especially when all here present know the falsehood of the charges."

At this Amy's eyes glistened and a harsh sob escaped her throat. "William, you are right. But, God forgive me, I am not sorry! She has ruined my life."

"Tell him," his mother said dryly.

"Mine . . . and that of the babe I carry," she added miserably.

"We thought you would come to your senses and return of your own accord, knowing the right thing to do," Margaret Cormac admonished. "We waited. Have ye something to say to us, William?"

William turned from his mother's grim, gray countenance, to Amy and regarded the shawl hiding her body, finally noted her face, swollen and round. "Why, my dear, I am happy for you! The child you always wanted."

"And do ye think you'll be father to your child?" his mother asked bluntly.

"Amy, my dear girl," he said softly, coming from behind his desk to kneel before her, "I am so sorry. I never meant to hurt you. And I cannot explain what Peg means to me without adding to your grief. Whatever I can provide I will . . . but think, would you want to be delivered in that place where Peg is held? Have you seen it?"

"I can well imagine," she answered, blowing her nose upon a handkerchief and wiping her eyes.

"No, Amy. With all respect, I don't believe you can. Two

months in that hellhole. Is that not punishment enough?"

"I have been summoned to court to give testimony next week. The date draws nigh."

"And what will ye do?" asked William, his trump card in the papers on the desk.

If Amy would not release Peg, he would file for an annulment swearing he had been duped, that Amy was no virgin on the night of their marriage. Most would see it for what it was, an attempt to rid himself of a hostile relationship, but there would be some who would want to believe this delicious piece of gossip. One way or another, the shame would be mortifying.

Amy sighed and cast a warning glance at Margaret. "I will not appear, and baring evidence, she will be freed. But, William, do you think . . . could you possibly consider coming back to us?"

How could he tell her that life and the love that fueled it, was more than appointments and dinner parties and Sundays at Mass. There was a banquet of the mind that needed feeding, a morality of politics, a courage to step where others dared not to ensure that justice was done. And there were needs of the body that she, Amy, would never be able to satisfy. This love, this intimacy of limbs and mind, was the cornerstone of his very soul, the fuel of his every waking moment. To live with Amy would mean to exist in the land of the dead. All his senses and goals, desire and ambition, his very breath, all would be effort and endless tedium.

William slowly shook his head and took her hands in his. "No, my dear. I could not. I am sorry, forgive me, but I cannot. I will always hold you in esteem and affection, but love . . . love is a thing that is boundless and cannot be explained."

Margaret stood and snorted. "If ye cannot change your mind and fulfill your duties, then I will have to do them for you. Forthwith, I am changing my will. All that ye stood to inherit will go to Amy and the child that is to be born. Do you understand, William? I disinherit you. I will give you until week's end to determine the course of your future and that of your legitimate wife and child. Then I will cut you off with nary a farthing."

She hesitated, adding ruefully, "And I will take on support of the maid and that babe to be born, if only ye will give her up. Think upon it." Without further word she stood and made for the door.

Following, Amy turned back to him and whispered, "See to her. She would not tell you, but she is unwell."

At the beginning of March, Peg was released from prison for lack of evidence. Greatly swollen with child, William welcomed her, and they once more took up residence in the small apartment. That she had suffered showed in the lines of her face and her diminished strength. Her thinness was frightening, all arms and limbs and great belly. In the evening, she would sit and rock her body, singing to the babe in her womb the songs of her own girlhood, running her hands over her swollen middle in a caress and whispering of the future and its possibilities. Only then did William realize that the babe had been Peg's closest friend in the months away. Like a thirsty man who cannot get drink, he suddenly knew the depth of his own yearning for this woman. Her courage filled his cup and made his will resolute.

The following week, the first of Peg's labor pains began, and she closed her eyes, overjoyed she no longer resided in the gaol.

As the contractions intensified, William left to find the crone who would help in the delivery. If they had held any doubts about what to expect in the future, all had been dispelled when William could persuade no doctor of his station to assist with the birth.

Hours passed and still Will did not return. A slow terror began to build. The contractions were harder now and close together, and the strength of body Peg needed for the difficult part of the delivery had not yet been restored. When the door finally opened, she felt a rush to the bed and heard her name through grinding pain.

"I'm here, Peg, I'm here," William whispered close to her ear.

The old woman moved toward where Peg writhed. With shrewd, cold eyes, she took in the sweat-soaked shift and wet hair, the eyes swollen and dark and filled with both relief and fear, and knew they had arrived just in time.

William grabbed the woman's patched shirt. "There's soap at the basin." His own fear made his voice harsh. "Wash before you touch her."

The contractions came quickly now, brutally strong, and Peg could not but wonder if this was God's punishment for her sin, for ruining the man she loved. Indeed, she asked if her very life would be forfeit, for as the labor progressed, the control she needed seemed just out of reach. Awash in the moment of intensifying pain, she would lose her grasp, unable to stop fierce cries, mortified that she frightened William. When the infant finally entered the world amidst great groaning and teeth clenching, the midwife held up the newborn to her.

"A girl!" William cried. "My darling, our very own child!"

Soon after the cord was cut and the afterbirth delivered, the old woman threw out an arm for her coin, anxious to be gone. Only then did William note the dirt still darkening the tips of her fingernails, grime from the streets covering her arms, and her hands stained with Peg's blood. With distaste souring his mouth, he reached into a pocket, thrust a coin in her direction, and was grateful when the door closed.

William carried the babe to the basin, and washing his daughter in water too cool for her taste, trembled under her squalls and wails, her cries breaking his heart.

"We shall call her Anne," he announced softly, after she had been warmly wrapped and placed in her mother's arms, "and she shall be a wonder for the world to behold."

"Oh, my love, is she not beautiful!"

"Like her mother. Now sleep, and I will rock the child."

In the days that followed, William seldom left the house. Often upon waking, the first thing Peg saw was him sitting in the chair, his eyes upon Anne's face, a look of amazed peace set upon his features. But if she could have looked into his heart she would have seen something else, a growing concern, for Peg was not regaining strength. Last night her skin had been warm, and now William looked anxiously at her flushed face and bright eyes, and knew a fever had taken hold of her body.

"How are my two loves today?" she smiled.

"Oh, aye, we're right fine. 'Tis a truth. And you?"

"More happy than any woman has a right to be."

"Peg . . ." William began, and she knew immediately he had something of importance to share.

"What is it?"

"My mother has died," his eyes sadly met hers, "and true to her word, she has left my fortune to Amy."

"Oh, Will, I am sorry for the loss of your mother. More, I am sorry that you could not reconcile with her."

"I had hoped she would change her mind. Perhaps when she saw Anne. But," he shrugged, "it was not to be. Mr. Reece, Amy's father, has posted a staff at the country home and is claiming it for his daughter, as well as the town house. He also asks for monthly payments for the upkeep of the properties and for Amy's personal expenses. In addition to her new inheritance."

"Will we be able to manage?"

"I do have something left, enough, but . . ."

"Your business is not doing well."

"No." He shook his head. "I have nary a client, at least none here in Ireland. I still have my connections in Jamaica. But you see, my abrasive manner with the court, outspoken politics, my moral state, why, Peg, even my immortal soul . . . all are a matter of great discussion among my peers. The upshot is that taken together, it seems I am being forced to abandon County Cork."

"Abandon? But this is your home!"

"No longer. There is nothing here for me anymore."

"I tell you again, I will not have you ruined. Let me go. Reconcile with your wife. Do penance before the church. Speak of what a fool you've been. Humble yourself and time will find something else for them to gossip about."

"I have a better idea," and he took her hand. "The Carolinas. I will take what I have left to me and we will go to this New World. Perhaps we will even find your brother Sean."

Peg gasped. "You cannot be serious!"

"And why not? There are many Irishmen in the Colonies, and things are not what they are here. Even an indentured servant may buy his freedom through hard work. The New World is not called new for nothing. It is a land for people like us . . . independent, willing to work . . . and perhaps somewhat marginal to society," he added with a glint of humor. "What do you say, Peg, are ye game? Will ye go to the Carolinas with me?"

"Are ye sure? Would ye give up all you know for me?"

"I could ask you the same. Will ye give up your dream for a free Ireland?"

A long moment of silence drifted between them, Peg finally fathoming there would be no return, and answered softly, "I would go to the ends of the earth alone, if you but only asked."

"Then, we will have a new start, the chance for a new life. You will be my wife, a common law wife, to be sure, but my wife nevertheless, and in no way common. I thought you might accept," he laughed, raising an eyebrow. "I've already taken the liberty of booking passage on ship. We take what is left of my fortune and my knowledge of the law, and when your lying in is finished, we leave for Charles Town."

"A new start."

"Yes," and he touched his lips to hers, and felt them hot, too hot. "A new start."

Part 2

Charles Town, South Carolina

April, 1716

William Cormac

Chapter Four

From the room where Anne sat at her lessons, she glanced from the window to see that the first buds of spring had finally given way to the pink and white blossoms of dogwoods, the air outside as sweet as new birdsong. She could just make out the stables, and longed to be on horseback, riding the length of the plantation, its fields well-tended, the orchard promising, the pond full of ducklings, new chicks in the yard, even the old sow with a fresh litter that would produce salted hams for the larder in the fall. Oh, but for the gentle sun on her arms, the wind in her face, the scented air in her lungs. Irish Rose, Rosie, the beautiful, brilliant black mare her father had bestowed upon her just days ago for her sixteenth birthday, would take the fences and hedges, and race through bright green grass. She would ride astride just as Father had taught her from the time she was a wee child, her seat as good, nae better, than any man's.

"Miss Anne," the voice of her Latin tutor reminded her firmly, "eyes out the window do not help in the translation of the Latin on your desk."

"Master Jennings, who could sit on a day such as this? My horse calls to me from the stables."

"Your father would insist . . ." Master Jennings replied acidly, his tall thin frame standing to emphasize his opinion. Turning, he cast a glance at the governess for support.

Simply there to chaperone the lesson, Mrs. Smyth sat to one side, the needle of her sewing poised midair, listening nervously to the exchange.

"My father, more than anyone, would know exactly how I feel," Anne interrupted, her eyes holding a glint that warned caution. Contemptuous of a man who would wear black clothing and short wig in a world filled with color, she added, "In fact, I shall ask him." And slammed shut the book.

Already the governess was on her feet. If the girl left the room to find her father, she would indeed ride for the day. The man overindulged her to the point of exasperation. Teaching her Latin and Greek was bad enough, but the workings of the field, the use of pistol and fencing lessons! Why, and she shuddered, what had that to do with the running of a house? Surely he must see that the girl was no longer a child.

As if reading the governess's thoughts, Anne paused, herself torn by the idea of adulthood. Although the mare was hers, a sidesaddle had come with the horse, and with it, a premonition of other boundaries that might lay hidden.

"Miss, ye shall sit and complete the lesson," Mrs. Smyth told her, cheeks reddening, breath panting, her cap bobbing on her head. "You do not have my permission to go."

A look out the window, an impulse, and Anne decided her future did not weigh against the moment. "I do not need your permission . . . or anyone else's," she answered tartly, flinging herself toward the door.

"Miss Anne!" the woman called. "Your mother shall hear of this, straightway!"

"Then ye'd better hurry," Anne retorted gleefully running down the great circular staircase to the foyer, light cotton skirts sweeping the floor.

"But . . . but ye don't wear your riding habit! Dear God, do not go astraddle in your skirts! Anne! Anne! . . ."

Almost knocking down the doorman, Anne rushed headlong to the stables, her dark hair released from pins, flying behind, a mass of waving curls.

"My horse," she called to the stable boy. "Now, Kevin! And do not give me that side-saddle!"

In the distance she made out the figure of her mother emerging from the house, and from Peg's determined walk making straight for the stables, already knew her purpose.

"Hurry!" she called to the boy.

"Your horse, milady."

"Your hands for a boost!"

She found her seat, riding astride, her stockings showing above her knees, just as Mrs. Smyth feared. Exiting the yard at a run, Anne presented a vision of beauty and skill, her destination the far meadow, delighting in the power underneath her and the knowledge that she could use that power to her own whim.

She had not yet reached the second of the fences when she heard the thundering hooves of another horse behind. Just before the jump, she turned to see Jupiter, the powerful stallion of William Cormac, coming up fast, her father clearly bent on intercepting her.

"Then I shall give him a run," she grinned wickedly, and spurred her horse forward, reaching the last of the fences before the forest road and freedom.

"Up, Rosie, up!" she cried and sailed over the gate, landing solidly, screaming her thanks to the mare as she raced toward the meadow a mile away with its wildflowers blooming and the grass tall and sweet-smelling.

Leaning forward over Rosie's neck, she pitched along at a run, knowing her father was close behind. The ditch before the meadow loomed. Anne felt the horse lift up and over to the turf, her path now through flowers and to the top of the hill, green mountains in the distance. Just behind, the big bay struggled to overtake, snorting with emotion, racing for the lead and dominance.

"Pull up!" William ordered.

Anne turned and was momentarily shocked by the red anger in her father's face and for the first time thought he might not consider this race of hers a lark.

"Have ye gone daft?" he cried when she had come to a walk. "Riding your horse like that! And where's the sidesaddle I've given you? You're to use it, do ye hear?"

"I only ride as you taught me," she tried, patting the neck of the beast in thankfulness for her stout heart.

"Daughter, am I so wild?"

"Yes, Father, 'tis a truth, ye are."

Trying not to laugh aloud, he intoned, "Anne, Anne, what am I to do with you?"

"I could not sit in that room a moment longer. Why, look about. The whole world is ablaze with spring. How can a dead Latin poet hold hope against a day like this?"

William regarded her appraisingly, and saw her mother in her—dark, untamed hair, cheeks flushed and rose-colored, her smile brilliant, lighting deep brown eyes, lips red and full, her waist thin, legs long, body tall—a beauty that took away the last of his resolve. In short, he could deny her nothing.

"I'm sorry," and he bowed shortly from the waist, with some mockery. "Sorry for your unhappiness. But even so, you are old enough to realize your position. In a few weeks ye'll have your ball and enter society. You must tame yourself, lass, for as surely as this day 'tis fine, no one can curb your own actions but yourself."

"But Latin, Father? What has it to do with the world? I can read, and I write a pretty hand. And my music, why, when I sit at the harpsichord, the house stops to listen."

"Indeed," he nodded, for true, she had rare talent.

"But I hate the Classics you insist upon!"

William thought back to her beginnings, to the two small rooms in Cork. Infection and fever had spread after the birth, devastating Peg's body. A wet nurse had been found quickly, and only his begging and the posting of a huge fee for the doctor he had known many years, had saved Peg's life. But Peg's health and strength had never been the same, and she was susceptible to colds and respiratory illnesses with any change of season. Worse, her body was scarred beyond hope for other children. One daughter had been given him, and although he loved her for herself, for the pride and abilities that were hers naturally, he loved her the more because she was akin to Peg and the symbol of their love and she was all the offspring he would ever have of that union. To this end, she would be son and daughter and heir to all that was his.

"Look about, Anne," and he lifted his eyes to distant mountains covered in trees, the road painstakingly cut through forest leading back to a house solid and rich and flourishing. "For sixteen years your mother and I have carved a life out of this wilderness."

Anne sighed deeply, and he recognized impatience and knew she could never understand. For all her memorable life, she had been given the world. How could he explain the first two-bedroom home in deep forest, unmilled wood and planking for floors? They had cleared land without slaves, with penniless freemen of good character, who'd worked and taken a section of land in exchange for their labor. Like Peg and himself, these men and women had gambled on opportunity in a new world, and had stayed to take part in the planting and harvesting of William's acres, slowly building their own homesteads. In the beginning William had traveled for days, plantation to Charles Town and back again to Cardiff Hall, taking legal cases and putting his profits into trading ventures in the Caribbean. With God's grace and good weather, the investments had paid well.

"When we left Ireland we'd a mind to leave you a legacy, for your mother's ancestral lands were gone, given away as spoils of war. Now this," and his hand stretched out to the horizon, "this is yours. And I've a mind to have it pass to you soon enough, for my work in town grows with the shipping."

"And I will make it prosper," she cried. "You know I'm good with the horses!"

"I've no doubt ye've skill and tenderness with the beasts. But," and his look told her he meant his words, "ye'll be doin' it with a husband. Would you be simply an ornament on that man's arm? Or an equal partner, knowledgeable and working by his side with a thing or two to say to each other in the evening?"

"The man I choose will not have me as an ornament," she answered with a haughty toss of her curls.

William narrowed his eyes, once again felt his blood rise,

and his voice hardened. "I will be clear with you on this point, and ye'll have to trust me, girl, and listen well. Ye'll not be choosin' your own husband. I will let you know when your mother and I decide." Then softer, "But do ye doubt that your happiness is always foremost with us?"

Disbelieving, knowing she could ask for anything, her eyes full of mischief, she answered coquettishly, "I can be a pretty enough ornament, if I must. I've watched the Charles Town women. The way they walk with lifted chins. Their curtseys and smiles. How they hold a fan to whisper and peer. Watch," and she gave him a look from beneath downcast eyelashes, lifting her eyes only for a moment, but the invitation so tempting, he gasped.

Anne giggled at the distress on his face. "Good, is it not? I practice before the mirror."

"Do not let your mother hear you speak such."

"Don't be silly. It was she who first showed me that glance."

"Anne," and he shook his head, "you will remember your place. Girl, you cannot be ruled forever by your passions. You love and hate in the extreme. Act without thinking. Impetuous and led by your own whims. I will expect you to play your role as hostess at the ball. Will ye take a grip of your emotions and act the grand lady? If not for yourself, then for me and your mother?"

She reached over, took his hand, and answered with the same passion he had just asked her to temper, "For you, I would do anything."

The stable smelled of hay and horse, and the dogs, frolicking in the straw, kicked up dust, rolling over and over in mouthing play until one of them yipped sharply. Peg stood next to a wagon in a plain cotton skirt and blouse, pointing out piles of wood to the stable boys and counting bags of nails.

"Out! All of you," she cried at the dogs, shooing the beasts from underfoot. "We've a wagon to load!"

"I believe the man said he'd his own tools, ma'am,"

Kevin told her, loading up the planks.

At that moment Anne rode through the barn doors, her eyes taking in the scene, and knowing something had happened.

"Ah, my prodigal daughter returns," Peg called, as Anne jumped down. "Have you cooled off that horse? I'll not have you leave her to sicken."

"Oh, Mother. You know I wouldn't have anything happen to her! I walked her the way home."

"Have ye no sense?"

"Just what my father asked in the last hour?" Anne murmured.

"And you will apologize to Mistress Smythe and Master Jennings, do ye hear? I've enough to worry me at the moment without havin' to fear that ye'll break your neck." Then, with some humor, added, "At least, not before the party. We've too many preparations already made."

"What is it that worries you? What is all this?"

Sighing heavily, Peg looked around at sacks of wheat flour, corn, salt and sugar, a barrel of apples, and a smoked ham. "There's a new crop of refugees just over from Scotland. They're taking that land over the ridge. Them that's left of the clan families. You've heard us speak of it ere now. Hangings and gaol for anyone thought to be a Jacobite. Many of the men transported, their families left to starve."

She lifted a bag of salt and placed it in the wagon. "Here. Pass those apples. There's space between the lumber." Then taking the sack from Anne, told her, "Those on the ridge have come mostly whole as families, but are in desperate need. The poor wee bairns thin as a rail. It's insufferable what hurt one man can lay on another. We can only thank God 'tis spring and the chicks can grow and the hens lay. The men will have to hunt if there's to be meat on the table, but this will get them started."

"Mistress, shall I load up the nails?"

"Aye, Kevin, and then I'll have this wagon gone. They'll have supper tonight if you hurry."

"So," Peg turned to her daughter, "what have ye to say for

yourself? I've had to listen to a good deal of prattle this afternoon from Mrs. Smythe about your . . . shortcomings."

"I *am* sorry, Mother. And it does me no good to see you work when I've had the afternoon to myself."

"Anne, my darling girl," and Peg took her arm and led her away for some privacy. "How quick you are to act!"

"I am trying . . . but the day. And Rosie. And I hate the Latin!

Peg glanced back to the wagon, her eyes angry at the want she had seen among the exiles. "You're right. Latin is unimportant when compared to other things. One day you will be mistress of this place. And when that time comes, I'll not have you forget those in need. Even if ye can speak French and Latin and read Greek, we'll follow what is most important. Do ye hear? What we've been taught. The corporal works of mercy."

"Aye. I know them. Have ye not told me them often enough?" And speaking from rote, intoned, "To feed the hungry, give drink to the thirsty, clothe the naked, shelter the homeless, visit the sick and those in prison, and to bury the dead." Anne took her mother's hand, "No, I'll not forget. 'Whatever ye do to the least of my brethren, ye do unto Me'."

Peg's face softened, her impatience and anger fled, for in truth, she did believe Anne. But William had given her everything, and it was she who was left to hold to the reins or Anne would indeed be wild. "Fine day or not, you will be about your lessons. By the way, where is your father?"

"He rides to the mash house to check on the brew for the festivities. He says to tell you he'll join us for supper."

"Take care of Rosie," Peg prompted with some sternness. Then with a breath of tenderness, "Afterwards I'll show you your gown for the ball. And I think I have time to brush out your hair before dinner. Goodness, what a mess," she declared lifting pieces of it off Anne's shoulders.

"I fear it is useless!" Anne cried.

"No, my dear. It is part of your beauty!" A kiss to her forehead, and Peg said, "I'll see you inside when you are finished."

Chapter Five

Cardiff Hall was well lit, a beacon that could be seen for miles. William Cormac had decided to host the ball at the plantation rather than the town house, because he wanted all to see what was truly Anne's dowry. Carriages pulled up a driveway lit with torches, to be met by liveried footmen wearing the green he had chosen. If he could not have Ireland, he would at least have a glimmer of its hills in the dress of his staff. Stunning flowers graced the entryway, anthurium, ginger lily, bird-of-paradise, torch flower, all brought from the tropics by Ambrose Worthington in a fast ship to honor his friend's daughter. Thousands of candles sparkled in rooms, balconies, and patios. About the house were tables spread with roasted meats and breads and cheeses, small stuffed pasties, fish brought from the coast and steamed, and sugared fruits and tarts and carrot pudding, pies made from last year's apples saved for the occasion.

Anne stood before the mirror and regarded her image. The emerald green dress she wore was made of the filmiest of silk material, a gift from France, and piped with sapphire blue, the fabric soft in the heat of early summer. The whole gown was cut provocatively low, a whalebone corset narrowing her waist and laced tightly so that her bosom rose full and high, giving the bodice its allure. Gathers at her waist emphasized a tiny waistline, the cloth spreading over round hips. The delicate Irish lace at the elbow of her sleeves was ample; the bodice covered in tiny pearls and trimmed with crimped lace. A petticoat from waist to floor and richly embroidered with gold thread, peeked beneath the front of the over-gown. When she'd first put on the dress, she had gasped, knowing her father meant to tempt, that he fished for the son-in-law who would run Cardiff Hall.

"You look beautiful, miss."

The housemaid sighed wistfully as she finished dressing Anne's hair.

"Thank you, Beatrice." Impulsively, Anne turned to her closet. "Here. I've something for you."

She removed a dress and carried it to the girl, considering the blue against her eyes. "What do ye think?"

"Oh, no, miss. I couldn't!"

"Indeed she could not," Mrs. Smyth told them both, scurrying into the room, overhearing and indignant, certain to wear her cap even to the ball. "Anne, it is not for Beatrice to dress above her rank. Why, it would simply confuse the other guests. Now, let me look at you. Yes, yes, wonderful." She plucked a piece of thread from the sleeve, and looked at her appraisingly. "My dear, your guests have arrived. And Anne . . ."

"Yes, Mrs. Smythe?"

"Your father has asked that you be mindful of your conversation with him when . . . when you rode together," and here she paused, still chagrined, even though Anne had apologized. "Remember your place, child."

Anne turned with her most elegant bow, skirts sweeping the floor, fan held just so, and said, "It will be my humble duty to honor my parents on this memorable evening."

"Well, yes . . . yes, that's it," Mrs. Smythe answered, not knowing whether Anne mocked. "Now come, my dear, your mother awaits."

"No need. I am here."

Mistress Cormac swept into the room in a gown of gold gossamer, a vision of beauty, riches, and stature, hair powdered for the occasion, her own breasts high and floating atop a low-cut bodice, a mole patch placed seductively next to her lip.

"Oh, mother, you look stunning! Will I ever be anything like you?" Anne murmured, taking her hand.

"My darling, you already have your own style. Here . . .

I've brought you perfume from Paris. You see, a little scent, and you could not be more perfect."

"When shall I powder my hair?"

"Not tonight. Tonight your father wants you just as you are. Now, I believe you are the guest of honor and are awaited downstairs. You may try the punch," and she laughed at Anne's anticipation, "but drink slowly, until you see the results. So . . . turn around . . . oh, yes, Anne, you are so lovely. This will be a memorable evening for you!"

Anne moved among the crowds, basking in the glow of her moment. But there was more than the dress that caused every eye to regard her. Anne had a presence that could not be denied, a confidence as she practiced the walk and fluttering of the ladies of Charles Town, her ivory fan displaying the gaiety of her mood.

William looked toward his daughter and the young men surrounding her, the laughter in her eyes, as she teased and cajoled. Her skin was delicate and white, bleached with creams Peg had insisted upon these last weeks, her cheeks lightly roughed, her lips red, hair wrapped and braided and woven with gold ribbon to match the petticoat of her dress.

"Most excellent, Mr. Cormac, most excellent indeed."

William turned to see Philip O'Conner at his elbow, gazing out over the party.

"Mr. O'Conner," he bowed, delighted that his client of sixteen years would make the journey from Jamaica, "ye do us too much honor, sir. The trip from the Caribbean was a generous endeavor."

"Not at all. Worthington wanted someone to look after the flowers," and he laughed, snorting through his nose, his eyes growing larger as they did when he thought himself clever. "But truly, I have a great deal of business to discuss with you before I return. I'm buying more land and slaves." His eyes strayed past William to where Anne stood. "I must say though, this party is absolutely splendid. Do you think your young lady will give me a dance? I thought perhaps if *you* put in a good word."

Interested in Anne? And why not. The man was still in his late thirties, with most of his hair. True, he was leaning to some weight. But experienced in the ways of the world. Wealthy, to be sure, mature enough, Irish and Catholic. But Jamaica was far away, and he was a slaveholder, a practice William abhorred, and a subject the two men avoided. On this one point both he and Anne absolutely agreed.

"Is it true you are thinking of taking land in the area, Philip?"

"Yes," he turned back to William. "I'm looking at a piece bordering Charles Town Harbor. Who would have thought the city would become the center of trade it has?"

"Why do you hesitate?"

"The pirates, sir. I daresay they are such a nuisance."

"If you don't mind my saying so, sir," William laughed, and held up a hand for a servant to bring drinks, "don't you think that rather odd coming from a man who lives on an island claiming Port Royal. Why, Henry Morgan and most of the pirates of the last fifty years have made Port Royal home. I believe there are as many pirates in the Caribbean as along the bays and inlets of South Carolina."

"Port Royal . . . the old Port Royal . . . is gone, William. Destroyed in the quake, some twenty years or so now. Swallowed by the sea, and what is left is not worth mentioning. God's judgment. We have a governor, Peter Heywood, who has sworn to rid the waters of piracy so that honest men can do business. Gallow's Point is already in full swing," and he chortled and snorted at his own crude jest. "What pirates we do have come quietly disguised as merchants, only there for supplies. But here . . . why it's plain as day pirates have leave to enter port. No one has authority or sufficient courage to stop them. I do believe if you remove proprietor control of the colony and ask to be made a royal province, things will look up decidedly."

"Good evening, gentlemen," Anne called gaily as she

stepped toward them. "Father, the dancing is about to start," and she bowed gracefully. "Will ye partner me for the first dance?"

"It would be my honor," he answered, returning her bow, glad for the opportunity to lower his head, for it gave him occasion to blink back an instant and unexpected moistness in his eyes.

"What are ye gentlemen so serious about? You must come into the party!"

"We're talking about pirates, my dear daughter."

"I say, Mr. Cormac," O'Conner regarded him. "Should Anne be frightened by such conversation?"

"Do not fear for me, Mr. O'Conner. The talk of pirates is all the rage in conversation these days. Why, everyone has a story. I have heard that some of the men are as handsome as you will find anywhere. And rich. Brave, as well, for they fight in the most desperate of circumstances."

"Why, Miss Cormac, you are a romantic! Indeed, all pirates are scoundrels!"

"Not at all," Anne teased, knowing O'Conner was serious about his money. "Just ask my father," and here she looked at William, laughing as she did, sure to strike a sour chord by repeating his own words. "They are simply men who have had ill fortune and are forced to desperate means. Men who crave the freedom of the seas."

"Ill fortune indeed," O'Conner sputtered, warming to his indignation. "They take from lawful men their hard-earned wealth."

"Would that be the hard-earned wealth produced by slaves stolen from Africa, Mr. O'Conner? Is that not simply another form of piracy?" she asked in her smallest, sweetest voice, thinking what a pompous ass the man was.

"Ah, the music!" William cried, intervening. "Come, my dear, let us take our places. If you will excuse us, Philip."

"Miss Anne," O'Conner bowed, conversation forgotten, and more to the point of his mission, "perhaps you will give me a dance later?"

"Why, sir," she returned his bow, her smile radiant with mirth, her eyes alight with a look meant only for him, "I would be delighted."

"Anne," William whispered as they walked to the dance floor, "go easy, girl. I need his business. Besides, 'tis not fair to the man. He's no match for you."

"Father, your nose is already red from drink. Do ye think you can dance?"

"I can best you at dancing any day. Drink or no."

From where he danced in the line of gentlemen, William gave some thought to the possibility of a marriage with Philip O'Conner, but found his mind wandered . . . just as surely as his feet moved unsteadily. The steps called for a turn and he found himself off balance, and sheepishly looked to Anne, for she had known him. Indeed, he had drunk much and eaten little, and he felt her laugh with unabashed mirth as she steadied his arm. Grateful to step to the side at the end of the reel, he applauded the musicians and thought to make his way to the tables brimming with food.

"Ah, there you are, William," Worthington called, siding next to him, a gentleman behind. "Miss Anne," he bowed, "many happy returns of the day."

"How wonderful to see you, Mr. Worthington. I must thank you for the flowers. I am overwhelmed by your generosity."

She curtsied deeply, flushed at the look of pride streaming from William's eyes.

"Not at all, my dear. Not at all." Then turning to William, "I've brought someone I'd like you to meet. I hope you don't mind."

"Your friends are always welcome, Ambrose."

"May I introduce Henry Lord Cavanaugh."

"Your servant, sir," William bowed. "My daughter Anne, the reason for this evening's festivities."

"Your Lordship."

Anne bowed gracefully, rose . . . and looked into the face of Henry Cavanaugh. For one long moment she believed her heart would stop, her composure gone, the brittle game she played disappearing in the blue of his eyes.

"A pleasure, Miss Anne. Many happy regards for your birthday. Mr. Worthington told me you were beautiful, but I do not believe words could possibly do you justice."

"A pretty speech, sir! Is it well practiced?"

Abashed William wondered what he would do with her tongue, almost spoke, but then saw the amusement in her eyes. Why, Anne was testing Henry Lord Cavanaugh, just as she would have tested a new horse, taken it out for a run to see the trueness of its heart, to see immediately if he was worthy of her time.

"Never uttered with a more humble or truer heart."

Something in his quiet tone caused William to peer closely at the man, then glance quickly at Anne. From the color that rose to her cheeks, he knew she had heard it, too, not the courtier's riposte, but a message meant only for her, his hand covering his heart.

"May I have this next dance?" he asked, smiling and gracing her with an elegant bow.

"Yes, milord. It would be a pleasure."

And without a glance to anyone else, she lightly laid a hand on the arm held out to her.

As William watched the couple take a place on the dance floor, he heard Worthington enlighten him in a low voice, "Let us hope I can make Henry Cavanaugh your friend as well as mine. He's got money, William, and he wants to invest here in the Carolinas."

"Where is he from?" William asked following his movements and begrudgingly admiring his grace.

"He's been living in France until recently. Surely you have heard the stories of his grandfather, the old Earl Cavanaugh. Cromwell hanged the gentleman."

"What was he doing in France?"

"Henry's father, Malcolm, was forced to flee Ireland after the Battle of the Boyne in '90. Took ship back to France with everything he owned of any value. Of course, his family went with him. Henry was a lad then, but eight years old. They made their home with James at court."

"Really."

The Battle of the Boyne had been the last attempt James had made in Ireland to secure his return to the English and Scottish crown. The Irish, led by the Earl of Tyrconnell, had been soundly defeated by William of Orange's forces, ending the few brief years of a Catholic Irish Parliament after the return of James in 1685, political power that was likely not to return.

Perhaps in his mid-thirties, Lord Cavanaugh was tall, wig fashionably long in the new style, clothes more than adequate, silk a deep shade of blue, the lace at his neck profuse and of excellent quality. When he turned, he presented a handsome, smooth face, ready smile, and eyes to match his silk.

"Has the man seen battle?" he asked Worthington.

"Aye. In the Rising." He paused, for the political effects of last year's Scottish insurrection were still raw and unsettled.

James had arrived in Scotland just before Christmas in December, 1714, and by the first days of February, had returned to France, the men who had gambled their lives, homes, and clan families for his cause now on their own, lost to their fate, just as had happened in Ireland. Tens of thousands of men, women, and children had attempted to replace James on the English throne, answering his plea for support. But he had left them to imprisonment, transport, starvation, and poverty, returning to his court and its comforts, saddened by his loss of throne and power.

"Malcolm Cavanaugh died of fever during the crossing. December it was, with rain and bitter cold. Henry inherited the title and stood by James until his return to France. But now, I believe he looks to something new. With his father's investments, as well as a number of good trading ventures of his own, Henry is as solid as they come and ready to buy here."

"He still holds to the Jacobite cause?"

"Aye. But between you and me, he's unsettled that James would leave the Highland clans to fend for themselves."

"And he is Catholic?"

"Indeed. The whole purpose of living in France! At least there a Catholic can still openly practice his religion!"

"Please, Ambrose, restrain your voice," William asked, none too quiet himself, for his drink had surely gone to his head and the noise, laughter, and music were loud in that room. "We are not in my study, and there are many here tonight, among them Protestants. As it goes for Catholics in Ireland, the same goes for Huguenots in France."

With the revocation of the Edict of Nantes by Louis XIV, Charles Town had filled with French Protestants seeking religious freedom. Many were there precisely because the town's constitution allowed freedom of worship. Truth was, Protestant or Catholic didn't seem to matter much to William anymore when it came to contracts. Business was business, regardless of a man's religion. Frankly, he was tired of Old World prejudices and politics. What concerned him more was the increasing importation of slaves for plantations appearing along the inland rivers.

"In fact," Worthington mused, "didn't Peg's brother have a hand in trying to secure arms for the Jacobites? Long time ago, true. Do I remember rightly?"

"A good memory, Ambrose. But do not spoil the evening by letting Peg hear his name." Sean had died in transport, buried at sea many years ago.

William said nothing more, but took drinks for the two of them from a passing tray. He watched Cavanaugh and Anne warily now, and made an instant decision. He did not want his daughter mixed up in Jacobite politics, perhaps to return to Ireland or Scotland or France for an impossible cause. The English would never permit the return of a Catholic monarch, terrified of France and the influence of the Romish Pope. William and Mary were both gone. Mary's sister, Queen Anne was ill and ailing, none of the five children she had born still living. The Hanover Prince, George, was already set to succeed her when she died. Only great bloodshed and unrest would return James to the throne, and unrest meant a disruption of shipping and his own fortune, and for what? Another series of bloody conflicts over an issue that was purely a matter of conscience, and even that depending on the family into which a man was born.

Downing his whisky in a great gulp, he reached for another. "Drink up, my friend. The dance floor calls. I go to my wife."

From the landing where Peg watched she could take in the entire evening, and all she and William had created over the years. The rooms were warm and glowing; no expense had been spared. Anne was dancing with a handsome man, her eyes alight, while William made his way through friends, shaking hands, establishing future contacts, picking up tidbits of gossip that would stand him in good stead.

Let him drink and laugh, for this is his party as much as it is Anne's, Peg thought. *May God bring many blessings upon our family from the fruits of this night.*

The music ended and immediately Anne was surrounded by a number of men holding out a hand, but instead of choosing one, she turned again to her partner, indeed stood too close, her head bent as he whispered into her ear.

The fan in Peg's hand fluttered impatiently. *Oh, Anne, what are ye thinking?*

Turning, she motioned for Beatrice. "Bring my daughter to me," she said quietly, holding the fan to hide the words from her lips.

Beatrice skirted the parameters of the dance hall, herself the object of more than one look, for although clearly a maid of the household, she was not more than sixteen, her face smooth and clear, eyes a deep blue, her step high, and she walked without cap or apron this evening, her hips swaying rather too much.

William watched as she made her way along the side of the hall, and knew from her intent look at the dance floor that she had a message for his daughter. At a side door, she slipped into the back hall where she would wait until the music was done, more than one pair of eyes following her.

Peg should have known better than to bring the girl into the light, he told himself, teetering on his toes. She's too pretty by far. Only trouble will come of her. Blue eyes, aren't they?

"Gentlemen," his voice slurred, "excuse me. Duty calls."

In the deserted back hallway Beatrice stood, waiting, tapping her foot to the music, taking small steps forward and backward with her own invisible partner.

"What are you about, dear Beatrice?" William asked, startling her. "Are you here on your mistress's behalf?"

"Indeed, sir," she curtsied. "I wait for Miss Anne."

"And what shall you do while you wait?" he asked leaning over her, his arm on the wall above her head to steady himself.

She did not drop her eyes, but brazenly looked straight into his.

God's blood, but I like the smell of her, fresh as new hay, and ripe, ripe as new picked fruit.

Without thinking, he reached out to caress her cheek, his blood quickening when she did not pull away.

"I have watched you, sir. The way you ride your horse. What else do you ride?"

If he gives me a child, I am no longer anyone's maid. He is drunk enough.

To his astonishment, she moved backward into the darkened entrance to one of the rooms. William felt an instant lust rise from groin to throat. A small part of reason whispered that he should walk away. The girl was no practiced coquette with whom to casually flirt at a party. Before he could turn, her fingers touched between his legs, and he hardened, her very lack of skill and the innocent attempt fueling his desire.

With one hand, he opened the door and walked her backwards into the room, closing the door behind.

"Perhaps we should see where my riding takes us."

Reeling from his drink he fell into her, and none too gently pulled at the bodice of her dress so that her breasts were exposed, white, while her neck and shoulders bloomed rose-colored with embarrassment. As he bit and sucked to raise her nipples, he moved, pushing her further into the room. Only when she was backed against the couch, did he lift his head to untie his breeches, releasing himself, gasping in his urgency.

"Sir, please, sir, I've . . . I've changed my mind. I'm . . . I've never done this before. I'm sorry, sir . . . "

When she had first thought to seduce, she had not imagined that his presence would be so huge, his body so strong, or that it would be this rough, fearsome thing of so many feelings and mortification.

But William could not stop, not now, and he roughly turned her over the back of the couch, lifting her skirt so that her backside was available to him, grateful women wore no further hindrances. True virgin, she was tight, and cried aloud in the raw shock of his first thrust, her throat whimpering small mewing screams as he plunged into her, the whisky taking all discretion from him, deeper, deeper, until she finally pushed back against the pain and he came in great shuddering gasps unlike any he had felt in years.

From somewhere in the fog of his consciousness he heard Anne's laughing voice, calling, "Just a moment, I'll be right back."

Without forewarning, she entered the room for a handkerchief from the bureau, a relief against the perspiration on her forehead, and held mid-step at the sight—Beatrice's skirts raised, and her father pushed against her, still holding tightly to her breasts.

Anne's hand went to her mouth, and absently shaking her head in denial, she backed toward the door, horror on her face.

"My God," William whispered, suddenly dead sober. "Anne . . . a . . . a mistake. For God's sake, don't tell your mother. Anne!"

Anne reentered the party at a run, moving past people who called her name, her face frozen, too shocked to know what she did. The crowds seemed to press upon her, and she gasped, the heat of the room oppressive, desperately needing air. At the first door she rushed onto the patio where she breathed deeply, over and over until her heart stilled its loud pounding and the pain in her chest subsided, until she felt her gorge settle.

Suddenly her mother was there, the very person she needed, but did not want to see.

"Ah, here you are, my love. I wanted to speak with you." Peg placed an arm around her shoulders. "Why, Anne, you are chilled and trembling. Did you see Beatrice? I sent her to find you."

"I did. I'm afraid she didn't mention it."

"Listen to me, my dear. You show too much favor to a single gentleman. There are others here who also want your attentions. Mr. O'Conner has asked at least three times if you will honor him with a dance. Anne, please, give your considerations equally to all this evening." Then, she laughed, "Although . . . he is handsome."

"Who?"

"Lord Cavanaugh. But this is not an evening to choose. Do not engage your heart so readily."

Even as she said the words Peg knew the futility of caution, for Anne had always been quick to know immediately what she wanted.

"Now go and enjoy. You will never have another evening like this one."

"I believe you are quite right, Mother. Not another like it."

Something had happened to unsettle Anne, and Peg hesitated. The night's dampness touched her skin and she shuddered. Now was not the time. On the morrow she would have the whole story. Instead she said, "If you should see Beatrice, would you tell her I have need of my shawl?"

The rest of the evening passed in a stupor, Anne smiling, dancing, making polite conversation, taking the floor more than once with Mr. O'Conner, her eyes always returning to Henry Cavanaugh. She saw that Henry watched her as well and was woman enough to recognize interest in his glance.

Breakfast was served at dawn, great tables spread on the lawn, and afterwards, the last of the revelers retired to carriages that would take them home and to sleep.

Anne was exhausted, emotionally and physically, and had no heart for her father. At one point he walked toward her, and she quickly made for another direction, confused, knowing life had changed in unimaginable ways and that she could never go back. Childhood was over. The raw, sexual energy that drove the world, that would soon demand her own complicity in marriage, had been too obvious. The scene replayed itself over and over in her mind—William's face distorted by passion, changing to shock at her presence, then horror, her crushing embarrassment. Innately, she sensed the passion that had fueled her own existence, and it was overmuch for her to comprehend

"A great success, Anne," her mother said, "a wonderful party."

Then she coughed, turning her head, hand to her mouth. "Come. I am for bed. I think we all are."

Chapter Six

The illness started as a slight cough on the day after the ball, progressed to chills, then turned to a great rasping as Peg's lungs filled with fluid. She labored to breathe, her eyes large and dark and frightened, holding the terror of suffocation. A fever burned through her body as she struggled. Anne changed her chemise hourly, wringing cloths of cool water to wipe her face. The curtains of her room were shut against the light, the better to keep out more illness, the room stifling hot in the summer heat, the smells of sickness overwhelming. The doctor visited daily.

William was never far from his wife's side, anguish stark on his face. He watched helplessly as Peg became weaker with each passing hour, guilt and remorse shredding his composure. To be sure, he had romped with other women in his sixteen years in the Carolinas, but in sobering he had completely understood what had occurred with Beatrice. After Anne had fled the room, he had turned to the weeping girl and paid heed to the blood between her legs and his callous handling. The ardor, the satisfaction of the moment, had ended with the knowledge that he had taken the girl against her will. Belatedly, he remembered she was the same age as his daughter. With what dignity he could still maintain, he'd found the handkerchief Anne had sought and had given it to Beatrice, smoothing her skirts and sitting her in a chair.

"All will be well," he had tried. "I am sorry for your discomfort." William wanted to plead the whisky, but the excuse fell flat within his own breast. "Stay to the kitchen for a few days whilst I speak with Anne."

But there had not been time to have a conversation with

his daughter, for even as he tried to form what he would say, the first of the fever had gripped Peg. Anne stayed in the bedroom, occasionally meeting him with eyes so accusing, he could not hold her gaze.

Hour after hour passed, Anne remaining at Peg's side, often to kneel in prayer, her petition fervent, believing her own force of will could persuade God to restore her health. Only with the possibiity of Peg's death, did she finally understand her mother was her touchstone, the strength and courage and source of her beliefs. Surely Father had been influential on her life, teaching her the land and its crops, the horses and animals, how to shoot, and even to Mrs. Smyth's horror, how to use a sword. But it was her mother who had first taught her to read, telling her stories of the little people and the silkies, broadening her imagination with images of the old world, the rain and sea and green of Ireland, speaking of injustice and the moral obligation to fight it. While her father was away in Charles Town, it was Peg who had made clear why there were no slaves at Cardiff Hall, and why she was certain as long as a Cormac owned the property, there never would be. Among those men and women who worked for them, there had always been materials for shelter and food enough to make it through a hard winter. No stranger, regardless their class, was ever denied hospitality.

Surely her mother would recover, must recover.

"Will," Peg whispered, her eyes delirious, "open the curtains. I would see the summer day."

William cast a glance at the doctor and when he nodded his assent, despaired. His wife was dying and nothing else could be done to remedy the outcome.

The freshness of the late afternoon breeze brought a sigh of relief from Peg, and she wondered why it had taken so long to demand that the living world be brought into the room.

"Birdsong . . . can you hear it, Will?"

Suppressing a sob, he answered hoarsely, "Yes, my love."

"Anne," she said softly, "my darling girl, you have a great adventure ahead. Marriage, children, the beauty of the world to remind you of God."

Anne held to her mother's hand, every moment spent in this room close to the surface of memory—dressing in her clothes as a child, wearing her pearls, stories and laughter and tales of the day.

Oh, dear God, please let her laugh again!

Drawing Anne close so that she might speak to her ear, Peg murmured softly, "Take care of your father. He will need you . . . and all your strength. For you are strong, my angel. Where will your strength carry you?"

"Will . . ." and he was at her side, leaning to listen to the weak voice, Peg's effort tremendous, "do ye remember what ye said when we first stepped foot in this New World? Ye said we would always be together. And we shall. Always. Whenever ye think of me, I will be with you. My lips at your ear whispering the things ye need to hear. Love is not a physical thing, is it?" she asked, her eyes bright. "It has a life in the soul. When I close my eyes, I feel your spirit. The essence of all that ye are. Around and in me, your mind so much a part of mine, that I cannot tell where I begin and you end. I have only to think of you and I can feel your presence. Know your smell. Feel your touch. Your breath on my neck. Your lips on mine. Oh, Will, whenever ye need me, think of me and I will join with you. Do not weep, my darling, my love is yours, even into the next world."

For a few moments longer her hand caressed his hair until she was unable to sustain the effort, and then, in a barely audible whisper, "Now, please, my love . . . call the priest."

Peg died a day later at sunset, waiting only for the arrival of the priest.

The entire house went into deep mourning. Black drapes were hung across the front doors where barely two weeks before tropical flowers had graced the entry. The joy of the great party of Cardiff Hall faded into whispers and condolences. Once again carriages lined the driveway, this time in somber procession, its occupants now to stand at the side of the freshly dug grave.

Anne was beside herself in anguish, missing her mother so terribly she thought she might not be able to walk to the gravesite. Forgotten for the moment was Peg's plea to take care of her father, for on this morning she had to see to herself, make it through this day, and the next, find something to fill the immense vacuum once filled by her parents. The dirt she threw upon the casket sealed a part of her heart with finality, and she felt the truth of it . . . she was alone.

"Miss Cormac, please allow me to convey my deepest sympathies." Henry Cavanaugh bowed and gravely added, "If there is anything I can do, you have only to ask."

Anne looked up into eyes deep and blue and for the first time since Peg's illness found a soft smile come to her lips. "Thank you, Lord Cavanaugh, your concern means a great deal to me."

"A great deal, Miss Cormac? Pray I am worthy of such trust." He bowed again and stepped back into the crowd so that others might make their condolences.

Tables were set up again under the trees and lunch served, and as the day wore on, Anne found she took up more and more of the reins of the household, for now she was mistress of the estate. The thought occurred to her that her mother knew her well, for the strength she had mentioned emerged as naturally as sunrise. Anne found that she greeted guests, saw to their comfort, accepted their stories and shared memories, waved them farewell in late afternoon. For the first time she called the head housekeeper by her given name, a signal to all the staff that she was taking control.

"Tomorrow, after breakfast, I will see the household accounts, Bess."

"Yes, milady," Bess curtsied.

When the tables had been removed, when all had been put back in place, Anne went to her mother's room, the bed newly made, the wash basins and damp cloths and medicines gone. Still, she could see her mother everywhere, remembering the hours of counsel Peg had given, sitting at the dressing table, the laughter in her eyes, sweeping back the untidy curl of her hair. Anne threw open the curtains to watch the sun set, wondering as she did so, how life could simply continue, one day done, another to come, and all the millions of people upon the earth about their own business, while Peg lay in the ground, gone from it. What of the pain of loss? How could the world continue with all the pain of those left behind? She shuddered where she stood.

"Anne, we have to speak."

William came into the room, looked around, and Anne knew his thoughts matched her own—he saw his wife everywhere in that place. Facing him directly, she looked into his haggard face.

"You are right, for certes, we cannot continue in this vein."

"I am sorry. The night of the ball . . ."

"Do not remind me of that despicable sight!"

As a dam bursting, all the hurt and rage of the last weeks spilled out in a torrent. "How could ye? A serving maid in our own house! I am not so naïve, Father, that I do not know that men have a roving eye and apparently insatiable lust, but I must have dealings with this girl each day. All the while knowing that she has had the favor of my father! How could ye be so . . . so stupid . . . as to bring this into the heart of our home!"

William blanched. "I am trying my best to apologize for my actions. None of what happened was preconceived or thought out. The entire exchange was a momentary whim."

"Is that how Beatrice sees it? A whim? Or does she have some hold on you?" Then with a new thought, "Is she with child?"

"I told you it was the first time and it was the whiskey. She could never have my heart."

They were much alike and he felt his own blood begin to

heat with anger and humiliation. Could she not see his pain? How desperate he was to hold on to what was left of his family? For God's sake, his wife, the love of his life, was gone! Had she no decent word of consolation for him?

"I do not yet know if she is with child, but truth is, we will have to face that possibility. It may arise."

"We?"

He cocked his head and said, "If you are still living in this house as my daughter."

"I will have no bastards in my mother's house!" she screamed. "The girl goes immediately!"

"Be careful, Anne. There is more than one bastard in this world." His face was a mask, beneath it, cold fury. "If you persist in this intemperate speech, I will make other arrangements."

"Whatever do you mean?" she asked, startled and coming up short.

"Do not presume to test your strength against mine. I will arrange a marriage for you to take you from this house."

"And I would be glad to go," she replied haughtily.

"In that case, I have someone in mind."

"I no longer trust your judgment," she dared. "I have already chosen."

"Have you now?" He raised an eyebrow, a small smile forming, admiring her courage in spite of himself. "I see we are not so different. We see what we want and take it. Who did you have in mind?"

And with eyes fiercely determined, answered, "Henry Cavanaugh. I shall be Lady Cavanaugh."

"So I thought. But let me make it clear. You will never have my consent to marry a Jacobite."

Abashed, Anne cried, "And why not? He supports the Irish cause!"

"Because it is a failed cause and promoting it will only cause more misery. As I said, I have another in mind."

The finality of his tone caused her pause, and she remembered the full power he held over her. "Who?" she whispered.

"Philip O'Conner. He is Catholic, Irish, wealthy, and his business interests serve mine."

"But, where would I live? The Indies? I thought you wanted a man to take over Cardiff Hall. Henry could be that man, a real man."

"Henry, is it?"

"You know as well as I that O'Conner's a fool. He's . . . old . . . his hands too soft for my taste."

Against her will, blood rushed to her face, for to tell her father what she desired was an intimacy that should have been hers alone. Between them stood the unspoken understanding that she yearned for someone with whom she could share the marriage bed, and Philip O'Conner was not that man.

"Perhaps you will like Jamaica," he retorted. "For if you cannot forgive me and offer me some civility, an island might be just the place for you."

Anne gasped at the audacity of his threat. Without a word, she turned and fled the room, racing for the stables as she always did when in distress.

"My horse," she screamed to Kevin.

"But, milady, the sun is almost down," he pleaded. "It's dangerous to ride in the dark," for all knew how Anne rode, and how would she ride on the day she had buried her mother?

"Now!"

And she was off racing to the gate and up the road, William only seeing the back of her, berating himself for his temper, his arrogance, for missing the opportunity to reconcile. He had not meant to frighten her. But he could not chase her either. Damn his stubborn Irish pride.

Anne took the roads at a fast pace until the first of the stars appeared and she could no longer see to gallop. Rosie was tired and Anne knew she must stop to rest when she finally felt the horse falter under her. With darkness gathering quickly, she wondered where she was to go, for she refused to return to Cardiff Hall and its misery. Instead, she noted her position and knew it was no accident that she was near Brambly Place . . . and that its guests included Henry Cavanaugh.

The company on the veranda observed her entrance into the yard, the moonlight outlining her shape in a silver glow. Only when the guests seated around the porch table realized who she was, did the entire assemblage arise, leaving their drinks. But it was Henry who came to meet her.

"You said if there was anything you could do . . ." she began, suddenly feeling very foolish with all eyes upon her, her hair once again disheveled from the hard ride. "I was out riding and it was dark before I knew."

"Miss Cormac, you have my gravest sympathies."

"I always ride when I want to clear my mind," she rambled, "but my horse was tired and I was nearby . . ."

"I am glad you came here, for I can fully appreciate your grief." He stepped forward and raised an arm. "Let me help you down. I'll get a carriage and escort you home. Your father will be worried."

Let us hope so, Anne prayed bitterly.

The carriage was deliciously close and she turned crimson at the feel of his thigh as they sat together under the bonnet of the vehicle, grateful for the darkness that surrounded them. The night was humid, too warm, and Anne was relieved for the wind that blew as they moved along a dim path cast by a quarter moon. Lord Cavanaugh drove slowly, in no rush, his hands firm on the reins, the horse sensing the road and moving leisurely. Now that they were together she wondered at her own audacity. Shamefully, she could still see the faces of those on the porch, their pitying glances apparent even in the dim light. By tomorrow everyone in the county would have heard of her night ride, another tale to add to the story of the funeral. She was more than aware that it would go round how wild she was, sixteen, going on her own to Lord Cavanaugh and escorted home without chaperone, her mother not more than twelve hours in her grave.

"Lord Cavanaugh, I am sorry for the inconvenience. I'm afraid I may have compromised your honor. Tongues will wag on the morrow."

"Nonsense. I can assure you my reputation is safe. As is yours. Indeed, I am inured to gossip, having lived with it for so long. Perhaps you can imagine the intrigue of James's court? Truth be told, I find this land refreshing, Miss Cormac, and have thought to make it my home."

"I am glad for you, sir. But I'm afraid you will find our society small."

"Not at all, Miss Cormac. I have already found it most enchanting. Far more than ever I expected."

"Lord Cavanaugh, if I might make so bold," and here she paused, but then thought to speak her mind. "This is not a land for the faint-hearted. Charles Town is a walled city because there is danger on the frontier. Are ye not aware of the many tribes and shifting loyalties of the Indians? Sometimes allied with the French, sometimes with the English, and often for or against each other. Do ye know that the Indians have their own creeds and customs? That they hold slaves and prisoners, and their methods of fighting and capture are . . ." again she paused, ". . . might not be . . . well, it is said they are unique to our experience."

"I am amazed that you mention it."

"And that is only to our backs," Anne ignored his stare in the dark, for honesty was exactly her point. "To our front we have the fear of pirates, some of whom have amassed more than one ship. How is a merchant to sail, only to be attacked by odds he cannot hope to best?"

"How informed you are, Miss Cormac!"

"I know my father's business, sir. I manage the plantation in his absence. When he has to return to town for his legal practice and shipping interests. But ye've not answered my questions. You call this land refreshing, but do ye have the courage for it?"

"No one who knows me would doubt my courage," he said softly. "But I do not think it is my sword arm that you doubt. Am I correct, Miss Cormac?"

"I would not doubt your sword either, not in battle or foray, for all are speaking of your distinction in service to King James. But the courage I speak of *is* different. The land you propose to purchase is west and south, is it not? Have ye the courage to create a new society in the wilderness? That is what I ask. My mother oft told me that the old rules do not apply. You will find that our women work alongside our men, as I do with my father. Can ye accept that a woman can ride and hunt? I shoot better than most men, and use a sword, rather well, I'm told."

To which Henry laughed, for here was a rare bird indeed.

"My family does not hold with slavery. *I* do not hold with slavery. My father says we Irish have seen enough of it . . ."

"Indeed!"

"A man must have his own self to call his own. And while King James has promised a Catholic Ireland again, here we mix equally, Protestant and Catholic, and we worship without fear of arrest, torture, and intimidation. We welcome Jacobites as our neighbors, but there is also room for Presbyterians, Baptists, and Lutherans. Is this the world for you, Lord Cavanaugh?"

For a long moment there was silence in the cab of the buggy, the horse's clopping footfalls and the rustling of harness the only sounds stretching out into the night. Anne held her breath, wondering if she had overstepped in challenging him.

"Then I will be equally frank," he said at last. "Maneuvering through the wars and arrests, the killing and torture of those who struggle for power in the name of religion, is as dangerous as Indians and pirates. And I have had my fill of it. If I must fight, then let it be fighting for a land that will allow freedom of conscience. I have come halfway around the world to hear the very words you speak to me now. And until this moment, I don't believe I understood exactly why I came . . . and if you will permit . . . exactly what I wanted."

"Might . . . might I ask, what that is?"

In answer, he pulled on the reins and stopped the carriage, Anne's heart racing so that she heard the blood in her ears.

"Anne," and there was no pretense in his tone, "there is already a connection between us, is there not? One from the first moment of meeting. I would like for you to see the property I would purchase. And if it suits . . . if I suit . . . will you receive me?"

"Oh, I would like nothing better! But . . ." dear God, a man who equaled her own impulsive soul, ". . . but . . . I'm afraid my father will refuse."

"How could he? A long engagement past the end of your mourning will allow us time to know each other better. None need know of the arrangements until the year is over. What say you, Anne, will you have me? For I swear I will never find a woman like you who matches my own heart."

"I will have you, Henry. But my father . . . has his own thoughts."

She looked up to the night sky just as a shooting star seared the dark horizon in a golden flash.

"Ah, did you see it? Beautiful!"

She wrapped the image to keep, quarter moon overhead, stars near the earth's surface. In the future she could take out this bejeweled remembrance, a reminder of a summer night and a handsome man and all God's creation.

Suddenly, he was leaning toward her, his lips soft upon hers in a first kiss, sweet, her mind stirring like gentle rain, rose petals, new silk, and she breathed in his scent of horse and whisky and cigar smoke, her body limp with emotion.

"Come," he said gently, "I will have you home. And there I will speak with your father."

"Wait," Anne cried softly, for she already knew William Cormac's answer. "Another kiss . . . that I might remember this night."

With a grin that could not be hid in the dark, he pulled her close, her breasts against his chest, and slowly, savoring the anticipation, brought his mouth to hers, the gentle first touching lost in this new embrace, his mouth opening hers, his tongue finding her own, her desire immediate, a warmth between her legs, a feeling new, terrifyingly out of control . . . and Anne knew for the first time that physical love might be a wondrous thing.

"One you will remember," he whispered close to her ear, brushing his lips along her neck, "always."

She felt him pull away and moaned softly, wondering if Henry were to touch her again, how her body might respond. Here was true adventure, a new frontier. Surely his desire must match her own!

The reins hit the backs of the horses, and they trotted off, Henry facing straight ahead, for he was no stranger to the low moan of pleasure Anne had sighed.

"You must think me shameless," she said into the poignant silence between them.

"No, Anne. You say and do what comes to your heart. Now . . . your father will trust me to bring you home."

At the entrance to the drive of Cardiff Hall, Anne tensed, for ahead she saw that torches were still ablaze near the porch and knew for a certainty that her father waited. As they stopped by the front stairs, William came out to meet them and accepted her lightly from the carriage, taking in the situation immediately. Without question Anne's reputation was compromised, how much so, he would soon learn.

"Good evening, Anne. Your maid awaits. We will speak in the morning."

Anne turned back to the carriage, her gaze bright and moist, her look intimate.

"Good night, Henry," and at the use of his familiar, felt the scrutiny of her father's eyes, "and thank you. For everything. I pray we meet again soon."

And she was off, taking the stairs quickly to her room.

"Sir," Henry began, "if I may have a moment of your time . . ."

"Lord Cavanaugh," William retorted without preamble,

clearly angry and seething, "although I thank you for escorting my daughter home, I must insist that you not see Anne again."

"I assure you, sir," Henry said stiffly, "my conduct was entirely proper."

"I can appreciate the position Anne has forced upon you, and again, my thanks. That is not the point. I believe we understand each other?"

"I am sorry, sir, but I beg to differ. Perhaps you do not understand my intentions. I would like to make an offer for Anne's hand in marriage. I believe we could come to terms."

William raised an eyebrow. "Your decision is rather quick, Lord Cavanaugh, is it not?"

The insinuation that he would take advantage of a sixteen-year-old girl given into his care infuriated Henry, and he struggled to keep the indignation from his voice. "Only that I believe she has a life and spirit that are rare, and I would have it in a wife in this new land."

For a moment they did indeed understand each other. "Of her spirit, I do know. But I will not have this union. I want something different for my daughter."

"If I may be permitted to ask, sir, what can that be? Anne speaks to me of a new society, one in which a woman can stand equally next to a man. How can you deny her a place in this world she envisions?"

"Does she now? Let me ask you Lord Cavanaugh, if you had an only daughter, would ye not want to determine where she would marry? My daughter is to be engaged to a man I have already chosen. Let it stand at that."

"Does she know?"

"I mentioned the possibility this afternoon. Do we understand each other now?"

"Yes, I believe so. With your pronouncement she took horse in the night, grieving sorely for her mother, and came . . . to me. Yes, I believe we understand each other perfectly. For the moment. Goodnight."

At breakfast table the next morning Anne sat at its head, her mother's old position, her father at the other end watching. He'd given some thought to Cavanaugh's words and ruefully had to admit he admired the man.

"Forgive me, Anne," he tried. "I seem to have made a muddle of things. My anger is quick to rise. You know I only look to your own happiness. I . . ."

For the first time since the ball, Beatrice entered into Anne's presence, nervous, her eyes only on the floor, a serving tray of hot porridge in hand. William stopped mid-sentence, mute with the flare of instant hatred that burned in Anne's eyes.

The world slipped away as Anne watched the girl move toward her. If not for Beatrice, she would have remembered the ball and her momentous entrance into the world, with fondness instead of disgust. If not for her, she and her father would have shared in the death of her mother, rather than as separate empty shells with much between them. They would have reconciled, rather than be locked in this battle where he would assert his dominance, the price for her independent thinking, marriage to a man she detested and exile to the Caribbean. If not for Beatrice, she could have Henry and the promise of the kiss in the carriage.

Time seemed to stop and Anne could not remember until later the images of that moment, the edges of the world going black. Beatrice came toward her nervously carrying a tray. A step from where Anne sat, she looked up . . . and wavered at what she saw in Anne's face. The tray tipped, hot cereal spilling into Anne's lap. Beatrice gasped and brought a hand to her mouth in disbelief, her eyes swinging round to William in horror. Leaping from outrage, oblivious of anything else, Anne lifted the knife at hand and stabbed into her flesh, the blade bouncing off the collarbone.

"Dear God!" William leapt up and grabbed the girl as she fell to the ground. "Anne, Anne, what have you done?"

But she had no words, bravado fled, and she shook uncontrollably, her heart pounding fiercely, appalled and not knowing how it had happened.

No one else was in the dining room that morning, and it was given out that the stabbing had been an accident. Anne had stood and turned just as Mistress Beatrice reached her with the porridge. But the servants looked at Anne's dress covered with oatmeal, knew her temperament and passions, and surmised differently. Although the wound was clean and simple, the doctor was called. Beatrice would live. Her courses began the day after the stabbing.

News spread and took as many forms as there were people to tell the story. In the end, the wags had their day, and William Cormac was forced to come to her with news.

"It seems O'Conner will not have you." Then with a wry smile, he added, "I do believe he is afraid of you, Anne. Perhaps his hands are too soft after all."

Chapter Seven

The town house in Charles Town was a well-appointed, three-story brick building facing the bay and near the customs office, the better for William to attend to the business of trade that was now outstripping his legal practice. After the incident at Cardiff Hall, he moved Anne away from Beatrice and the servants, determined not to bring her back until he had settled money on the girl and found her another position.

Anne found some comfort in the upstairs bedroom with its large bay windows facing the water, the room filled with light, another place of memories and images of her mother. Grief stricken at losing Peg, her first love, her reputation and self-respect all in the week, she took refuge in the parlor harpsichord. Music filled the house at all hours, her eyes holding all the drama of dark tragedy

After several weeks, there was a shift in her temperament. The indoors seemed too contained, stifling, and she walked the cobblestone street along the waterfront, her eyes following the dozens of ships in port, their masts a forest reaching the sky, the breath of the wind filling the sails of those headed out to open sea. With the departure of the merchant men, she began to dream of what it might mean to have the whole world in the form of a ship that could take a person anywhere one had a mind to go, some place away from tedious unhappiness.

While William tended to his needs at the plantation, Anne walked in all kinds of weather and at all hours of the day. Only her clothing gave evidence of her social status, and because people looked and wondered, she sought to costume herself in simple cotton and linen, somber colors and little lace. Scandalously, she went about without cap, her hair more and more left to fall the length of her back, curled and restless upon her head in the humid air. When she returned she held color in her face, a rosy glow from the fresh air, but her skin was turning an unsightly shade of brown. The head housekeeper, Mrs. Stewart, begged her to carry a parasol, for she feared the explanation Mr. Cormac would demand upon return.

So it was that one late afternoon a new ship put into port, and she stood with others along the quay and watched the men disembark, pay in their pockets and looking to the pleasures of Charles Town.

"Pirates," an old man muttered and spat on the ground.

"Really," Anne asked, "where? I've never seen a pirate before."

"Well, ye just have to give a look-see there. Watch yourself, missy."

Anne regarded the longboat putting ashore. Among the men one caught her eye, and she watched his movements with bold interest, for he was young, the sway of his body a curiosity, his dark brown hair his own and cued, no cropped hair and powdered wig for a seaman, a straight nose and clean shaved face, a glint of gold at his ear, and his hands . . . rough. Trying to take his measure, she noted the wide-brimmed hat, white linen shirt with billowing sleeves, knee breeches, and boots, his lack of waistcoat or jacket. Across his chest he carried a thick leather belt holding a sword that hung at his waist, and he wore the weapon as an old friend. From the shingle he looked up and his eyes were brown and they could not fail to notice the girl who stood alone and singled him out.

"Well, lass," he called as he jumped to the boardwalk from the sand, "and where be ye off to?"

Taken aback that he would speak to her, Anne said the first thing that came into her mind. "Indeed, sir, I am out for a stroll."

"Sir, is it?" And he looked at her with some curiosity, for here was a strange whore, fresh, and he wondered how long she had been about her business. "Would ye like to walk with me? I've money in me pockets," and he shook them so that she could hear the jingle.

"I walk home, sir. But . . . I could go part way with you . . . if you will tell me about your ship and the lands you have visited."

"Why, I've been to England just now." He warmed to her game, her acting the innocent immediately arousing him, although after three months at sea, it would not have taken much. "There with a load of goods. Tobacco, rice, and cotton. And back again, with China plates and pipes and wools and silks. Tea as well. For sure, the East India Company has made the world a smaller place."

"Then you're not a pirate?"

Warily now, "Why would ye be thinkin' such a thing? Piracy is a hangin' offense. Better to watch what you say, girl."

"Hanging? I beg your pardon, sir. That old man," and she gazed in his lumbered direction, "he said . . . and well, pirates are so rich and brave . . ."

"Ah, if that be the case, then pirate I am, for truth is, I've a pocket of pay and as brave a sword arm as any." He leaned close to her ear. "Have a drink with me, lass, and I'll tell you stories of the sea, as sure as I'm a seaman," then he bowed so prettily and laughed with such glee, that all Anne could remember was how long it had been since she had laughed.

To his bow, she curtsied, "I shall be honored. But where shall we drink?"

"Follow me."

The streets he led her down were those she had never traveled before, away from the large homes that lined the bay, away from the bastions and soldiers guarding the walls of the city. Although late in the day, the sun was still high, for it was summer, but Anne was well aware that if she did not watch the time, it would be dark when she returned through these very streets that looked none too safe in daylight. Suddenly, she wished for the small pistol she carried when traveling from town house to plantation.

"My name is James . . . James Bonny. What shall I call you?"

"You may call me Anne," she said bravely.

Bonny turned down an even narrower street, buildings close upon each other, the second-story cantilevers making a dim alley. A loud group of men who had obviously had much drink were gathered there, and with them, women with rouged cheeks and red lips, laughing too loudly. As they made their way up the lane, heads turned toward them, for here was a fresh pair, James, tall and brown from his work aboard ship, and Anne, clean, her eyes wide with wonder at all she saw, drawing her cloak more tightly and trying not to touch those who pushed against her.

"Belay, James!" One of the sailors keeled in his direction, his gaze none too steady, his voice slurred, teeth cracked and brown in a lopsided, drunken smile. "Here now. Jus' in? Give up a shilling for a pint, will 'e?"

"I'll stand you a cup later, Ned," he told the man, pushing him aside, "but right now, I get my own throat wet."

Bonny took Anne's elbow and tried moving toward the entrance of a tavern, but before he'd traveled three steps, a woman grabbed his arm and whispered hoarsely, her face hard for all she tried to smile with some allure. "Any takings, James? Any pretty bauble from a Spanish ship?"

"Not today, my pretty," and he grinned, giving her a wink. "This time I was aboard a merchant. Straight back from England I am with a load of proper cargo."

The inn he stopped before was half-timbered, dark wood beams framing wattle and daub, white-painted, with a stout wooden door for an entrance and a second-story. A sign swung on a metal hook naming it the Ship and Shore. James reached for the door handle, but found that Anne hesitated, eyes questioning.

"You . . . you *are* a pirate."

"Of course, girl, everyone knows that. I thought you did too."

"But," and the reality struck, "it's pirates that disturb commerce. Steal what belongs to others. Rapes and tortures. Or so I'm told," she added hastily, blushing at the mention of rape with a man she had met scarce fifteen minutes ago.

"It depends on the pirate," Bonny told her. "Each has his own style. Like you, lass, we takes what comes our way. Would you ply your trade if there was enough to go round? You risk the fort's dungeons just as I do."

"Whatever do you mean?" she queried, stepping back slightly.

"A man's got to make a livin' any way 'e can. Or a woman." And now he looked more closely at her. "This is real Irish lace, ain't it?"

"Why, of course. Is there another kind?"

"Aye, and not as rich as that on your sleeves," he answered, and regarded her again more closely.

"What about that drink, then?" she asked to take his eyes from the lace at her bodice.

"Come along," and he pushed open the door.

The tavern was too warm for summer, closed in upon itself and lit by candles. Anne stopped just in the door, suddenly mindful of what her father would say . . . what he would do . . . if he saw her alone and unaccompanied with a man such as Bonny. Along one wall stood a great hearth, hot and roaring, pig upon the spit, the smells of roasting meat filling the inn. The noise was great, for as the drink flowed, so did the voices. A fiddle and a hand accordion played lively music and a few of the sailors danced, one precariously upon a table. She drew back, sensing a danger, a knowing that anything could go wrong and that she was out of her element.

"Changin' your mind, girl? Are ye afraid of me?"

"Not at all," she said sharply.

"Where do ye want to sit?"

"There," she nodded, her cloak still tight about her.

The tables were long planks crudely fashioned and unfinished, filled to bursting with merrymakers, but toward the rear, rough-hewn booths offered some privacy and there seemed to be space enough in one corner. Anne made her way through thick tobacco smoke and between men who rubbed against her without pardon. James pushed toward the bench, his walk a swagger, holding her before him like a prize and guiding her to the place she had chosen. Gratefully, she slid into dimness, a spot where she could observe, aghast and shaking.

"What'll it be?" the serving girl asked haughtily, eyeing Anne with distaste. "Come on, James, name your poison. I ain't got all day."

"And how are you, Betsy?"

"Same as last time. Who's the doxy? I 'aven't seen 'er before."

A rush of anger and Anne blushed scarlet to her shoulders, too stunned to say a word.

"Rum. From the Indies."

"Rum, is it?" Betsy glared. "Your share must be good this run. Sure you want to put it into this?"

James placed a hand on Anne's arm to hold her to her place and nodded, "Aye. Rum."

With a shrug, the girl was off and back, quick, with a bottle and cups. Bonny filled a mug, smiled, and held it out to her. Gingerly, Anne took it, sniffed, the fumes pushing her head away.

"Go on," he encouraged, "drink up."

She sipped, letting the liquid sit on her tongue, sweet, then swallowed, and choked, feeling the burn all the way to her stomach.

"So this is rum," she gasped. "My father ships a lot of this to England."

"Ships, does he?"

"Yes. And he drinks a good bit of it, too."

Bonny tipped his head and threw back the liquid, and to

prove she was man enough, Anne followed, drinking a hard mouthful, coughing, close to retching, while James merely grinned and poured another round.

"Here's to beauty . . . to you," he called, his voice louder. He emptied his cup, then waited with challenging eyes, while she took a deep breath and drank, breathing deeply to let the drink settle.

On the third glass Anne suddenly cried aloud, "To the sea . . . and to freedom!" her eyes watering as she drank, but the burn less, a great numbing taking hold, the picture of her father with his hands grasping Beatrice's breasts fading. "And to you James Bonny, the pirate, to you, because you are my first pirate and my first drink of rum . . ."

"First?"

"Another!" she shouted, and saw that Betsy watched with a look of sheer hatred, but Anne was beyond caring what anyone thought. "And because ye are handsome . . ." now she looked at him, unabashedly, leaning close to see every angle of his face, her voice slurred, tongue thick, words taking some time to form, "and because your mouth is soft . . . tell me James . . . tell me once again where you've traveled . . . James . . . James Bonny . . . for my name is Anne and at the moment my father . . . he's at the plantation . . . getting rid of the serving girl he compromised . . . on the night of my coming out ball." Then, with another shout, "To parties!"

"Jus' who'd ye say ye were?" Bonny asked, his own words blurred, the bottle wavering as it moved to fill her cup.

"No . . . no . . . don' worry . . . I took care of it . . ." and Anne leaned in close, "I stabbed her. No . . . nothin' to worry about . . . no problem. She lived . . . and . . ." lowering her voice still further, "she's not pregnant." Grinning, satisfied that was out of the way, she murmured, "So tell about foreign lands . . . tell what it's like to live on a ship . . ."

"Lemme unnerstand . . . you're not a whore?"

"Why, sir, at any other time I might be insulted, but . . . I know now that I am to whore for my father . . . for his business interests. You see, he will marry me where he will make the most money." And again she drank. "He already tried to marry me off to some man of little stature . . . a tall man really, but his . . . his character is short . . . and his hands," she said tellingly near his ear, "soft." Then she sat back and pronounced, "But it seems the man won't have me . . . rumor you know . . . seems I stabbed the serving girl . . . and now he's afraid of me."

And she laughed uproariously.

"Then, Anne, you're the girl for me," he avowed, his breath warm on her neck. "I likes a girl what's can take care of her own interests. That's the code of the sea. Someone does you wrong, you take care of it. Are you fearless, Anne? For 'tis courage you need to sail into the unknown."

And he began to tell her stories, of waves and winds, of ships he had met in battle, of the daring of men like himself who risked all so they might find a moment in a tavern with a pretty wench such as herself.

"We live on a bit of wood for many months and no one knows when the devil may take us. Our job's hard, my pretty, and we scuttle upon the masts to take up the sails, the foam lappin' at the ship's sides, and many's the time we battle the wind and pray we cheat Davy Jones. 'Tis a struggle each day t' see what wind and water and sun and the men of other nations might pour upon us. Our fare is poor and the disease harsh . . ."

"But . . . you may go where you will. You are free!"

"Free? We sell ourselves to the cap'n and the company what hires us! It's poor wages and ill treatment more often as not." And forgetting himself, "That's why the piratin' and the smugglin' past customs is the job. It's the only way to make a decent wage."

Anne tried forming words. "Piratin'? I . . . I thought we weren't goin' to talk about piratin'?"

"And so we shan't. At any rate, not 'till I know you better. But come, drink another cup with me, for I've made me journey and am alive and well and on shore."

The first kiss was soft, and she could taste the rum on his lips, delicious, his breath fueled by the alcohol of his lungs. Now she could understand why her father liked his drink, the numbness of the body while at the same time feeling everything. And oh, this wondrous thing called passion, how it filled the limbs and fired the belly and became a great force that wanted to suck in the world. He kissed her again and she responded, warm and happy to be loved, to feel love, her body melting into his, this new astonishment of not knowing where her own self ended. Then his head was at the top of her breasts, and she leaned back further into their dark corner, grateful the neckline of her dress was low, the lace thin and narrow, wishing his lips would follow his breath down her cleavage, already sensing how it would feel to have his mouth upon her nipple . . . how she *yearned* for his lips to suckle. She pushed against him with her body, her arms reaching up to caress his hair, his neck . . . from a distance she heard him ask the serving girl for a room . . . the brilliant flash of fire between her legs at the thought . . .

"Miss Cormac?"

From a dream she woke, double vision coming gradually into focus.

"Mister . . . Mister . . . Hempstead?'

A man stood before them, rather short and knowing a good table, his wig powdered, his clothes dark and practical, without weapons, most certainly a merchant.

"Why . . . why, yes, Miss Cormac. I . . . er . . ." he glanced toward Bonny with indecision. How on earth had the young lady wound up here? He himself would never have entered this particular tavern if the ship's captain unloading his goods didn't like the fare. But this dark corner . . .

"Miss Cormac, how is your father? Is he well?" The man must be out of his mind to let the girl out alone! "I am very, very sorry to hear about your mother. Please allow me to offer my sincerest condolences."

"My mother . . ." and Anne began to cry, softly, drunkenly,

but tears hot and heavy.

"Dear God," he turned to a bewildered Bonny, undone by the intrusion, "do you know what you're about? Why the girl just lost her mother not more than a month ago. However did you meet? And do you have her father's permission to . . . court her?"

"Blimy, if I know a thing. We met on the shoreline. Tha's all I know. I thought she was a whore. I can assure you I would not have cheated her." The words were heavy, run together, but still distinguishable.

"A . . . a whore?" he gasped appalled and indignant. "Miss Anne, where is your father?"

"Gone," she answered, still crying, "gone to the plantation."

Hempstead spoke sternly. "This lady is of good character and good family. This is some madness to do with the grief of losing her mother. I will escort the lady home."

Bonny pitched himself up and forward. "Somethin' wasn't right," he nodded. And to himself, *but she knows how to use her body, for certes.* "I will accompany you."

"That will not be necessary."

Bonny stumbled and placed a hand on his sword. "I think it will."

Chapter Eight

Arising from her bed the next morning, Anne reeled to the washbasin on its stand near the window and vomited, full, foul, gut wrenching fluid that told her she'd had little food and much rum the night before. Streaming sunlight hurt her eyes. Never before had she felt this sick, her legs trembling, her stomach heaving. Remembering scenes from the night before, she felt the more ill, realizing all she had said . . . and done. And Mr. Hempstead! What would he say to her father?

The serving girl brought food, the very smell of bacon causing her to retch again. "Take it away," she ordered weakly. "Take it away or I shall be sick. And stay out!"

Only when Mrs. Stewart came personally from the kitchen to see to her with unbuttered toast and light tea, did she allow anyone to enter.

"Come, I will help you dress."

The household was too quiet, and she knew every tongue wagged. Refusing to be intimidated in her own home, she sat at the harpsichord and played, her heart in her hands. Last night had been a confusion of emotions—curiosity, anger, courage, and lust. Yes, she had known lust, no romantic notion of what lovemaking might be, no soft yearning as she had felt with Henry Cavanaugh. The fire of that desire had touched her whole body and changed her. The man she had met had been a pirate, an adventurer, but, she told herself, he had also been a gentleman and had seen her home under the disapproving eye of Mr. Hempstead. James Bonny had used what little money he'd had to buy drinks and had told her tales of the sea, of sunsets on the horizon, storm and wind, of parrots and monkeys and the dress of people from Africa to the Indies, of the great city of London itself, and even of his adventures smuggling through the port of Charles Town. As the sickness of the morning passed, and the day turned hot and sultry, she wished for the air of the harbor, the sight of ships that sailed to freedom . . . and she longed for James Bonny and his stories of his world.

Just after mid-day, and to the horrified gasp of Mrs. Stewart, her hands slammed against the harpsichord, loud and discordant, and she left the room in a rush to her bedroom, changing into modest clothing, grabbing a light cloak and the small traveling pistol for her purse.

"Miss," Mrs. Stewart called, as Anne made for the front door, "please. Let Roger accompany you!"

"I'll have no footman slowing me down, Jane. I am mistress of this house and I shall have my own time."

The street where Bonny had led her to the Ship and Shore was still alive with people and more than one watched as she pushed through the crowd, quick, wishing no interactions with any of them. She felt no small amount of relief in finding the tavern on her own, and entered looking about for James.

Even at this time of day tankards were delivered to busy tables, and the whores, for certainly they were, sat in the laps of patrons. But only a lone musician played a sad fiddle, for this was still the night-after crowd. Although the fire was lit and the roast for the evening meal already upon the spit, the rising energy of the dinner hour with its new complement of patrons wanting food and drink, had not yet fully arrived.

"'Upstairs, ducky," Betsy called, "and if you're lucky, 'e may be alone."

Anne started toward the stairs, then turned back, and thinking herself bold, said, "You've been with him. That's why you dislike me. Do you want him still?"

"Well, that's comin' right out with it, ain't it?" Betsy regarded Anne then, saw the youth and inexperience, thought she'd get hers soon enough and softened enough to give answer. "Nah, not really. It just rankles, you so high and mighty as all. But would ye leave 'im to me if I cared?"

"I hardly know him. Here . . ." and Anne removed a thin gold bracelet and handed it to her, "for your worry. And that we may friends."

Betsy grabbed quickly, before the wind blow in another direction.

"Well, now, this makes things different. Awright, then, friends it is. Go on up . . . 'e's alone. Top o' the stairs, first room right."

No locks held these doors. Anne pushed, the rough bottom scraping the planking, and hesitated at the scent of unwashed sheets and old food. Her stomach, still none too steady, gave a lurch at the smell, and she almost turned to go, knowing this was not for her. But then the thin light from a small cut-glass window showed Bonny, shirtless and bootless, sharpening his sword, his face astonished at her appearance. Surprised, but still handsome. For the first time she guessed at his age, young, perhaps five years older then herself. All right, she would stay, but she resolved then and there, she would never give herself to any man in such a place.

"Well, now . . ." and he stood slowly, walked to her, his chest warm, his muscles hard and crossed with the scars of his fights.

"No," Anne told him, as he reached for her. "Not here."

Instead, she took the sword from his hand and felt the balance of it.

"Come now, my pretty. You're 'ere for only one reason."

"Aye," she grinned, holding the sword between them, point near Bonny's chest, making clear her distance. "I want to hear your stories. And I've a mind for a bit o' practice."

"And what is it ye'll be practicin' at?" he asked softly, gently pushing aside the blade and stepping close.

"Swords," she answered, turning away from him, swishing the weapon through the air and hearing its hum.

"Do you mean to say you can use a blade?" His eyes

narrowed, skeptical, yet he was curious to see if she spoke true. "All right. I can borrow one downstairs and you can show me what ye have to offer. Unless you'd rather do something else?"

"I believe swords will serve for the moment."

The days passed and still William did not return from the plantation. Anne in her heart of hearts knew that his dalliance was not simply with the labors of the field. Beyond doubt, a common wench had already supplanted her mother. She shook her curls and stiffened her resolve. If William would have his way, so would she.

Every morning she left the house alone and joined Bonny at the tavern or along the shore. Sometimes they met in the small room where they practiced at swordplay, and although Anne had technique, James began to teach her the finer points of street-fighting, those tricks she would need if she were to encounter a serious opponent bent on taking her purse, or worse. She learned quickly, and he became unsettled when she could back him into a corner, her lightness of foot and greater maneuverability unbalancing him. She had a disconcerting way of using his strength against him, and even when he swung hard enough to disarm her, she moved with the blow, the force of it dissolving into her very retreat. The day came when he no longer wanted to practice, fearful of humiliation, but she insisted if he was to have her company.

In this new world, the simple sailors and women of the street suddenly became more comfortable as acquaintances, than those who inhabited the three-storied houses along the waterfront. Most were without pretense, speaking their minds and telling true. Here were real people who lived on the edge of life, one day to the next. In their existence she sensed a vulnerability that brought them closer to the great belly of life. Why, closer to God, she thought. Clearly she was her mother's own daughter, for she understood their poverty, the small wages, the persecution and social circumstances from which many of them ran—debtor's prison in England, branding, thumbscrew and boot, whip and cane and cat o' nine tails, long, arbitrary sentences for petty theft or for being on the losing side in some religious war. Almost all had been born on the wrong side of the blanket, bastards, orphaned or abandoned as children. The men, outlawed, turned to theft as the occasion rose, and protected each other better than any army or police. Together, sword in hand, they would take back from the world what had been taken from them. Piracy was the way the books were balanced.

"Here's to fair winds and calm seas," Davis called, lifting his tankard to the half-dozen who sat at table. His eyes were as blue as the deep sea he called upon, hair the color of flax, unwashed and pasted to his head beneath a red scarf.

Anne raised her cup of ale with the others at the Ship and Shore, unable to conceal the livid anger that consumed her, appalled they would take their lot in stride.

"Aye," Morris nodded, "to fortune."

"And to you, Bridget," Anne cried, "for God knows you deserve praise for endurance!"

Perhaps in her early twenties, Bridget seemed a woman grown to Anne. But Anne's esteem simply caused a shrug, a wave of the hand to push the past aside. The woven braids of her hair fell long over one shoulder, and about her neck lay a string of shells, white against skin darkened by the sun.

"Lord, it wasn't just me as was stolen. Hundreds of children come on dat boat wit' me to Barbados, all terrified and not knowin' what was t' become of us. Dem all has dey stories."

"But Bridget, you were *kidnapped* from the streets of Dublin so that you might be sold into slavery. Only ten years old! It is unspeakable!"

In answer Bridget leaned back in her chair, one slender hand languidly holding her cup. "Yeh see, dey tol' us we was indentured fi seven years. An' I can tell you each and every one of us looked forward to de day when we would be let go.

But dey always found an excuse to add more years, so's dey could keep us bound in slavery. Yeh unnerstan'?"

"However did you get away?"

"Aboard a ship, but six months ago. Stowed away by de mate. None too easy leavin' de picknies dem, mind you, but," and again that impervious shrug of acceptance, "me din' own dem, yeh see?"

"Oh . . . I . . . I see."

"Do ye, Anne?" Bonny asked. "Can ye see that men and women are forced to be fieldworkers and breeders, so's the planters will have their labor?" And he eyed her thinking of her own plantation, not knowing her father kept no slaves.

"When de captain found I was aboard," Bridget told her, "he was none too happy, mind you. Sailors dem, dey fear de woman, to be sure. And I was an escaped slave. He could have held me in de brig until he returned, and de master would have paid plenty to get me back."

"Why didn't he?"

With some amusement at Anne's innocence, Bridget answered, "'Cause me was busy liftin' me skirt de whole journey. De price fi me freedom."

"Oh," Anne whispered, breathless.

Finally, Morris took pity on her ignorance, for the lass was green raw. With a flourish he removed his hat, cast it to the table with a soft thud, and looked directly in her eye.

"Have ye seen a slaver, girl? I was pressed onto an African trader dealing in black ivory two years ago. Swore I'd fight and die before forced to serve aboard one again."

"Well, no, although I have heard they come with more frequency."

"Have ye been to the market in town what sells human flesh?"

Anne shook her head, a hard, anxious knot growing in her stomach. "There's many that don't hold with slavery."

"A losin' game thinkin' you can stop slavery," Bonny made plain. "Look about. Slavery's big money. All these planters are puttin' down rice. What man's goin' to work those fields but a slave?"

"If you look in the harbor," Morris told her, "ye'll see the *African Crown*. But ye'll not see 'er close up to shore, for the good people of Charles Town who'll buy 'er cargo, don't want the smell of 'er. All those wretches . . . pukin' and shitin' and layin' in it for the months of passage from the African coast. Why, Christ's balls, you can smell the fear as easily as the offal. Even those that sail 'er are lucky to make the coast alive."

He swilled deep, trying to drown the memory of fear and stench. A tremor ran involuntarily through his body. When he looked up Anne saw revulsion in his eyes.

"Took us a good four to five months to collect the cargo, 'cause the captain wanted men of different tribes, see? No sense in 'avin' 'em speak the same language so's they could make a mutiny. No, let 'em fight amongst each other, for often the hates among 'em are as great as the hate they hold for their captors. Once I had to accompany the cap'n ashore t' guard his back with pistol. There's a sight, I can tell you. Stockades filled with black men t' be purchased, sold by their own people. The Ashanti, them's the one's. They goes about and collects men, women, and children from their enemies and brings 'em to market."

He took a deep breath and slowly shook his head. "We sat on that pestilential African coast while waitin', jostlin' with other ship's captains for the best o' the bunch. I watched me mates sickenin' one by one with tropical fever and scurvy, forever fearful of attack from the mainland."

"An' the captain," Davis interjected. "I can tell you it's the hard man who's goin' to run a slaver."

"Aye," Morris nodded. "The only thought to the cargo is just which tribe will bring the most coin. Some of them Africans are warriors, t' be sure, and the planters won't 'ave 'em. No, it has t' be jus' the right tribe, see. When we finally took sail, the whip wouldn't stop the moanin' and chantin' until the water ran low and it was too much for 'em to use their voices. The stench so awful, we nearly puked our guts up havin' to smell it. Not even a brisk wind took it away. I swear to you, that putrid smell settled into every piece of wood and cloth on ship. And to eat, why, Christ, even a piece of damnable maggot-ridden hardtack was a misery."

"Do ye begin to see why men are pressed aboard?" Bonny asked her. "Who would sail that voyage except for the captain and his officers who will make a heavy purse."

"Each mornin' we would open the hatches and the wretches below decks would pass up five or six corpses to be thrown overboard," Morris continued. "And as quick as that we closed 'em back again, for the captain was deathly afeared of an uprisin'. Hell, he would tell stories he'd heard to make the blood run cold with thoughts o' the black men takin' over the ship. And at night . . ." he looked away from the table, his eyes on the memory, "at night we quietly slipped our own dead into the sea, so's they wouldn't see our dwindlin' numbers. For every black man as went over, so did a member of the crew, and sometimes one or two more. We lost a full third of our cargo by the time we reached Port Royal, and as many crewmen. Given way to bad food and water and disease and cruel treatment by the captain and his officers."

A pause, and he added bitterly, "I meself spoke a wrong word to the mate. I've the scars of a dozen lashes with the cat on me back as reward. No, from now on, I'll keep clear of the slavers and the press gangs, and choose me own captain and me own ship, and I'll take me due from them's that's takin' from me."

"Perhaps . . . perhaps," Anne suggested, aghast at his story, "the importation of indentured whites will serve. The legislature recently passed laws encouraging the practice. At least after seven years the men and women are free and have a chance for their own land in the west . . . that is, if they can wrest it from the Indian."

"Anne, Anne," Daniel Davis answered, shaking his head at her ignorance. Mid-twenties, he had escaped from indenture on the frontier and made his way to the coast. "I will be tellin' you plain and true, there's precious little for a man what's poor. But even poor, at least me family 'ad a home. Until the day the landlord wanted the land we'd lived upon. Raised the rents, 'e did, to force us out, an' put fences around what used to be the farms of many. You see, he would have sheep to run the land, sheep instead of families. Sheep for the new manufacturin' in the cities . . ."

"Aye, so's the wealthy can make more," Morris nodded resentfully.

"I took me wife and bairns to Manchester," Davis explained, "for we'd nowhere else to go, and I went to work in the same factory as bought the wool. Toiled from sunup to sundown, I did, for a wage that couldn't feed me alone. So I borrowed, and when I couldn't pay, they took me to prison, leavin' my family to fend on their own."

"And do ye know where they are now?" Anne asked, shaken.

Davis shook his head, blue eyes turned on her. "My indenture was in the backcountry, fellin' trees and uprootin' stumps. When the rumor of a chance to make me own wages came, I hid and slowly found me way to port. There I joined up with the first ship I could find, makin' my mark below the Articles."

"Now there's a free man's creation, to be sure," Bonny told them.

"Articles?"

"Why, the Articles of the Brethren, lass," Davis answered. "The Brotherhood of the Coast."

"The . . . the pirates' code?"

Bonny nodded, for she might as well know. "The Articles allow us to choose our own captain and captain he'll be 'til 'e's voted out. Every man of us is a freeman and stands for his own self, but a man serves his best interests by standin' with other free men. We don't hold to color or class or wealth. A man's not born with his rank, but earns it."

"Aye," Morris nodded. "We make our own laws and we accept 'em, as well as the punishment for breakin' 'em. No captain or company makes 'em for us, nor breaks us for what we know is unjust. No pirate captain's goin' to scar a man's back."

"And that, Anne," Bonny told her with some fervor, "is the true freedom of the seas. It's not the ship what gives us freedom. The ship only takes us to places, and to get there we face peril. If you have nae respect for the sea, t'will come at you and carry you away. But to be able to choose how to live and how to die . . . that is freedom."

"Well put, mate . . ." a voice boomed through the room.

All eyes turned to the man who had just entered the tavern and stood close enough to have heard James's speech. Tall, handsome, and imposing, he filled the room with his presence, for if any man knew himself it was Benjamin Hornigold.

Anne recognized him at once. Lace adorning collar and cuffs, long coat to his knees with silver buttons, embroidered waistcoat, good knee pants, and shoes with buckles. The captain had been to Cardiff Hall several times to make arrangements to ship William's cotton. But what was this? Did her father suspect that the good captain was into piracy? Knowing the man and knowing his tastes led Anne to question whether all was as democratic as James believed.

". . . and indeed I am taking on crew."

"Captain Hornigold," Bonny stood, "when do you ship?" For his money was low and the tavern keeper could not afford to keep him indefinitely. To his way of thinking, he had two options, back to sea, or if Anne would have him, marriage into a wealthy family and all its prospects.

"Within the week. I take on stores now." His arm indicated the large man who stood beside him, beard the color of bootjack, and by way of introduction announced, "My mate, Edward Teach."

Hornigold strode to the side of the tavern and tacked a bill to the wall. "Any man wanting to sign Articles will meet here tomorrow afternoon. But make haste to spread the word, for I want to fill the roster quickly. We go to do the work we know best, and that's the taking of French and Spanish ships. Each man gets a share according to his station and the extent of his wounds."

"I believe you can count on every man here, Captain," Bonny told him.

"Aye, sir," Morris stood and nodded, "and good timin' it is. We was just talkin' about a slaver that's unloadin' and puttin' off again."

Captain Hornigold cast his eyes around the room taking in what men were to be had, gave a second glance to the women of the tavern, then suddenly stopped, his eyes falling on Anne, her face tuned away, hiding behind Bonny. "Miss Anne?"

"Indeed, sir," and she stood and bowed in her best manner to bluff her way out of embarrassment, for surely now all of Charles Town would have their proof of what was only being speculated upon in the parlors. "A pleasure to see you again, Captain Hornigold."

"What are you doing here?" he asked, so surprised he could not help but be blunt.

"Why, having ale and food, Captain," came the quick answer, for Anne suddenly found her position so absurd as to be humorous.

"Forgive me, but . . . this is not Cardiff Hall."

"Indeed, it is not, and I am glad of it. I wish you well, Captain. Good hunting and good fortune."

Captain Hornigold made an elegant leg, "Your servant, milady." And then added with some amusement, for he was certain William Cormac knew not at what the girl played. "My respects to your father."

"I'm sure he will be delighted to receive them," she answered matching his tone exactly and gracing him with a bow.

Hornigold gave her a parting grin and turned to the door, gesturing to his mate. 'Blackbeard' some called him. And a handy man he was in a fight, his strength and fury such that no man would meet his sword. To their horror, he would swing over the side, bits of rope twined in his beard and set afire, flames and smoke framing his face so he looked like the devil himself. Rather than follow Hornigold's lead, Teach doffed his hat and made in Anne's direction. Horigold seeing his intent, stopped him with a single word.

"Edward."

The voice cut through the room like a pistol shot, hard, Hornigold's eyes narrowed with a mixture of menace and authority. A long silence filled the space between the men, then Teach smiled, his lips curved, eyes cold.

"Aye, Captain."

He made a flowing bow to the group at table, eyes lingering on Anne, pondering, then made for the exit, his bulk filling the doorframe.

The door had not finished closing behind them when Bonny turned on Anne, real anger in his voice, something she had not heard before, for he had removed his hat to Captain Hornigold and had been the picture of deference.

"How is it ye can speak so with the captain?" he asked hotly. "You speak as his equal!"

"I beg your pardon?" and she looked at him with some astonishment. "I am any man's equal."

"But if you are to be with me, ye must be respectful! You're but a lass. A ship's a small world and I'll not have myself compromised!"

For a moment she simply stared at him bewildered, then before the whole assembly answered, "I believe you are speaking of submission, not respect. Have ye not just told me that the Code made all men equal? By what right do ye tell me how to speak . . . or what to think? I'm here precisely because I will have no man tell me what I can or cannot do."

With a turn, he kicked out at a bench, clearing a path, and was out the door, furious that she would seize his manhood in front of his mates. Anne watched him leave with regret, for she did not want to argue, but when she sat back onto the bench, she noticed a quiet and that all eyes were on her, the initial intake of Betsy's breath and the laughter of the others gone. Well, then . . . she would simply leave as well. Standing calmly, she shook out her skirts and drained her tankard.

"Hey, poppet," a burly voice called. "Looks like your sword just left."

The man had been staring at her for days, and Anne was naive enough to have missed the fact that she went unmolested because she was under Bonny's protection. Around her, she felt those at the table stand and move away, these men with whom she had just eaten and shared stories and a joke, and was surprised.

Ah, so this is the pirate's way. To think first of self . . . for that is all they know . . . how they've come this far.

"Ah, leave the girl alone," Betsy tried.

And almost as much as gold, they love good theater. The drama has begun and I must take the lead. Every person in this room wants to see how I handle myself, for indeed, this is not Cardiff Hall and I must prove my mettle. So be it. I will give them a good show.

"My name's Dalrick McKenzie," he said moving slowly, approaching her stealthily, as one might a cornered animal, "but they call me Red." And he tugged at the red beard on his face, laughing loud to show rotted teeth.

"Go find James," Betsy whispered to Bridget.

Anne saw the stripes of his pants, three quick steps moving across the floor, the wide belt buckle jab into her side as he drew her close and grabbed at the sleeve of her dress, then the rough tug, the pull so that her breast was laid bare. To everyone's surprise, rather than scream or cry, Anne turned, and with a backhand, smashed the man hard and full across the face, a ring catching his lip so that blood spouted. So shocked was he that for a full minute he could not respond, but merely stared dumbfounded at the blood on his hand.

"Don't you ever lay a *fucking* hand on me again!" she said into the dead quiet, pulling up her sleeve and covering herself. Her face, her father's face, was white with rage, her first use of the profanity tasting good in her mouth.

Pandemonium ensued, for he lunged, his own fury matching her own. Numb from drink, he roared, crashing into bench and table, but Anne, faster, had already moved around and to the other side.

"A sword!" she cried, and one found its way into her hand.

Laughing uproariously now, Red pulled his own sword. "Come on then, poppet, let's see what you've got!"

His laughter did not last long. Amidst great cheering by the assembled, he found himself met by skill and some cunning, and by the fourth or fifth rush at her, found that he fell and crashed and was maneuvered so that the very force of his attack was turned against himself. Stunned, nae terrified, he found himself battling for his life against a skirt.

Anne took her time, remembering her father's lessons in style and Bonny's practical ploys, taking a cut here and there, the crowd with her, enjoying the spectacle, his blood covering his shirt and pants, his face permanently scarred, until she had him backed against a wall and on his knees.

"Now, apologize," she demanded, holding the sword to his windpipe, blood slowly trickling down his neck.

From the cold hardness of her eyes, he was unwilling to chance that she would not run him through. With embarrassment, sobering quickly from the shock of the wounds, unable to hold her gaze and dropping his head, he mumbled, "Sorry. I'd only a mind for a bit o' drink. No need to take it so hard, poppet."

"My name is Anne," she told him coldly. "Remember it."

From that day Anne always wore a sword once she entered the tavern, kept by Betsy in her own room, and she did not need Bonny's protection. Indeed, men warily watched her and none dared approach the 'hell cat', for that is how they spoke of her.

When Bonny heard of the incident, the tale told over and over, he was not surprised, for Anne had been his sparing partner. No longer was she the girl he had met on the quay weeks ago. Instead, she had steadily made her way into the world of the tavern and seafarers, his world, and gradually she was earning their respect. His position was now even more precarious than before, and he resolved that he would have Anne one way or another, or he would be a laughing stock.

Chapter Nine

The weather was changing, autumn approaching, trees beginning to turn, and still William had not returned. The entire household knew of Anne's change of habits, indeed she was rarely at home and they knew she was not out walking. When they did see her, she seemed happy enough, though clearly she was into drink. Mrs. Stewart was beside herself. Anne was her mistress, true, but the girl was in trouble. So, after some soul-searching, Mrs. Stewart sat on a cool September morning to write a letter to Mr. Cormac at Cardiff Hall.

Five days after the letter had been sent, Anne rose and dressed for the world she had begun to call her own. Even though she wore somber cotton, she had come to realize that her dresses were far more elaborate than those worn by Betsy or any of the other girls at the Ship and Shore, for there was a certain quality of cloth and handsome workmanship involved. Beneath her gown she wore a dagger tied to her leg. Bonny had left port for some weeks, sailing with Hornigold, and she felt the safer for having it while he was away.

A cup of tea, a bit o' bread, and she hurried to leave, for she was increasingly uncomfortable in a house with the sudden silences of staff as she approached and the glaring disapproval of Mrs. Stewart. On her way out, she stopped in the hall to glance at the mail on the side table.

"Mistress," Mrs. Stewart said, approaching from the kitchen, "are ye leavin' so early?"

"Yes, Mrs. Stewart. I am," she answered, her attention focused on the letters so as to avoid the housekeeper's eyes.

"Mistress Anne, I must speak with you," Mrs. Stewart pleaded.

"I'm afraid I'm about to leave. But I shall put some time aside tomorrow morning if that suits."

"Mistress," she answered, screwing up her courage, "it does not."

"All right." Anne put the envelopes down and looked at her directly, for she knew this conversation was overdue. "Now then, what is it?"

"I believe you know, miss. You . . . ye cannot continue like this. Have ye completely forgotten your place?"

"Perhaps I have. And good riddance to it. For it is a place in a society filled with hypocrisy, one that preaches its own superiority as an excuse to enslave people for profit."

Jane gasped. "You cannot be serious, miss. No one who comes to this house would even think . . ."

"Is that so?" Anne interrupted. "Perhaps you have Philip O'Conner in mind, a man who at this moment fits out a ship to bring captured Africans to South Carolina? Men and women kidnapped and sold into slavery. Would you like to hear stories of the slave ships, Jane? The torture of men? The rape of women? If food gets sparse on the passage, why, simply tie a number of weights to some of the cargo and drop them to the bottom of the sea. Have you thought what it might be like to drown in this way?"

Discounting the woman's stricken face, Anne continued, taking small steps in her direction. "Or perhaps you have Colonel Birmingham in mind? Did he not recently burn an Indian village because it stood in some settler's way? What of Monsignor O'Brien who preaches that the Huguenots and Jews who have arrived are condemned to everlasting hell? Or the stolen Irish children sold to plantations in the Indies? No, Jane, you will have to do better to convince me of the integrity of those who purport to be our friends and who have neither nobility, honor, or courage in the face of greed."

White-faced, her eyes filled with tears, wringing her hands, Mrs. Stewart replied in a small voice, "I've written your father."

Instead of the furious rush of anger she'd expected, Anne merely shrugged. "My father cannot be bothered with us. He's far too busy taking care of his own needs. I'm sure he and Mistress Beatrice are quite happy."

"Miss Anne!" Mrs. Stewart cried, aghast. "Do ye know what you say?"

"Perfectly. My father is in an illicit love affair with my mother's serving girl," she answered bitterly. "Now, if you will forgive me, I'm off."

At that moment, the brass knocker on the door thundered through the house.

"Now who could that be? Certainly not a visitor. Or if so, the first since my mother died. What tremendous support I have had from our neighbors," and she cast a leer toward poor Mrs. Stewart. "See to it, please."

"Yes, miss," she answered nervously.

The door swung open and Lord Cavanaugh stood alone, his shoes black with small gold buckles, his stockings white silk over knee breeches, elaborately gartered, a long brocade waistcoat worn under an overcoat with tremendous cuffs folded back and buttoned to hold the turn in place, copious amounts of lace at throat and wrist, a diamond pin in the lapel, powdered wig, sword at his side, eyes the color of a still, shallow sea and searching her face. Anne's heart rose in her throat, once again enamored.

"My Lord," she rushed to the door, "please, come in! How wonderful to see you!"

Lord Cavanaugh entered, made his most elegant leg, and said softly, "Your servant. But Miss Cormac, am I no longer Henry to you?"

Anne matched his bow. "Of course. Mrs. Stewart, tea in the parlor, if you please."

"Yes, miss. Your Lordship," and she curtsied before hurrying off.

"Come this way, Henry, and tell my why you have made this visit," she said leading him to the parlor. "I am glad for it. How have you been?"

The fire had been set that morning, but now burned low. Henry walked toward it and placed a hand on the mantle, his back to her while he gathered his thoughts. With a deep breath, he turned.

"Anne, I am not sure where to begin. Will you sit?"

And when she'd found a seat, he unabashedly knelt before her on one knee. "I have missed you," and she heard the sincerity in it. "We said things to one another, and for my part, those things were not said lightly."

"Nor on mine." But she was of a mind to give him no quarter. "Tell me, have you started to build your house? Cleared land? For you see," and she looked into his eyes, "I have not heard where life has taken you since I left Cardiff Hall."

"You do right to admonish me. I should have called sooner. But your father said you were to be betrothed . . ."

"And you lacked the courage to challenge him," she said with directness.

"Forgive me. Once you asked if I had courage."

"You assured me you did. I was not to doubt you."

"Truth be told, Anne, after your father rejected me, I confess I did try to make my way through society. But the company introduced to me were not to my taste. Nary a woman I met had your beauty or your spirit."

"Henry, all of Charles Town knows my father sought to marry me to a planter of Jamaica and that the engagement never took place. And all must know why."

He turned to her and asked evenly, "Did you stab the serving girl?"

"Why, Henry, I see that you will be frank! In answer, yes, I did."

"With good reason?"

Anne paused, for she knew that Beatrice had been complicit in the seduction of her father, that the act was not his alone. Perhaps she played with him still. Yet she shook her head, "There is never good enough reason for an act so harsh."

"Then why, Anne?

"In truth, I do not know. And if I am to explain the secrets of my heart, it will take more than an afternoon conversation over tea."

Not yet ready to discuss her father and Beatrice, her fears for Cardiff Hall, the moment of darkness when she stood and raised the knife, or the priest she had sought afterwards for solace, she patted the seat beside her.

"Please, sit here next to me and let us speak honestly to each other. I will ask you simply . . . do you love me enough to fight for me?"

"If I must. I understand there is a sea faring fellow. True?"

"Why," her gaze held some mirth, "wherever do you get your information? But yes, true."

"Then I will fight," his hand went to his sword, "simply name the time and place."

"No, my dear, you mistake again. That is not the fight I would have you make. The fight I speak of is against gossip and prejudice. In the end, can you accept me for who I am? For as surely as we both sit here, I believe you do love my free spirit. But do you want it in your wife?"

Henry looked away and Anne could see the questions about Bonny roll across his face.

"I would be true to you, Henry. There would never be another, and I would go anywhere, do anything you asked." And she smiled, "But I would be bringin' my stubbornness and my will with me wherever we went."

"And you would use that will in our interests? Be a true partner in marriage?"

"Always."

A discreet knock on the door and he stood and crossed to the window, his back to the room, the better to hide his face, flushed as it was with emotion.

Mrs. Stewart put the tray down looking neither right nor left. What was happening with her young miss was more than she knew. What was it Anne had said about her father? What in dear God's name was going on? She closed the door quietly, anxiously knowing Mr. Cormac would never approve this unchaperoned visit.

"I would have you, Henry," Anne said softly. "And I speak true when I say I will go anywhere you ask. Back to Ireland to fight for James. Or make a new start in the wilderness." She stood and came to him, the very softness of her breath and the words she spoke, rousing him to both desire and protection. Suddenly she was in his arms, pulled close, the warm length of him causing her to tremble. "And I would love you for all my days," she whispered, her mouth close to his.

His kiss was not the sweet kiss of the carriage, nor the drunken kiss of easy exploration she'd had with Bonny. This kiss was new, bestowed by a man in his prime, hard, sucking the breath from her, a man taking possession of his future. The newness of it, the very difference from anything she had ever known, the fresh sense of body, the strength of emotion, the smell of his skin, all mixed together to become the wanting of something more.

"Then I will ask again of your father," he whispered hoarsely, his lips traveling her neck and reaching for her mouth again.

"Henry!"

She held him at arm's length, the better to look into his face, her eyes bright, her lips swollen and red, her breathing hard, bosom heaving. "You do not understand. I will marry you because we so choose, not because my father gives his permission."

"Anne, we cannot marry without your father's permission. I am Lord Cavanaugh, a title our first son would inherit. My family has lost its estates in Ireland, and I would rebuild them here in the colonies."

"You . . . you want my dowry." She pulled away, feeling she might weep.

"Of course, I do. Any man who says he does not, lies. But surely you know that is not why I marry! Forgive me, but quite frankly, there are any number of engagements I could make. I am here, in spite of all, because I want you!"

"If I might make so bold . . . in spite of all what?"

"In spite of gossip and rumor-mongering. So much is said. Surely you know your reputation suffers. Maiden or not, I do not care!"

Stunned, she answered, voice shaking, "Then am I the only one who does? For as surely as I live, I am a maid."

"I did not mean . . . that is . . . I did not believe . . . should not have suggested . . ." And for once in his life, Lord Cavanaugh appeared completely undone.

With eyes large and bright with tears she refused to shed, looking suddenly the young girl again, she asked, "Without my father's approval ye will not wed, Henry?"

A catch in his throat, desiring her more than any woman he had ever known, he was forced to answer, "As I will be a father myself one day, in all integrity, I cannot."

"Then we are doomed, for William Cormac will never agree."

Anne turned to the tray Mrs. Stewart had brought.

"Tea, Lord Cavanaugh?"

Chapter Ten

October gave way to November and the air turned bleak and cold. Anne refused all of Henry's overtures, unsure of his motivation and angry. Had not her mother repeatedly said how little the conventions of Europe really mattered in this place where great changes could be made. What truly counted was a man's character, the strength to take life and make something of it rather than have it make you.

Along the quay she stopped to look out to sea and saw the beach where James had landed the first time she'd set eyes upon him, the sun bright, the day fair. Now the sky was grey and the air blustery, the waves high and crashing on shore. Only five months, but a lifetime ago. She pulled the hood of her cloak close round her ears and turned to make her way to the Ship and Shore . . . and saw that James Bonny stood watching.

"The place where I first saw you," she told him, smiling.

"Anne, I've come to ask you something, and I do not ask lightly," he placed her arm in the crook of his and they continued leisurely along the water's edge. "You've said your father looks for a man to run his plantation. Marry me. Let me be that man."

Anne laughed, and the sound drifted away with the wind, brittle and hopeless, fraught with absurdity.

"Oh, James, is that what you want? A ticket to what you see as an easy life. Believe me, running a plantation is not so simple as it seems. I was bred to it and know it inside and out. I can tell you it is hard work."

"You know that's not what I'm about. I love you, Anne, and there is promise between us. Let me try to make you happy."

"My father will never consent to a marriage between us. Never! Good God, he has refused a lord! Tell me, James, would you marry me on your own without his permission, knowing we would be penniless?"

"Ye know I would. But 'e'll not take away your inheritance. He could not be so cruel."

"I can assure you, I will be without dowry or home. This you must know for the truth. He will not recognize the marriage. You do not know my father."

"Do you really think 'e would cast you out? His only daughter?"

"Beyond doubt."

"Then we will make our own way. Do you love me, Anne?"

For a long moment she could not answer, for truly she did not know. What she felt for James was different than the thoughts that arose when she thought of Henry Cavanaugh. But she also knew what she felt when James put his lips upon hers, how her body became a torch, burning for consummation, and yet . . . he had not insisted. Even when she'd had too much to drink, he had not taken her to that dirty room to make love to her. No. Wisely, she knew he waited because he wanted something more than her body. He had seen the house in town, knew of the plantation. His needs and desires were no different from Henry's, but he was willing to commit even if they were penniless. And James was a road away from her father's door and what Charles Town expected of her.

"We will marry with a priest," she said suddenly, resolved, "that way there can be no going back."

"Then you agree?"

"I shall have Bridget and Betsy as my bridesmaids. And who shall stand as your witness?"

"Why, I shall ask Captain Hornigold. When?"

"Today, if you like. Don't you think you've waited long enough?" She laughed and clapped her hands gaily, for this would be her wedding day.

The very thought that they might finally fulfill months of foreplay—touching not just with hands and mouth and tongue and swords, feinting in and out, trying to best each other—was cause for arousal.

"Today, then."

And he kissed her full and deep.

The wedding took place on board ship attended by members of Hornigold's crew and patrons of the Ship and Shore, and it was the captain himself who bribed the priest to perform the ceremony. The poor man, wishing only the money for his destitute parishioners, closed an eye to the posting of the banns, and had no idea what he was unleashing in offering the sacrament.

For the first time, Anne stepped on ship . . . and fell in love with the beauty of the frigate's lines, the polished wood, and the promise she offered. Facing the mouth of the harbor, she gazed out toward the ocean, knowing she could leave the small world of Charles Town behind. She had no idea what might await, but the horizon was endless.

From a great chest in his cabin, Captain Hornigold took out a white dress of lace, another woman's bridal gown, captured from a Spanish ship. Dark hair dressed, a small bouquet of flowers provided by Bridget and Betsy, pearl earrings from a jewel casket, and she walked to the altar on board, wind blowing off the sea, taking her vows, her eyes wide and moist. Not until the end did she think to ask if this was what her mother would have wanted for her.

The wedding feast too had been hurriedly orchestrated, the food brought on board in baskets, the rum and ale flowing. On this evening she drank freely and laughed loudly, reeled to the music of fiddle and recorder, sang songs with sailors who were drunk and had a mind to sing their hearts out, and when it was time to bed, she lay on clean sheets in the captain's cabin and did not return home for the night.

The promise of her body, the longing to touch the fire that had been only a whisper, flared brilliantly. Now she could feel his lips upon her nipples, and gasped as he kissed along belly, buttocks, and between her thighs, the great burning between her legs finally taking in the hardness of his ardor. James, surprised, knew her to be a virgin, and afterwards, they lay wrapped in each other's arms, she soft and white and pliant, him with hardened muscles and sun dark skin from head to waist. While James slept, Anne took comfort in the moment and considered this thing called marriage, and thought it a small word to describe how a man and woman could become one being.

Thus it was that on the morrow, when she left ship with James to gather some of her things, she found that William had finally returned the day before and that he was waiting in the parlor.

For all her bravado, Anne went in to face him with an ashen face, James at her back. Trembling, she took stock of him, for five months had passed. His hair was his own, grown out, his wig gone, his face dark from the sun. He sat upright in a chair near the fireplace, hands resting atop his cane, and did not rise to meet them.

"You will explain," he said too quietly.

"Father," and her voice sounded to her own ears as if it came from far away, "may I present James Bonny . . . my husband. Married yesterday afternoon before God and the priest."

"And consummated?" he asked.

"As is the normal course of events."

"Are ye daft?" he shouted, finally rising, his face red with suppressed fury. "To take such a man to wed? A penniless sailor, and pirate by the looks of him!"

"Please, sir, if you will . . ." Bonny tried.

William rounded on him, "I most certainly will not!"

Then he spun on his daughter.

"What can he offer you, Anne? Does he share your love of music?" and he brought his hand down hard on the harpsichord. "Does he speak Latin or French? Or read the books you do? How will he dress you? Good God, what can you have been thinking? What . . . what is it you even say to each other? . . ."

"Sir, I love your daughter. I can assure you . . ."

"You can assure me of nothing!"

"And you," Anne said coldly. "I hope your affair goes well with Mistress Beatrice."

"The girl left Cardiff Hall the week after you arrived in Charles Town. Five months ago. I have not seen her since and never again will."

Shocked, Anne asked, "Then where have you been? Why haven't you been home?"

"Has it occurred to you that I might need to grieve for a lifetime with your mother? Do ye really think because of a moment's indiscretion, I didn't love her. That she wasn't my whole world? I went west to the frontier to look at land and found a measure of peace in the beauty of what I saw."

"Could ye not have told me?" Anne cried. "Instead ye let me think the worst!"

Bonny, restless, began to dimly imagine that Anne had married him for reasons he was only beginning to suspect. Nor did he like the picture William Cormac presented of this other Anne. He had never heard her at the harpsichord, nor seen her with a book, and as he looked around, he sensed a world of which he could only dream.

"Anne, we've come to get your things. I think it's time to go."

"You have one chance at annulment," William told her, "for I will never accept this man into my house."

"Just a minute, sir, no one is asking you for anything!"

William turned and for the first time really looked at him. "No? Can ye honestly tell me you did not have certain expectations?"

"I had some, but they was for Anne. She deserves her inheritance. It's only right."

Without a response, William turned his back on Bonny and again faced his daughter. "A pretty mess you've made, Anne. What will it be?"

Anne took steps through the room, turning, looking. The house was beautiful and rich and comfortable . . . but it was also stifling, the prospects for her own future if she lived here, narrow. If she turned to her father now, she would give over every shred of self-respect and self-determination she possessed. Living in this world of parties and social gatherings, she would be expected to be someone she knew she could never be, gossiping with the rest, listening to the whispers about who she was and what she did. Yesterday had been a door to another world, the ship a road to the future. Her heart longed to make the journey out of port, reach beyond all she had once known, trust in the kind of person she might fully become.

Both men watched her, waiting, and she finally turned.

"I love you, Father, and I wish to be reconciled. I am sorry I could not have told you sooner . . . but I go with my husband."

"Then you will leave this house and never return," William told her, devastated, knowing the choice would bring her to disaster and there was nothing he could do. "You are no longer any daughter of mine. Leave. Ye'll take nary a thing from this house."

"Only this," she answered taking up a small, framed portrait of herself as she looked approaching her sixteenth birthday. "So that I might remember what could have been . . . had ye been true to my mother."

As she passed toward the door, William grabbed her arm and whispered close to her ear. "I spoke with Lord Cavanaugh. I gave my permission for him to call. He still wants you, Anne, and he's waited decently."

Aghast, Anne said nothing, simply gave him one last look, and walked from the house.

Once outside, the door slammed shut against them, James let out a great, deep breath. "We cannot stay here longer, not in Charles Town. We are out of money and I must find work again. Hornigold sails for New Providence in the Bahamas before setting out for warmer waters."

"The pirate capital."

"Aye, lass, 'tis. Will ye sail with pirates, wife?"

And suddenly, Anne felt free, truly free for the first time in her life. "Oh, yes, James, I am ready to take ship."

"The men won't have you on board as a woman. Will ye wear pants and act the man?"

Anne laughed thinking of the many times she had worn breeches, all to the dismay of her governess. "Aye, James, I'll wear your pants."

"You know we won't be havin' the captain's cabin. I've empty pockets until I get my next pay."

"We'll manage."

"Then let us hurry. The *Ranger* sails on the tide."

Part 3

New Providence, Bahamas

1718

James Bonny

Chapter Eleven

The noon sun was overhead and Anne still lay abed, her head heavy and stomach none too sure. She turned a naked shoulder to look upon James in disbelief, wondering if she had heard him true.

The room they shared on the water's edge was small and when the tide was low, seaweed lay upon rock and shingle, smelling of rot, attracting flies and sand lice. Even though she tried to close the windows against the buzzing and biting, the wooden slats were broken and the wee beasties found bare skin. A thin layer of damp salt from the sea air covered everything. On this morning, the bed of filthy sheets she had sworn never to sleep upon, was actually a comfort, for after a night of grog, she needed a place to throw herself down. Last night's oblivion had left the remnants of some meal upon the table, while an ancient, forgotten soup oozed up in the kettle, fermenting in the heat. With the beginning of June, temperatures had intensified, and Anne found that a perpetual stench covered her body, the rank odor of sweat mixed with the musty juices from between her legs. Washing either the sheets or her body was near impossible, for both soap and the wood to boil hot water was too dear if they were to fund other pleasures.

Furious, she jumped from the bed, hands on her hips. "Did I hear rightly, James? Well, let me tell you for a certainty. I'll not whore for you! You, nor anyone else! Do I make myself perfectly clear?" Her eyes were torches, sparks flying. "What in God's name do ye think you're on about?

"Well, jus' look around . . ." his speech was still slurred from the night before, his mouth dry, his stomach craving food, and he carelessly threw an arm out over the room, "wha' d'ye see?"

"I see exactly where you've taken us," Anne cried. "To be sure, *I* would never have chosen this shite hole for a dwelling place!"

He rolled from the bed, unsteady, and attempted to stand tall, pretending to a dignity. "You knew when we married I had no money."

"And you knew that I did. You staked all on it, didn't you? But if you will recall, I told you my father would never accept a marriage that was not his say. I told you, plain as I'm standin' here!"

"Tha's all behind, Anne, and no goin' back. We're here. We need to eat and . . . and I think maybe you could work the tavern a little."

"And I think maybe you could go fuck yourself. Or maybe sign on. Captain Hornigold goes in and out of port with regularity. And he's been lucky, takin' more than a few prizes each time he's out. Or there's Captain Teach. He's here and he's got a handful of ships."

"I'll not sign on with Blackbeard. He's a crew of three hundred men and four ships and I'll not get lost in the numbers."

"Stede Bonnet, then. He's about as gentle as you can find. Him with his books and manners."

"But 'e doesn't know the sea! He's all about playin' at his boat! I tell you his crew will either mutiny or slit his throat. Jesus, Anne, 'e even *bought* his ship! What respectful pirate wouldn't steal his craft? And 'e's nervous 'e is, about his *reputation.* He's a pirate, for God's sake. Why does 'e care wha' people think. The only ships 'e sinks are those goin' back to his home in Barbados, so no one will *tell* on him."

"James, I will not *fucking* whore. Are ye listenin'?"

"Well, then, wife, you tell me where the money's goin' t' come from. The only work I know is the sea, and I'll not leave you."

"So, then . . . we have come to this."

"Indeed, we have come to this. So, what do you say?"

She looked down upon her clothing, saw the stains and

patches, the dirty lace, remembered Betsy's grab for the gold bracelet she'd once cast her way. How could she know this kind of poverty? Were someone to offer her a bracelet, anything, she would grab at it with the same fierce resolve.

"I'm off, James. I'm goin' for a walk. I want to think."

"Shall I come with you?"

"No. I need to be alone."

James mustered a deep voice. "It seems to me you want to be alone a lot these days."

"I like my own company, that's for certes."

"It was jus' a thought . . . the whorin', I mean. I don't think I'd take to it well anyway."

"No, James," Anne said quietly. "I don't think you would. Nor would I."

The wooden door swung open and she made her escape, glad to be away from him and his moonstruck face, wondering how she had reached this impossible place. The more she pushed for her own freedom, the more he smothered her, refusing to take a job on ship, sulking when she was out of his sight. Two years they had been together and the dream she'd held as a raw maiden of sixteen still eluded her.

On that first and only voyage from Charles Town so many months ago, Anne had experienced a mystic moment when land had been just a speck on the horizon, then, had disappeared entirely. Suddenly, she'd felt as if she were flying, wind in her face, spray in the pitch, and her eyes never tired at looking over the horizon, each wave different, mesmerizing, no two alike. They'd traveled south, gray sky evaporating, the air warming. She had taken to it, the roll of the ship, even the cramped quarters below where she and James had secretly tried to touch as they lay swinging in hammocks, for they had been newly wed. When they'd boarded, Hornigold had known her, of that she was certain, but it had been a measure of his courtesy to take her on in spite of her costume. Pirate, yes, but also gentleman, who had come to piracy after His Majesty's privateering license had been rescinded at the end of the War with Spain. Too soon, the voyage and the ship with its smooth wooden decks and billowing sails and promise of passage to the wide world was over, and the joy of being at sea had been hers only for the brief journey to New Providence.

With great disappointment she had disembarked and found herself forced back into skirts. In this rough town she'd had to go armed, dared not walk the streets without weapons, sword at her side and pistol in a makeshift belt over the pleats of her hips. Only once had she been assailed, and she had drubbed her attacker with such ferocity that the story from Charles Town caught up with her and the name 'Hellcat' was again bestowed. Newcomers might cast an eye to her dark hair and full lips, but when the man learned who she was and that Bonny stood behind her, she was well enough left alone. Certainly there were plenty of working whores. And before God, she was determined never to become one of them.

Damn you, James, God damn you to hell! You have all the freedom I crave and won't use it!

For almost two years she had continued to study the names of the sheets and ropes of the rigging, asking questions, learning the special language of sea farers, and in this place, the law that formed the Articles of the Brotherhood. On occasion she had drunk men under the table, joined in singing sea shanties, and had bested more than one with a sword, her soft parlor voice traded for the curses and rough speech of sailors, for by God, she would be one of them. But she could not take ship because of her sex, and the sights and knowledge she had expected, the foreign lands, the power to come and go as she saw fit, all unfulfilled, frustrated dreams.

Had she been a man she would have sailed with Hornigold, straight off. Oh, but the captain was a man touched by good fortune. A dozen large prizes or more in the last months alone. If James had spent as much time with the captain as he did in the tavern, they could have put down on land by now. Somewhere south of the Carolinas, near the coast in Georgia. For the idea had occurred to her that with land she could build a future, that the numbing, nameless, tiresome days drifting with no purpose but the next night's drink, might end. But she was marooned in New Providence, as surely as on some desert island.

As she walked along the sand, she breathed long and hard the clean air, the better to rid herself of the stench of the hovel in which she lived. The day was already half gone, the sun hot and high. The wind was up, the sky blue with white clouds on the horizon. Her feet sank in sand and she kicked at water tickling her toes.

Looking out to sea, an unbidden thought forced itself upon her. What had she possibly seen in James? Honesty, compelled her to admit to his attractiveness, muscular body and charming smile, his lips. When they'd first met he was five years older, more experienced in the ways of the world, traveled, but now she'd heard his stories, and heard them again, and he wasn't making any new ones. Bonny was no leader of men, in fact, he could hardly handle himself, certainly not her . . . and it rankled. The more he tried to control her, the less she wanted to do with him, and the less to do with him, well, he followed to the point of suffocation.

Truth be told, she looked for a way out.

When Anne finally made her way to the Rose and Garter, the sky had turned a silvery blue, for there was a moon, and stars hugged the corners of the canopy. At the door she stopped at the smells of roasting meat, hot bread, and ale, a reminder that she had not eaten all the day and thought to search her pocket for a pence or two.

Better to eat first before confronting James, she thought, for she was determined to have it out with him.

Already the tavern was boisterous and too warm from torch, candle, and hearth, and her ears reached for the music that was sure to be there. Even as she listened for laughter and song, she knew that tonight she would be the entertainment, for what she had to say to James would be repeated the island round, until every speculation, gloat, and eyebrow raising be gleaned from her misery.

Yet the music she'd expected was unheard, the atmosphere tense, and instead of laughter, raised voices assailed her, angry, loud, all speaking at once.

"Grace, what is it?" she asked, grabbing the passing barmaid's arm. "What has caused this uproar?"

"New gov'nor's set to arrive tomorrow, and 'e's to put down piracy," she laughed. "There's upwards to two thousand men that goes out to sea from 'ere. And the new gov thinks it will all end, just like that, just 'cause 'e's offerin' a pardon. What that compared to a rich prize?"

"The name of this new governor?"

"Woodes Rogers. Used to be a privateer 'imself I'm told, although never took to outright piracy. Always sailed with letters."

So why was there such a furor? Any governor could be bribed, for that was exactly how they enjoyed such security as this, these pirate captains. A governor who once held letters of marque, would surely understand, for he himself had once been a legitimized pirate to those enemies of England. But never had she seen the ship's leaders in such chaotic conversation.

In the center of the room the drama heightened as several captains squared off against one another, Charles Vane, come from the south and with a prize in the harbor as well as his own ship; Benjamin Hornigold, his hat and plume conspicuous in that inn, a man Anne tried to avoid lest he remind her of what her family expected; and Stede Bonnet, gentleman pirate of Barbados and if rumor be true, taken to sea robbery by a whim.

"Anne!" James yelled above the hubbub. "Where've ye been? Have ye heard?"

Charles Vane stood, took a pistol from his belt, and banged it loud upon the table until the noise subsided. "I call a meeting of the Brethren!" he roared focusing the attention of the tavern's boisterous occupants. "You've all the heard the news."

"Aye," came shouts.

"What use 'ave we of a royal gov'nor?"

"We can lay all this at Blackbeard's feet," Vane spat. "Takin' ships at sea is one thing. Blockading Charles Town harbor with his fleet's another. And what treasure does he ask for after all the trouble? A box of medicine! Christ's blood! Can't you reel him in, Hornigold? He's your man."

"You know as well as I that Teach no longer sails for me. And he does no more than the rest of us. In fact, perhaps more, for he cares for his crew enough to get the medicine to try to cure the damned pox from his men."

"You defend him?"

"Aye," Hornigold answered. "Truth is, I've yet to see a man die by his hand or order, except in honest battle. When he took the *Concorde,* he put her crew on a sloop and set free her slaves. Is it you've some envy for what he's done? Remade the *Concorde* into the *Queen Anne's Revenge?* Ye cannot deny she's the best pirate vessel on the water."

"I've me own ship and me own business to look to. I do well enough without havin' to envy Blackbeard anything."

"Look here, Vane. What I know of Teach is that he's a man what knows his business. The stories he spreads about himself are simply a good enough trick of battle, reason enough for ships to lay down without fight when they see his flag. More than blood, tis' treasure he wants. He plans to marry soon and he'll be usin' his takings to start his family. Can ye not admit that we have all served to bring the storm upon ourselves? This governor is not only about Teach, but his arrival concerns the rest of us as well."

"Then why's the man comin' now?"

"He's been on his way for at least a year. It's nothin' sudden. But you are right about one thing. The outcry against pirates is rising. Those rich merchants that we take from are . . . well, rich . . . and have influence. Eventually it had to end this way."

"End?" Vane sneered. "Explain yourself, Hornigold."

"Simply that we are going to have to choose and soon

enough. I've had word that the governor is here to offer us pardons if we give up piracy and settle into honest trades."

"Honest trades!" a voice yelled. "Why, pirating is an honest trade! There's not a man 'ere what doesn't abide by the rules of the Brethren and the Articles!"

"That may be well enough for some," another called, "some as 'as somethin' stored away. But what about us that's spent what we 'as?"

"Aye," another ventured. "The officers makes the most, and we get but a share and that's gone soon enough."

"Would you have the captain's share, then?" Hornigold shouted. "Pray God you never have the responsibility of ship, chase, and battle!"

"Even if it's only 'ats ye be chasin'," a voice shouted, and the majority laughed loud, for all knew the story of how Hornigold had chased down a ship simply to have the hats off the crew, the sun being hot and his men having thrown their own overboard with too much drink.

"If you need more in your pockets," Hornigold ignored the jibe, "I suggest you put out to sea with all possible haste and take what you can before you're forced to choose between the gallows and a pardon."

Over a furious new racket, Vane shouted, "I'll not be bowin' to any of this new gov'nor's orders! We're pirates, come here by our own ways and means to do the job we 'as!"

"The killin' and thievin' will stop," Hornigold insisted coldly to an audience that did not want to hear. "Teach may have assembled a fleet, and we could join him with our own ships if it's a war we want. But the king's navy is larger, more deadly and more disciplined, with a treasury to back it. No, my friends, I see the handwriting on the wall."

"As I stand here before God," Vane shouted, "I'll not sit in port and grow old looking out to sea. That is no life for a man."

"This governor can surely be bought," Stede Bonnet offered. "All the governors have been bribed."

"Not this one," Hornigold answered with some disdain,

for Bonnet was a joke amongst them. "Take your ship and go back to your wife and plantation in Barbados, Captain Bonnet. Before you hurt yourself and every man that sails with you."

"Here," Bonnet pulled his sword from its scabbard, "I'll have none of that!'

"Hold," Vane stood between them, "we've no time for this now. Settle up later, if ye must. The gov'nor arrives tomorrow and I say we give him a warm enough welcome so's he goes back to England."

"I'll not side with you on this one, Vane," Hornigold told him. "The wind's blowin' in a new direction. Take what ye have, man. We've enough to start honest trade. My crew and I came together from the War and are still mostly whole. We had nothing and put to sea to take what we could from those who had more. But we've our share and we can do something with it."

Bonnet still stood with his sword poised, his face red with anger. "You'll answer to me, Hornigold!"

Ignoring Bonnet, Vane pledged, "I'll tell you what I'm goin' to do. I'm goin' to lay a broadside across the good gov'nor's bow in fair warnin'!"

"Then you'll be doin' it five times, for Rogers arrives with a fleet of three warships and two sloops. Fire your cannon at the *Rose*, for that is his flagship."

Bonnet lowered his sword and the room went quiet, the impact of this news settling into every heart, for this was no idle arrival.

Vane narrowed his eyes. "You're amazingly well informed, Captain."

"It's a dangerous business we're about, Vane. I intend to survive and to do so I must be informed."

"A fleet," Bonnet repeated. "Aye, 'tis bad business, it is. I'm away on the tide. I'll take my work further south."

"And further south you'll run into Governor Nicholas Lawes in Jamaica with the same commission. As we speak they're hangin' pirates at Gallow's Point and leaving them to rot at the mouth of the harbor as a warnin' to us all. Gentlemen, I will take the governor's pardon when he arrives, and I will build my home. No different as Henry Morgan."

"Then you are a coward, sir," Bonnet shouted, his ire still inflamed.

Men moved back for no one would ever assume Benjamin Hornigold a coward, and indeed, he drew his sword, "By the devil, I'm sick of your ranting, Bonnet. Have ye no sense of decency? This is a matter that concerns us all and impugning my honor does not serve!"

Bonnet stepped forward, and in response, Hornigold's mate rushed to his captain's side, his own sword in hand. A touch of blade to blade and like dry tinder, the room was soon a tempest of furious swordplay, the fight spreading like a pebble thrown into a pond.

That's when Anne saw him. One of Vane's men.

"Who's that?" she asked the serving girl, pointing.

"Why, that's Jack Rackham, Vane's quartermaster," Grace told her. "A pretty picture, 'e is, don't ye think?" and she laughed at the lost look on Anne's face. "Careful, dearie, I believe your own dear James fights."

Anne watched him, this Jack Rackham, his movements catlike, smooth, his skill with the blade better than most she had seen, and she wondered absently if she could best him, for there were not many men better than herself. The thought flashed across her mind that she could enter the fray and test against him, but she let it pass. No, now wasn't the time to test against Jack Rackham.

From his swordplay, she looked to the rest of him. Hatless, light brown hair streaked with gold and tied with a dark ribbon, his face clean, skin sun-browned, blue eyes lit with fire and mouth smiling, a man enjoying the fight. An expensive waistcoat rife with embroidery, long jacket, white shirt with good lace, boots, and calico breeches. Jack was indeed a pretty picture and Anne's heart quickened.

For the first time in months she looked to herself and

knew her face to be brown and freckled with too much sun, her hair dull from bad diet, but the worst was the cracked and broken fingernails, black with dirt, her patched dress not so bad on its own, but smelling and filthy, the old lace a dull gray, her shoes covered with caked and dried mud and sand, her arms and face sweaty and smelling sour. She backed away into the safe shadows of the tavern with the other women who laughed and watched and applauded the fight, but the only protection she wanted to give herself, was out of the sight of Jack.

That evening, Anne told James what she had wanted to say for many months. "It's over, James. I can take no more and I want to be on my own."

"You are my wife, legally wed before the priest, and you know as well as I there can be no divorce."

"Don't give me your shite, James. There *can* be a legal divorce."

"Let me be clear. I will never give you a divorce, Anne. You are mine and always will be. Always."

For a brief moment Anne thought to bludgeon him, then thought the better of it. A prison was not where she had in mind to go. It was freedom she was after, always had been. Freedom from the stifling conventions of Charles Town and the expectations of a narrow life, freedom from the hypocrisy of dogma, freedom to grow into herself, and at the core of her being, she trusted what she was.

"I was never yours. I was always myself, and I gave myself to you gladly. But now, I see no way to continue. This farce of a marriage ended the night you asked me to whore for you."

"That was despair talkin' after a night of too much drink! You know I didn't mean it."

"Must you take what little respect I have left for you and trounce that as well? Do not presume to lie to me, James, it is beneath the both of us. I'm not drinkin' anymore. I'm tired of wakin' up three faces to the wind and pukin' my guts up. It doesn't suit. I'm on my way to somewhere else. And it's without you."

"You will not have a divorce. Never."

"We will see." Then she added, "Hornigold's leavin' on a last excursion before Governor Rogers appears to make his offer of pardon. I suggest ye go with him. We need the money and no tellin' how things are goin' to change."

"And if I choose not to go a'pirating?"

"Then I will murther you in your sleep."

From the look in her eye, James finally relented, for he had an uneasy suspicion she might do just that.

"All right," he said. "I sign on."

Anne breathed a quiet sigh of relief. That gave her a few months to put her plans in order.

Chapter Twelve

True to Captain Hornigold's information, the *Rose* carried the new governor into New Providence harbor the next day, but Hornigold was not there to watch, for he had sailed on the morning tide, taking James Bonny with him, out for one last foray before the governor handed out his ultimatum.

Anne stood on the quay with the crowd and watched Charles Vane give Governor Rogers the warm reception he had promised, setting afire his captured ship in the harbor, billowing black smoke seen for miles. As Vane rapidly sailed out of port with every sheet of canvas unfurled for speed, he sent two cannon balls over the bow of the *Rose*. From where she watched the spectacle, Anne could see Jack Rackham holding tight to the forward yarn supporting the jib, leaning out over the water, his smile bright, hair blown back in the wind, his sense of joy and freedom so profound, that she swore the next time she saw him he would take notice. Then they were gone, out of range of guns, only the white sails growing smaller on the blue horizon, heading south toward the Caribbean Sea.

With James out of the way, the first thing Anne did was change residence, paying for the room with coins she had hidden from him. The lodging was not much better than the last in terms of size and composition, and was still on the sea, but it was away from the small stretch of seaweed-lined coast that smelled of decay. When she walked into this new room, Anne opened the windows and breathed in fresh air, and then for the longest while, she sat, merely gazing from the window, the changing sea holding her captive. Not until the sky turned pink, and the clouds on the horizon edge purple, and her stomach rumble, did Anne realize how long she'd sat there. She left only long enough to buy rice and peas cooked with thyme, a small piece of chicken, boiled water, and a little oil for the lamp. Then she fell onto the bed and slept peacefully for the first time in many months, alone, her pistol under her pillow, sword at the bed head.

When she woke in the morning, the window was still open. Early, the sun rising fast, a great finger of light fell across still water that had not yet been whipped into waves by heat and wind.

The new landlady was all too happy to give her soap if she was to clean, and Anne began first to scrub the house, top to bottom. Poor she might be, but she would have something fresh and unsoiled, and as she washed away grime, resolved that James would never live in this place with her. With what moneys she had left she bought wood, then boiled water and scrubbed the brown marks from her bed linen, and with them, the memory of every time James had touched her.

Her clothes went the same way. With a solution of soap, and laying them in the sun, the lace came white again. She took to braiding her hair like the Creole girls and wearing a bright red scarf. At the Rose and Garter instead of spending her nights at drink, she took a job as a serving girl, where she made merry and served with such good will, that she earned a pretty pair of gold earrings from a passing sailor who'd insisted he'd fought a Frenchman well for them. Allowed to eat before she served, she began to fill out, and the half-starved waif took on the appearance of a real woman, her curves coming back, her walks along the shore giving her a stamina she had not possessed in a long while.

On those walks she reflected on past decisions, among them, leaving her home and father. Damn, but William had been right about Bonny and about where it would all end. Homesick, she longed to see him, hear his voice, even if it was only to curse her and tell her to leave once more and never return. Occasionally, she heard word of Charles Town and knew that two months ago he'd been in negotiations with Blackbeard for the return of certain of the port's citizens, captured and held for ransom until the city forwarded the box of medicine he'd demanded. From this, she thought her father to be alive and well.

And what of Henry? Well, Henry by now had surely found another bride, perhaps even cradled the heir he'd wanted. Reluctantly, she admitted that he had indeed done the honorable thing, while she had married a man simply for adventure. Sweet Jesus, her choice had taken her to this, one room with a bed and a job as a tavern wench.

The only thing she had not pawned or sold, was the small picture of herself in its silver frame, taken the day she'd walked from her home in Charles Town. She had kept it, fighting James for the privilege, a memory of a girl from another world. Now it sat on a makeshift shelf and stared down at her, questioning, accusing.

So Anne continued to walk miles during the day and serve at night, read from the book she had borrowed from Captain Bonnet who'd returned to take advantage of the amnesty, practice at her swordplay with anyone foolish enough to take her on, and more importantly, to save money. For at last she had a plan. In the same way she had come across the sea to this place, she would begin to travel away from it. With her savings she would purchase cotton strips and men's clothing. When she was ready, she resolved to bind her breasts, dress as a seafarer, and put out that her name was Will. Will Brennen. Brennen . . . her mother's name.

When Anne worked at the tavern, she hung her sword at the door of the kitchen for easy reach, and only two or three times had she grabbed for it. By now, most knew not to mess with her, for although cheerful enough when things were the way she liked them, cross her and beware if the hard glint appear in her eye.

"Anne," Grace called to her, passing with a tray, "'ave ye 'eard? *The Ranger's* just put in. Captain Hornigold's on his way to see the gov'nor. Your man should be comin' this way any time."

Anne steeled herself for the moment, for the last person she wanted to see was James Bonny. But before she could turn back to the kitchen, he was there, jiggling the money in his pockets, and that more than she could imagine. For two years she had been wife to a sailor blown by the wind, happy to drink himself into his cups each evening, take her to bed, and wait for something to change his life. The one chance he'd ever been given was to marry into her family, but when his expectations had collapsed, he'd simply taken ship with her in tow. By God, he was certainly not the man for her, and the price of separation was half his earnings.

"I swear to you, Anne, we had the best fortune. Took half a dozen prizes, we did, and I only took a small scratch on the forearm and even that has healed fairly well," he told her joyfully, swooping her up in his arms, and reaching for her mouth with his. "What's this? Come now, you're not still mad about the whoring thing, are ye? I've brought enough money for us to live quite nicely for a long time."

"Leave off, James," Anne told him. "I'm workin'. And how long is a long time? A month. Year? Do ye have enough to start a business or buy land?'

"Aye, Anne, if you wish. Bring me some food and drink, won't you. There's a good girl," and he smacked her bottom before taking a seat at table with his mates.

Anne heard the orders for drinks and wondered how much he would spend this evening before she could get to him. From tables round the tavern she saw other furtive eyes cast a look, knew desperate men would wait, and while unwary and drunk and retching up all they had just spent in a dark alley, those fresh to shore would be bludgeoned and their purses emptied of what they had worked so hard to obtain.

Ah, no, I'll get to James first and then we'll divvy up, and she reached down to feel the dagger kept tied to her leg, certain to watch over him this night.

As the evening wore on, the tavern grew loud and merry was the song, the fiddler and the piper in good form, and there was dancing on the floor and a great clapping of hands. Only twice were a few of the rowdier thrown from the place, and Anne found herself infected by the gaiety of the evening.

"Let's hear it for Captain Hornigold!" the shout went up when he entered later in the evening. "Hip, hip, hoorah! Hip, hip, hoorah!"

"What can I get you, Captain?" Anne asked. "The Mistress says it's on the house."

Hornigold looked at her carefully, "Why, Anne, you look . . . different somehow. What has happened to make this change? A new lover perhaps, while Bonny's been gone?"

"Don't be silly, Captain. I would have to find someone better than meself and that's a hard enough thing to do."

Hornigold eyed her with merriment and admiration. "I had a long talk with young Bonny while we were at sea."

"With all the pirating you was about, I'm surprised you had the time."

"He says you play the harpsichord."

"Does he now? Strange thing to say, for he's never heard me play."

"I just happen to have one I picked up on my last voyage. Could I presume upon you to play it for me one evening?"

Anne stepped back to look at him sharply and said plainly, "What kind of playing do you have in mind, Captain?"

Lowering his voice for her ears alone, he said, "Anne, I know your family, both mother and father. I've shipped for your father for some years now."

"Is . . . is my father into piracy?"

"Actually no, but I have contracted with him on several ventures in the past, and we have spoken of new enterprises. I thought he might feel more . . . secure . . . knowing that you had some of the things he'd want you to have."

"Does . . . does he ask of me?"

"No. But I thought to tell him. He *would* want to know."

"That's kind of you, Captain," she said hurriedly, wiping

the tray, "but I think my harpsichord days are at an end. I'll get your drink."

"Wife, wife, over here, my love. Give us a kiss," James called, his tongue thick, "and more drink. Much, much more drink!"

Jesus Christ, it didn't take him long to get shite-faced.

The first off the tray went to the captain, then she carried tankards to James and his friends, yet when she got within grasping range, James was all over her, a hand at her breast, his tongue in her mouth, another hand reaching up under her skirt as if they were at home and not in the center of a tavern.

"Enough, James," Anne told him, pushing him off. He was almost ripe enough for her to pick clean, just a few more drinks.

Suddenly, without warning, his mood changed, and he said loudly and provokingly, slurring badly, "Who the hell do ye think you are anyway? I've been at sea for two months and I espect somethin' when I return. Is that too much to ask? By God, you're my wife, and I will have you when I want you." From the look in Anne's eye, a few patrons began to give space and others to place bets on just what she would do. "We're leavin' . . . now . . . and I will have my way with you!"

"Who the hell do I think I am? Are ye so drunk James Bonny that you do not know? I'm Anne Cormac, my father's daughter. And if you ever lay hands on me again, I'll slit your gizzard."

"Don't play miss high and mighty with me," he leered into the deepening silence. "I know who you really . . . really are. Jus' as' the Cap'n. Right, Cap'n?" And he fell over the bench, stumbling mightily to regain his footing.

Anne cast a glance at Hornigold and saw he had gone white with anger. The look he threw Bonny would have silenced the dogs of hell, except that Bonny was too drunk to notice.

"Yea," he continued, swaying where he stood, "really, really are. You're a common bastard . . . just like the rest of us."

All who had drunk with Bonny knew his mother had sold him to a sea captain when he was eight years old, there being no father and a brood of other children she could not feed.

"What are ye sayin'? Speak it plain."

"Why, don't you know your father was married in Ireland?"

"Of course I do."

"But to whom, thas the question . . . to whom?"

"My mother, you git."

"Wrong," and he held up a finger to stop her there. "Wrong. Your father, bless his soul, your good father . . . that I hear so much about . . ."

"I don't speak of my father to you. Why would I? You would never understand a man like my father."

". . . that you *think* so much about . . ." he reeled, badly trying to form words, "was married to someone else. Your saintly mother was a servant . . . in his household and, well . . . ye did come along . . . and so they left . . . and *pretended* . . . pretended to be married . . ."

Before James could draw another breath, Anne had ripped the dagger from under her skirt and held it to his throat. "That's a lie! Take it back, James. Take it back or I'll cut out your lyin' tongue."

"Jus' as' the captain 'ere." James gave him a cross-eyed look, too drunk to feel the point of the blade and the slow, thin trickle of blood down his neck.

"How ironic, Bonny, that you will sustain more wounds in this tavern . . . from your own wife . . . than you took the entire time aboard ship."

"Does he tell true, Captain?" Anne turned on him, the blade still at Bonny's throat.

"Aye, lass, he does," Hornigold said sadly. "I told him on ship, but it was not meant to hurt you, or to have it told to you in this manner. My thought was to help him to understand, because . . . well, there's no denyin' the trouble betwixt the two of you. I'd no notion he'd bludgeon you with the news of it in a tavern, and I am sorry for it."

The knife she held began to shake and without further word, she turned and left hurriedly, racing along the water's edge searching for the beach, for she had to think. Think. Everything she had thought about her life was a lie. Why hadn't her mother told her? Of course . . . floating at the back of her mind she had questioned why her parents never took Communion at Mass.

My God, James is right. I'm no better than the rest of them. A bastard like most of the others. Outcast at birth and bound to the prison and pirate ship!

Then she stopped and turned to face the water.

Ah, I'll not feel sorry for meself. What I got from my father and mother was love, more than many here can say. I read, for Christ's sake.

And she had a further glimmer of what her father had tried to do for her.

I have brains and talent, both with sword and harpsichord. Now I will just have to decide how I'm going to use it.

Yet as she walked the beach, she could not help but feel, at last and in truth, that she was indeed one of them.

Chapter Thirteen

Early the next morning, the sea a brilliant shade of blue, white caps lining the length of reef, Anne returned to the tavern to find if Bonny had survived the night. In a room above the hall, she found him passed out cold, a woman in his bed. She felt no jealousy, for she knew he would remember nothing, not even his speech before the tavern. Christ, but he had been at sea for two months and deserved a woman.

Quietly, she lifted his coat and took most of what was left of his prize money from the pockets, then walked backwards to the door, her eye on him, remembering for a last time what they had shared.

In the inn's great hall she regarded the evening's damage. The remains of left over food and spilled drink needed cleaning, and she thought to help, for last night she had run from her work. A few of the patrons slept where they'd sat the night before, heads down on the table, snores echoing against the walls, whilst a few still drank sloppily, and a single fellow held one of the girls in his lap and laughed.

"Here now, get me some food, would you, Mistress Bonny?"

Anne turned to see Stede Bonnet make his way down the stairs. "Ah, Captain, are ye just wakin'? Stayed the night upstairs?"

"Thought it best."

"And what'll ye be havin' this morning?"

"Salt fish and fritters, if you please," and he found a chair at table. "Anne, I'm sorry for the words your husband said last evening."

Without answering his regret, she turned from him to take up a tray. "I've your book to return. Shall I bring it to the ship?"

Stede Bonnet regarded her a moment longer. "I knew you could read. But Hornigold . . . goddamn the man . . . Hornigold has said you can read more than English. True?"

"English, of course, French, Latin, and some Greek. My father insisted upon it for some reason that has yet to make my acquaintance. Perhaps he thought I could use the skill in my work," and she glanced around the tavern laughing good-naturedly at the absurdity of it all.

"Are you familiar with this?" He took a book from his bag.

Anne read the cover. "Ah, my old friend, Cicero." How long ago she had fled the classroom from this very work! "I'm well acquainted with the gentleman, Captain Bonnet." Then more to herself. "And lucky ye are to have such a book."

"In fact, Anne, I have a library aboard ship and thought to discuss my readings with one who is like-minded. Would ye care to see the whole library instead of a single copy?"

"Why, it seems I'm fairly popular these days." She tilted her head thoughtfully. "Indeed, Captain Hornigold just offered me use of his harpsichord. What purpose would *you* have in mind, if you don't mind my askin'?"

"Conversation only, girl. How many in port can speak about anything other than treasure and drink and a good fight?"

"And women, Captain. Don't forget the women. Food, drink, a bit of cunny, and the exhilaration just before the fight. The life of a pirate, surely. Men of simple pleasures."

"Perhaps life is not so simple for some of us."

And his look was such a boy's, that Anne wanted to clasp him to her bosom. Instead she leaned forward and said quietly, "If I might make so bold, it's not just Benjamin Hornigold says you should go home to your wife, back to your plantation in Barbados, Captain Bonnet. They say you're out of your element and that you took to piracy not because you had to, but because you thought it some game you could do as a hobby. And now this business with Blackbeard . . ."

His face darkened. "Yes, Blackbeard. Most unfortunate."

"More than unfortunate, I'd say. The rumor is he cheated you. Stede," and she used the familiar to get his attention, "how is it you expect to remain a captain if the crew and all on shore know you've let yourself be hoodwinked?"

Bonnet looked about the tavern and saw that no one listened, then began to explain. "Off the Carolinas we met up, Teach and I, and he asked me to sail as part of his flotilla. But when he saw my . . . unique . . . style of sailing, he invited me aboard the *Queen Anne's Revenge* and put one of his own men aboard to captain my ship."

Again his gaze swept the room, and he further lowered his voice. "Truth is, Anne, I was a prisoner. Oh, the word was never exchanged betwixt us, and he left me the run of the ship and the library. But prisoner I was. With the help of my own crew he took a dozen or so prizes, then put me back aboard the *Revenge* and convinced me to come here to accept the governor's pardon. Without sense, I sailed away, only grateful to be free of him. It was not many hours until I realized the bastard had my share of the loot, and although it is promised, he'll never give it in this life. I've got my pardon, Mistress Bonny, but I'm soon to sea, for I will have my fair share from Blackbeard."

"You intend to chase him down?"

He nodded.

"Captain Bonnet, have ye thought about your style? There's no other pirate captain what's bought his own ship. That's part o' the grace of bein' a pirate. Captain's elected. The men take a share of the prize. Workin' together toward a common goal. There's no pirate as gets paid unless he's fortunate to take down a ship. But you . . . you pay your men, like the hired muscle of any ordinary merchant or man o' war. You see what I'm sayin'?"

Indeed Bonnet seemed not to hear, but stared past her into the air. "I can still see Teach's face as I sailed away, smug and laughing. I'll not have it from any man, not even Edward Teach." He ran his hand through his hair, and his face hardened with thoughts of revenge.

"Blackbeard is no man to challenge lightly. Think upon what you do. Is Barbados so bad?"

"Mistress Bonny, I must satisfy my honor, or I shall have none." Then he smiled. "But while I wait, I would be happy to share my library with you. And perhaps some conversation?"

She sighed, for he had his own mind. "All right. Friends, is it, then? Nothing more. For I will be equally frank, I've had me fill of men and one in particular."

"Aye, friends."

The great news of the day was that Benjamin Hornigold had accepted the governor's pardon and had sworn off piracy. On his return he had gone directly to the governor's office, so as to make no mistake about his intentions. Already the city had changed, for pirates had fled by the hundreds, not liking the look of the king's armada sent to suppress their livelihood. Nary a pirate ship stood in harbor; the only ships remaining were those whose captains had taken the pardon and sailed under new colors and one or two legitimate merchants brave enough to test the waters. For many the transition proved to be difficult, and more than a few sailors felt as they had after the end of the War, once again put ashore without work.

Among the remaining ships, the *Ranger* rode at anchor, and within a few weeks Hornigold posted a bill for a crew to sign on, this time without Articles. Instead, the crew would sail with laws dictated by His Majesty's navy, the purpose of the voyage to chase down those men who refused to accept the pardon.

"Ye cannot seriously be thinkin' of signin' on!" Anne exclaimed to James as soon as he mentioned he would be a crewmember.

"And why not? Isn't that what ye wanted. Me at sea with Hornigold?"

"Aye, when he was an honest pirate! But it's unethical of the man! He goes to hunt down our friends, men with whom ye've fought and shared drink!"

"Captain Hornigold has made the right decision. He's out of the game."

"Perhaps so. But it doesn't mean he has to turn on the rest of us."

"Us?"

"Ye know as well as I why so many have come to piracy. Have we not spoken of it many times? Have ye forgotten Bridget's life so quickly? Her kidnap and forced indenture and the things she had to endure? Or . . . or . . . or any of the others? James, think. If you play this game, who will be next in line for the gallows? For they mean to hang the men Hornigold captures. Look at him, for God's sake! He's no ordinary seaman. He settles onto a gentleman's plantation with the governor as a friend. And he buys his own comfort by tracking down the very men with whom he's sailed! The irony of the matter is that he's still pirate at heart, his own self-interests first. If you help him, ye put money into his pocket, flogged from the backs of men of acquaintance. And know this for certain, it's not you who will sit with him at the governor's table."

"I hear Bonnet's shipped."

"Aye, the fool, off to pursue Blackbeard and take what he can along the way."

"What do you know of his plans?' James asked, jealousy and accusation deep in his tone.

"Just what he's told me. I've tried to convince him he's no sea captain. But all he could say is that he said he'd show me."

"And why would he be havin' to show you anything?"

"Because we are friends. Because we have shared a glass of wine and a passage from a book and sometimes a poem. Do not presume to make me explain myself to you. Ye know we are done."

"Then there's no reason I shouldn't sign up with Hornigold, is there? In fact, he goes after Bonnet and Blackbeard and Charles Vane . . ."

Without warning, a picture rose of Jack Rackham laughing as Vane's ship headed out to sea. "Vane? What news have you of his ship and crew?"

"Only what I hear from Captain Hornigold. Vane's been taking ships off the Carolina coast. Some say he's heading south, others north. But I think he's joined up with Teach until the furor dies down in Charles Town. Seems Vane tortured several captured passengers looking for where they'd stashed their valuables."

"A bad business," Anne agreed, "but it doesn't mean his men should suffer for his decisions."

"Come now, Anne, who d'ye think's doin' the torturin'? Besides, it's not just Hornigold who's puttin' out. William Rhett is fitted and makin' ready to sail. And there'll be more, like a vise squeezing shut. I thought you wanted somethin' different. I thought you wanted land or some such."

"That was before. I'll have none of you, James, so I've said over and over."

"And I tell you, we're married and I'll never give you a divorce. I'm signin' on with Hornigold and I'll be after those pirates who've refused the gov'nor's pardon. I'm doin' what I know best, makin' my way by the sea. And then I'll be back."

Chapter Fourteen

After several attempts Anne finally succumbed to Hornigold's plea to play the harpsichord in his parlor, and there she practiced, generally when he was not at home. But on the day he returned early and followed the music, he stood at the door enraptured as she played with the same fierceness with which she lived her life. How could a woman who tended tavern, cleaned her own house, counseled the wretched, and fought like a demon, play so that his heart would either take flight or break?

"Captain Hornigold!" she stood when she saw him. "I did not know you had returned. I shall leave you to your peace and quiet."

"Quiet is not what I desire, Anne. Not when I hear your music. And I will have you call me Benjamin."

"Thank you, sir," she curtseyed, "but I will be off."

"Wait. I've a proposition for you. I have a certain amount of influence with the new governor, but I would have more. Accompany me to the governor's dinner on Saturday. Play for him as my guest and you will bring me honor. No one on this island will have heard music like this unless they have recently been to London."

"You grant me too much favor," and she bowed now, slowly and deliberately. How easily the words and demeanor all came back! "But I am afraid I must refuse. Besides, why should I increase your influence when you use it against the very men who were once your friends?"

Hornigold smiled and indeed he was handsome, his face full of life at sea. "What makes you think I would turn against friends?"

"Begging your pardon, Captain, but everyone knows

you are an informant to the governor. Indeed, that you have personally hunted down known pirates and many of them have hung."

"True. But those I've captured were those who will not be missed. Those men I've known, those good and true, still have a berth on some ship." He looked toward the harpsichord, then at her hands close to the keys, finally, straight on, into her eyes. "Anne, 'tis a dangerous business we're about, for the Admiralty is more than serious about ridding the waters of sea robbers. I must have influence if I am to secure a future for any number of men, my crew included. I am asking that you meet the governor and win his favor. Knowing him, I am best able to recognize what he will do next." Then he smiled and offered a challenge, "Unless you are afraid of what people will say. In both worlds. Those who will sit at the governor's table, and those who carry stories in the tavern."

"Not in the least! I am my own person and care not what others think!"

"Then come on Saturday as my guest."

In truth she was curious about this new governor who had changed life in New Providence. Perhaps it was not such a bad idea, for who knew when the occasion might arise when she could claim familiar with him.

"What's in it for me?" she asked. "If you're to have more influence through my efforts?"

"Why, the harpsichord. After listening to you today, it could belong to no one else."

"You jest."

"I jest not."

Anne took a deep, satisfied breath. "If you are serious . . ."

"I am."

"Then, yes," and she smiled wide and with true delight. "Yes. Saturday."

The governor's mansion in Nassau was alight with torches and candles when Anne stepped into the great hall on the arm of Benjamin Hornigold. At once she fell back into the lady she had been bred to be. Here was society, and with more than a little curiosity they regarded her, wondering what ship had brought her to port and how she had come to be with the captain. The overdress she wore was emerald green silk, the underskirt a lighter shade of moss green. A fresh whalebone corset pushed up her bosom to advantage, the rigid bodice embroidered with gold thread, ambitious lace at the sleeves and collar, and in the center, a huge diamond pendant on loan from one of Captain Hornigold's chests. Under the skirt strapped to her leg, the dagger she could not forgo. Now she glided across the floor, all her wits about her, and Benjamin could not have been more pleased.

The table to which they were led after introductions and drinks, was set for an intimate dinner of fourteen. Anne regarded the art on the walls, family portraits and one magnificent painting of a ship at sea, the white linen table cloth, the china, crystal, and silver, numerous candles on the table and in sconces, thinking that one alone would have given her light for quite some time, and wondered from whom it all had been stolen, for it was no secret that Woodes Rogers was a privateer before he'd become the king's man.

"I say, Captain Hornigold," Colonel William Rhett said when they had been seated, "your old friend, Edward Teach, is at it again." He held his glass out for more wine and a liveried servant stepped forward with white gloves and powdered wig to fill his cup. Like Hornigold, Rhett wore his natural hair tied back in a queue with dark silk ribbon, for a wig and the shaved head required to wear it, was a nuisance on ship. "If nothing else he does make for a good story."

"Indeed," Hornigold returned, the silver thread of his brocaded coat sparkling in candlelight. "What is the black-guard up to now?"

"Seems he lost the *Queen Anne's Revenge* at Beaufort Inlet. Run aground, I take it. Insisted another smaller vessel in his fleet try to assist in freeing her, and lost that as well!"

"That should cut his navy down," sniggered a gentleman

at table, fat of belly, his lips too fleshy, his face round and cut with the deep furrows of his age. "And pray God it cuts down the rabble with him. Convicts, vagabonds, escaped slaves, whatever. . . vermin, all of them," he added with disgust. "Of every color, white, black, mulatto, even Indian. The scum of the earth, and all living together on ship. Can you imagine? All in equal partnership!"

"About the devil's business," agreed Reverend Shaw, drinking deep the red wine in his crystal goblet and smacking his lips. "But then, violence is natural to those who live without morals, governed by lusts of the flesh and drink."

"I say piracy 'tis treasonous. Treasonous!" rejoined the fat man. "Interrupts the very thing that makes us a strong nation! The very thing that grants us wealth, strength, and glory! Damned anarchists . . . begging your pardon, ladies . . . but the very thought causes my bones to shudder."

"The best bit of the story is the part about his crew," Rhett continued. "There is some speculation that he deliberately beached the two ships, for he deserted twenty-five of his own men! Marooned them on a rocky ledge without provisions! Only took a picked crew with him, and, of course, his treasure!"

"What happened to the men he left behind?" Anne asked, aghast at the betrayal.

All eyes turned to her, for she had been silent for most of the evening. Now they saw that her hand shook and that her gaze was intent and waiting for answer. Only Benjamin Hornigold knew that it was not in squeamish fear, but in rage.

"There, there, my dear, you mustn't let yourself get upset by this barbarous conversation," consoled an elderly man with some civility.

Hornigold cast his eyes to the ceiling.

"Are you certain you care to hear the outcome, Mistress Bonny?" the governor asked. "Tis true the story is unsavory and I do beg pardon for the offense."

"Not at all, Governor Rogers. Please continue. I am

merely excited by thoughts of dreadful danger."

"Well, then, to be sure," continued the colonel, relishing his platform, "they were rescued by Stede Bonnet . . ."

"Bonnet!" Anne exclaimed. "The gentleman from Barbados?"

"Why, yes. Wherever did you hear such a thing? Although how much a gentleman is uncertain."

"Surely you know, sir, that pirates are all anyone talks about in New Providence."

At this the table laughed heartily and a chorus of agreement went round.

"Well, then, I shall tell you that Bonnet persuaded the men left behind to sign on as crew in exchange for rescue. The whole pack immediately set out to take ships and plunder. Did quite well I'm told . . ."

"That is," and here the governor intervened, pointing toward Rhett with his fork, "until the good colonel here chased Bonnet down with the *Henry* and the *Sea Nymph."*

"There was a splendid battle!" the colonel gleefully told the table.

"And Bonnet? How did he fare?" asked Anne, a quiver in her voice.

Relishing her breathlessness, the heave of her bosom, and her reddened cheeks, Colonel Rhett exclaimed, "Battled for his life, my dear! I had the good fortune to find him near the mouth of Cape Fear River near Charles Town. Between the *Henry* and the *Sea Nymph* we carried some sixteen guns and about a hundred thirty men. Bonnet thought to be clever and rename the *Revenge* in an attempt to hide. The *Royal James* he called her. We saw through the deception immediately. There he lay, just inside the mouth of the river, outmanned and outgunned, him with his forty men and ten guns. But then the most damnable thing happened . . ." and he paused to sip his wine.

"What?" she asked huskily.

"Good God, Colonel! This is no conversation for ladies!" the older gentleman called, noting Anne's distress.

"No . . . please. The outcome?"

"Well," Colonel Rhett continued with some delight, "ahead we could see Bonnet's mast upriver, but in trying to get up close, both my ships were run aground! Seeing us helpless and waiting for the tide to float us over the sandbar, Bonnet tried to slip by. Why, my dear, the *Henry* was a mere seventy yards away, and the *Sea Nymph* four hundred yards, when he tried to make his break. But the inexperience of the man! In sailing downriver to the sea he hugged the shoals too closely. Shy of our cannon, he was . . . and ran himself aground! We took to firing at each other with cannon for the better part of an hour. A bit dicey at this point for whomever floated first would have the other at his mercy. Fortunately for me, the *Henry* was closest to the middle of the channel and was lifted before the *Revenge.* I sailed in raking her sails and deck . . . and Bonnet surrendered!"

"He's been taken to Charles Town for trial," the governor told her offhandedly while motioning for a servant to bring a tray of meat. "I hear he writes letters daily pleading for forgiveness and reform. It seems he would now like to honor the pardon I once so generously granted him. Unfortunately, his reform is somewhat late. I believe they'll make an example of him."

A woman at table with an admirable diamond necklace and earrings moaned, "Must we talk about pirates? Mistress Bonny is right. I do beg your pardon, Governor Rogers, but ever since your arrival that is all the conversation to be had! Please, sir, have pity!"

Governor Rogers smiled and nodded to her deferentially, "I hear the East India Company is sending spices our way," and the conversation moved to the price of cinnamon and tea, and as the wine flowed, voices rose, and Hornigold leaned to Anne.

"He's doing quite well," he whispered. "Crew's in prison, but Bonnet has a room in the marshal's house and every amenity afforded a gentleman of his station."

"What will they do with him?"

"Why, I am sorry to say it, but they will hang him."

A pause, and Anne stood abruptly. "Governor, I do beg your pardon, but I need some air. If you please . . ."

"But, of course." And every man at the table stood just as abruptly.

"I will see to it," Hornigold nodded, and took Anne by the arm toward the garden, the words, "I told you this was no conversation for ladies . . ." following them.

"It's very warm in there," she said, "and I haven't worn a corset like this for quite some time and . . . oh, Benjamin, are ye certain . . . so certain that they will hang him?"

"Shall I tell you truly?"

"Always."

He nodded. "He does have a chance, although not much of one. Many are trying to persuade the governor to change his mind. Planters who have known Bonnet in Barbados, men who have the governor's ear, myself. Believe it or not, he has taken in the society ladies of Charles Town. Why, they've even formed a committee to write letters in his favor, inquiring how anyone with a library could be bad!" He held out an arm to a bench, but Anne could not sit, rather paced on that small, private patio. "I told you, Anne, it is a serious business."

"That poor miserable man, who is only a romantic at heart! For God's sake, he sees himself as the hero of one of his novels!"

Now Hornigold regarded her with narrow eyes. "Ye asked for the truth and ye shall have it. Have ye seen a sea battle? Have ye felt the rush of fear and exhilaration in swinging over the side of a ship with cutlass and pistol? Have ye watched other men desperately fight for their lives? It's not all romance, Anne, and he's done it more than once. Enough to know the killing. Besides, this is about his wife, something to prove to her. Hell of a way to end a marital spat."

"You said you are taking Bonnet's side? I don't understand. I thought you were all about bringing in the 'brigands', as you call them," she asked, her voice tight.

Lowering his voice, he explained stiffly, "I'll not be the governor's spaniel. But I walk a thin line. I told you before, those I've chosen are deserving of justice."

She turned upon him then, and said quietly, fiercely, "Is a sea battle any more killing than at the prisons or gallows, Captain Hornigold? I have heard the stories of torture, of brandings and floggings, of the rack and thumbscrew. In the tavern, I've seen the mutilation of tongues and feet and fingers and heard stories of brutal rape. The women I've known have cried in anguish for the loss of a child, taken and sold without recourse, slave born and merely property. I know personally the hopelessness of poverty, its ugliness, and I understand the desperation that drives men to take what they can. Like you did, when ye had nothing but your knowledge of the sea, a ship, and a crew. And like you and yours, every man aboard Bonnet's ship has a story. You know as well as I that Teach marooned those men to die a lingering death, and Bonnet, God bless his twisted heart, took it upon himself to save them. I will not turn my back on Bonnet simply because he is a fool. You see, Captain Hornigold, he is my friend."

When Hornigold finally spoke, he first cleared his throat. "Would that I had a friend like you," he said softly. "What will ye do, lass?"

"Why, nothing, Captain Hornigold," she eyed him innocently, looking up at him from beneath lashes, a trick she had not used in many years. "Now, let us return to eat from this banquet. I have seen too much hunger."

Chapter Fifteen

The chest in her room held a number of items Anne had been preparing for months. From the bottom she removed a long roll of cotton fabric and began to wrap her breasts, flattening them, and over this cotton, she placed a long sleeved sailor's shirt and vest. She wore breeches and boots, wrapped her hair in a scarf, and then placed a hat on her head. A duffle bag with a few items and she was ready.

For years she had wanted to return to sea, but only with the threat of Bonnet's fate did she actually have the courage to take ship. The original plan had been to sail out and away from all she knew; now, she had to sign aboard a ship that would take her back to Charles Town, for she was determined that Bonnet would not hang.

The ship was a merchant vessel bound for Charles Town, New York, and then Liverpool, and although she had made it her business to learn every sail and rigging by name, and remembered the jobs she had done on the voyage to New Providence, it was apparent to all that she was as green as they come. But she managed by following orders with such enthusiasm, that one of the older seamen took the boy under his wing.

Once the ship cleared port her heart rose, and again she felt as if she were flying, skimming over the water, eyes ever outward, the great moving picture of sea and sky changing color and never the same from one minute to the next. The hardest work was done with song and rhythm and she lowered her voice to sing the words she had learned in the tavern. Her concerns about washing were unfounded, for sailors never washed except when it rained and then they washed themselves and their clothes while wearing them. Below decks was dark and the privy was a private corner, its use considered the most natural function in the world, unquestionable. No man was going to look too closely into the toileting of another, or else run the risk of an ungodly name. So Anne was set, and unless someone searched too closely the bag she carried, she would make her way into Charles Town with ease.

The alley where the Ship and Shore stood was the same . . . and yet different. Men staggered with too much drink, women plied their trade, seamen went about their business. But there was no one she recognized after two years away, and she passed unnoticed. What a picture she must have made when she'd first arrived with James! Wealthy, well-dressed even in the clothes she thought were so ordinary, hair flying. Her main concern now was whether Betsy still served at the tavern, for she had need of a friend. At the door she looked into the great room and a thousand memories flooded her thoughts, but by fortune, there was Betsy, and Anne moved toward her and whispered in her ear, "Can I see you alone?"

"Why, Lord, of course, ye can, m' dear," and Betsy ran a hand along Anne's face. "Such a pretty boy. I 'as a good price for you too. I'll just drop these off," she nodded to the drinks on her tray. "Go on up. First door, right."

Anne shoved the duffle bag higher on her shoulder and made for the stairs, gave a glance back and saw that Betsy grinned provokingly.

"Just off the ship, are we now? And anxious, eh?"

The room was as she remembered and she unbuckled her sword and began to unpack the duffle, shaking out the dress she intended to wear for her visit to Bonnet, removing shoes, stockings, corset, and hat. The door opened behind and there was a startled gasp, a hesitation, and then with more professionalism, "So tell me how I can pleasure you, m' boy. Do you wear the dress, or do I?"

Anne turned laughing, "Do ye not know me then, Betsy McDonald? For I'm not your own sweet boy, but Anne

Bonny, straight off the ship and come to visit!" And she pulled off her hat and scarf.

Betsy's eyes went wide with wonder and question. "Anne . . . how . . . off the ship . . ." Then, she took Anne in her arms and, boy or girl, gave her a hug laughing. "How come ye to be here? You were always a wild one, Anne, more bollocks then many a man! And James, where is he? Onboard with you?"

"No, Betsy, I'm afraid that's finished."

"What, the marriage?"

"Aye. I'm done and makin' me own way. I've a mind to stay at sea. There's somethin' about the feel of the boat, like a livin' being, and when we hit open water with all the sails unfurled, why, I could go on forever."

"Well then, let's keep the truth between us, for I'll not have the worry of it. If the two of ye are truly done, ye won't mind me sayin' that James has had his fun here . . . with me . . . on his travels."

"Nah, I don't. I've not slept with him for months so he's got every right to take his pleasure where he can find it."

"Well and good riddance to that off me chest." Betsy nodded toward the dress. "What's that for? What are you about?"

"I've a friend whose been captured and arrested along with his crew. He's being held at the marshal's house."

"Stede Bonnet? Why the entire city's in an uproar over the good captain. Have a care, Anne. Ye'll stir up the hornet's nest."

The guards at the marshal's house were by now accustomed to any number of citizens of Charles Town visiting the gentleman pirate, idealizing his folly and forming committees to petition the governor on his behalf. A cursory look at Anne and they thought her no exception, allowing her to pass into his quarters for a private visit.

The room where he sat was comfortable and clean, with a bed, good chairs, a writing desk, quill, and ink. His long coat was well tailored, the sleeves elaborate, and his head had been shaved so that he might wear a wig. Seated at table, Bonnet was having breakfast, but upon her entrance, he looked up, rose when he saw a skirt, then almost fell back into his chair when he recognized Anne.

"Good morning, Stede. Enjoying breakfast?"

"Anne," he gasped, shocked, "how come ye here?"

"To make sure you don't hang, my friend. I could not bear the thought of it. How many times did I tell you to go home? Now this."

He threw down his serviette and walked to her, taking her hands. "It's good of you to come. Truth be told, it doesn't look good. Even with the sympathy of a great many people of influence, the governor and the judge, one Sir Nicolas Trott, are set against me."

"I do not have much time. Just a few minutes the guard said, but I have a plan if you will hear it."

His look was one of gentle condescension. "I thank you for your thoughts, but there is nothing anyone can do to help me escape. Although there are comings and goings from this house, I am closely watched."

Anne glanced back at the door, then opened the cloak she carried over her arm. From its folds she took a dress and stockings. "I think they may fit. Donated by one of the larger women at the tavern in New Providence."

"I'm . . . I'm to escape as a woman?"

"If you care to save your life, aye. If not, you can swing as a man."

"But can it be done?" and a glimmer of interest rose in his voice.

"I think it's worth a try if you use my cloak to cover your frame. After the changin' of the guard, call out in your own voice that you have a visitor leavin'. Then go out yourself. There are only two sentries and they march, one on either side of the door. When they turn their backs, walk calmly between them. Here, hide these things. It'll take courage and nerve to carry through. Once you're out, go to shore and steal yourself a boat. You just might become a real pirate," she teased. "Then get as far away from here as quickly as you can. Go home to your plantation and write your memoirs so that one day I may read them. It's a chance, if you want to take it."

"It just might work. Blood and wounds, it just might!" he cried quietly, and took the things from her and stuffed them beneath the bed.

"So tell me how you spend your days, Stede Bonnet . . . and tell me how this all came to pass."

"I suppose all the uproar is about the ten vessels I took off the Virginia coast," he told her proudly.

"I don't see how they can rid these waters of pirates," Anne mused in return. "There's a thousand inlets and coves all along the coast, with as many islands. What about your crew?"

"Doomed, I'm afraid. They're dead men and nothing to be done about it. The Admiralty has already said they will bury them at the low water mark. Food for crabs. I'm sorry for them, but at the moment, not as sorry as for myself."

"No hope at all?" for she believed a captain's duty was to see to his men first.

"None, I'm afraid. I can only pray that my rank gives me an edge."

Sadly, she shook her head, then, "Come. Show me what you read before I go, and one day, I shall make it my business to get to your island, my dear Captain Bonnet, for I am to sea."

That very evening Stede Bonnet made his escape. A great hue and cry arose, and many of the same people who had petitioned for Bonnet's release, now turned toward the governor with accusations of bribery. Fearing the wolf had been let loose among the lambs and that Bonnet would once again murder and plunder ships of commerce, a new local movement worked just as diligently to have him returned to prison. The governor offered a reward of seven hundred pounds for his capture and return, and Anne, who could not see leaving until she knew Bonnet's fate, watched the ship she had enlisted on sail away to New York. Instead, she waited at the tavern, to all eyes a young lad attached to Betsy.

The story was passed round soon enough and was a great source of mirth to all. Bonnet, the tale went, had escaped in women's clothes, stolen a small vessel, and was off on the seas, none knew where. But nary two weeks had passed when word came that Captain Bonnet had been recaptured.

When the ship returning him to Charles Town dropped anchor and Bonnet was brought ashore, Anne stood among the crowds to watch him arrive in chains. So intent was she upon her thoughts, that she did not notice the man who came to stand behind her. Not until she felt him take hold of her arm did she draw away with a start, at the same time reaching for her sword.

"Hornigold," she hissed, looking into his eyes. "What the devil are you doin' here? Unhand me."

He placed a finger to his lips. "Come with me."

"How is it you recognize me?"

To which he merely raised a sardonic eyebrow. For a moment she wondered, then nodded and followed him from the crowd.

"The truth is, t'would be better if Bonnet did not recognize you. Women's clothing, Anne?" He smiled with some amusement.

"Why do ye think t'was me?"

"I believe we've already had this conversation at the governor's mansion."

"Curse it all," she raged when they were farther from the shoreline and a press of people took their places on the quay. "Why in bloody hell didn't he make straight for home where he has influence?"

"I think he tried, but the boat he stole was badly provisioned and the weather equally foul. He had to put in to Sullivants Island for supplies. But you're right, it's too close to Charles Town."

"How could he have let himself be found out?"

"Because he was betrayed. And that by the first person who recognized him. Seven hundred pounds is a lot of money, wouldn't you agree? When the governor got word he asked Colonel Rhett and myself to bring him in. Unfortunately," and here he cast her a knowing glance, "my ship was out of service. The good colonel went on his own and has the honor of the capture."

"I see. Have I misjudged you, Captain Hornigold?"

To which he returned no answer, instead he said, "Anne, there was nothing anyone could have said to him. He's a man who's made his own choices. The pity is he had more choices than most. Did ye actually think ye could save him? If not this time, then he would have been captured another. Bonnet would not have given up piracy. T'was in his blood. Not the wanting of wealth, for that he had before he started. No, it was the lust of battle that he sought, the chase, the knowledge that his life was more than ordinary."

"How would you know?"

"I will not deny it, the thrill still beckons. Can ye deny that you did not feel the excitement as well? The thrill of danger as you slipped in and out of Bonnet's room, the guards watching closely? Helping Bonnet escape would have put you in prison for a long time. Possibly hung, for you'd be called pirate as well."

"I'm no real pirate, Benjamin!" she cried, the thought so disconcerting she called him by his given name. "And surely they will not hang a woman. Besides, as you can see, I'm merely a lad."

With a start she looked up at him, a thought just come to her. "You are here to make sure I am not caught?"

"Perhaps I am."

"Why?"

"Your mother . . . if you will not accept your father as reason enough."

Completely thrown off her guard she finally nodded. "All right . . . all right." Bonnet had passed and the crowd followed, moving toward the prison. "What will happen now?"

"He will go to trial. You will find Judge Trott a . . . religious man. He will see to Mr. Bonnet's soul, quote scripture, and explain the evil of his ways. Then he will be found guilty and hung. And very quickly, I believe."

"Has he no defense?"

"None that anyone will believe. He's taken over thirteen vessels just recently, and he's responsible for the deaths of many. No, Anne, it's time to go back to New Providence." And with a hint of his old humor, asked, "Will you join my crew, lad?"

"Benjamin, why are you really here?"

"In truth, because you disappeared. And I thought you might be up to some foolishness. Who would play the harpsichord for me when my soul needed food?" He looked toward where Bonnet had disappeared up the street. "And because I had business with the governor."

"Ah . . ."

"Perhaps. But that 'ah' extends to your husband as well."

Anne stiffened. "James is here? He sails back to New Providence on your ship?"

"Not any more. I've a job for him."

Anne narrowed her eyes. "He spies for you and the governor, does he not?"

"If you really hate your husband, you will repeat that speculation every opportunity you get, for if anyone hears, his life is not worth a farthing."

"What business are you and he about?"

"I have your promise of silence?"

"Go on."

"This business has to do with Teach."

"Blackbeard? What about him?"

"'Tis Teach the governor will have next. One by one, they

will take the captains down."

"But Teach is your man! He sailed under you . . . you . . . you created him! He's a fast, bonnie ship and many men. Tell me, how can they honestly think to rid these waters of piracy?"

"Will you give a mind to what I say? Must I make my case over and over? Teach makes himself too big and I tell you, Anne, they will have him and there is nothing anyone can do."

"And ye'll join them in the hunt," she said flatly.

He stopped, then, where they walked, and with some seriousness regarded her. "There is one more thing. Would you like to see your father while you are here?"

With a vehement shake of her head, she answered. "I cannot. Not with this thing about Stede. My father will be right up front in the courtroom. I'd be obliged, Captain, for a place on the roster. When do you sail?"

"This evening on the tide. Can you handle the job?"

"Better than most. I'd better get aboard. It seems as if James will be taking my place in Betsy's bed."

Part 4

New Providence, Bahamas

Spring, 1719

Jack Rackham

Chapter Sixteen

The wind of the sea was blowing warmer, a sure sign that the heat of summer was on its way and with it, the possibility of the great hurricanes that every sailor feared. Anne was on shore with money in her purse, for she had just returned from a voyage to Charles Town and Boston on board the *Ranger*. Shipboard rumor was that Captain Hornigold was meeting with partners in a legitimate trading enterprise, all the more reason to clear the seas of pirates lest his new business be bankrupted by the very trade he had once pursued. Anne could have simply asked his plans, and he would have told her, but she avoided that intimacy. The asking would mean that she was more than the crew, and being more than the crew was a problem she did not want. No, for the first time in many years she had found a measure of happiness—able to choose work aboard ship as a boy, the freedom to come and go in and out of port, money enough to live, and while on shore, skirts and a book, friends, song, grog, and merry-making in the seaside taverns of New Providence.

Grace laughed at her with a crooked smile. "Are ye daft as well as blind?" And when Anne was slow to answer, added, "That wasn't really a question, dearie. Of, course, he's smitten with you!"

"Don't be silly, Grace. Captain Hornigold is simply a good friend. Though only God knows why I call him friend," she answered testily, for in spite of herself she liked him immensely.

"But you're just back from shippin' with 'im."

"Not after pirates, we wasn't. The captain and I have an understanding on that point."

"And what's that, if I might ask?"

"Why, I cannot countenance gaol and hanging for those with whom he once sat and drank!"

"Where *is* the good captain these days anyway?"

"On his way to Mexico on a trading venture, 'tis said. But truth be told, he's too close to Spanish waters for my taste. The temptation of it all. How easy to slip into old habits."

"Worry about 'im, do 'e?" Grace grinned.

"You know well enough that I care for a great number of people," came the tart reply, "and Captain Hornigold is only one of many."

"So," Grace leaned in close to her ear, "what's it about with you and James? Are ye gonna settle with the man or not? Me, I'm gettin' tired of 'im moonin' 'round here and cryin' in 'is cups."

"Ah, Grace, I have settled with the man, but he will nae listen."

A rowdy party entered the tavern, boots on the stairs, boisterous voices, the rattle of swords, and hands slapping the tables calling merrily for drink. Anne turned at the noise . . . and found her heart leapt in her chest. Jack Rackham strode into the middle of the room with a laugh and great wave of his hand to the assembled, his hat with dancing red plume set jauntily on his head, his crewmates behind, full of equal laughter, even a few voices raised in song. Many were the greetings of welcome from around the tavern, and more than one woman's face brightened with expectation.

Anne had not seen him since the day he and Captain Vane had set sail with the arrival of Governor Rogers. For once she was pleased that she wore skirt and a billowing white cotton blouse, that a new gold necklace lay bright on her sun-darkened skin, that her earrings glistened when she turned. Without thinking, she ran her hands through her uncovered hair falling in waves down her back, and forgot for the moment the red sash at her waist that held a pistol and the belt carrying her sword. As she watched Jack's confident smile, she thought he looked like clean sunshine.

"Drink up, mates," he called, "for today we are free men. Liberated men. Men with the king's pardon in our pockets," and he held up to the cast the source of his merriment, a signed paper excusing all his pirating. "May God forgive us, but we are back on land, and safe from the hangman's noose."

Anne grabbed Grace's arm and begged an answer, never taking her eyes off him, "Jack Rackham, am I right?"

"Aye, *Captain* Jack Rackham. Left 'ere a quartermaster and come back a captain." Grace watched the sparkle in Anne's eyes. "Ah, so's you're interested, are ye? Come along then. Time to meet the captain."

But there was no need, for Jack had looked over the tavern in the first seconds and could not take his eyes from Anne. With mug in hand and great strides in her direction, he made her a generous leg, and said upon rising, "What would someone of your beauty be doin' with sword and pistol? Shall we put them down for awhile and take in the evening?"

"I'll just be gettin' on, Anne." Grace grinned and lifted her tray, but not before Jack grabbed the bottle upon it.

"A whole bottle, Jack?" she teased. "Plannin' on settlin' in?"

"Anne, is it? I'm Jack. Captain Jack Rackham."

"Anne Bonny."

Jack knew the name but not the woman, had heard stories of the lady, the 'hell-cat', beautiful, cold, allowing no man near, friend to governor, captain, pirate, and scullery maid. But this Anne Bonny did not look cold. Whatever block of ice she held in her breast would certainly be melted by the heat that radiated from her eyes.

"I watched you leave with Captain Vane some months back. He put a broadside across the governor's bow."

"Aye. Slipped out of port, every sail unfurled and flyin' like the wind. Bollocks he had, our good Captain Vane. Ran up the black flag, spread plain and broad, so's the Governor could make no mistake as to who we were." Jack threw back his head and laughed.

"How fortunate our governor is so forgiving."

"Fortunate indeed. For the moment."

Jack set eyes on the pistol she carried, noted her hand resting easily on the hilt of the sword. No, she wasn't a tavern wench, but something apart, just what, well, he would carefully make his way through the shoals to find out. In her uplifted chin was a challenge, a narrowing of the eyes, an unspoken question asking if he was worthy of her interest. Unaccustomed with the necessity of impressing a woman, he could not have torn himself away from Anne at that moment had he wanted, his body drawn to hers like a compass to the north star.

"Are you any good with that?" he nodded to the sword. "Or do ye wear it as decoration."

Anne laughed loud and gleefully. "Would ye care to find out, Captain? I can assure you, most men would not. Something about the humiliation of being bested by a woman in a skirt, I'm told."

"Indeed not, Mistress Bonny," Jack answered putting the bottle down on the table. "Fighting with you is the last thing on my mind. I merely asked."

"What *did* you have on your mind, Captain?" And she gave him the look from between lashes she had practiced long ago in the mirror, filled with suggestion and promise.

"Will you sit and have a drink with me?" He bowed. "And I will tell you a story."

"Tell me first about Captain Vane. I am wondering what could have possessed the good captain to give up his ship and make you captain instead. He doesn't seem the type to walk away from things readily."

"Why, the last I saw of him he was sailing off on his own."

"Happily?"

"Perhaps somewhat put upon," Jack grinned. "He let a French man o' war slip by us without a fight and the crew accused him of cowardice."

"Cowardice? Vane a coward? The same Vane who fired

at the governor's fleet? Come now."

"The crew's call."

"And yours?"

"Aye and mine. For I believe we could have taken the ship. We had plenty of hands on board and good guns. It was simply a matter of boarding her. After the vote Vane was asked politely to take the small sloop that rode alongside. If rumor be true, I believe he's traded up, and now he's back in business with several seaworthy ships."

"An honor to be named captain by your own men, to be sure. I take it you are no coward."

"Indeed not. Will you sit, milady? Will you drink with me?"

Anne nodded, unhitched the sword and placed it on the table between them. Jack sat and poured into two cups, and Anne thought it might be fun to drink pure rum instead of watered down grog, and tease and laugh and if the mood struck, to dance to the fiddle and pipe. As surely as she was Anne Bonny, she knew she wanted this man, only how much and how long need be determined, him with his fine clothes and sure words, a commander, and more than a step above the others. She would take him for herself, because she was a free woman and could choose her own partner. All that surprised her was that she *wanted* to be with a man again and knew irrevocably that she was over James and at liberty.

Jack pointed toward the sword. "Is there any reason it must sit between us? Come closer, girl, so that I might whisper tales in your ear."

"My hearing's fine right where I sit, Captain. And I am no girl, but a woman true. How come you are back in New Providence?"

Jack took the hat from his head, slapped it against his thigh, and swallowed a great swig of his drink, for he knew here was trouble.

"Because I've come back to the beginning," he told her honestly.

Edging closer, Anne could smell him, the sun on his skin,

the rum on his breath, a scent of wind and warmth in his clothes. In the heat of day his shirt lay unbuttoned to his waist, his chest bare, yet he wore a long overcoat, calico breeches, and sea boots to his knees. When he spoke again she barely heard the words, only reveled in the beauty of his face, skin darkened by sun, the gold of his earring brighter because of it, his hair streaked blond, long to his shoulders, and clean, for he had washed in coming ashore to meet the governor. The rum worked its magic, and soon she found herself laughing at his stories of captured ships and silver doubloons, watching his lips, listening to the sound of his voice, marvelously true as he sang of the women of Kingston Town and the loneliness of the journey and glorious sky at sunset. For a great while she longed for the harpsichord of Captain Hornigold, but found that she could join him in song, and after more rum, it seemed all the better.

"Have ye luck then, Jack?" Anne asked, her head beginning to swim with drink.

"That's why I'm here, lass," and he held wide his arm. "To find a ship and take to sea and try my luck again. I've the money and a worthy crew."

"What has happened to the ship you took from Vane?"

"It sits in Havana harbor. But that is another story."

"Will this luck you're to be tryin' be as a pirate?"

"No, for I've the papers in my pocket that gives me a new chance. A new life."

"Oh, ho!" Anne laughed, and reached for the bottle. "And where shall you begin this new life of yours?"

"Why, right here," and Jack reached for the bottle as well, covering her hand with his.

Anne felt her breath quicken and saw that her hand trembled when she pulled away and let him fill her cup. Lest he take advantage of her weakness and try boarding her, she lowered her eyes. But Jack watched her mouth and the heave of her breasts, recognized desire, and knew he must have her.

"'Tis true I have told other women that they are beautiful,

Anne. But you and I, we both know, this is no ordinary drink in a tavern." He stood and offered her a hand. "Come along. I have a room. And we can talk more fully in private."

Anne did not take the outstretched hand, nor rise to meet him, instead said plainly. "I am married."

"Aye. Bonny. I know the man."

"It has been over for a long time. I have not slept with him in a year. But he swears he will never let me go, for we married before a priest."

He reached out to caress her face with the back of one rough finger. "I'm a good captain, Anne, and I know the sea. I can maneuver through any storm he sets upon us. And I have a home. Out of the way, to be sure, but I do have safe harbor if need be."

"Then I am yours . . . if you truly choose to begin again. I'll not share you, Jack. Not with any other woman. I've heard of your conquests and there be many, I'm told." Anne stood and delivered the further terms of the contract. "And ye must know now, here at this beginning, that I want more than a life of piracy. About this, Captain Hornigold is right. Piracy is being smothered. One by one they will take down the captains and their crews, and as they catch them, they will hang them as a terror to others. Already Stede Bonnet and his crew are dead and buried. And Edward Teach is next I'm told. Any number of others. If you and I are to be, I want more. I never want to know the dread of putting into port and fearing for your life. Never able to bring in a ship to refit, or careen, or take on supplies. Where is the freedom in that?"

In answer he leaned toward her and ran an arm around her back and drew her close up against him, her breasts pressed against his chest, her legs running the length of his, pelvis against his hips, his eyes never leaving hers, and she permitted her body to feel, to give way to the soft, building current of erotic love. Then he closed his eyes and in front of the assembled and to the great cheers of the tavern, kissed her, long and deep, so that tears came to her eyes, for dear

God, she felt again, every passageway of feeling opening, the life flowing back into her like water into a river after a drought. When he released her, they no longer heard the sound of the room, knew only the face of the other.

"On my soul," Jack whispered. "I love. I truly love. Will ye come with me, Anne, right now?"

"Aye, Jack, to seal the promise."

Jack's lodging was a fine one, for if he had not ship, he still had money. The room overlooked the sea and had a window box blooming with red geraniums. He lifted her at the door and carried her to a fresh bed and laid her upon it. She watched as he removed his own weapons and set them aside, then his coat and boots, breeches and shirt and stood naked so that she might see him. The muscles of his body were hard, his skin browned above the line of his waist, his buttocks and legs white to the knee, his waist narrow, his skin unblemished yet covered with the scars of battle.

He slipped toward her, took sword and gun from around her waist, and laid them aside the bed. With expert fingers he released her bodice and pushed back the folds of her shirt so that her breasts were revealed, white and soft, her nipples pink, and as he gazed, they hardened.

"Anne, you are so beautiful," he whispered.

"Wait," she said softly, and stood on uneasy legs.

With her own hands she took down the skirt and pulled off the blouse and wore only the gold upon her body, then turned so that he might appreciate the round curves of hips and stomach, the very things she tried to hide when dressing for sea, now glad they were hers to share with him.

"What think ye, Jack?" her voice quivered, uncertain. "For I am all of eighteen years and no longer a young maid. Do ye like me?"

"Like you?" he cried, lunging for her, casting her to the bed, and standing above her. "More than the whole wide world!"

"I am yours, now and always," she whispered hoarsely, making her vow.

His hand began at her face, carressed slowly down her neck, the backs of his fingers gently moving over the length of her skin, his lips following to touch her eyes and mouth, then softly brushing every curve of her body.

"Jack," she murmured, somewhere between a whisper and a moan, "I need you . . ."

"Aye. And I you," he cried softly, his feelings passing over him like pounding storm waves. "Now and evermore. My promise."

In the next moment he was upon her and in her, mouth hard on hers, and Anne cried out, for she was tight and virgin new after the year alone. They moved like the sea upon the bulkhead of a ship, gentle as a boat moored in port, then with more strength as in the pitch of a tempest. Anne sought to consume him, to take him into her own body and soul, and to never again know a separate self.

After, he held her and she him, whispering secrets, touching, rum dizzy, filled with lust and curiosity, and then once more before dawn, he entered her again, exploring, before both drifted off into contented sleep.

Even before the sun rose on the next morn, word had gone round the island that Jack Rackham had tamed the 'hell cat'. So quick had the news spread that George Fetherston, master among Jack's crew, reminded those at table that if a body sneezed on one side of the island, someone on the other side said, "Bless you."

Thus it was to whistles and cheers that Anne and Jack entered the Rose and Garter the next afternoon and heard a song already making its way round the streets of their amorous affair. Richard Corner, quartermaster, stood to toast the couple, stating, "Well, Cap'n Jack, seems like it's every sail unfurled, straight up alongside, a broadside to slow 'er down, and the prize taken."

Anne laughed in her happiness, arm about Jack's shoulder, occasionally turning to kiss his lips or nuzzle his neck, and they ate, and joked, and sang, and finally danced.

No wedding party could have been more joyous . . . until James Bonny appeared.

Bonny's face was white with fury, his body taut, a sword at his side, his hand dangerously placed upon a pistol in his belt. The room quieted, for here was a new verse to the song in the making. Several of the regulars shook their heads, others placed bets, the money on Anne, for most knew she could best Bonny with either sword or words . . . and Jack was the best swordsman on the island.

But the pistol was another matter.

"So it's true then," Bonny said tightly.

Anne stood slowly and faced him. "Aye," she said simply. "Do ye want to talk alone. Or are ye plannin' on spillin' your guts before this crew?"

"A bit late for privacy, don't ye think, Anne?"

"James, I've told you for a year now. We are done." She would not say what she knew about his own exploits in Charles Town, and if sleeping with whores there, why, certainly in the brothels of every port along the seaboard. "I've no wish to shame you, but my feelings for Jack are not casual."

"You *dare* say that to me," his voice rose. "I am cuckolded before this entire assembly. The laughing stock of the island!"

"You need not be. Just let me go. Divorce me."

His eyes narrowed, red and dangerous. "No. Even though you are just what I thought you were the first time I laid eyes on you—a whore."

"Here," Jack stood. "None of that."

Bonny turned on him malevolently. "When I speak to my wife, you will not interfere."

"I have a proposition for you, Bonny," Jack said stepping away from the table, his body alert and ready to move quickly if need be. "There is a means by which I can buy Anne's marriage papers from you. An old law, to be sure, but on the books nevertheless. A Common Law Divorce. You will be the richer and wiser, and you will have your freedom. As will Anne."

"I know the law. If you buy her, she will be yours, and you shall never have her. Do you hear, Rackham. Never! I will never give Anne a divorce. Whatever you do, you will have to choke on the fact that she belongs to me!"

"You mistake, for Anne is mine and always shall be. She graces my table and my side. We care not for rules and paper in affairs of the heart."

All the while Jack spoke he circled closer to Bonny, squaring off against him, slowly, moving foot over foot, turning him away from Anne.

Anne saw and marveled that Jack stood behind her and beside her, and found her eyes fill with tears, for it had been a long time since anyone cared, really cared, about her. With reluctance and sorrow she thought again of her father and grieved for him.

In haste, Bonny chose his course and drew sword, leaving the pistol, for he would not add coward to cuckold, and Jack answered with the song of his own blade escaping the scabbard.

"James, for Gods' sake, let it be!" Anne cried. You cannot expect to come out of this fight unharmed!"

But he found it necessary for his honor to test the waters, and the sound of their swords in play rang through the tavern, benches pushed back, men to the side and away from the slashing. Anne longed to interfere, to draw and smite James over the head with her own weapon, but could not. As independent as she was, this fight she knew, was something between men.

"There's no need," Jack told him quietly. "I've no wish to kill you. Lay down."

Bonny looked about and knew the odds. "Perhaps I'll not win this one. But fight there will be. For if Captain Hornigold has taught me anything, it's that there is more than one way to fight."

With a furious rush he was out the door and gone. Anne came to stand next to Jack watching the door left open by Bonny in his flight.

"What do you suppose he meant by that?" she queried, turning over the possibilities.

"I told you, Anne. I can handle rough weather. Now come. It is as I say. You are mine."

And as he kissed her solidly, the music began again. Along with food and drink and laughter, the room was filled with speculation and new story, the details of which were already an embellishment of the facts.

Chapter Seventeen

The days of the next week passed in a happiness Anne dared not think possible. True, time with Jack was spent in the taverns along the waterfront, but more was spent alone, and Anne found that she poured out her heart to the man who walked by her side, the story of her mother, Beatrice and the break with her father, Henry Cavanaugh, the marriage with James. More than talk, she listened and took seriously his dream to have a ship again and the legal trade he could begin. A plan began to form, where they would buy land and start a plantation Anne would manage, grow the cotton that Jack would sail to England or north to the factories of New York.

They slept late until the room grew hot with the sun, then opened the windows for the breeze and made love in the bright light of morning, all the better to know each other. The beaches took their footprints, the sand hot between their toes, and surf bubbling white about their feet. Anne would insist that they swim when the sea was still, and they floated together in the salt water, holding hands, arms and legs outstretched. They hiked along trails left by wild pigs and found an isolated lake, the water warm, and went back three days running, bringing food and tobacco and Madeira wine. Jack would strip her of her clothes, to stare, to rub against her, and she would feel the sun and breeze on her skin like velvet, and know a sensuality that left her breathless and dazed. On the banks of the lake, they would lay wet and chilled, and cling to each other, and afterwards, they would fish, roasting the catch, and ramble through forest to collect wild guava and banana.

At the end of the first week of their meeting, she brought him to Hornigold's house, for the captain was at sea on his

Mexican venture. There she played the harpsichord for him, sitting at the bench and playing with such passion and love that for the first time she saw Jack cry. When she had finished and her hands lay softly upon the last chord, he had taken her into his arms and whispered that he must have her, and she had smiled, aroused by the music and his hands, and had turned her back to him. Lifting her skirt, she had invited him to his pleasure, laying over the cabinet and sighing that this was the first time she had used the harpsichord so.

By week's end she and Jack looked out to sea and knew how good it would be to take sail, for the world beckoned and they could go anywhere.

"There's a beauty of a ship I want, Anne, the *Curlew.* She's sleek, faster than many a ship on the sea."

"Is that fast to catch another ship, Jack, or fast to escape from one chasing?" she asked, cautious of his answer.

"Why, my dear, the faster to get cotton to market, surely."

"Aye, Jack. Right answer."

For Anne was serious about the future she wanted, and her vision proposed a plantation with room to grow, a solid house of two stories with columns and a porch, a kitchen, and quarters for families who would work the land, for she would have no slaves. On this she was adamant.

The land would be on a river that ran to the sea with enough deep water to moor Jack's boat. Together they would make a life and there would be children and horses and dogs and a great sow that would produce a litter to be made into hams for the winter larder, and when her eldest daughter was sixteen, she would give her a beautiful black mare named Rosie. So they talked and dreamed and held hands as they walked.

Another week passed, and for the first time, instead of heading to the taverns and parties with the crew, Anne wanted to stay at home after the sun had set. Jack, to her delight, agreed. They shared a quiet supper and a mug of grog, and while she mended a shirt and afterwards read from a book she had borrowed from Hornigold's library, Jack ran the figures of his accounts, adding up what he should offer for the *Curlew.* The ship had a few years on her, but he thought the price fair.

Finally, Anne stretched and called to him, "My dear, it is late. I am for bed."

"I'll be right along. Let me put these papers away."

Anne blew out the candle on the side table, took off her clothes, and stood at the darkened window, outlined by the candle light Jack still used. The water was calm and silvered with moonlight, gently lapping at shore, the air still, the heat already moving into high summer.

"Perhaps we will leave here before August," she said softly into the perfect stillness of the evening. "A dreadful month for the heat."

"Indeed. I pray we may take ship before that."

Without warning, into the quiet of the room, the door burst open, kicked in by burly men wearing masks, the sound earsplitting and unreal. Anne screamed and Jack jumped to his feet, the smell of fear and uncertainty crowding that space.

"No, no, Captain," Bonny said, holding a blade to Jack's throat, "don't reach for your sword."

Jack turned to see that Anne struggled between two stocky men who were desperately trying to tie her hands. They had come disguised knowing Jack would kill them afterwards. Suddenly, terrified for her, he stepped forward, only to feel a trickle of blood flow. Held, unable to move, he sensed his sword just out of reach.

"What the hell do you want, Bonny?" Jack yelled above the tumult, his rage the more so for being caught unawares.

"Why, my wife, of course."

"For the love of God, grasp it, man. She's not a slave. If you take her, she will only return."

"You son of a whore!" Anne screamed, never so hate-filled or furious in her life. "You're dead, do you hear, James? I will kill you myself!"

"Gag her," he told one of the men, and a scarf was tied around her mouth. But it was not enough to still Anne's screams, so James took the pistol from his sash and aimed it at Jack's head. "Quiet, Anne. Or the next sound you hear will not be to your liking."

Anger gave way to fear. What would he do?

"Now, Rackham, my wife goes with me."

"Where do you take her?"

"To the governor."

"The governor?" Jack's eyes narrowed. "What has Rogers to do with this?"

"Everything. I have charged my wife. You see, adultery is a crime."

Jack looked at him with incredulity. "You would have her gaoled for her affair with me?" The thought was preposterous.

"Sentence will be pronounced by His Excellency. Now, you will excuse us." And he nodded to his men.

"Wait!" Jack cried and looked about him. Anne stood naked, ready for bed, only her breasts covered by her hair. "Let her dress," he said quietly.

"I don't think so. The governor will have her just as she is . . . without harpsichord or silk . . . so that he can see the truth of the matter."

"Let her dress . . . and I will let you live."

But James laughed unnaturally, an otherworldliness filling the room, so that even the henchmen cast a glance at each other. "Go ahead and try to kill me," he cried recklessly.

"For God's sake, man, at least wrap her to take her through the street!"

James thought about this. "True. I would not want the world to see my wife unclothed. That spread," he pointed with the pistol, "roll it round her."

Jack leaned to scoop it from the bed and placed it under her arms tying a knot to hold it in place. "I'll come for you. Ye know I will," he whispered.

"None of that."

With a tremendous blow the pistol came down on Jack's skull and he crumpled to the floor.

Anne screamed and struggled to reach him, but James only said, "Bring her along."

Then he was out the door, alerting the carriage driver that their passenger was ready.

Governor Rogers was more than a little annoyed at being bothered so late in the evening. Putting on his longcoat and wig, he lifted the small bit of fluff he called a dog into his arms and walked out into the antechamber.

"What's all this about, Bonny?" he demanded.

"I've brought my wife, sir," Bonny told him. "I accuse her of adultery. Living openly with Jack Rackham."

"Oh, that. So I've heard. Damned bad business, Bonny. I don't want to interfere between a man and wife. Why can't you control her better?"

"Have you seen my wife, sir?"

"Indeed I have. She has come to play the harpsichord with your Captain Hornigold. It is only my relationship with him that allows this presumption of yours at this late hour."

Bonny could not say that he'd had to wait until he was sure Jack and Anne would be unarmed before entering Rackham's room. What better time than after they'd bedded? "But have you seen her on ship, sir, or with sword in hand?"

"You don't mean to say that your wife is good at sword-play?"

"Not just good, sir. She's not called the 'hell cat' without reason."

"We are talking about the same woman who came to my table?"

"I have her outside. Wrapped in a bedspread. As naked as the day of her birth. The way I found her with Rackham."

"Good Lord, man. Bring her in."

Bonny nodded, went to the door, and opened it. The two men dragged her forward, Anne fighting each step, her hair disheveled, her eyes bright with hate and malevolence, the spread wrapped loosely around her torso, held by her bound hands. She was beyond caring about her nudity. All she cared was that she resist the ordeal with every breath she take and wanted nothing so much in life at the moment as to get to James and rend him apart.

"Mistress Bonny," Governor Rogers said when she stood defiantly before him, "I can understand your perturbation, but you must calm yourself and show some decency of deportment. You, fellow, remove the gag so that I might hear what she has to say."

"Decency?" Anne spat, working her mouth, sore and twisted from the gag. "You dare talk to me about decency? I am taken in the dead of night and dragged through the streets without clothes! The marriage is over! I told him more than a year ago that I was finished with him!" Her voice rose higher. "Fuck you, James! I will eat your liver before I am through with you!"

"Is this the woman who sat at your table, Governor?"

Governor Rogers shook his head with distaste. "My wife's maid," he said to a soldier at the door, "ask her to bring a set of clothes. I cannot continue this discussion unless she is decently dressed. Put her in that room," he pointed, "until the clothes arrive."

"Before I go," Anne said, nodding to the men on either side still wearing masks, "I want to see their faces so that I might press kidnapping charges against them."

"Is it illegal to take one's own wife, Excellency?"

"Bonny, this is a bad business. Mistress Anne, when you are dressed these soldiers will take you to the gaol until I can sort through this in the morning. You men," he gestured to the ruffians holding her, "be available to answer to me then."

"Gaol? I've done nothing to warrant gaol! This is an injustice, sir!" she said with the haughtiest voice she could muster, for now she saw that she had fallen into the trap James had laid, had acted the part he'd wanted the governor to see. Oh, why hadn't she thought! If she had just been the wronged lady instead of the tavern whore, she would be dancing out the front door even now!

Chapter Eighteen

The night in prison served to convince Anne of the seriousness of her predicament. Even though the walls were damp and slimy with salt, the straw bed filled with vermin, the food nothing she could recognize, the toilet a bucket whose reek made her gag, what troubled most was her isolation, the unknowing. Suddenly, she wanted her father, the barrister.

In the darkness, she remembered the stories he'd told her in a candid moment about the men in Ireland he'd once represented. Criminals, aye, but alone, without funds, and not knowing whether they would live or die. She had a sense of what her father's presence must have meant to them, and with it, a new respect for him.

If he had stood with her before the governor, he would have known the law, and she most likely would not be in gaol. Perhaps he would even understand about Jack. Had he not left all that was dear to him to go to Charles Town with her mother? As certainly as she believed the sun would rise and the wind blow, she knew she would give everything she cherished to begin a life with Jack Rackham.

So she stood in the center of the room, alone, and waited, refusing to sit, for this was not where she belonged and would take no comfort from it, not even a bit of straw for a seat.

"Mistress Bonny," a voice at the door called, "the governor awaits you."

Morning had come and the chamber held some light, although she could not guess the time. Doing what she could to straighten her appearance, she followed the guard.

Already waiting before the governor's chair were James Bonny and Jack Rackham, Jack's face enormously relieved to see her. "Anne, are you all right?"

"Leave off my wife!"

Ignoring James, Anne nodded to Jack. "And you? Your head . . ."

"A lump and sore, but still in one piece. I've had worse."

Then she turned to Governor Rogers, and with a graceful curtsy, said in a clear voice, "Good morning, sir. I am sorry to bring this trouble upon you."

"Your Excellency," Jack bowed politely, sweeping his hat from his head.

"Captain Rackham, I thought our business finished with the pardon for piracy. What is this about? Mr. Bonny has accused you and his wife of living in open adultery."

"Your Excellency, I have offered to buy the marriage contract from Mr. Bonny, but he will have none of it."

"As I said to you last evening, Your Excellency, my marriage has been finished for over a year. I took myself for divorced, sir. And I would have Captain Rackham as my husband."

"And I would have Anne for my wife. I have a plan to buy the *Curlew* and settle as a merchant shipper. My wife . . . that is, Anne . . . and I want to start a cotton plantation. I believe we deserve a chance to make a life, your Excellency."

"And what say you Bonny?" the governor asked.

"That we were married before God with a priest and that we are in danger of our immortal souls if we do not heed our marriage vows. I claim the law, Governor Rogers. My wife must submit."

"Will you not take the marriage price Captain Rackham offers?"

"You could be master of your own vessel, Bonny," Jack told him. "A fine offer and not one I'll make again. I would swear to forego all vengeance against you for the kidnapping and the pistol to my head."

"Mr. Bonny?"

Yet the governor watched the slow shake of Bonny's head.

"Then so be it," he pronounced, "although I believe you a fool to try to take back a woman who does not want you. I have no choice in this distasteful matter. Mistress Bonny, you are to return home with your husband. If you are found with Jack Rackham again, you will be publicly flogged . . . by Captain Rackham himself . . . a dozen lashes. Am I understood?"

Anne gasped, "But, sir, I have not lived with James in over a year! I have my own home. Will you send me to this sniveling toad?"

"Indeed I will. If you appear before me again, you will feel the lash. Now I have pressing matters," and he turned his back on the group.

Outside the governor's house Anne and Jack looked at each other, a conversation in their glance. Jack removed his hat with a flourish, bowed, and parted.

Distracted, thinking to the future, Anne turned to make for her room, but found that James followed. She stopped, turned to him, and said quietly, "If you enter my home, I will slit your throat. You had best be getting to your own den and think upon those words."

"Will ye not 'ave me, Anne? Think on the last years!"

"I am. Heed my words."

That night Jack slipped in through the window and they fell into each other's arms with kisses and caresses as if there would be no tomorrow, for surely they did not know if they had one together.

"As soon as Captain Hornigold returns he will champion you, Anne. He has the governor's ear and his favor. In the meanwhile, I will back to Bonny and try to make him see reason. I offer a lot of money."

"I will not be bought and sold like an animal at auction!" Anne cried angrily. "I am my own person and God knows, I have earned my right to choose."

"I know that, but the law does not recognize your struggle. Or appreciate your abilities like I do." His arms were close about her, and she felt the tremor of his subdued laughter.

"It is not a joking matter," she pushed him away petulantly.

"Come, Anne, I will shield the candle, and we will sleep. In the morning I will be off before the light of day."

Yet in the morning, the sun was well up before they woke, and Jack was seen slipping away by spies Bonny had set upon her.

Anne was immediately arrested and sent back to gaol.

For two months Anne was held, Jack fighting the order for the flogging, begging the governor to wait while he made arrangements with Bonny. And during that time Anne changed, for she could no longer ignore her surroundings. Each day she rose fearful that this would be the day she was publicly flogged and wondered if Jack would wield the lash if ordered. The worry was not about the pain of it, or the humiliation, but rather that she would scar and Jack would see her as less beautiful. As day after day slipped by and no resolution came, her world became small and her thoughts turned to the other prisoners who shared the loneliness and isolation of the prison.

In her despair she began to ask fundamental questions about the very nature of prison itself. Surely prisons had been in existence for as long as anyone remembered . . . but why? The place that held her was one of such sorrow and pain and evil, that it became hard for her to grasp how such a thing could exist.

Praying, she thought to take some comfort in the fact that Jesus had been a prisoner as well, the victim of some other plot, but all she could come round to was the same thought—the men who had tortured Him were still alive and well this day. In wild dreams she was released and would wake startled, for surely an angel had appeared and led her away, just as St. Peter had been released from his shackles and freed by another angel long ago.

The prison guards who brought food, who taunted and leered, who grabbed at their crotches and laughed, those men pretended to a superiority, not because it was earned, but simply because they held power over the bodies of the incarcerated. Anne watched the beatings and withstood the barbed comments, knew starvation and sickness, closed her eyes when the girls in the dungeon traded their pleasures to the gaolers for food, and asked . . . who were the real criminals?

Around her were women who had been jailed as pick-pockets, or for thievery, debt, public drunkenness, whoring, and in one case, murder. Because there was nothing but time, she heard their stories, and saw that they were poor, from a foreign land, or spoke another language, often a patois, a mixture of English and French and African. The women were no strangers to hunger or homelessness. Some knew the darkness of despair and looked to find solace in drink. In the one case of murder, the girl had been beaten until she rose up swinging the very bottle that had been thrown at her. True crime, Anne was growing to understand, was hunger and poverty and social systems that created a class destined for the gaols, a system that fed upon itself by giving birth to its own prison economy, nurturing a livelihood for those who appreciated dominance.

Anne listened and looked upon them . . . upon herself . . . and knew injustice. As she walked her daily circle round the small room, she wondered that no one understood what was obvious, and why in all of human history, no one had found an alternative to incarceration. Indeed, why no one had thought to find solutions to the very causes that created criminals. In pronouncing sentence Governor Rogers had said it his obligation to make an example of her, so that others might be deterred. If punishment was supposed to deter crime, why then, were the prisons full? And the answer came. Because it was easier to lock away trouble, out of sight and mind, than to have to find a real solution for it.

At the end of two months of fear, of a stomach constantly

heaving and bowels rumbling and watery from rancid food, of cold and sleepless nights curled up with the other women, of having to shit in a room of onlookers, of seeing the world through a tiny window high in the ceiling, nary a book to pass the time, and alone with the bitterness of her thoughts, Anne hardened. Never again would she be the lass of Cardiff Hall, because for the first time she truly knew with her heart what she had only known with her mind before. Poverty and injustice walked hand and hand. Forevermore, she had joined the ranks of the demeaned. As she looked to the high window, she resolved that once out of this place, she would fight to the death rather than submit to the system again.

He has finally agreed to an auction, Jack wrote in a letter delivered to the prison, *but he will not sell me the marriage certificate outright. I must bid for you. What I can tell you is that he has seen some reason, and I believe he knows his life would be worthless if he forced you to fulfill your conjugal obligations. Instead, he will give you your freedom, both from marriage and gaol, if the price is right. Courage, Anne, your ordeal is almost over.*

On the day of the auction Anne was brought to court. There a number of men awaited the bidding, for Anne was known as a beauty and an accomplished woman. Three of the men were older and needed a wife to help in the raising of children, one was interested in her musical ability. Of all the men attending, only Jack was there for love. Yet when Anne walked into the room, the toll of the last months was obvious, her hair dull and unkempt, her face thin, her clothes unwashed, her nails black with dirt.

Clearly, even the governor was shocked, for he sat her in a chair and asked kindly, "Mistress Bonny, before we begin the bidding, have you anything to say?"

Anne stood. "Yes, Your Excellency," and she smiled so sweetly that several seconds passed before her words registered with the group.

"I will slit the throat of any man who dares to put a price upon me. I will not be bought and sold like an animal."

The look she gave each of them had the blade poised. Not a man doubted her, and they began to think back on other rumors they had heard and now believed true, for wild she did look.

Abashed, the governor cried, "If that be the case, Mistress Bonny, you would hang for murther!"

"And it would be my pleasure to do so," she said with equal sweetness.

With some disgust, Governor Rogers asked, "Are there bids for the lady?"

Not a man among them gave a sum. Nor did Jack.

"Then it seems, Mistress Bonny, that you are free," the Governor told her.

"What?" James cried. "But my money?"

"There have been no bids, there can be no profit, Mr. Bonny. You have lost your wife to herself."

Furious, for now he felt himself tricked, James demanded, "Then I claim the flogging . . . and a branding with an 'A' for adulteress. It is my due under the law!"

"Your Excellency, perhaps we should wait until the arrival of Benjamin Hornigold before proceeding further," Jack interjected. "Let us see what the captain has to say, for he knows both Anne and Bonny well enough."

"I agree, Captain Rackham, it would be a blessed event if Captain Hornigold were here, for I have always found him steadfast of mind and more than intelligent. But I am afraid we would have to wait a long time. You see, word reached me this morning that Captain Hornigold's ship hit a reef far from shore in Mexican waters and all hands are drowned, sadly, including the captain."

"Oh, dear God," Anne moaned, "not Benjamin!" And felt another part of her old world die with the news.

Jack stepped forward to steady her for she looked none too strong, but her eyes held steady on the governor's face.

"He was a dear friend," she said softly.

"How dear?" Bonny asked.

Only witnesses prevented Jack from murdering Bonny in that room, but Jack waited, for he was learning to be a patient man.

Governor Rogers turned from Bonny as if he could not bear his sight, and said, "You may have your lashing, Mr. Bonny. The dozen promised. And Captain Rackham will wield the lash as ordered. But I will not order the branding. In the interest of justice."

Without warning Anne's legs folded under her, and Jack grabbed her before she fell to the floor.

"A glass of water for the lady," he called, and in the noise of the room as a glass and pitcher were found, he whispered pointedly, "You are not the fainting kind."

Anne smiled and whispered in return, "No, you're right. I am with child, Jack. Your child. I'm a little unbalanced these days."

Awestruck, completely without words, Jack wanted to leap for joy and at the same time howl in frustration. "How long have ye known?'

"Not long."

"You cannot go back to that place."

"If I take the lashing, will I be free?"

He nodded, his face grim, "But there will be no lashing. And I certainly will not wield the whip."

He turned to the governor. "Your Excellency, may I take the young lady home on the understanding that she will return in three days."

"If you post bond, Captain."

And Jack threw to the clerk the money he would have paid for Anne . . . or the *Curlew.*

On the morning of the third day, Governor Rogers arose to find his peace already shattered. During the night the *Curlew* had been boarded by a pirate crew and had slipped from port. Without asking, he already knew who had taken her, and knew also that Anne Bonny would not appear as ordered. Jack Rackham had forfeited his bond by taking the girl out of harm's way. A part of Rogers admired the man.

Yet the truth was that Rackham had broken the amnesty he had been granted, and was once again outlawed, and Captain Rackham, no fool, knew that as well. In which case, he would set to taking ships again. All damnably inopportune.

"Bring that scoundrel Bonny to me," he ordered.

But when a guard went to fetch him to the governor's home, the news was that Bonny had fled the island in terror after Anne was released from prison, shipped two days before on the first vessel he could find leaving port.

Chapter Nineteen

On a bay on the north side of Cuba, Jack kept a home in the Spanish style, *La Rosa,* and here Anne found delight. The house boasted an arched front door of dark wood, studded with iron flowers, pale-pink stucco walls, and a heavy, red-tiled roof. Tall windows of glass opened to sea breeze and light, hurricane shutters secured against the walls. From their bedroom on the second floor, Jack could watch the *Curlew* moored in the bay.

La Rosa lay situated at the edge of a small town where the crew made merry, many keeping their own families safe from the travails of pirating. Music drifted from its taverns and public square, and Anne listened as it flowed into the garden where she sat growing large with child. Never before had she known such contentment. She spent her days sleeping late on a feather bed, putting back the weight she had lost in prison, cutting roses in the garden, and playing the harpsichord that Jack brought into the house, an instrument once bound for Boston and taken from its ship. The music seemed to soothe the child, for it slept while she played, then kicked lustily if she walked. Anne reasoned that if the baby heard music, it could hear other things as well, and began to sing and talk and tell tales of Ireland and the New World and the lands of the Indies and made promises of happiness. Now when she and Jack made love, she could feel her entire uterus spasm with pleasure, setting the babe to dancing in her womb. Into this perfect world Jack strode one morning with purposeful step, and as she watched, thought him more beautiful than remembered, for her love grew with each passing day.

"Anne, there is something we must discuss," he said, sitting beside her and taking her hand to kiss. "Well, I'll just be plain about it. Master Fetherston has come to say the men have inquired of him when we'll be puttin' out to sea."

Anne laughed. "Don't be silly. How can they possibly think of shipping? Whatever they need is right here, their women, children, their homes."

"Money grows short. What you see is bought."

She paused, some premonition afoul in her breast. "Would they be puttin' out for piracy, Jack? Can we not stay here and live our lives? We're safe here."

He tightened his grip on her hand and looked into her eyes, for surely she must understand. "You know we can't. Not since I took the *Curlew.* I've sealed my fate."

Anne looked out to sea and knew there was no hope for it, but still she tried, "I'm sorry for it, Jack. But can the men not find their own way on board another ship?"

Slowly he shook his head. "I've an obligation. They are my responsibility. They named me captain."

"Then give them the ship and have them name someone else!" Anne cried. "I am too large to go to sea and cannot hide under a man's apparel! And I need you, Jack. In a few weeks the child will be born and I want you here!"

"Anne, Anne," he took her in his arms. "I love you more than life, but the birthing room is no place for a man. I am born to the sea and I must have it. Let me go willingly that I might fill our coffers once more."

"No," she said coldly, her body stiffening. "Let them go alone."

"I have lost my amnesty, and I did it willingly for you."

"Will you take these risks and lay them at my feet?" she cried. "No, Jack, I am not the problem. It's you. You cannot stay in one place very long, can you? You must always be moving and scheming and . . . and you like the battle. Something Benjamin said to me once . . . about Stede never being able to quit piracy, for he liked the thrill of the chase and the moment of boarding, where everything, even his life, was a gamble. It's the excitement you're after, isn't it?"

"I am here, outlawed, because I chose to carry you out of harm's way," he said stiffly, standing and turning away from her.

"This has nothing to do with me. This is about you and what you crave, like drink to a man who must have it or his limbs shake."

"Drink right now sounds like a good idea."

"It's morning."

"I would go to sea with your blessing, but if you will not give it, then I will go without it."

"What if I said we would be finished if you left?"

"Then you will have to make that choice."

And he walked away from her toward the town and the sound of music.

Two days later the *Curlew* was ready to sail on the tide and Anne watched as Jack packed the last of his things.

"Please believe me, I do have an obligation," he begged. "I will be back before the babe is ready to come. Some months remain before your time. What say you? Will you part with me as friends?"

"Aye, Jack, I'll part as friends. But I had hoped to live together as husband and wife."

"Then kiss me, for I go into battle, and it is your face that will bring me home again," and he reached for her.

Anne stood tall and proud, clutching a thin scarf around her shoulders in the predawn chill. She held up a hand to stop him. "We'll talk about it when you return. If you return. Why should I open my heart to the sorrow that would pierce it if you came nary again?" She poked a finger into his chest. "You're a pirate. How do I know you will ever come back at all?"

Jack knelt on one knee. "I swear to you, Anne, you hold my life in your hands. I am yours. Give me honest leave to go and I will return richer and wiser."

Her face softened and she leaned toward him, "You don't have to do this. You will bring the king's navy down upon your head. Stay with me, Jack. We can do something different. I swear to you, I will do anything you ask as long as you keep us a family and safe."

"Cap'n," Fetherston called up the stairs, "tide'll turn soon, and if we're not about our business, we'll miss 'er."

"Will you kiss me good-by?"

"Once you're with the crew, you'll drink and carouse and act the man. I know you. But no matter," she said off-handedly, "either you'll be back or not. If you die in battle, well, we'll just make our own way. Meself and the babe. And if you find someone else . . . then stay with her. Better to know the truth of your character now."

Jack backed away from her, disappointment heavy on his face. "You're a hard woman, Anne Bonny, with a tongue sharp as my sword. But I will forget these words, for I understand that you are put ashore and I am to sea. A hard thing it is to watch a loved one sail away. But men have put to sea for as long as there have been ships, and they'll not be stoppin' now. I will be back. Whatever you think, I love you."

He turned and made his way down the stairs and across the sand to the longboat. There, he took a place forward, watching where she had followed him to the shore, alone and solitary, pride, anger, and sadness drawn upon her face.

As the *Curlew* sailed out of sight, try as she would, she could not explain the guilt and hopelessness that overwhelmed her.

As whenever she was troubled, she returned to the harpsichord frequently, reminding herself how glad she was that she had stayed and what a fool he was not to be with her to savor the music. Yet with each passing day, she missed him more, and slowly, the anger was replaced by pain and an ache of longing for his return, for the touch of him, the smell of him, a glimpse of the light in his eyes. Her one consolation was the child within her womb, and the midwife told her it was a good sign that the babe was quiet, for he was gathering strength for the work of entering the world.

On a bright spring day with a sky so clear and bright that it hurt the eyes, Anne's labor began. At first she was not sure what the sensations were, but then her water broke gushing between her legs, and there could be no doubt her time was nigh. The real pains began sometime after sunset, and the midwife had her walk in spite of the need to stop and breathe through each of the contractions. A moment came when she believed she needed to lie down, for each of the pains came closer together. Now she began to moan through them and to think of Jack. With a desperation she had never known, she wanted him, for some deep animal part of her believed that if he were there, the pain would be less. As the moon traveled overhead and toward morning, longing turned to terror, the great rending inside her coming with keen regularity and with such strength, that she did not know she screamed. A part of her hated, for if Jack had been with her, she might have the will to live. Another part of her cried with sorrow for the babe, entering the world in suffering. Near dawn, when she was too exhausted to care for any thought, the midwife called in her ear that she should bear down, and this she did with great exertion, grinding her teeth, releasing guttural raspings, until the child slipped from her body.

The sun had just broken into a golden arc on the horizon, when she took into her hands the tiny son she had struggled to deliver . . . and her heart was lost. If she thought she had loved before, it was nothing compared to what she felt for the swaddled infant who looked curiously into her face. While the midwife laughed and disposed of the afterbirth, Anne placed the baby to her breast and winced as he settled.

"Ooch, a strong lad he is," she murmured. "What a tongue. Something of his father in him already."

"A fine boy, mistress! Wait until Master Jack sees 'im. Proud as a peacock 'e'll be! I'll get the kitchen girl to bring you some bread and broth with chicken and small beer. You've got to eat to feed that babe and beer is the best thing in the world for mother's milk. You goin' to feed 'im yourself?"

"Oh, aye, Mistress Devon, for I have never had anything before that was mine, so truly mine, and I will see to him," then added in a whisper, "always."

She began to hum, and the babe held tight to her nipple and gazed in her eyes and sucked slowly.

"When do you suppose Master Jack will be back?"

"Why, before the child is born, to be sure. You know, since the birth is so many months away," and to her great surprise, from nowhere, tears began to stream down her face.

Mistress Devon chuckled and took the liberty of sitting next to Anne on the bed, passing her a handkerchief, "There, there, dearie, we's all sensitive at a time like this. And the truth of it is that men are terrified of the birthing room. I've known Master Jack for many a year. He was but a lad when he first came to this island. A boy on ship. But I can tell you for fact, Mistress, that he dearly loves you. And wait until he sees the boy. The funny thing about men is that once the babe is in the world, they puff up likes it was them that did the growin' and the birthin', with nary a thought as to the hard work, only a mind to the joy of how it all started in the first place. Come now, dry your eyes. The master will be here soon enough and tellin' you how sorry he is and makin' his excuses."

"I'll spit him," Anne wailed.

"Will ye now?" Mistress Devon grinned.

And Anne laughed and cried at the same time. "Yes, just after I kiss him so that he smothers from the length of it."

"So's I thought."

"I shall call the wee one John William. John, after his father . . . and William, after mine," Anne said softly.

"A fine name. All right, I'll be back shortly. We'll get you some clothes and we'll have a wash and I'll bring some rags to go between your legs, for you'll bleed for some weeks. You must drink the tea I give you to help with the bleedin' and to pull that stomach of yours back into shape." Mistress Devon laid a hand on the small head of the babe. "Then you will rest and I will take care of young Master John."

Word went round the village that the *Curlew* was sighted and making its way along the coast and into port. Anne went to her upstairs bedroom and stepped onto the balcony. As she watched the sails come into view, her heart leapt in her breast at the beauty of the ship. Every sail was full and white against deep blue sea, making great headway, as if the very timbers of the boat rushed to harbor and what waited on shore.

"Oh, Jack," Anne sighed, "you're home. God damn you, but you are home."

Not until she saw the ship drop anchor, the longboat lowered, and Jack with the distinctive red plume of his hat step aboard, did she feel the tears well in her eyes.

I must stop this, she told herself, *this weeping at nothing.*

Admonition was no use, and a dam of thoughts broke, tumbling one upon the other. All the animosity she had held crumbled, and what remained was only the wanting to touch him, to look into his eyes, to watch his face as he saw John for the first time. The boat hit sand and Jack jumped ashore and made straight for the house. Then she was running, down the stairs and out to meet him, throwing herself into his arms, her face wet with tears that would not stop.

"Here, here," Jack cried. "I'm home and I've come to see the babe. I won't be leavin' you again, Anne, for I've not the stomach or the heart for it. The ache is too harsh for my taste. Come, don't cry. Show me the babe."

"Kiss me first or I shall die if I do not feel your breath on my body."

Jack swept her into his arms and placed his lips upon hers. "That's just for starters, there's more to come."

For as long as she lived, Anne would not forget the look on Jack's face as he saw his child for the first time, a mixture of tenderness and pride that she thought would break her heart. For here was a child that was all his hope in the world and a place to put the love of his heart, and he whispered his own marvel that such a being could have come from joy with his wife.

From his cabin on board ship, he brought a jeweled chest with iron bands and placed it before Anne and told her to take her pick of what was there. Of all she could have chosen, she selected a small gold cross set with the emeralds of Brazil to wear about her neck.

The schedule of the entire household revolved around that of young John. Together the family spent their days in the garden, air smelling of roses, blowing across the skin like the feel of silk, and when Anne played the harpsichord, the babe watched with open eyes, as still as he'd been in the womb.

Master Fetherston called frequently, as well as the quartermaster, Richard Corner. Other members of the crew made their way to the house to see the newborn and to sit and drink the wine that Jack had rolled off ship and set in the cellar. Great was the song and music, for a fiddle and drum was often added to the harpsichord, and with the grog passed round, the dance became a mixture of African rhythm and Highland reels and Irish stomping. Anne sat at table and took from the bounty laid before her, never once daring to ask from whence it came. The thought that Jack had put his life in danger for the coin that bought these things, facing sword and pistol and noose, was terrifying.

Yet as she woke each day to him beside her, to his lips across her body and the warmth of the length of him, hard and solid and real, she asked if this would be the day when he tired of the house and family and the monotony of happiness, if this would be the day when he told her he must set out again to sea.

As the months marched into July and the sun rose already too warm, another ship made its way into port to great exclamation and excitement, the men arming until they know the score. Jack watched from the upper balcony with his glass, noting the details of the boat, and then smiled.

"Why, it's Captain Bellows. Bless my soul if he doesn't have the *Kingston,* the old pirate. That must be a tale worth telling. And just in time for dinner. Master Fetherston, meet the good captain on shore and ask that he join us."

"What is it, Jack?" Anne asked. "You look thoughtful."

"It's the *Kingston.* My old ship. I took her from her owner at sea and the man had the audacity to steal her back while I was docked in Jamaica. That's how I came to be in New Providence seeking a new ship. Now it seems that her owner has lost her again. I can't help but wonder why Bellows would bring her here. Something is amiss."

The table was laid with good fare, but the mood was subdued. Anne had a premonition that with the coming of the *Kingston* things would change and she felt a shiver run the length of her spine, the hair on her arms stand and prickle. For the first time since the birth of John she went armed, a dagger strapped to her leg under the skirt, a pistol neatly tucked into her belt. When she came to table she noticed that Jack wore his sword, as did Master Fetherston and four of the other attending crewmembers. Wee John was introduced to Captain Bellows, then Anne sent him away with the maid, for she feared.

"Tell us why ye've come, Andrew," Jack asked over fish soup. "I've a feeling you've brought news and that it is not good."

"I'm afraid you're right, Jack, and I am sorry to be the one to bring it. Four months ago, Charles Vane was captured and brought to Port Royal. Now 'e rots in jail and they plan to 'ang 'im 'at Gallows Point. A warnin' to pirates as to what fate awaits them."

"I am but amazed that Vane let himself be captured!"

"As am I. But fate is fickle, and in the end, it was not very generous with your Cap'n Vane. A sad tale, to be sure. It seems after 'e lost the vote and confidence of the crew and you took command of his ship . . . beg pardon, Cap'n Rackham, but we all know the story . . . Charles sailed away in a small sloop. Well, it's just like Vane to trade up quickly, for 'e was always one to be about his business. T'was the *Pearl* 'e acquired and with her, another nice little sloop. After 'e refitted and cleaned their bottoms, 'e set out once again, but a storm separated the ships. Damn hurricane. Disabled 'is rudder and threw 'im up on the reef of a small island . . . somewhere near the Bay of Honduras, I believe . . . then the sea tore apart what was left of the boat and drowned every last man but Vane who by God's grace made it ashore. Damn but that man did 'ave the devil's own luck at times! Here, pass that bottle again will you Jack . . . there's a good man . . ."

"Marooned himself, did he?" Jack asked.

"Aye. Except that 'e had turtle and fish given 'im by some poor fishermen who lived on the island."

"Fishermen? Why didn't 'e just take the fisherboat?" Fetherston ventured.

"That's just what Cap'n Holford asks of 'im."

"Holford?" Jack asked, surprised. "That ne'er-do-well pirate from Kingston?"

"That's 'im. But 'e's taken a pardon and no longer considers 'imself pirate." Bellows took a long drink. "You've a tasty pantry, Jack," he wiped his mouth across the back of his hand. "At any rate, Holford comes upon Vane on that small island and Vane begs for a place on board. But Holford only says if 'e takes Vane on, 'e won't make it back to Jamaica with 'is own ship. Vane would find a way to turn 'is crew against him! That's when 'e told Vane to steal one of the fisherboats. Funny part is, Vane refuses. Says 'e couldn't take from the men who'd saved 'is life. Holford went away laughing, saying, to the devil with 'im, if 'e'd gone and got a conscience at this stage of 'is life."

"So how did he escape the island," Anne asked, "only to be threatened with the hangman's rope?"

"Again 'e 'ad a bit o' luck. As it 'appens another ship comes by not long after and takes 'im on board as a common seaman. Works 'ard, for Charles Vane 's a good sailor, 'e is. Why I knew 'im when 'e was but a youngster and learnin' 'is trade. I can tell you 'e took to the sea and knew 'ow to bear down on the crew and the ships 'e took after."

"Hear, hear," Jack cried. "A toast. To Captain Vane!"

"A toast!" and the men at table stood and lifted their cups to drink.

"But," Captain Bellows sighed, seating himself again, "'ere's where 'is luck run out. The ship 'e sailed on met up with Cap'n Holford at sea, and Holford . . . the devil take 'im . . . knowin' the captain of said vessel an' comin' aboard to dine, saw Vane at his work. Says t' the captain 'is friend, 'Don't ye know who ye've got on board? A brave man ye are.' An' the cap'n, fearin' for 'imself and the ship, 'ad 'is mate take Vane by pistol. Clapped 'im in irons right off. No matter that 'e was the best seaman in the crew. Put 'im aboard Holford's ship, they did, and Holford . . . God rot 'is soul . . . sailed direct to Kingston. Once there, it was a wonder to see how quick 'e was brought ashore and t' the prison. And there's the whole and the truth of it."

"I am sorry to hear it, but there's more, isn't there. The reason you're here."

"Aye, there's more, Jacky boy. I've come t' warn you that Jamaica's gov'nor, Nicholas Lawes, is much like Gov'nor Rogers in that 'e's a mission to complete. T' rid the waters of piracy. But unlike Rogers, 'e's a bee in his bonnet and it's all rather personal with 'im. An old sea cap'n friend of 'is was tortured to reveal the whereabouts of 'is treasure after being boarded. The man died, 'is crew conscripted. Forced t' join up or take a swim. A long one, for the ship was set afire to sink to the bottom and there she resides in Davy Jones's locker."

"Well, good luck to the man. Governor Lawes, is it? Surely he has his work cut out for him."

"The gov'nor's a true hazard, Jack, for 'e's fervent in 'is avowed task and 'e means business. Nae like Rogers, a man you can get around. Rogers understands, 'im bein' a pirate 'imself once."

"Privateer," Anne told him, "different. Thinks his piracy was patriotic."

"Humph," Captain Bellows snorted. "I will not tell you at table what I think o' that. But Lawes is different. Mark my word. The good governor 'as formed a navy and a system of lookouts along the island coastline with a relay system to bring 'im news of passing ships. When 'e gets word, 'e sends out one or more of 'is ships to track down the pirates. Cap'n Vane is not the only one who's to be 'anged at Gallows Point. The 'angman's been kept busy and it's the wealthy man 'e's becomin'. A black day for the Brethren, I tell you."

"Have ye come to warn me, Andrew?"

"Aye, Jack, and any others that I can."

"It's good of you."

For a long moment the room was silent, each man pondering his own thoughts.

"May I offer you my hospitality for the evening?"

"'Tis tempting, for your wine is strong. But no, I think I will sleep best in me own bed. My crew feasts in the town and I will 'ave order as they board later this evening."

"When you are ready, Master Fetherston will see you to your boat."

After they had gone, Jack went upstairs and Anne followed. He stood by the window, spyglass in hand, and watched until he saw that Captain Bellows had made it safely aboard ship.

"Is something wrong?" she asked.

"I'm not sure. Only that Captain Bellows didn't steal the *Kingston,* and that he is about the governor of Jamaica's business. Although why he would want to warn us, I do not yet know. Perhaps he picks and chooses who he will betray, as Hornigold once did. And as to that, who can say what motivates a man to choose? Or perhaps he spies for the governor, to see what we are about. There is always the possibility the governor feels he can frighten men out of piracy by spreading rumor of his intentions."

"Aye, and a good idea to frighten them out of it rather than have it hanged out of them. You're not thinking of going to sea again, are ye, Jack? For then you and I will have a problem."

"Anne I'm twenty-nine years old. What else do I know? I have been trained at my job since I was a lad and am captain of a ship. Other men . . . those who do not take to leadership or responsibility . . . they look to me to give them a livelihood. What else can I do?"

"What livelihood is in the rope? Can you think of no other way to support those in your care except lead them into danger?"

Jack turned and leaned against the balcony rail, his face shadowed by dim candlelight. "You knew what I was when you came away with me."

And Anne sat, for here it was, the difference between them, no longer on the fringes obscurely intruding, but come to rest on the porch. "Jack, I understand now that it was a girl's romantic notion. I believed pirate captains to be handsome and strong and brave, and you . . . the first time I saw you . . . I could see sunlight filled your eyes and I loved you from that moment. You are still all these things and more. But the truth is that I have John and I want to see him grow up. I want him to read and play music, and yes, know life on ship. But I want him to live. I want home and family and a husband and father who believes we are his life and does not grow bored with us."

"Oh, Anne, I would never grow bored with you. How could I? You are like the sea, changing minute by minute, and I am eternally entranced, wondering what you will do next. But how is it you expect I am to support this family of mine? I cannot take to sea as a merchant sailor with a warrant upon my head and in a stolen ship."

"Then let us send to Governor Rogers and ask if he will receive us."

"I'm afraid he will insist on the return of the *Curlew*."

"I will take whatever he imposes."

"The lashing?"

"Even that, if it be for John."

"Then let us hope he still insists I wield the whip, for right now I'm of a mind to do so."

Anne's face reddened, and her temper flared like oil on fire, "Are ye now?"

"In fact," he said stepping toward her, warming to the idea, "a bottom made bright red by my hand has a certain attraction. Why, my breeches tighten at the very thought."

With nary a word Anne pulled the dagger from underneath her skirt and held it before her.

"So ye'd draw upon me, would ye?" he asked, amused, for he believed he could take her and do anything he'd a mind to do.

"You'll come no nearer with that kind of talk. I will take the governor's flogging and I will do penance. But I'll not be whipped like a schoolgirl."

"What else, Anne? What are your terms?"

She softened, "Nor will I give you up if the governor insists. If I have to, I'll track Bonny down wherever he is on this earth and make myself a widow to have you."

"Ah, who's the pirate?" he smiled.

"Those are my terms."

"Then I suggest we send to the governor and wait to see how he responds. And in the meanwhile take as many ships as possible to fill our treasury, for we will have need of money to start again."

"Indeed, Benjamin Hornigold had it right. Take what you can, then beg pardon."

"Perhaps we could put away the blade?"

"Only if you promise to take a good look at my bottom."

"My dear, my breeches are still tight. What say you, Anne, will you bend over my knee and give me one good hand print?"

"Yes, my darling, if you allow me a stroke with the lash across your bare buttocks."

"Like the sea, Anne, you are like the sea."

Chapter Twenty

Two days later Captain Bellows sailed out of port, and five days after that, Anne woke in the night to John's cries. She lit a candle and groped her way to his bed, touched him, and recoiled.

The child was burning with fever and she cried out for the kitchen maid to bring cool water and a cloth. By mid-morning the next day the fever had fled to be replaced by violent chills, the tiny body wasting before Anne and Jack's horrified eyes.

'Swamp fever,' the household whispered, and the word passed quickly through the town.

By evening John was limp, pale and deathly white. The shivering had brought him back to fire and sweat once again, and he was but a thin, emaciated tiny human who had lost much of his body weight quickly, his eyes sunken and dark. Nothing Anne did, could get him to drink.

In the darkness of that following night, she listened to his whimpering cries and rasping breath, and despaired. She had heard that same breath in her mother before her death and knew John's lungs were filled with fluid. With her own hands she baptized him, there being a church but not a priest in the town.

The household tiptoed through hallway and rooms, and members of the crew sat in the garden and kept vigil. In the town the music was silenced, and the night had an unearthly feel to it, alien, the only sounds the distant laping of sea on shore.

Sometime after midnight John's eyes rolled back in his head, his body in rigid convulsions, and Anne, busy at her task of trying to comfort and nurture, did not feel the moment when he slipped away.

Although Jack sat at her side through the night, it was not until morning that he took her arms from around the tiny form. When finally he looked directly into her eyes, he felt his heart so pierced by a dagger, he thought his end had come. But he pulled her away, promising she could return to wash the body and dress the babe for burial, and held her against him. The world had gone mad and they both needed to feel what was real and solid or surely the floor would open and swallow them both. He wiped her tears and half carried her to the chair on the balcony where she could see the sunlight and sea, away from the dark room where John lay.

"Oh, dear God," Anne wailed, "oh, Jack, I do not think I can bear this pain. Please help me, for God knows that I cannot."

"Hush now, my love," he murmured, kneeling at her feet. "We will take one moment at a time. John still needs us. We will do him the honor of a burial. And Anne, I do not think John would want you to despair. God has called him before us, that is all. He is baptized and enjoying eternal peace."

Though he said them, the words made no sense, for how could one explain the death of a child, and one so happy and handsome. Sure enough, the heat of summer would bring out sickness, but why John?

"Is God punishing me for something, Jack? What have I done? I have done nothing but love you. Oh, Jack, I will not believe our love is wrong!"

"Swamp fever is common enough, and why it strikes, I know not. But Anne, you are not to blame. I will not let you take this upon yourself."

On the following morning after Anne and the ladies of the household had washed John's body and the ship's cooper had wrought a tiny coffin and the crew members who could stand after a night in town walked past to say a farewell, they buried John under an almond tree in the yard. Food was served and music played, but the mood was somber and the men could not remember such sadness, refused to remember, and one by one they slipped away, leaving Anne and Jack to each other.

The house was empty, but more, life was empty. All their plans had been for John—the pardon, a home somewhere safe, business both of horses and ships. Jack took Anne in his arms and felt her tense.

"Don't shut me out, love. I need you. Let your sadness come out of your body any way you wish—scream, cry, pommel me—but let it come so that when it's done, I might have you with me again."

"Oh, Jack," Anne cried, throwing herself against his body. "There's a part of me that blames you. Maybe for not being here. Maybe if . . . if anything had been different, he would still be with us. But God knows, it's not your fault. I only wish a place to put my sadness, for truly my heart is broken."

"I will do anything you ask."

"Then take me to sea. Please, Jack. Let us to sea, together!"

He hesitated, for this was unexpected, and the issues large.

"The men will not have you aboard. A woman would ruin any chance of good fortune."

"I'll put on trousers as I have before, and bind my breasts. A few cups of grog and no one will know me."

"I will know you."

"Then while the crew sleeps, I will come to you."

"Anne . . ." and still he hesitated. "On board ship, you must realize, there is only one captain. You're an able seaman and know your work. But ye'll be hidden among the men and I'll not be able to show you favors. When I give an order, it is not to be questioned."

She stepped away from him, a hurt and answering spark of anger in her eyes, for she would ever be his equal.

"Listen, lass. You must hear me out, for I know your mind and independence. True, you've sailed, but not on a pirate vessel, and you've not been in a fight before. I'm asking if you can accept me as your captain and honestly sign the Articles of the Brotherhood. You see, lives will be at stake."

Anne sobered. "All right. I do understand. But I must

get away from here, and quickly. John is everywhere."

"The men will be glad to leave port. Three days then. We ship in three days." His hand softly traveled the length of her face, regarding her. "So, Anne, you'll finally join as a pirate. It'll be different from the merchant ships you've sailed on before."

"I swear to you, you'll find no better crewman. By my soul, I want nothing else but hard work, anything . . . anything to make me forget the sound of John's pitiful cry."

"When our coffers are full and we are ready to hear the governor's answer to our proposal, we'll come ashore to find a home. No need to decide where. When you're ready."

"Just now, I need to be remade. But I fear that may never happen, for my sorrow is such that the ocean cannot hold it."

"Anne," Jack whispered, holding her close, "God's world will remake you, true enough. But don't change too much."

"I will always love you," she promised. "That will never change."

"Come with me to the water's edge. Today we grieve. We will make footprints in the sand and remember our son."

Again the sea began to work its magic, for when they returned, Anne's tears had stopped, her skin wind and sun burned, her body tired, but her eyes focused on the changing color of the sky, on the prayer in her heart, the feel of Jack next to her, his arm around her shoulders. If she could just make it through this day and know a new dawn, possibly she could believe that one day she would live again.

As they walked up the stairs and he kissed her ear and neck, softly, gently, she thought to make love to him. Certainly not of lust or desire, but in hopes that if she allowed herself to feel, let something out, instead of holding all in the pit of her stomach, then perhaps she could face tomorrow.

Jack carried her to the bed and there her hopes were tenderly realized.

Part 5

The Caribbean

Summer, 1720

Mary Read

Chapter Twenty-one

A few days out from the coast of Cuba and they sat aboard ship, the breeze easy, and grateful they were for it too. Some time had gone by with nary a breath of air to fill the sails and there was no going anywhere, just a sit down on the sea with the sun squeezing every last drop of water from the men, baking them alive on its glasslike surface.

Anne's lips were parched and cracked, a sore in one corner of her mouth. The toileting she was always uneasy about was no longer a problem, for there was not enough liquid to urinate, even swallowing the cup of water she was given as ration four times a day. The grog at each meal went right to her head, her body absorbing all liquids, even the rum, and she found she roamed the deck and went about her chores in a stupor.

But hours ago the air had freshened and even now the *Curlew* made for dark clouds in the distance and the rain that fell in black sheets. Drink would be had for the taking, her body would be washed, and her skin cooled by cold water that for a little while would block the summer sun.

The wind whipped up further as they approached the short squall. The sea darkened and waves tossed the boat. Then they were into the rain, and the sea went dead and flat with the weight of it. Blessed, Anne raised her mouth, closed her eyes, and let the water pour over sunburned and tightened skin, cooling her body and drenching her hair so that the headache from heat and drink lessened. The crew reveled and filled water casks and buckets and drank until they could drink no more.

Suddenly, the storm was past, moving away to the east, while the sun moved closer to the western horizon, the sea splattered with golds and reds, and the breeze perfect in the dying day.

"Sail, ho! Sail, Ho! Off the starboard bow!"

At the cry, men jumped to the rail, for a sail meant they would either be prey or predator. The lassitude of moments before vanished, each waiting, ready to take to his post.

"Two sails, Captain! No three!" came the word.

"My glass!" Jack commanded, and he searched the horizon.

"Saints protect us," Master Fetherston murmured loud enough for Anne to hear.

"You are right to ask for God's help," Jack told him. "That man o' war flies the Spanish flag and carries forty guns . . . a fourth rate . . . and she makes for us. Look there," he passed the glass to Fetherston. "She's an escort of a neat frigate, three-masted, and she's caught the wind. With every sail aloft, she's running faster than the flagship. She'll be upon us first with her twenty guns."

"The third sail?" Fetherston asked, placing the glass to his eye. "Might as well 'ave it all."

"A sloop. We can count on more men and guns. We'll have to make a run for it, George. Three leagues back, there's a bay . . ."

"Aye, I know the place." He pushed closed the spyglass and turned to face Jack. "The bay's roomy enough, but the channel is a bottleneck. If we enter, we'll ne'er get out! They'll 'ave us boxed in."

"True enough. For the moment. But if we hold at the end of the channel and keep our guns broadside, the Spaniard won't be able to follow us in. She'll not be able to maneuver in that tight space." He took the glass from Fetherston and judged once more. "Look at the frigate. We can't outrun her. God's blood, but she's fast and gaining! If she reaches us she'll slow us with her guns long enough so that the galleon catches up, and then they'll pound us to death. No, it's the channel for us. It's our only hope."

Turning to the gunner, he ordered, "Mr. Howell, make ready the guns."

Then to the crew, cried, "Muskets and all the shot for a fight. Swords and cutlasses in hand! Bear up, let her fall to leeward. We need all speed!"

"All hands! All hands! Lay on every inch of cloth. Jump to! Make ready to run!"

The *Curlew* turned, fled away with the wind, and reaching the estuary, sailed into it, ropes straining and creaking, the pound of the sea loud on her keel.

True to Jack's foresight, the frigate arrived and waited, for it was near dark, and the captain could see the *Curlew* was going nowhere. The man o' war sailed into the bay, sometime behind her, and blocked the channel, but could not turn to use her guns in the narrow passage. Night was quickly descending, and Jack breathed a sigh of relief as he watched the flagship drop anchor, her fast frigate taking a place behind, and the smaller sloop settle away to her port side. Safe they were for the night in the little bay, the galleon the cork in the bottleneck, and the *Curlew* anchored just out of range of her guns.

"She's a beauty that frigate. Clean, well built, and of some craftsmanship." Jack stood with Fetherston at the railing, ships turning dark on the water. "A trim ship. All her wood polished."

"I'm more interested in what sits in front of 'er. The galleon and its marines will come for us in the mornin', Jack. She knows she has us. Our only way out is right through 'er."

"And right through her we'll go."

"What's that?"

The surprised look on Fetherston's face caused Jack to laugh heartily. "We've no moon tonight. Call the men together. I've a plan."

The crew gathered on deck, disquieted, a low rumble amongst them, and Jack looked them over.

"What say you? Afraid of the Spaniard?" and he boldly eyed his quartermaster, Richard Corner. "A round of grog for the men here, and make it heavy on the rum. A bit o' fire in the belly and your courage will soon return. I've an idea, if you're with me."

"We're listenin'. Let's hear it, Cap'n," one shouted amongst the general murmuring.

"Aye," came another voice. "It's a pretty pickle we're in."

"Then listen up. There's no moon this evening and t'will be dark. We've enough longboats to slip away . . ."

"Will we abandon the *Curlew* and put to sea?" cried an astonished voice.

"Yes, we'll put to, but it's not to sea in a longboat we'll be goin', nor to the devil. We'll be takin' the frigate that rides just beyond yon galleon. We'll trade the *Curlew* for the *Santa Maria,* for that's the name painted aft, and by the looks of her, she's a better ship than the one we have. I'd bet my share of the spoils on her worthiness and offer any man here odds that she's faster then the *Curlew.* What say you, will you take what we can from the *Curlew* and make the gamble of slippin' by the flagship in the night?"

"She'll be watchin' us, Cap'n, while waitin' for daylight," one of the men called.

"Aye, and we'll keep our lights ablaze so she keeps her eyes in this direction. If luck holds with us, we'll be out on the open sea before she realizes that the frigate has a new crew."

A mighty shout went up, and Jack ordered the lanterns lit, put fore and aft and in the yard arms so there could be no denying that the *Curlew* rested at anchor and waited for new day to do battle.

Once the sky had turned and air and sea were ink dark, the longboats were carefully lowered and the oars removed from their pins. Instead of rowing, the men were to paddle quietly past the galleon. Several trips would have to be made to ferry each sailor, and Jack swore to the crew that not a man would be left behind. Each among them remembered Blackbeard's marooning of his own men in straits very much the same—a few picked seamen, some carefully chosen articles for navigation, his treasure, and Edward Teach was gone, never to return for the rest. It was a measure of their confidence in Jack that those left behind followed his orders to stay aboard and make the noise that would keep the galleon's eye upon them.

Not much was taken from the *Curlew*, only that which each man could bear upon on his body. Only Jack carried more, his navigation maps, and the monies and treasure in the small chest he held for the voyage.

Anne, dressed as a man, her secret still intact, sat in Jack's boat and wore a blanket rolled, wrapped, and tied about her. Inside it were those items she could not leave—the picture from her father's house in Charles Town, the cross of Brazilian emeralds, a lock of John's hair. Grateful that no one suspected she carried a silver frame and gold cross, she dipped her oar and made for the channel, all the while praying that the watch aboard the galleon would not look to the water.

When she had first asked Jack to take her to sea, she had been bereft, her mind too numb to understand the full measure of what she sought. Certainly she ran from pain, but into what? Not for all the world could she have foreseen the danger of her choice. The absolute knowledge that she and all these men might die, that at any moment, a sound, a wayward glace from the watch of the galleon, anything, might betray them. The thought caused her heart to pound, while at the same time, her breathing seemed to stop.

As she looked toward Jack sitting forward in the longboat, she had a new sense of his abilities. He had immediately understood the danger upon seeing the sails on the horizon, had known the fill extent of the impossible situation, but rather than fear, had taken all to hand and made a plan. Just weeks ago they had argued, and as she sat huddled in the boat, his words came back to her. "I am captain of a ship. Other men, those who do not take to leadership or responsibility, look to me." Now she understood. Jack lead where other men could not. She, certainly, would never want the responsibility for so many lives. Without him, they would all at this moment be at the bottom of the sea, or wearing the chains of the Spanish governor of Cuba.

The flagship had plenty of lights on board, but, for the most part, the ship's crew was quiet. Words of conversation drifted, and Anne could hear someone singing below decks. Then, a splash, something emptied overboard, and Jack held up his hand. All rowing stopped. Anne's body folded in on itself as if to hide, and they drifted on still water with the movement of the last paddle, until Jack motioned them forward again.

The danger was greatest near the frigate, for they had to board without rousing the crew. Quietly the boats slid alongside, the watch visible on deck, lantern light illuminating the outline of a body. A single man stood alone, the crew asleep, for they hid behind the galleon and no one dreamed that anything untoward would happen before daybreak.

When the sentry turned his back, Jack was up the entryway stairs and first over, sliding into shadows, Fetherston right behind, careful to make no sound. A warning shout and all would be lost.

In moments Jack was upon the guard, a knife at his throat, Fetherston pulling the musket from his astonished hands and the pistol from his belt. Eyes wide with fear, the man shook uncontrollably, while Jack whispered into his ear in his own language that if he wished to live another minute, he would not so much as breathe.

The rest of the pirates came aboard without misstep, and when the full complement was on deck, they stole downstairs to stand over the sleeping sailors with cutlass and pistol, holding a single lantern to lead the way, threatening all the ravages of hell if a man as much as coughed.

Signaling to his officers, Jack stealthily made his way to the captain's cabin and turned the knob of the door. Startled, the Spanish captain called out at the light that interrupted the dark. Pistol cocked and to the ready, Jack put a finger to his lips and hissed, "*Silencio!*" The man froze and regarded Mr. Fetherston's cutlass too near his mouth.

"I protest!" the captain cried, taken off-guard.

Jack removed his hat to the man, "My sympathies, Captain, for I understand your loss, but I will insist on your silence and cooperation. A single word and it will be your last. Now, I hurry, sir. This way." From the look on Jack's face, the captain did not doubt him. Indeed, Jack was a bow-string ready to let go, for one misstep and they were all dead, and with them Anne.

"Con permiso."

In the hallway Mr. Howell, the master gunner, and Mr. Corner, quartermaster, held the other officers. Much to the captain's dismay, and livid with anger that he should be made prisoner aboard his own ship, he and his officers were led below with no distinction for their class, and forced to stand close together with the crew in the ship's brig.

Then began the most dangerous effort of the evening, for the longboats headed back to the Curlew, attempting to make the treacherous journey in silence to ferry all those left, so that Jack's promise might be fulfilled. Again the men paddled rather than rowed, and it was with a great exhalation of breath that Jack saw every man quietly aboard.

In the hour before daybreak Jack felt the ship rise with the tide, saw the water run from the bay, and cut the anchor to float slowly and silently out to sea. When the *Santa Maria* had cleared the harbor mouth, he caught the wind in his face and quietly ordered the sails hoisted. The ship gave a small uneven lurch as her sails filled, and then moved off. Just as Jack had surmised, she was graceful, and he praised God for this fresh life that had been given them all. As they made to sea, the sun rose with all the glory of a new day and the wind picked up further with the warming of the water.

"God be praised, gentlemen," he cried, "for we have our lives, a new ship, and the means to become wealthy men!"

A moment of quiet followed, for not often was there a sense of prayer on a pirate vessel. Nor were they often called gentlemen, for in truth, it was gentlemen who had set them to these straights. But if it were to be made known, it's gentlemen they would all have been. Called blackguards and curs, they would surely act the role, but gentlemen, why . . . a few removed their caps in salute to the captain, and yet, none knew if they were far enough away from the galleon to let go a cheer.

Only then did the crew below decks feel the rolling of the ship. Unnerved and confused they shouted out that the hatch was locked and themselves below decks. Jack merely laughed loud and handsomely, ignoring their cries.

"In a few moments, the captain of yon galleon is going to realize what's happened, and then we will see some fun!" he called.

Sure enough, there was a great deal of furious activity on board the Spaniard, as she understood the pirate had duped her. Then the cheer went round for Captain Jack, and they rode the wind fast into the rising sun of the eastern horizon, her speed suggesting good care of her hull.

Once on open water, the galleon behind, Jack ordered an inventory taken of her stores and found she was very well outfitted, indeed with better victuals than the *Curlew*, certainly better wine. She was entirely seaworthy, strong enough to ride out a hurricane in a sheltered bay, and her pumps in good working order. The rum was passed out and they raced, testing her strength, this time with a mind to being predator rather than prey.

"A job well done, Captain," Anne whispered when there was a quiet moment on the deck and the men too drunk to notice how close she stood.

Jack looked at her and grinned. "I appreciate your admiration. Perhaps you could come to my cabin tonight and show me just how grateful you are. Would that it could be now!"

"Jack, I've a concern. This ship's fine, but she's larger than the last. We'll need more crew to man her properly."

"Indeed, you are right," and he looked over her decking. "I've a mind to rechristen her. What think you of the *Lady Anne*?"

Abashed, unexpectedly remembering when she'd dreamed of being Lady Anne, she said too loudly, "As a crew member I'd say you were a milk-sop pining for a skirt on a bay in Cuba!"

"No matter. That's her name and pray God luck be brought with it. She's a warship, for certes, and there's little we'll have to be doin' to convert her to a pirate vessel. Below decks we'll tear out the bulkhead walls so's everyone has an equal place for a hammock. Men and officers, share and share alike."

"And the captain's cabin? Am I to show my appreciation with egalitarian eyes upon me?"

"The captain's cabin is the exception," and he gave her a small bow. "A benefit of the job and its responsibilities."

"It's a big bite we're takin' here, Jack. She's twenty guns and that smacks of Blackbeard's style. Remember it's him that got the ants' nest all stirred up, him with the *Queen Anne's Revenge* and her forty guns and his armada of ships. Do we want this kind of vessel? Or would we be better off with a small, fast sloop, easy in and out, not makin' too many waves or takin' so much that it throws the weight of the king's navy against us?"

"What you say is true. Between you and me, I'm startled that we ran into these three ships out searchin' for pirates. That tells me the Spanish governor of Cuba is just as serious as Lawes or Rogers. I think it a good idea to head to New Providence to see to that amnesty as soon as possible. We may need a back door if forced to it."

"What will you do with her Spanish crew?"

"Why, I'll put them ashore as soon as I am able."

"And will ye wreak havoc amongst them?"

"No, a deed unnecessary. I do not hurt indiscriminately. Surely you know that about me?"

"I've not seen you pirate before, Jack"

"All will be released, unharmed."

"Will we put into port to enlarge our crew?"

"Bless me, but no! We'll take our crew from the next ship

that becomes prize. But I'll have no Spaniard, for there's no trustin' them. At least none from amongst this lot." Then he said thoughtfully, the fun gone from his voice, "Are you ready for battle, Anne? It will be your first and I worry."

"No need," she answered testily. "I've signed Articles and I'll take my chances with the crew."

"Then stay by my side. I will feel the better for it."

A moment later all seriousness fell from him and he doffed his hat with its bright red feather, then turned his face to the wind, tanned and brown, his smile bright.

"Master Fetherston," he cried, "send the ship's carpenter. I've a mind to change the name of our new vessel. Now, give me the wheel. I'll have the feel of her!"

Chapter Twenty-two

On the next day the *Lady Anne* sighted sail on the horizon and gave chase. Here it was that Anne had her first encounter with outright piracy, for the crew was determined to plunder the vessel, a small Dutch flute. Hurricane season was upon them, but captains and ship owners hoped the worst of it would come in late August and September, and the shipping lanes were rife with merchants attempting to sail cargo to port before the hottest months. As expected, the *Lady Anne* flew towards the sail, fast and sure. Laughing, Jack called for the black flag, and with more than a little pride, the pirate unfurled.

For the better part of half a day the chase continued, the *Lady Anne* gaining steadily. Toward evening they were close enough to lay a single shot near her aft hull. Not wanting to continue the chase into night, Jack cried across the water that she should strike and take up her canvas. Instead, the captain of the flute left on every inch of sail she could carry and attempted to turn east and away from him.

With a roar of cannon, the pirate let loose with a full broadside, taking the flute's mizzenmast, a man of her crew killed, her rigging tangled, on-deck anchor blown away, and pieces of shrapnel and splinters of wood flying through air to injure and maim.

"Bring us alongside, Master Fetherston!" for the Dutchman had been stopped in the water.

Amidst smoke and the shouting of orders and the screams of men, grappling hooks flew, the pirate crew frantically drawing in the lines, while the Dutch crew worked just as diligently to cut them away, all the while firing at the attackers who used both hands on the ropes.

"Quickly there, secure before she regroups!" Jack ordered.

Anne shaking and terrified, heard the whine of a pistol ball as it landed in the boom near her shoulder. A moan from the man next to her and she felt him fall away. Then, a second shuddering broadside erupted from below, a great heave, a trembling of timber, a confusion of smoke and new fire on the deck of the merchant, and Jack bellowed from his perch on the upper deck. Pulling his sword from its scabbard and grabbing a line, he flew over the side toward the trapped victim.

Too fearful to think, Anne yelled with the other men, cursing as she swung over, sword tightly gripped, pistol at the ready, and found herself fighting hand-to-hand in mortal fear. She had fenced and won before, but never had she known the terror of fighting for her life against a man fighting for his, knowing no quarter would be given, and wondering from which side the next blow would fall. The fight was not long and as it ended, she found that she'd slashed a man with enough hurt so that he'd fallen back, and that the new seaman who'd taken his place had no stomach for the contest.

The sailors of the Dutchman, looking toward those shipmates cut down, knowing they were greatly outnumbered and carried someone else's wealth, laid down arms and struck colors.

Dazed, visibly shaken, Anne followed the lead of her shipmates and surrounded the men of the merchant, her gorge none to steady at the sight of blood on her blade.

Immediately the rest of the crew of the *Lady Anne* set about securing the ship, seeing to those crewmembers who were still armed, and putting out fire. Jack went below to access the cargo and found himself pleased, knowing he could smuggle the goods into one of the ports of the mainland colonies.

"I am sorry for your loss, Captain," Jack told the dejected commander once on deck again. "There was no need for loss of life, for it is only your stores that I want. We shall take what we need and you shall have your ship returned.

Mr. Corner, if you please, begin moving the ship's stores to the *Lady Anne.* You'll find a good quantity of sailing rope, as well as salted fish, rum, and molasses." Turning back to the captain, he added, "And I'll have your money."

"There is none. All I have is in the goods. Take them and be damned to you!"

"Come now, sir, I've been at sea all my life and we both know a ship does not sail without some purchase power. I will have your treasure and I will only ask for it once more . . . nicely."

When the captain stood stubborn and face set, Jack looked around the captured prisoners on deck. A young boy, barefoot and with ashen face, stood out among the cloistered group. When he saw Jack's eyes fall upon him, he trembled and cast his face down.

"Bring him," he pointed to the boy.

With a flourish he removed the pistol from his belt and held it at the boy's temple. "Your coin, Captain. I do not make idle threats."

"Indeed I cannot imagine that you do, you scurvy knave, you damnable excuse for a man, you cowardly cur . . ."

"Hold there. Enough. What is it to be? Will you watch your crew die one by one for a few pieces of metal?"

Anne watched Jack, and this a Jack she had never seen before. All the softness was gone from him. Instead she saw the pirate, the man who risked all, brazen, his face put forward along with his action for all the world to report, his sword bloodied in one hand, boots spread apart and arm outstretched to hold straight and sure the pistol. The blue eyes were hard and cold, and she shivered. For the first time she truly understood that Jack was wild, that he would risk all, and knew to the depths of her soul that she would never be able to tame him, that the pirate's life was the only life he would ever lead. To her great shame she wanted to weep, for she saw that she was doomed. Her love for him would take her where he would lead, even into the mouth of disaster.

"It's in my cabin," the captain said disgustedly, "under a

floorboard. I'll take you there. Let the lad go."

Jack lowered the pistol. "That wasn't so difficult, was it? After you, Captain."

Later that evening, after night had fallen, the pirated goods stowed and the men's wounds bound, Jack had dinner for five served in his cabin at the large table of the former ship's commander. He had ordered a feast—fresh turtle soup, albacore and dolphin fish cooked with onion, one of the chickens from below decks roasted, a fowl Jack had to promise to replace for the eggs the hen produced were precious, boiled potatoes with plenty of salt, even a dessert, an extraordinary pudding made of eggs and flour and sugar. The cook had just opened the bottles of wine found stored in a special locker and served the first course of the meal when Jack held up his glass, for on this evening they did indeed dine with real glass and the plate of the Spanish captain.

"I have invited you here," he told the men around the table, a gleam in his eye, "to give praise to your actions this day. George Fetherston," and he nodded to his ship's master, "you took us right up alongside. Got the feel of her, have you?"

"Aye, Captain," George answered with some amount of pride, his graying hair neatly combed back, "and easy does she go."

"Richard, to you." Jack held up his glass to his quartermaster, Richard Corner, thin and tall and on the sea from a young lad, now in his early twenties. "Goods over the side and stored neatly away."

The man drank deeply, and with a satisfied grin exclaimed, "Thank 'e, Cap'n Jack. The more in our hold, the more in our pockets."

Fetherston, suddenly uneasy, looked at Jack, his back stiffening, for he saw Jack's purpose as he moved around the table.

Jack reached for a bottle, poured red wine into his master gunner's glass, "John Howell, your shot stopped the

Dutchman dead." Approaching thirty, of good body and handsome face, the gunner had a scar over his right eye and by the looks of it, had been lucky to keep the eye.

Now Jack leaned back in his chair, his voice low-pitched, "And here's to Andy." All eyes turned to Anne, uncomfortable and wondering just what Jack was about. "Andy, who went over the side with the crew and fought like a demon."

"First fight?" asked Howell, questioning why the boy sat amongst them.

"Aye," Anne answered, "and a good feeling it was." For during the conflict and true to her purpose, she had not once given thought to tiny John, dead in his grave.

"Clever work you made of it, lad," Howell nodded. "You've earned the crew's trust this day."

"I am glad to hear it, Master Gunner, for perhaps you are not aware of the whole truth about our lad here," Jack said.

"Is the lad's privacy a matter for others?" George Fetherston cautioned, for he had spent too many hours in Jack's home not to have recognized Anne, and he worried what the crew would do if it were known that a woman was aboard.

Jack raised an eyebrow, a gesture that reminded Anne of her father, and she shivered. Already she was not sure about their actions of the day. Poor, yes, set upon by outrageous fortune, true, but what she and the others had done was outright theft, and a part of her was ashamed.

"I believe so, George. For the lad has a story to share with the crew. *I* have a story to share, for his story is my story as well."

The room was too quiet as each man at table tried to guess what that story might be.

"Let's hear it, Cap'n. If it concerns us, we might as well know the truth of it now," Howell told him.

Jack stood, smiling, confident, and raised his glass. "This lad is no lad, but my wife, my Anne, dressed as a boy and brought to sea. But I will have my wife at my side, for she has proved herself, both as seaman and fighter. I will have her openly a part of this crew, for she has signed Articles and knows what she has signed and is true to her word."

The astonished table looked closely at her. She stood to meet their eyes, removed her scarf and shook out her hair.

"Tis true, my breasts are bound. Will ye have me?" she asked, looking each one fiercely in the eye. "For my heart is with the ship and the men, and it's to sea with Jack I will go. I'll not be without him. Not since the death of wee John." And here her voice almost faltered, only Fetherston noting the quiver, for she would be hard, like the look in Jack's eye that afternoon. "And if ye will not, I'll fight any man who dares to try to put me ashore."

"We'll have to leave it to the men, lass," Fetherston answered for the table. "There's no denying that you're capable. But the crew will be jealous that Jack has a woman aboard while they eat their hearts out wishin' for one."

"I have asked you men here this evening for your favor. Talk to the crew before the vote," Jack told them.

"Truth is," Fetherston rubbed a hand along a jaw line needing a shave, "it's not going to matter what the crew says, is it Captain Jack?"

Jack threw his head back and laughed uproariously, then pointed to the food on the table. "Let us enjoy this fine meal." And he sat and refilled the glasses again.

The news of Anne's presence on board went round the ship, and as if someone had struck a match to powder, it sizzled and ignited. Before first watch the crew had voted, and to her immense relief, found they voted with her, although there were one or two she might have fought for her place aboard. True to Fetherston's word, a good part of the ship was jealous of the captain, for he had it all, title, woman, chest of treasure, and cabin. And it was here that he very conspicuously took Anne on the night of the raid, and brought her to bed. Unbinding her breasts, he ran his hands over them, feeling as if he had come home.

"I hope you know what you do, Jack Rackham," Anne

whispered hoarsely, his mouth and tongue around her nipple, the passionate flame spreading through her body. "Ah, Jack, perhaps you do."

"I could not go on as we were. I must have you, Anne. I will say it so that you will understand. With John's death . . ."

"Sh-h, I know. Touching takes away the pain. Here . . . pull off your shirt and lie next to me."

"I will have you naked. I will feast my eyes."

"Then remove your breeches, my love, and I will bring you joy."

"Today, Anne," he said tugging at his boots, "you were magnificent."

"No. I was terrified. So much so that all I could do is yell like a banshee and fight for my life. It does not serve me, Jack, this killing. I take no pleasure in it like some of the men do. And you, would you have shot the boy?"

"No. But I had to make the good captain think I would. I'm with you, Anne. I do not like to kill or torture. True enough, there are some that do. But I am for the treasure without the blood."

"I saw a look in your eyes . . ."

"I am a leader of men. They must believe me just as the captain of a captured vessel believes. Now come and let us celebrate your first real act of piracy," and he poured straight sweet rum into cups. "You are bound to my soul by your work today, for you share the condemnation of all pirates. Men were killed, gold taken."

Anne drank deep and felt the warmth spread to her head, a softness take over her limbs. She came to him, and the feel of him along the length of her body was exquisite desire. Women spoke of their trysts, but none ever spoke of a man like Jack, who thought first of her pleasure, who had learned all the ways to tempt so that the fervor of her wanting rose with each breath he placed along her body. Lost in the rum and the feel of him, warm and real and the smell of his skin, she sighed as he worked his way down with lips and tongue, until she cried aloud, a sound that slid beyond the cabin walls and more than one man wished for a private place to spill his own semen.

"Jack . . ."

She moaned and not until he lay against her, finished and still and sweat soaked in the hot cabin, did she remember she had taken no precautions against pregnancy.

"Jack," she whispered again softly. "I believe we might have made a child."

"Why, Anne, then a perfect day . . . a prize, a fine meal, you . . . and a child to take my name."

"Aye," she murmured, closing her eyes. "Surely the life of a pirate."

Chapter Twenty-three

In the weeks that followed, Jack and Anne slowly made their way toward New Providence by sailing through the Caribbean, taking in the waters of Hispaniola, its bays and inlets. As Anne advised, they avoided larger ships, hoping the news of their exploits would not run before them. The smaller defenseless fishing vessels were theirs for the taking, furling their sails the moment the black flag appeared, and the hold of the *Lady Anne* filled with goods that would be smuggled into port past English tax collectors, much to the glee of the citizens of the seaboard cities who would pay less for their wares. During that time Jack walked a line between serving Anne's caution and securing a future for the crew—until the day a large Dutchman appeared on the horizon just at sunrise and not even Jack could refuse so plump a prize.

"She's fourteen guns," Master Fetherston told Jack. "But she's sitting heavy in the water. A merchantman, to be sure."

"Lay on sail, Mr. Davis!" Jack called to the boatswain. "Every piece of canvas you can find. She turns to run! You've the helm, George."

Anne slipped into Jack's cabin and changed out of the skirt she wore on deck, instead pulled on breeches and boots. About her head she tied a red scarf to match the waist sash that held a pistol. Once more she looked the lad.

Just as she climbed onto the deck to stand beside Jack, the black flag was hoisted to a great cheer from the pirates, for here was their nation and their law and a symbol of their pride. Rackham's flag they called it, white skull above crossed cutlasses.

Taking Jack's spyglass from him, Anne gazed across the

water and could just make out furious activity. The merchant vessel had seen the black flag, and although she scurried with the wind away to the west, clearly, she was preparing to give them a fight. A shudder went through her involuntarily, for it boded no good if the merchant would defend. Someone would die or be maimed. Pray God it was not Jack or herself.

By midday they were upon the ship. As Jack always did, he sent forth a single shot from the *Lady Anne's* cannon, and called out for her to dip her colors before loss of life. Instead the merchant rolled with the kick of her own cannon, putting a hole through the forward topsail and taking out a railing and a man's leg with it.

"Let go, Mr. Howell!" Jack shouted to his master gunner. "On the roll. Fire!"

The cannon released its ordnance, belching dark smoke and powder, grime covering the ship. When the smoke had thinned, Jack looked out to the Dutchman, only to see the red flare of ignited powder and seconds later, hear the sound of their cannon. With just enough time to shout a warning, he flattened down on deck. The volley shook the *Lady Anne* violently, and she took a hit so near the water line that several of the seaman made for the pumps.

"Damn, but she's a feisty catch!" Jack shouted, "and what's she on about? She can't stand against us! Prepare to bring her close up before I have to let loose upon her and there's nary a ship left to salvage!"

"She's preparin' another broadside!" the gunner called.

"Another round before she fires, Mr. Howell!"

At the ready, a roar shook the ship as the gunner fired, wrenching a moan from the ship's timbers, while the air became a great choking smoke.

"Muskets in the topsails! Soften her up!" Jack ordered. "Mr. Fetherston, swing toward her. Hard to starboard and straight at her. The rest of you men, grappling hooks, prepare to board!" He drew his sword, took hold of a line, ready to lead the charge.

The musketeers cleared her decks, and the quick broadside of John Howell delayed the Dutchman's gunner long enough to allow the *Lady Anne* to slide alongside. As the ships came together, there was a great creak of wood, a crackling from taut lines, the roar of men and the shriek of shot.

Jack was first over, Anne beside him, once again screaming like a wounded devil. The men eyed her and no longer thought of her as a green boy, but a woman, and found that they tested their own courage against hers and waited to see how she would take to battle now that her sex was out. They needn't have worried. Anne was everywhere at once and bound to the same blood lust as they, fueled by fear and the prospect of treasure and her own reputation. Not only did she want to stand out in the minds of the men, but she wanted to prove to Jack that she was his equal in a fight, and her sword ran as red as any of the others.

On her right she watched Jack battle with a young seaman, blond hair and deep blue eyes, and thought it a pity someone so handsome as the lad need die, but then, the sailor was giving Jack a good fight and she kept an eye on the exchange.

To the side of her face, a rush of air, a swoosh, and a blade whisked by her eyes, so quick it was but a blur and she turned to face her own adversary, a stocky man, big in the chest who had chosen a fight he thought he could win. The near miss recalled her to the moment, and all else was forgotten. As if a lamp had been lit, everything was extraordinarily clear, every movement controlled, for just that quick, she could have been gone. She stepped into the fray with some anticipation of its results, and the sailor found he had chosen the wrong battle. Anne ran him through neatly, her own instinct for survival acute, and quickly spun to see who else might be upon her, behind or to the side, poised with a blade and ready to take her out of the action.

Secure for the moment, she turned back to Jack's fight just as a great roar of approval from the pirates was sounded, for the captain of the Dutchman had ordered his men to lay down. Even so, the young man who dueled with Jack continued his fight, until his own captain knocked away his sword.

"No point in giving up your life for a lost cause," the captain told the lad, then called out. "Who among you leads this band of cutthroats?"

"That pleasure would be mine," Jack answered, giving him a bow. "Captain Jack Rackham at your service."

"So you're Jack Rackham. We were warned about you in New Providence."

"Your name, Captain?"

"Van Horn. Captain Van Horn out of Amsterdam."

"And might I ask who gave the warning?"

"Governor Rogers warned us that these waters are pirate-infested and mentioned you by name. Took a ship from the harbor, did ye?"

"Indeed, but that vessel is gone and this has taken its place."

Then Jack turned to the crew of the beleaguered ship. "I'm looking for good men who want to make their fortune amongst honest pirates taking the sea's bounty. If any want to ship with me aboard the *Lady Anne,* step forward." Jack faced the young man who had defended so bravely. "What about you? You're a talented fellow. Are you as good a seaman as you are a swordsman?"

"Aye," the man answered. "I started early as a cabin boy many years ago. But I've also been in the army. At first a foot soldier, then in the cavalry. I'm back to sea now."

"An Englishman? Aboard a Dutch ship? How did you come to this pass?"

"T'was where I left the cavalry, sir. In the Netherlands."

"We can use a man like you aboard, especially another Englishman. You know that as war goes, perhaps we'll have letters of marque in the future and the protection of the king. Who knows if we'll fight the Spanish or the French or the Dutch. What say ye?"

"I say I'm your man, if you can guarantee me a good share."

"Don't be foolish, boy!" Captain Van Horn cried. "Signing on with pirates! They'll take you to a bad end!"

"But I'll never fill me purse this way. No, I'll take the pirate's life for awhile. You know as well as I that's the way o' it. Why, 'alf the 'onest seamen 'ere 'ave been sea robbers at one time or other." He turned to Jack. "Ye've me sword, Cap'n, if ye'll take it. My name is Mark."

"Well spoken, lad. Anyone else?" Jack asked.

And there were several more. Anne saw that the crew would swell with each attack upon a merchant ship, and that the men would come and go as their purses came and went. But this Mark had a sober manner about him, knew what he was about. No, this Mark was different from the rest.

"Mr. Fetherston will show you the Articles," Jack told the new men. "You'll have to agree and make your mark before we cast off lines. In the meanwhile, Captain Van Horn, let's see what holds you so low in the water. If you please, I'll have your escort below deck."

Captain Van Horn gave up his dead to the sea in Christian burial, and sailed away as best he could in a crippled ship. His crew was all the smaller, for several had come aboard the *Lady Anne,* and his surgeon could only wait for time to heal the wounded. The last view the crew of the *Lady Anne* had of the ship, was of her limping away, back to New Providence and the company that had hired her. And to tell the governor new tales about Jack.

As the sail of the Dutchman became smaller on the horizon, Anne leaned against the rail and asked, "Do ye think this is a good idea? Letting him off. We're on our way back to ask for a pardon."

"Aye, and so much more will the governor want us off the sea. No, Captain Van Horn is doing exactly what I want him to do. If he makes it, praise God and let him work for us. If he goes to the bottom, well, then there's no loss, is there?" Jack turned to her, a smile on his face. "Would you have me kill the crew?"

"I could not do it, but in truth, perhaps it would be best if they did not arrive in New Providence."

"Why, Anne, you've become bloodthirsty!" And he threw his head back and laughed loud. "Well, then, I think it's time for a drink, don't you? In celebration. Our hold is filling and our chest has new gold."

The sun was bright overhead and many hours were left to the day. Since John's death Jack was drinking more heavily, starting earlier with each sunrise. Something bothered Anne, but she had yet to put her finger on what that was. Their lives had grown into a continuous routine of thievery, drink, a good meal, drink, sex, and drink. The freedom of the seas Anne had expected was turning into monotony, for there was no freedom in the running and hiding, and she had begun once again to long to build something, to work toward a future. In her memory she heard the hooves of Rosie pounding beneath her, and she dreamed of raising horses, of planting a crop, of shipping the fruits of her labors to a port and sailing when she cared to do so. The thought crossed her mind that she would fight any pirate who tried to empty the hold of her own ship. She knew the labor involved in running a plantation and would be loathe to lose her hard work. It occured to her to feel for the ships she took at the moment. But she and Jack needed a stake, and she risked all in hopes of getting it.

"Go ahead, if you want. Have your drink," she told him. "I'll settle in the new seamen."

By evening something remarkable had happened to Anne, and what that might be, she daren't guess. But she found her eyes followed young Mark all the day long, and his eyes in return, bluer than Jack's, would hold hers for some moments before turning away. Soon she wanted to know everything she could about the man, and when the music was loud in celebration, and the sun set, and Jack and the crew too drunk to know the thing next to them, Anne found him in a quiet corner. The man held a cup of grog and drank slowly.

"You are a soldier come to sea," Anne ventured, taking a seat next to him.

"Aye," he answered. "And you. I've 'eard the men call you Andy."

Anne nodded, for it was Jack's place to tell the new men there was a woman on board.

"I was just nine when I found meself aboard a merchant sailin' as a cabin boy. But then, you yourself must 'ave shipped early. I watched you in the fight today, all fury and no qualms. Born t' it, I imagine."

"Ah, no, there you're wrong, for I'm new to the sea just this last year or so. But I'm well practiced with sword and pistol, and I've learned to hold my own in battle."

"That's the crux o' it, ain't it?" Mark grinned. "Holdin' your own. Fight like the devil, show no fear, and there's not many a man who'll take you on. Sea or land. Now your cap'n there, 'e fought me good enough, laughin' the whole time. Enjoyed the swordplay, 'e did. I figure 'e was testin' me. T' be sure, 'e's the reason I decided t' sign on. I want a purse and I've plans for it. I think 'e can get it for me."

"You will save? What will you do with your money?"

Mark looked at her with some interest. "Why, I've plans for an inn, if you'd really like t' know. I 'ad one once, but, well, I lost me love, died of a fever . . ."

Anne heard well enough the hurt, and because the pain of death was fresh with her, said sincerely and softly, "I'm sorry."

Surprised by tenderness in the seaman's voice and wary, Mark answered simply, "I went on with the business for awhile. But with the war endin', the soldiers went away, and I couldn't make ends meet. So I sold the place and rejoined what was left of the army. When my regiment was disbanded near the coast, I took ship on the Dutchman."

"And where will you have this new inn of yours?"

"I've a place in mind. In Virginia near the sea. And

there'll be no lack o' seamen."

"I wish you well in your dream, Mark."

"Why . . . why, thank 'e," he stammered. He looked around and saw that many of the crew had started to sleep where they lay on deck, the drink and celebration having done its work. "Well, g'night then. I'm t' quarters and the hammock."

"Come on. I'll show you where to hang up."

Below decks was quiet, the only sounds the creak of wood shifting on water, ropes pulled tight to groan, the fruitful snores of those who'd made it downstairs, already passed out and abed. The light was dim, a single lantern to shape the shadows. Anne grabbed a hammock, walked to a darkened corner and fastened the bed to the supports. "This will do."

In that private place they stood, and there was no reason for Anne to stay, except that she was drawn to the man and looked for an excuse. But none was needed, for Mark leaned toward her, a magnetism so strong that the force was physical, and without thinking, Anne found herself pulled, closer, surely, then on impulse, a kiss, and found a warm response with soft lips and tongue, and an embrace that covered her body.

Suddenly, she realized the absurdity of it. "Is it men ye like?" she asked, her voice quivering.

With a most curious glance and a smile, Mark answered, "Aye, for my first love was a man. And ye, I take it that ye like men as well?"

"I . . . I do . . . but there's something you should know . . ."

"You don't 'ave t' say more, lass."

Anne gasped. "How is it you know?"

"The embrace, for certes. I know a bosom when I feel one."

And Anne realized she had not bound her breasts before battle, no need with the crew knowing her sex.

"Then where does that put us, Mark?"

"It puts us 'ere . . ." and he began to remove belt and sword.

"Wait! First you must know, I am with Jack. The captain."

"No problem. I'll not go against the captain . . ." he continued to remove his coat and unbutton his shirt, Anne's eyes wide, wondering if she could refuse him, ". . . for you see . . ." and he pulled back his shirt to reveal the breasts of a woman, smaller than those of Anne, for Anne had nursed a child, but breasts, none the less.

For a long horrifying minute Anne could not fathom, until it dawned, and she began to laugh softly, "Oh, dear God, Mark . . ."

"Mary."

"Dear God, a kindred spirit. A woman who would be free to make her way in the world and the only way to do so is to become a man."

"Ah, so ye understand."

"Indeed. For the only way I could to sea was to bind my breasts. Mary, Mary, my name is Anne."

"We still need t' decide where that leaves us, Anne. I want no man t' know my sex, for I'd lose my place . . . or worse . . . if it be known."

"They'll not hear it from me. But you and I have many stories to share, and I am ripe for friendship."

Mary looked directly into her eyes and stepped forward. "The kiss . . ." she began.

Anne grinned. "Aye, a good one." Then cocked her head to one side. "And one I would have again, if you wish."

Mary reached out, her body as hard as Jack's, her confidence in every move, like Jack's, and with fingers bound in Anne's hair, drew Anne to her lips and kissed with love, moving her free hand across Anne's back and pulling her so that their hips locked. For a long moment they let the feeling wash over them, emotion raw and floating, then Anne backed away. "Something's missing," she said quietly. "For me."

"And for me. But in truth, you are my first kiss since I lost my husband."

"I am missing Jack's hardness between my legs. Do ye understand?"

"Aye. I understand," she nodded. "Friends, Anne?"

"To the death."

And both laughed and almost cried, for they knew the truth of the risks they took.

Chapter Twenty-four

Over the next days Anne and Mary were never apart, and there was a great deal of muttering among the crew, interspersed by great silences, when Anne and Mark passed together. A tension was building throughout the ship and the men eyed Jack warily to see what he would do, for surely, he could not be blind to the love Anne and Mark had for each other. The two were inseparable and never stopped talking although no one ever heard their words. In the late afternoon they could be seen in a quiet corner near the bowsprit where they had privacy, and from the look on their impassioned faces, the talk was deep, and once, one of the men swore he saw Anne wipe away a tear.

"I was born second of my mother. I'd a brother who'd come before me, but 'e died when I was but a wee babe. My mother was married to a sailor, and some dozen or so months after 'e left port, I was born. You see? Loneliness can be a terrible thing, can it not? And me mum was a young woman. Alone for the long months of a sea voyage. Why, t' be touched . . . indeed, to be a woman . . . well, the need must 'ave been great. And from what I've seen of my good companions, I don't believe the man was any less active in whatever port 'e 'appened t' drop anchor." Mary looked over the bowsprit and out to sea. "In honesty, there was a time when I condemned 'er. But life has taught me that there are things one must do."

"Mary," and Anne placed a hand on her shoulder, "my own parents were not the original of the marriage. My father left his wife for my mother and moved to Charles Town. But, oh, if you could have known my mother. She was more lady than any I have met."

"And you've met a few, have ye not? For you yourself are a lady born and bred."

"Only when I remember to be," and a gleam filled Anne's eye. "But to fit in amongst the crew . . ."

"And t' act the man. Aye, I know what it takes. Some hardening of speech and attitude. It was not always so with me, Anne. There was a time when I was soft and a woman and 'appy t' be so. But, I go ahead o' me story."

"Here now, I'll have it all."

"Aye, that ye shall. I was too young t' remember the words, but I do remember the tears, even though I could just walk. Mum cried for she'd 'ad news that 'er husband 'ad perished at sea." Mary sighed hard, and shook her head. "I remember because it was the first I'd been away from 'er and I wailed meself. You see, she 'id me with a neighbor whilst the man's mother came for a visit t' see the grandson. Oh, I suppose she liked the lad well enough, for she decided t' send money each month for 'is upkeep. But," and she shrugged, that same shrug Anne had come to know about the table of the Ship and Shore as men and women accepted their lot, "the boy died shortly afterwards, and t' keep the money comin', Mum dressed me as a lad and gave it out that I was the dead son. I'd no idea I was dressed as a boy, you understand. I simply did those things any wee child does. But we were found out, and the money dried up. Still, me mum 'ad set her course, and she already knew we could do much better if I was a lad, so's a lad I stayed."

The sea was beginning to roll, the pitch of the ship to strengthen, and Mary glanced east to see the approaching weather. "Storm's comin'. Captain'll want the sails furled."

Anne followed her gaze, absently remembering the dresses she had worn as a child, miniature versions of those clothes her mother and the women of her station had worn.

"Aye. We'll be gettin' wet soon," she said. "But your story."

"Well, then. I suppose I was about four or five when I began to ask questions. I'd been given strict rules about wha'

I was t' do and not do and about 'ow I was t' toilet. Wha' I was t' say. And I noticed. I knew what was a girl and a boy and 'ere Mum was tellin' me t' say I was a lad."

"And if you were to eat, ye were to say what she taught you. True?"

The wind came up and Fetherston barked an order, but so involved were the women that they kept to their seats, while the crew who climbed topside eyed them with more than a little disgust.

"When I was seven I became footboy to a French woman living in London. My job was t' hold t' the back of 'er carriage, and when it stopped, I was t' step right off t' open 'er door and put down the footstool. A mean one she was. But by now I knew my place. I knew my class and my place and somethin' of 'ow the world worked, and I knew 'ow t' 'old me 'ead down and say, 'Yes, ma'am' and 'Yes, sir'. That's the trick, ain't it? Keepin' your 'ead down and out o' sight, but always lookin' around t' see the way t' break through."

Mary remembered and thought to speak of the insufferable—a child of not more than seven years of age, the rhythmic sounds of the carriage wheels rolling along cobbled streets, her head nodding sleepily with the early morning hour, for her mistress kept a late night. Only the sudden quiet roused her from the slumber into which she had slipped, arm locked into the handrail, and close behind, the harsh voice of the coachman urging her to the door and footstool of the vehicle.

"I do not intend to wait for your favor," the lady had said, with more than a little irritation, barely casting Mary a glance. She released the small hand held to steady her trip down the carriage steps, and turned to the driver, "See to it."

"Aye, ma'am," and the driver tipped his tricorner hat, nodding his head.

When the woman had flounced away up the steps of the great house to her bed, the coachman had turned to Mary, and with his long whip had lashed the boy, again and again

. . . and again . . . until he heard the pitiful cries and knew he had made his point, and indeed, Mary had learned to keep her head down.

"Then when you do catch a glimpse o' opportunity," she continued, "you've got t' run like hell toward it, anything that gives you a better chance. Like the offer the captain made t' me. I just ran t' it."

"Aye, Jack's a fine one."

"And you've true feelings for 'im?"

"We . . . we buried a child recently, and the two of us, we're not back yet. Not to bein' ourselves. I wonder if we will ever be right again, or if the bite the sadness has taken from our souls is too large for repair."

The ship dipped and the bow cut water through a sea that had begun to roil white caps. Spray broke across the bow, and the timbers strained and sang, while the boat danced to the pitch of gathering waves.

Mary absently rubbed salt water off her arm, thoughtful, then said softly. "My Edward was such a fine, good man. And when 'e looked at me, there was no tomorrow and no yesterday, just the love in his eyes. You see, there was a winter o' ice and snow and a fever, and even though I tried everything, well, it wasn't enough."

"No, Mary, no. Do not say it. I know you did all you could and certainly enough." And she thought to how she had prayed for little John.

"Anne, do ye think so? I tried, I did try."

An adult at nine years, knowing what she must do, she had finally escaped the lady and her carriage. No longer able to bear the meager food, the insults, and the whippings, she'd run straight to the docks on the quay, believing a ship could take her far away from torment and the reproach of a mother who would no longer receive the poor pence of her wages.

But once on ship, reality crowded into her world, and she hardened to meet the challenges of each new day. The life to which she had escaped was perhaps worse than the one she had left behind. The food was not only small, but ridden with weevils, the thirst acute, for water was hoarded against unknown disaster, the men rough and teasing and once or twice a hand caressed her buttocks, and she learned to slap hard and heavy with anything within reach until she was left alone. Although the lash was not for her own back, the cat knew many, and it was more than a dozen men she'd tended, smearing ointment on skin open and raw. The captain's word was law, the work hard, physical, the pay poor, and she was hard-pressed to send money home. Yet she grew in strength, muscled and firm in body and spirit, and again, blended into the background, unobtrusive, quiet, calling no undue attention to herself.

At fourteen she jumped ship in Dover and made straight for the army, for she needed wages and her choice was between factory and soldiering. The factory would be a prison, a living death for one accustomed to the boundless sea. She chose open air, and as a man, felt a new camaraderie, a sense of her worth and power, the musket in her arms the great equalizer. Her arms were strong after a life of lifting sails and yardarms, of tying off halyards, of swabbing and polishing, of loading cannon and carrying powder, and she had learned the swordplay that would save her life in meeting pirate or enemy, for the world was at war.

At eighteen years she transferred to the cavalry and right glad was her captain to have her, for she was fearless, able, and uncomplaining, taking on tasks others avoided, positioning herself in the front line of battle, wielding horse and saber. Close to the men, but reserved, she held their respect, and more than one officer had asked if she would join their ranks. Regretfully, Mary had shaken her head. Without the money to purchase her commission, she had to remain in her place.

In the spring of 1716 Edward joined the company. One look and Mary was smitten, and for the first time in her life, was out of control, tongue-tied, her emotions twisted. With some maneuvering, she managed to partner with him to share a two-man tent. Then came the night, a single candle stub aglow, when Mary made her choice. The sound of Edward's movements in the small space pierced the silence, while her eyes never left his body.

Edward turned to her with some discomfort. "What is it, Mark? Is there something you know about tomorrow's fight that I do not?"

Mary weighed her future, her answer the tipping point, a crossroads. Whatever she answered, her life would never be the same, but would follow a different path.

"There is something I know," she finally answered. "But it has naught t' do with tomorrow's engagement."

Edward sat down on the camp cot and regarded her face, thoughts bouncing between them, everything said without words. Mary slid to the floor, her arms on his legs.

"Easy," he whispered.

"Can ye feel it?" she whispered.

"I cannot," he said coldly, a hint of regret in his voice. "I care for you and I am glad you're in this company. In battle there's no one I'd rather 'ave by my side. But this . . . I cannot do." And he pushed her arms off his legs.

In answer, Mary began to undo the buttons of her jacket. Edward made to rise, to leave the tent.

"Wait!" she cried. "Look upon this . . . my secret, Edward." And she pulled back the front of her jacket to reveal the breasts that spoke her true sex. "I am a woman. Come to the army t' support myself. That is all. Yet, it seems, I am besotted and can no longer keep my own counsel."

Edward closed his eyes, swayed, then looked again with astonishment, "And what shall I call you? Tell me your true name."

"Mary," she answered softly.

"Mary," he repeated, then tenderly reached out to touch her cheek, pulled the hat from her head, and let down her hair. "Dear God, Mary, I hardly know what to say."

"Would . . . would ye 'ave me?" she asked with some

trepidation, for no one had loved her before, not for herself, for the person who was Mary.

"Have you?" he murmured, tracing the length of her jaw, her neck, moving slowly to her chest, down to the tip of her nipple, then suddenly, hungrily, taking her breast in his hand. "Aye," his voice was husky, "I'll have you, and I'll have you now, if ye will."

Mary shook her head. "No, Edward. I give you my secret because I'll 'ave it a secret no longer. If ye'll 'ave me, it will not be for now, but for all the tomorrows and everyone will know our love. What say ye? Will ye wed?"

He grinned, scooping her up in his arms, the better to feel her breasts against his chest, and his laugh was light and his lust had risen. "Wed? To say true, I've no objections."

But turning her head from his mouth, from lips hard with desire, she pushed him away so that she might look once more into the depths of his eyes. "Now, solemnly plight me your troth. For then we shall be married in all but ceremony."

With her demand he stood very still, all the laughter gone from his face, for at last, he understood her true purpose.

"Will ye 'ave me, Edward?"

A long while passed, while Mary waited desperate, for she had gambled much.

Edward thought to her strengths and integrity, believed that to have them in a wife might be just the thing. Where else would he find someone with Mary's qualities and one who loved him? With all solemnity, he had taken to his knees before her. "I do solemnly swear my love and fidelity. Until death do us part."

"And I," Mary returned, kneeling beside him, "I do solemnly pledge my love and fidelity. Until death do us part."

Then she had removed the jacket, shirt, and trousers, and for the first time had let a man gaze upon her body, tight and hard and scarred as any soldier's or seaman's was.

"I am a virgin," she whispered.

And Edward had trembled.

"Oh, Anne, I did try. And although I loved 'im with every part of my body and soul, it t'weren't enough," Mary moaned, despair thick in her voice. "I could not save 'im."

"I tell you it was enough!" Anne cried quietly. "You did all you could. As I did with my John!" and for the first time believed the truth of it. "But it wasn't up to us. God's choice, for certes! I've no doubt that this short time on earth will bring us to everlasting happiness with each other when our own time comes."

"Do ye truly think so? I've told this t' nary a soul, but, Anne, I feel as if I failed my husband. Oh, God, I could not save 'im!"

"Mary, Mary . . ."

If all eyes had not been upon them, they would have held each other to lessen the grief, and even as Anne cried, the ship slipped into rain.

So it went for several days, Mary and Anne sharing their lives, knowing their differences, one poor, the other privileged, but beyond all, one of mind and heart and understanding the other.

Jack threw the tankard across the cabin, his roar heard from stem to stern, and none was brave enough to come near. Drink had been poured into his gullet right from the bottle since early morning, and all aboard tread gently. For the past days the captain had disintegrated into a drunken stupor, his temperament lethal, a raging green jealousy stinging him, for he believed himself cuckolded. Now Anne stood before him, her own voice raised in disgust, and the shouting enough so that several of the crew looked to Mark and thought him lucky to live through the day.

"I'll slit his throat, I will, I swear it, Anne! Have you no honor? You are my wife, and I've foresworn all others for you. Hard enough to do, but you bid me do so on our firs' night."

"Oh, and those months you were away while I was in Cuba," she cried, her voice heavy with sarcasm, "you will swear that you were celibate?"

"Well . . . almos' . . . but it was a different thing. You were not there . . . and if you had been, why, your belly was large and in the way . . ."

"I have not cuckolded you," she screamed, "but do not play the hypocrite with me. I'll have none of it. How dare you expect me to be that which you cannot be! And do not try to tell me that because I am a woman, I must have a different set of rules, for God knows, I have earned my place as an equal. I am a crew member and entitled to all the privileges of any man here."

"While you are on board ship, I am your captain. You swore to that as well."

"By the Code, you are only my captain as long as I say you are!"

"And I tell you that I will have that man's gizzard!" Jack bellowed and reached for her.

"Let me go. I will come to you willingly or not at all, do you hear?" But he had her hard and fast, his hands clumsy, his breath foul, tearing away her blouse, ripping it from her shoulders, her breasts his, and lowering his face to them.

"Damn you, Jack, as if I have many clothes or the means to replace them. Let me go!"

She felt the shift in her position, him pushing her back to the bed with one arm, while with the other, he tried undoing his breeches, already spreading her legs with his knee.

"If you rape me, Jack, I'll kill you in your sleep! Worse, I'll never come to you again. Can you hear me through that drunken head of yours? Let . . . me . . . go!"

Releasing his hold, the better to undo his breeches with two hands, Anne was able to push, and unsteady, he stumbled back. Instantly, she was on her feet, a kick to his groin, and she reached for her sword. Jack crashed to his knees, doubled over, the pain making its way to his brain even in his stupor.

"Now we will talk," Anne told him, holding the sword to keep him at a distance and watching as he struggled to stand, only to fall again.

"Anne," he moaned, "there was no need . . ."

"You know, and I know, there was need. God knows I love you, Jack, but it's time we talked. You've been crazy of late. Now listen to me. First there's the drink mornin' to night. Using John's death as an excuse is wearin' thin. He wouldn't want to see you as you are now."

"The lad would be joinin' me."

"Oh, no, Jack. If you loved him, the lad would be about his books."

Suddenly, there were tears, and Anne thought her heart might break for she had never seen Jack cry in sorrow. On his knees, he looked at her imploringly. "You're right, you're right. He should be about his lessons, and he should have the home we would have given him. That's what rankles so much, that you go to that man whilst I mourn our son."

"Do ye think I am without sorrow? It's Mark that lets me speak of him, for I know your sadness and would not burden you. I had thought to leave you to the runnin' o' the ship, but . . ."

A knock at the door startled them, for who in their right mind would interrupt Jack in a rage.

Anne pulled up the ripped shirt and wrapped it around as best she could, still keeping an eye to her sword, for she was uncertain of too many things. Opening the door, she gasped, because Mark stood there.

"I have something t' confess, Captain. May I come in?" Without answer, Mark stepped in and closed the door behind.

"I'll rip out your tongue, you pox-ridden, scurvy excuse for a man," Jack screamed hoarsely, rising from where he knelt on the floor and making towards him, "if you've come to say that Anne is yours!"

In answer Mark quickly removed hat, belt, sword and pistol, and before an astonished Jack, unbuttoned his shirt, holding it open so that Jack might see breasts.

"This is what is taking the time of Mistress Anne. The friendship of another woman on board. And an understandin' of what must be faced by any woman who needs t' care for 'erself in a world that threatens t' knock 'er down for 'er sex. You see, Captain, I spent years as a foot soldier and in the cavalry dressed as a man so that I might make me livelihood. And I was not alone. There's many a women in the army, and some at sea, who hide their sex so's they might 'ave the life they choose and the coin t' pay for it."

Jack stunned, perhaps for the first time in his life beyond speech, fell to his knees upon the floor again, the wind taken out of his sails, while all on deck waited for the screams and curses, and were even more terrified when none came.

"Dear God," he whispered, "why didn't you tell me. Why let me believe . . ."

"It was not my secret to share," Anne told him, "and you needed to trust that I would do the right thing. But I see that you have judged me by your own standards, by those things you would do. It pains me, for they are not my standards."

Jack stood then, ashen and reeling. "What can I say, Anne? I am a man and a pirate and I have a certain way of life." Then, as if a new idea struck, he began to smile, "But this is a fine piece of luck. Two women in my cabin and both with bared breasts."

"Oh, Jack," Anne sighed.

"Beggin' your pardon, sir, but I'll 'ave no relations unless there's love. I've only been with my husband before 'e died, God rest his soul. And I'll wait for love again before I give myself. I'm no loose whore."

"How is it you came to be on the Dutchman, Mark . . . or . . ."

"Mary, sir."

"Aye. Mary. How come you to be here? A woman . . ."

And so Mary spent the next hour telling him of her experience on ship as a lad, how she ran powder to the gunners, how she'd made as good a foot soldier and cavalryman as a sailor, but could move no further in the ranks without buying her commission.

"But, as luck would 'ave it, I fell in love . . ."

And here Mary smiled, her eyes faraway, remembering the day she and Edward had told the regiment their story. The troop had had a great laugh and put together a fund, enough to buy them a small inn, the Three Horseshoes in the Dutch country.

"Strike me, if them was not happy days. The smell o' food and tobacco fillin' the great room and Edward and me workin' side by side. Tankards flowin' and laughter and song amongst all those soldiers so far from home. Well, then the illness . . ." and she cleared her throat. "After 'e was gone, it was just me t' do it all, but the fun was out o' it, you see. Little by little the soldiers disappeared with the war's end, and I was left with debts and a failing business. I sold the inn then, paid me debts, and joined up with the army again. When I got near t' sea, I took ship on the Dutchman you just met up with. That's me story in a nutshell, captain."

Jack looked from Anne to Mary and saw no competition for Anne's affections, or at least, not the part that really mattered to him. He thought to ask once again if they might not consider a romp in his bed together, but then thought the better of it, for Anne still stood to one side, sword in hand.

"My apologies, Mary. All right, Anne, put the blade away. The shock of it all has sobered me, perhaps too much."

"They'll be no more drinkin' today," she declared. "The ship needs care and the men are asking where we're sailin' and what prize we're to be takin'."

"Indeed. Call Master Fetherston to me and we'll have council. Ask Mr. Corner, the quartermaster, to come along as well."

"And I think you'll be needin' the gunner, John Howell."

"You're right. It's time to get back to business." He turned to Mary. "Anne wears skirts until battle. I offer you the opportunity to do the same. I've seen your work and I've seen you fight. You can stay aboard and be your own female self if you like."

"No, Captain," Mary smiled. "I thank 'e, but I'll have you keep my secret. For in it lies my freedom."

Yet for once Mary's hidden ambiguity could not be concealed, for somehow, within hours, every member of the crew knew the nature of her sex. The worthy seaman and swordsman who had held even against Jack Rackham, was a woman named Mary Read.

Then was the jealousy so profound as to be unspeakable. For there had been an hour of quiet in the captain's cabin, the two women alone with him, and what a great unfairness that the captain should have not one, but two, opportunities for pleasure, whilst they had only the dream of putting in to port.

Chapter Twenty-five

The *Lady Anne* sailed north along the Atlantic Seaboard with a full load of pirated goods stowed below decks and a large crew ready to take a share as soon as the goods were sold. On the coast of the Carolinas near Charles Town, Jack sent two emissaries ashore—one with a letter to the governor of New Providence asking for a pardon, and one to a merchant who would take the cargo in the hold. To his great relief, the cargo sold at a fine price, shares were distributed, and the plan was proclaimed. Any man wanting a pardon could sail on to New Providence and start anew with his earnings, on condition that the hoped for pardon would be granted. Those who wanted to continue in the pirate life, had only to wait for another ship and the opportunity would present itself.

Not many days later, word came. Governor Rogers would indeed grant the pardon, if Jack would surrender his ship. The *Lady Anne* would be exchanged for the *Curlew* he had taken in port, and the captain of said vessel, waited anxiously for word that Jack would agree to the transfer.

"Can they not buy the ship from us, Jack," Anne asked. "We could use the money to set up again."

"Like we bought the ship we took?" he laughed. "No, Anne, we'll have to give her up, if you've a mind to go ashore."

"Do we have enough for another ship?"

"Aye, if we want one. We can hire out to a merchant company and in time, we'll get your land on the river."

"All right, I am for it, for we have a fine crew. Mary included." Then she thought, "What about the flogging? Is the governor's order still in effect?"

"Indeed not. It's part of the amnesty. I would have it no other way."

Anne laid her head against his chest and he put his arms around her. The simple pleasure of his touch caused her to sigh deeply. "I believe we might actually have a future."

What she did not say, was that her courses were missed, her breasts tender, her stomach queasy in the morning. She was almost assuredly pregnant and even knew the night the babe began to grow.

"Then we are off to New Providence on the tide," he said softly. "The sooner we arrive, the sooner we see where we stand."

New Providence was like an old friend, and it was with a great deal of joy that Anne learned Bonny had not been seen since she'd left with the *Curlew*. It gave her no pleasure to hear him laughed at in the taverns for his cowardice, and it was with some surprise that she heard the songs sung about herself and heard tales she could scarce believe, most told to her before the storyteller realized who she was—she'd stabbed and killed a serving maid in her house, beaten a man who'd tried to rape her within an inch of his life, she was wild in combat, the 'hell cat', and a sorceress, a dangerous claim, for she trapped the men who loved her. She was wanton, having many lovers, and deep into drink, cursing and swearing like any man. Even Captain Jack Rackham, handsome, affable, the pride of many a tavern, the 'Terror of the Caribbean', had fallen victim to her spell.

"'Terror'? Whatever can they mean?" Anne laughed. "He is a lamb among wolves!"

Mary shrugged, drank from her tankard, and smiled over the rim, for Mary knew, as did Anne, what the rumors were about. Simple jealously, it was. That Anne could make her own way at sea, had chosen Jack as an equal, fulfilled her duties aboard ship, and had her own money without asking a man for it. Strength, power, choice, these were things the gossipers could not understand. Meekness, feigned innocence, constricted clothing, and complete subjugation to the politics of men, was the way of the day. Had not Anne spoken of how her father had complete say over where she married? Those women who did not fit the mold, who lived on the fringe, were undone, outcast, as was Anne, considered whores, insane at best, witches at worst.

"Only in time o' warfare," Mary told her, "when a woman can be of service t' do the dangerous jobs of spyin' or carryin' important information simply because of 'er sex, then do men congratulate 'er. But when the conflict is over, they'll 'ave back their power. Why, do you suppose?"

"Who knows?" Anne shrugged. "But I have come to understand that it is we who are powerful, Mary." For she was in the full throes of pregnancy and deeply felt the life she carried. "That we bleed from between our legs and can grow a child and give birth. That we nurture from our breasts. What can be more powerful than that?"

"True. The power of a man's different, ain't it? They control with force. With the strength of their bodies, the law and the prisons. What else 'ave they? They can compel us by their threats, while we must use all our skill and knowledge t' move the mountains they are." Tankard in hand, she tapped against Anne's cup, her eyes alight. "Unless, of course, like you and me, a woman can make things happen with a sword."

Anne and Jack received the governor's pardon and carefully put the paper in the sea chest. Then with some sadness, they vacated the *Lady Anne* with all their possessions and took a house on the sea with stuccoed walls and a red-tiled roof that made Anne homesick for the home that was her own in Cuba. At first the time passed quickly, for there was much to do in the cleaning and ordering of the home, and when it was done, Anne asked Jack to see to the possibility of a ship.

One he did find to his liking, the *William,* small, but adequate, and a vessel that could be traded up. Do what he could, Jack tried not to think like a pirate, but in the boarding of her for inspection, his thoughts went to how she must be remade, where to add guns, and how to clear below decks to make room for the large crew needed to board a prize.

Then he learned the price and was astonished to realize that the William was beyond their means.

Some weeks later, with home established, a ship considered, and most of the crew about their business, Jack came into the house one afternoon and sat in a chair. Anne was busy with the cook, the house in order, the pages of her harpsichord music strewn about the table, a book placed next to her chair. Anne, he could clearly see, was happy. Then he reached for a bottle as he had nothing else to do, and wondered at his life.

As he drank, he put his disquietude into words. He was a man of action and was best in the thick of it, every nerve and muscle straining to meet the challenge. For the last months they'd had one thought in mind, to get the governor's pardon and to make a new life free from the fear of the hangman's noose. But what life did he have, this sitting in a chair with nothing to do and no one to lead and worse, marooned on shore? The glimmer of an idea occurred to him that he was not ready to be a man with his memories and stories and the bemused and pitying glances of those who wondered at the truth of what he spoke. The thought sent such a shudder through his body that he feared it might affect his heart.

With hardened resolve, he knew who he was and what he had to do. Anything was better than a life of mediocrity, following laws made for the wealthy, by the wealthy, and determined to keep those without in their place. Servants must be had. Slaves must be had. Rising capitalism in the merchant class must be served. In a great mystic view of the future, he saw that the laws would squeeze the small man until he survived but did not live. In that moment he resolved he would be himself, whatever the cost, ply his own trade as a free man, and make his own laws with those of his brethren.

Without telling Anne he was leaving, he went in search of his crew.

Everyone who had known Mary aboard the *Lady Anne* watched her with interest. Dressed as a lad while on shore, she mooned about the tavern with a love sickness that would have been amusing if not for the severity of it. Mary herself recognized the symptoms, the same as those she had felt for her Edward many years past. At that time she could think of nothing but him, longing for his presence, never removing far from his side. In battle she had gone before him, certain her own courage and skill would make the difference in a fight as to whether he would live or die. She made sure to lead the way in charge and hand-to-hand fight, to stand before him and take what blows she could, the better to protect the man, for the thought of his death was more frightening than the sabers and pikes of the enemy.

And like her first love, the man of her affections was the last to realize her desire.

John Howell, master gunner, had first caught her eye during a fight. Mary had brought powder to the cannons, moving from stores to cannon quickly, a job she knew well, and there she had watched him, his attendance to detail and knowledge of the ship, the feel of it as it rolled with the wave, placing his shot with precision. The scar over his eye was white at most times, but in the heat of battle, she had watched it redden. In the watching, she had noted the many ways his handsome face changed color with his emotion, and after that, well, she found that indeed his face was handsome. On the day he had looked into her eyes with the thrill of danger everywhere around them and praised her for her resolve and work, then had smiled with white teeth in a powder-blackened face, her heart had leapt unexpectedly, and she was lost.

Today she sat at table with him and others, a little apart and too silent, listening to the tales told, her eyes naked and lovelorn, while the men around wondered when she would declare for the man.

"Here now," said one of the crewmen, "looks like there's

plenty ashore what's given up on piracy."

"Aye," agreed another, "and it's rough seas for sure. What we needs is all provided on board, and always the hope of gettin' more. But here, there's a price for everything. And soon the coin runs out with no prospects."

"You could sign on a merchant."

"The wages is small, and the food worse than we've known. And ye well know the lash is always at hand. Damn it all, I'm no of a mind to put gold in the purse o' the ship owner with only a few farthings in me own pocket for m' labor."

"Him," John nodded in the direction of a man who sat near. "Didn't he sail with Blackbeard?"

At that moment the man looked up and gazed with red and watering eyes upon John's glance, then, his speech slurred, yelled toward him, "What in Christ's name do ye think you're lookin' at? Put yer damned eyes on somethin' else or you'll have a taste o' m' blade!"

"Enough!" Mary stood and shouted. "Ye'll hold yer tongue, ye scurvy son of a cur. Devil take your eyes if you don't mind your own manners and your own plate!"

"Does the lad fight for you?" the man leered at John.

To which John was on his feet in an instant, only to be met with, "Hold. You're a fine man with a cannon, John, but not with sword. I'll shut 'is mouth for 'im."

John turned to her, his scar dangerously red. "Will ye shame me?" he muttered under his breath. "We all know what you are. Will ye have the crew say I need a woman to fight my battles?"

"My name is Tom Needham." The man rose unsteadily to his feet. "Who is it I will fight?"

"There's no reason to fight any man," a voice called from the doorway, "for you've had much to drink and I think you'll be wantin' to keep your life another day."

All eyes turned to the voice they knew well. Jack Rackham stood at the entrance, and the cold steeliness of his tone caused every man to pause. Even Tom stepped back a foot.

"Cap'n Rackham," the man managed, "I've heard you're lookin' for a ship. I'm a good seaman and I've a mind to sign on. I mus' take to sea." Lifting unsteady hands, he gestured to the space around him. "I've got to get out of here."

For his honesty, Jack took pity on him. "I'll post when we're signin' on."

"Thank 'e, Cap'n," he lifted a hand in a form of salute, suggesting his military beginnings. "Thank 'e."

Jack sat down at the table and called for rum and many were the glances that passed among those present, for the captain had not been drinking hard rum of late.

"Where's Fetherston?" he asked when he had their full attention. "It is time we talked."

"Oh, Jack, are ye daft? The governor will nae pardon you a third time! Come to your senses! We're close to realizin' our dreams!"

"How do ye think we'll finance these dreams, Anne? The *William* is beyond our means. Let us go back to pirating a bit longer and we'll get the money we need."

"Only in that she is not the *Lady Anne* or the *Curlew*. We could find something else, smaller perhaps, but . . ." and she stopped dead in her thought, as if slapped. "But truth be told, they're my dreams, aren't they? You'll never quit piracy. It'll always be one excuse after another. You . . . you can't quit."

"What I would do . . . have done . . . is for you, so that you can have your house and the horses and the harpsichord."

Stunned, Anne said quietly, "Those are things, Jack, and they have naught to do with what is real. But . . . I cannot ask it of you. I cannot ask that you live the life I have in mind if it's not the life you want. We have only the time God has given us, and the greatest part of it is our freedom to choose how we want to spend it. You must choose the life only you can live."

"Then come with me, Anne, come back to sea!" he cried.

"To feel the wind again, and to sleep or eat when we are hungry, to drink with the lads and play at cards, to dance to music on the deck!"

"To hide in the bays and inlets," she answered sadly, "to cruise a town to see if there's a warship in port before buying goods. To be wary of every ship at sea. To careen a vessel on some far off bit of sand for we cannot bring her into port . . . and wonder when they will take us . . . when they will hang you . . ."

"Don't say it!" he said, taking her shoulders. "Words have a power and it will never happen. Do ye hear, Anne? It will never happen."

"Jack," and she was hard pressed to keep her voice level, "it's not the words. There's no magic to it. It's simple common sense. There's fewer pirates now than before, for most have taken the governor's pardon. And them that still sail, they're hangin' them. One by one. Mass executions. Will ye not take a house with a garden of flowers and horses in the pasture and a river that leads to the sea?"

"We cannot have it without money. And to get it, we have to become one of them, like Hornigold who ate at the governor's table. I won't have it. I won't turn in those men who gave me their loyalty. They have come to me already asking for money and it's not all for women and drink. If I retire what will become of them?"

"They will have to make their way in the world just as you or I. You cannot be responsible for the world, even though your heart is large enough to hold it. But what you've said is only part of it. Tell me truly, how bad is your need to stand on deck and feel the thrill that rushes through your veins just before you swing over, sword in hand?"

Jack stiffened. "I'll only ask once, Anne, are ye with me? For I will do my job."

To think of Jack without her was to pity him, for without her, what was he but a man of honor among a band of thieves. His world would be the dregs of the Caribbean and she knew he would drink away his sadness. But it was more than pity that bound her to him, for he had a heart of tenderness, and he loved her beyond the moon and thought her a beauty as no man ever would. In his own world he was a lord, a leader of men with a strength of spirit that was heroic, and after all was said and done, for whatever reason, she was his, body and soul. The thought of breaking with him was to walk ghostlike upon the earth, half a being. And, he did not yet know, but she carried his child. Nor could she tell him, for if she did, she'd be put ashore without him to give birth alone, crying his name, like once before.

"Then so be it, Jack. We will follow this path wherever it may lead. But when we get to the end of it, I expect you to stand with your head up . . . whatever happens . . . with pride and dignity. Are we agreed?"

"Aye."

"I'll not have you moanin' and dreamin' about what might have been. I mean it. Will ye stand on this decision?"

"Aye. Wherever the road leads."

"All right," she nodded. "All right."

"Then we are off, and Mary with us, and most of the crew!" His excitement was tangible and he grabbed her and held her dear. "The *William* is in the harbor. We have but to take her."

A few days later, in the dead of night, Jack boarded stealthily with his crew, ordered the anchor hoisted, and by morning was away and commanding the ship.

When Governor Rogers heard what had happened, his fury knew no bounds, and his first task after his fit of outrage, was to send messages to authorities in every part of the Caribbean and Atlantic seaboard with news that the 'Terror of the Caribbean' was again at sea.

Chapter Twenty-six

The *William* sailed south, straight to the Caribbean, and once there wasted no time in flying the pirate flag. On the first three days of September no less than seven fishing vessels were seized, their crew threatened, their hauls confiscated, tackle rolled and taken aboard, strongboxes emptied, and anything of value seized.

In each encounter Anne took a line over the side and played her part, yelling and threatening in her man's breeches, but afterwards, was quiet, for while Jack drank and made merry with the crew, she trembled quietly for the secret she held within her womb. If Jack knew she fought with the babe at risk, great would be his anger. But she had come along to be at his side, and to stay there she had to be crewman and fight with the rest. And as much as she tried, she could not push away some intuition that their time was running short. Could Jack not see that they had precious few places left to go?

She stood alone at the bowsprit on the evening of the third week, staring at the stars, listening to the music of hand organ and pipe drifting up from the crew's quarters, trying to come to terms with her confusion. Once she had believed that these men had no choice in their thievery, but that line of argument was wearing thin. Each raid forced her to consider the harm she caused, the men killed, fortunes lost, dreams shattered. Niggling at her thoughts was the sense that what she did was wrong, yet she was torn by those who also stole and yet called themselves authority, those who controlled the armies and navies, the courts and prisons, who sailed the slavers and thought the common man expendable. On leaving New Providence she had believed that once at sea, Jack would understand how small the world of the ship could become if he had to live in fear of capture. But she saw that it was no good, for she heard his rich voice and knew this was the life he loved, and regardless the dangers, the life he would have.

Without turning, she sensed him behind, felt his arms encircle her.

"Where is your heart tonight, my Anne?"

"In the mystery of it all, dear Jack."

"Do you regret coming away with me?"

"In truth, I cannot imagine life without you. But, I fear."

"Sh-h. We shall not say it, nor speak it."

The glow of a single lantern gave outline and shadow to her body, and he looked deep into her face in the dim light, trying to read what lay hidden. Below decks the music was gay and the voices loud, yet a quiet surrounded the space where they stood.

"Kiss me, Anne. Tell me you are happy."

"I am happy, but . . ."

"Sh-h. A kiss, my heart."

His lips met hers with such tenderness that she felt tears fill her eyes, unexpected, and knew they coursed down her cheeks.

"Here now," he said, "what's this?" And he brushed a drop from her face.

"My happiness, Jack. Surely, my happiness."

"I've not known you t' cry, Anne. Only once. After John left us. What is it?"

How could she tell him of the new child, of the fears of his arrest, the hopefulness of a life they had foregone? Instead, she answered, "Let me feel your lips again."

"Where?" he grinned.

"Why, Jack, you've not had a problem deciding ever before."

"Ah, my choice is it? Then I will start here," he touched her mouth with his fingers. "I don't believe we've ever made love on deck, have we?"

"Are ye so drunk that ye cannot remember?"

In answer he pulled the forward staysail yard a little higher for privacy. "They're all below."

"Jack, I don't think . . ." she whispered, never believing he was serious.

But this was why she loved him, the surprise of him, the knowing that one day would always be different from the last. His eyes were soft, the blue even deeper in the dim night, his smile a flash of white, and as he bent to her and pressed his lips to hers again, she closed her eyes to take in the whole sense of him—his body like her own skin, the gentle probing of his tongue to create the old flame, immediate and demanding, the smell and taste of his skin, salty, like the very sea itself, his hands reaching into her shirt, her breasts larger and more firm, pressing against his hands—filling her spirit with all that he was, so that she took deep breaths with her mouth against his.

"Oh, Jack," she moaned.

"I will insist on quiet," he murmured. "I'll not share you with the crew."

"Then let us hear your own silence," she whispered in return, pulling at the belt of his breeches and releasing him from confinement. "Sh-h. I'll not be doin' this for the whole crew."

"No," and he took her by the arms. "But I'll be havin' you now, all to myself. Turn around."

"No, Jack," she answered quietly, "I'll see the lust in your eyes and know the wanting of me."

"You'll see the bottom of my soul, is what you'll see. For truly, Anne, no man ever loved as I love you."

He lay her down upon sailcloth and lifted her skirts, his own breeches just past his knees, but they knew their own fit, and the heat of her caused him to close his eyes for a moment, then open them once again as promised. Close they held their gazes, moved together, and what they saw in each other carried them to a world apart. When they had finished and he lay atop her, moving gently to draw out every last sense of ecstasy, he whispered, "The stars give witness to my troth,

Anne, for never shall I know such bliss. You are my entire heart, now and always."

"As you are mine."

Three leagues off the island of Hispaniola, just after dawn, Jack heard the cry, "A sail! A sail!" and went on deck with his spyglass.

"Aye, Mr. Fetherston," he told his first mate, "a sail indeed. Let's come closer and get a better look at her."

"She turns, Captain. She'll away from us."

"Then all hands on deck and put on every inch of cloth we have. If she runs she has something worth keeping."

"Shall we hoist the black flag?"

"Not yet. Let me get the lay of her first."

The *William* gave chase through the morning hours until Jack cried, "Bless my soul, Mr. Fetherston. There's not one, but two sails, and they sail close together for protection, but here . . . yes, the first is armed, looks like, eight guns, I believe. I can never understand why the merchants carry guns. They generally lay down as soon as we run up the black flag, and the weight not only slows them in the water, but takes valuable cargo space. And yes, the other is a sloop as well. What do you say, Mr. Fetherston, ready to board two ships?"

"At your command, Captain."

"Then every man to his post, weapons around, and guns at the ready, for we're coming up fast. A single broadside should stop them."

Jack slipped down below decks to talk to Anne who slept on his bed.

"Anne," he shook her gently, for she had seemed unwell of late, tired, and he worried. "There's a fat prize close by. Two actually." Then with some uncertainty added, "If you would rather not join the crew. . ."

"I'll not have the men thinkin' I'm soft," she told him roughly. "And Mary. Their fight is mine. We'll board." And she threw back the light blanket.

"All right," he said quietly, but more and more he did not like it. Just for a moment he thought how good it would be if Anne were at home in Cuba, in the house with its clean stucco walls and the garden in the back, and buried near the tall tree, their son.

"Captain," he heard Fetherston call from above. "Straight ahead."

"On deck then. I'll see you after the battle," he told her.

Once near the wheel of the ship all Jack's reservations disappeared, for the wind was with them, and the *William* had been careened before the taking of her, and was fast. He drew his cutlass and called, "Now! Go to't! Let them know us! Let fly the black flag!"

With the tip of his sword, he pointed to the master gunner. "Below decks, Mr. Howell, lay one across her bow! Stop her quick! We want the second ship as well!"

A great rush of activity claimed the gunners below. Cannon ports opened, wooden covers crashing against the side of the ship, and the high-pitched metallic whine of wheels sounded as the guns moved into place. Each gun was manned, six men to a cannon, powder and ball readied. On Howell's cry, flame to fuse, the cannon roared, the eight-pounders recoiling, while the men rushed to reload amidst deafening noise and short visibility from smoke and powder.

With some bit of surprise, the merchant returned the broadside in answer, and great was the flash of her cannon and the thunder of their belching. Some minutes passed before Jack was able to see that the sloop had swung away.

"Another volley, Mr. Howell! Tell her we've a mind to have her!"

Again a great rumble lit the air, fire hot from the mouths of the cannon, the shot taking the top of the merchant's main, wooden projectiles floating through air, and the screams of men impaled and burned carried across water.

"If she doesn't heave to, give her one below the water line, Mr. Howell! Stop 'er and let's be quick about it! We want the ship that sails away. Damn them for lily-livered cowards! They run to leave their companion to fight on her own!"

"Reload, mates, and be quick about it! We'll stop 'er with the next round, or we'll send 'em all to the devil!"

Close now, the crew of the *William* managed to toss a series of grenades. As the smoke drifted, Jack could see the faces of the sloop's crew, and filled with fear they were.

"Mr. Fetherston," he rejoiced, for the fight would be quick, and only one or two need die before the others lay down. "Bring her up along side! We'll secure her and leave a crew aboard while we chase down the other ship!"

Anne and Mary were in the first rush over the side, once again screaming like madmen in hopes of frightening the defenders, swinging at those who did not disarm quick enough, seizing weapons, and securing men. And once again, Anne moved in terror for placing the child in her womb at risk. Of a sudden she realized she was trapped, trapped in a life where she would never have anything but the thrill of theft and the prospect of death. Soon Jack would know about the child, for he knew her body. Only his drinking had preserved her this long, and his wits were not entirely about him. And then, where would that leave them?

"My compliments," Jack told the captain of the merchant. "A fine decision to surrender, saving unnecessary bloodshed. You'll have to forgive me, but I do rush, for your companion sails far out on the horizon and I would have her. A pity she did not defend with you, don't you think? Your brig, sir, where is it?"

"Below." He nodded to a young seaman, resignation heavy in his voice. "Show him where. Give him the keys."

"Mr. Fetherston, take the crew below and lock them up for the time being. The ship is yours. Investigate the hold and the captain's cabin. Be ready to bring the cargo aboard the *William* when we return."

"Aye, Captain. You 'eard 'im, lads. Below decks with you."

"My wounded . . ." the captain of the vessel began.

"Mr. Fetherston will see to it. Point out your surgeon."

Then Jack was off, a skeleton crew left behind, the majority of his force back on the *William,* chasing down the sail now barely visible on the horizon. Just at sunset he caught her and lucky too, for she could have done much maneuvering in the night. But she had watched her companion and knew the score and saw that the *William* was serious in her work. A single shot over her bow from the swivel gun, and she struck her colors.

Jack took them up alongside, grappling hooks holding the ships together, and to make sure there was no planned resistance, the crew went over with their terrible curses, frightened themselves at any boarding, and knowing that bluster was half the battle.

At the end of the day Jack and his sea robbers took stock of the two ships with their cargos of tobacco and pimento, their fishing tackle and cash. A number of new seamen threw in their lot with the men of the *William.* Those who chose not to come aboard, Jack released to continue on their way as usual, intact and unharmed except for the wounds of battle. And once again, Anne wondered where it would all end, for it could not continue.

The trouble had already started between John Howell and Tom Needham on shore, born of Tom's drunkenness and Mary's offer of protection. As the days moved forward, they continued to clash in small things, for Tom had signed on as seaman. Before long, the entire crew watched the growing enmity, in part, because Tom would not let up about Mary's unrestrained watchfulness.

Shortly before leaving port with the *William,* a word from George Fetherston had finally made John aware of what Mary was about. The man was torn, for how wonderful to have his own woman aboard, and true, when he looked into Mary's blue eyes, the world offered promise. Yet the fact that she was so capable when she wore breeches, threatened him.

The words she had used in the tavern, that he was good with cannon but not with sword, stuck in his craw and he could not swallow or spit out. In the end, lust won in his battle to decide, and he plighted his troth. After the couple had announced their intention to marry before the entire crew, Mary had exuberantly taken to his bed. Indeed, he was more than happy with Mary when she was a woman. Yet when she was seaman, it galled.

So it was that on a morning in early October with dark clouds forming large on the horizon and the threat of downpour in the air, Tom finally managed to cross the line by asking John if he sometimes wore a dress, as his wife wore trousers. At once swords were drawn and the clashing of steel brought Jack to the deck bellowing an order for them to belay.

"You'll take it ashore," he told them, feeling for his gunner and knowing him for many years. But he would not insult the man by protecting him as would his wife or Needham's jibe would be the worse. "You'll settle it once and for all. And if I see it aboard ship again, I'll settle it for the both of you. Understood?"

The men turned to each other. John nodded. "This afternoon. On the beach."

When Mary heard she was stricken with fear, for she'd no doubt that Tom was the more capable swordsman and would kill her John. Without thought, she made straight for Tom Needham and challenged him then and there.

"You're not afraid, are ye? Not of a woman, for certes," she goaded.

"All right, then," Tom rejoined, grinning. "Ashore. Now. You and me."

A boat was lowered, and when a few of the seafarers saw what was to happen and understood the quick secretiveness of it, they climbed aboard and made for the beach with the duelists.

"You've a minute to say your prayers, if ye have any," Mary told him when her feet hit sand.

Tom laughed and drew his sword. "Let's get this over

with so's I can go to work on your . . ." and here he paused and his inflection was clear, ". . . man."

With nary another thought Mary drew and went straight for him, hell-bent and with a mind to frighten him before the final thrust. She had no doubts as to his meanness, and knew he'd not lay off until John was dead, for he'd invested too much spite in the game. Three thrusts and as many parries, and she ran him through with such ease that those observing the drama on shore, gasped. Tom Needham died quickly, his heart pierced by blade, surprise and shock still on his face, only a few shuddering breaths and convulsing limbs before the end. A few were kind enough to bury the body in sand.

When all returned to ship and John heard reports as to what Mary had done, his anger knew no bounds and his humiliation was beyond repair. Once Mary understood that he meant for them to separate, no amount of pleading would do. Anne could have wept for her friend, for she saw that it was over. At some point Anne took her away to the captain's cabin and there she allowed Mary to cry out of sight of the crew, for Mary had never cried, not once, not ever.

"It's better that ye know now what kind of man he is," Anne said softly to her. "Let him go before the priest blesses the union."

"But, Anne, dear friend, you don't understand. I'm t' 'ave 'is child! And no one is t' know, promise me, no one!"

Anne, understanding exactly why she kept her secrets, answered, "I promise." Then took Mary in her arms to hold her.

The death of Tom Needham and the sadness that pervaded Mary's every move, served to unsettle the crew, for many were reminded of the brevity of life and fleeting happiness. Suddenly there was more drink to be had from early morning to late night. The ship roamed with some idleness, hugging the coastal waters of Jamaica and harassing small fisherman rather than rich merchant vessels farther out to sea.

"This cannot continue, Jack," Anne said fiercely, sickened by the stupidity of it. "We've been warned. Governor Lawes has lookouts on the hills and if he knows we are in warm waters, he'll be after us like lightning!"

"We shall not be here much longer. The hurricane season is almost over. Let us keep to the shallows for another week or two and then we can take to open sea again."

"I don't think it wise. I'm serious, Jack," she told him, unable to put into words the premonition she felt. But he would have none of it.

"Cap'n, a small boat dead ahead. Shall we have a look?" one of the men called.

Jack looked forward and saw a canoa, a small sloop with a single triangular mainsail and mizzen, out to fish, he supposed.

"Let the small ships be," Anne whispered. "Think on it. We take bread from the mouths of those who struggle!"

"We've not had a take in days. Let's see what she's about." Then turning to Mr. Fetherston, ordered, "Bring us up. No need for the flag, she's not going anywhere."

When they approached, they found that the fisherman was instead a fisherwoman, brown-skinned and bonnie, and the crew, at sea for some weeks, began to make rumblings with some real threat to her honor.

"No," Anne tried, "we'll not add rape to our charges. Are we to be animals, or true men who look to our work?"

But Jack had been drinking all the day and could not command, and the crew was beyond caring about tomorrow. When the woman finally realized that the ship held a pirate crew, her jaw slackened and fear was visible in her eyes.

"Hoist 'er up," John Howell cried, casting a glance at Mary. "Let's see what it feels like to have a woman on board!"

To which insult, the crew laughed.

Anne watched Mary go rigid with anger, and thought this to be good, for it was time she took her own back and gave as good as she got.

Strong hands pulled the terrified woman aboard, while others jumped down to the boat and started unloading the meager fishing tackle in her bottom.

"Here now, I'll just have a look at you," John cried taking the woman by the arms.

"Jack," Anne whispered, "if the men have her we'll surely hang! We've hurt no one deliberately to date, save what's been in true battle. We've not tortured or marooned or thrown captured crewmembers overboard. Think on it!"

"The man needs to get his balls back," Jack said, quietly slurring. "If it takes the woman to give 'em to 'im, then I say he takes 'er."

"It's against all honor! You can stop this," she continued to whisper fiercely. "What . . . what if it were me? About to be raped in front of a crew mad for a bit of cunny?"

"Hm-m. Something to think about. Why, the very th . . ."

And here Anne slapped him, the first and only time, hard, and full across the face, and even in his stupor, Jack came up swinging, but being unsteady, missed. Anne drew and knew she was in for it, for she had never seen him so furious. All these years thinking the day would come when she would test against him, had finally arrived. And Jack drew as well.

"Okay, lass, let's have at it. Let us see once and for all who will best the other."

With a rush he was upon her, swinging hard and powerful and skilled even in his drink, and she had a feeling that the anger had cleared his brain, and that she fought a man more sober than drunk. To a chorus of cheers, the men gathered, and in truth, cheered for their captain, for all of them were tired of the challenge that a woman could equal a man. That they would do so only made Anne more determined, and she put everything aside, all feeling, all history and future, the babe included, and thought with her head and her skill. Something of her father entered her, and she fought with his voice in her ear. "Remember, Anne, a man will always be the stronger, and ye cannot hope to best him with your own strength. Use his strength against him."

The crew was delighted, for life had been tedious of late, and here now was a good show, forward and aft. Only

Fetherston shook his head, for he was the oldest man aboard and knew it was a bad business, all of it. More than anyone, he knew that Jack adored the lass, but that she had called him out in front of the crew, well, Jack had to fight, put her in her place or he could no longer be captain. That was simply the way of it.

Below on the main deck, John was having his way with the woman, in full view of anyone who cared to watch, laying her stomach down over the hatch cover, too ashamed to look in her face, yet torn by excitement, his lust enhanced by the woman's terrified screams. Only when Mary could bear it no longer, did she roughly push him off the woman, ignoring the incredulous face he turned toward her, one swiftly turning to red anger. Pulling down the woman's skirts, Mary stood to guard her while the fisherwoman slowly and with great effort made to move from the drubbing she had just received.

"Dear God!" Mary cried looking at the men surrounding her and wondering how far the fight would go. "Have ye no sense? No sense at all? Now we'll 'ave t' kill the woman lest she tell the authorities and we all hang for certes!"

"My name," she turned to face the group, crying and begging, "is Dorothy. How can you kill me now that you know I am not a faceless, nameless body t' be had?"

"Let off, Mary," one of the crewman called, "let us have a turn at 'er. It's been awhile since we've 'ad a woman and we've our back up watchin' John have a go. You don't know what it's like t' be a man. Move off, I say."

Tom Brown, another crewman stepped forward, his voice menacing and filled with hard desire. "Noah's right. You can't fight us all. And we'll 'ave the girl, one at a time."

The circle tightened and Mary saw the odds were bad. With damning insight she knew that they could just as easily turn on her, and here she remembered the real reason she had kept the secret of her sex—she could not trust the males in her regiment, any more than she could trust these men.

"I'm sorry," she murmured to Dorothy. "I cannot protect you."

On the aft deck Anne held her own against Jack, so much so that she could see the surprise in his eyes, and then something else, some concern.

In the first of the fight, he had blundered, chopping at her, trying to overwhelm her by the sheer force of his strength, but he had learned quickly that she simply moved away, dissolved, while he merely chased. As he sobered from the intensity of his own anger, he mastered her style and understood finally why Anne was good—she simply withdrew through the force of the onslaught, then returned when the rush of the blow was finished and the man unbalanced. Suddenly, he was moving with her without over-committing his forward thrust, locked in a deadly dance of love, their knowing the other now played out with swords on the quarterdeck, the rhythm set, and the clash of swords both beautiful and deadly to behold.

The blows she took quivered up her arm. Without hesitation, she reeled and parried and felt his style for the first time against her, with all his tricks and maneuverings. From one corner of her mind she heard the cheers of the crew for Jack, from another, the screams of the woman below, and thought disgustedly that she had put herself and the child at risk for the entertainment of a band of cutthroats. Time to finish it, she thought, and was certain she could take him, for she still had ploys to use, and he lumbered without full control of his limbs.

Jack saw her smile and redoubled his efforts, face reddened with anger, slashing hard, thinking to move faster than her parries, trying to disarm her before any real damage, and yet . . . her blade always met his, as if she knew his next move. Try though he would, he could not get past her defenses easily, and for the first time had an inkling of what she had freely given him. Anne could have been anywhere, with anyone, yet she was here, counseling and protecting the men and the ship—his job. Never for a moment did he doubt that he would win this contest, but to do so, he feared he would have to hurt her, and this he could not do, but . . . he must win.

Anne saw the hidden hesitation, for she alone looked into his eyes, the better to know his next move. And wondered . . . what to do? If Jack were not captain, who would control this crew of motley men? Some sense of pity for them all overwhelmed her. Jack could not falter, she could not let him falter.

The clash of their swords interspersed with the calls of her mates, finally brought her back to the moment and away from that place where she stood alone and on the edge. With instant decision, she let him come at her, hard and wild, backing up instead of circling round. At the rail, she spread open her arms, vulnerable, lowering her weapon.

"I yield!" she called, and all cheered but Jack, for he knew the truth of the contest.

More furious than before, he looked toward the sport below, and turning his back, strode across the deck to the fisherwoman with quick, wide steps, thought to take his turn, let his anger sear into her with hard thrusts. Only he knew it was Anne who should be beneath him taking the prick of his wrath. Cursing himself for his thoughts and his crew for the deed, he turned away.

"Leave off," he shouted above the laughter. "Put her in the boat and let her be off!"

"But, Cap'n!" one cried who waited.

Jack still had his sword and he rushed the man, his face twisted into a kind of madness, his voice a roar, "Damn you to hell, I said leave off!"

From where she stood, Anne finally thought she knew men at their worst. Ravaged by lust and without a care to what they hurt, they would take where they willed, the larger and stronger among them foisting themselves on the weak, and the only thing that held them to sanity and morality was sword and pistol and skill and discipline. Silently, she prayed a thanks for William Cormac.

Mary came to stand next to her where she waited with Fetherston to see the outcome. "She'll have t' die," Mary told them. "She will probably want to. What has come over these men?"

"I am at a loss," Anne answered quietly, "but, for certes, part of it is the drink."

"It's truly over with John, is it not? He'll never forgive me this interference."

With some pity that she should still want the man, Anne told her, "You did the right thing, but now we have to look to the aftermath."

Over Anne and Mary's protests, for here was a fine witness against them, the woman was freed. The last they saw was a crumpled form in the bottom of the canoa too hurt and tormented to move.

But on the *William* a fiddle and accordion started up and the men settled in for the evening, the rum flowing once again, the sun setting, the air still and heavy with heat. As day darkened and night was upon them, bright spokes of lightning seared the sky, illuminating clouds hidden by the dark.

Jack was restless and roamed the decks, not sure he was ready to face either Anne, Mary, or George Fetherston, for the three of them had challenged him in different ways. George had said nothing, but would not look him in the eye, and because he respected George's age, knowledge, and sense of law among the Brethren, that careful avoidance shamed him. By all the saints, Anne and Mary had been right! The woman should not have been touched. They had understood her vulnerability and had tried to stop a rape that would take them to the gallows, even if they were not tried for piracy. If ever there was a chance they would avoid the hangman's noose, they had just lost it, for according to law, rape was worse than theft.

With a leap he took the stairs to the place Anne stood near the wheel, still angry, no longer quite so drunk, and already thinking to the bottle awaiting him.

"I'll see you in my cabin," he told her. "Now."

"Aye-aye . . . Captain."

Chapter Twenty-seven

The morning after Anne's fight with Jack was already hot an hour before sunrise, filled with humid air and without a breath of wind. They had entered Jack's cabin to make love in the night, angry with each other, and their foreplay had been wild and filled with pain, Anne giving as well as she got with teeth and nails . . . until Jack picked up his belt and threatened her.

"You've nary touched one of the men with the lash, and yet you would beat me, Jack! By God and the devil, I'll not have it!"

"It's different with the men," he'd answered hotly, his face red with fury, the other hand holding tightly to the strop. "'Tis naught to do with the Articles. You're my wife. For Christ's sake, Anne, you've humiliated me! In front of the whole cursed crew! I've a right to discipline you. An' hang or lash you, if I've a mind, or put you off ship, for you challenged me!"

"'Tis you who thought to offer me to the crew, you bloody bastard!"

She had never realized his true physical strength, but his outrage with her and himself knew no bounds, and turning her, he'd swung the strop, then entered her, hard and punishing, his weight slapping roughly against her bottom.

When it was over, rather than reach for her dagger, she'd cried aloud in a husky voice close to tears, "We are even, Jack. No more will be said about the fight today . . . or the woman raped by the crew . . . or what you've just laid on me." But she would not say what both of them knew, that the true contest between them was not finished.

"How is it," she asked, words quivering uncontrollably, "that we fight? We have never fought before. What is it that is so out of balance? Where is our love?"

Her words took him aback, for he wondered exactly what he had foisted on her, and regretted . . . so many things.

Near morning when he was finally asleep, she had left the cabin, worried, for she knew a danger. The woman of the canoa would have found her way home, and news of their activities and whereabouts could even now be on its way to the governor.

The crew had spent the night drinking dark rum, and because they waited for the breeze, for the moment, they slept. Quietly, she found Mary and motioned for her to come on deck.

"How goes it?" Mary asked. "Are ye all right? I'm sorry, but the whole crew heard the ruckus."

"'Tis true we had things to say to each other. And I'm sore in places."

"And the man still lives?" Mary gave her a wry grin. "Ye must love 'im somethin' fierce."

"Jack would not truly hurt me. If so, he would have done so in the fight yesterday, but he could not."

"Aye. I watched. You laid down before the end of it," she said quietly.

"'Tis a fine mess the men have made of things, Mary." Anne led her to the side near the long boat, the watch dead asleep on the deck, and whispered, "I've not told you, but I too am carrying a child."

"Anne!"

"I feared that when Jack learned of the babe he'd put me ashore, so I've said nothing." She shuddered involuntarily. "If he was angry yesterday, what will he do when he knows I've fought with the babe growin' in my womb?"

"So what's it t' be?"

"I've made a decision. I'm taking the treasure . . . for us . . . for the children we carry. They deserve a chance. Only God knows what yesterday's actions will bring."

As quietly as possible, Anne and Mary let down the ship's boat knowing only Jack could have heard and taken notice, but he was below and unawares, sunk into drunken sleep. As for the rest of the crew, nothing short of cannon could have roused them and even that was questionable.

"I'll keep an eye open. Hurry," Mary whispered.

Anne began to row hard toward the limestone cliffs at the edge of the shore, her hopes for the future and the safety of the children in the chest resting at the bottom of the boat.

With her face to the horizon, she watched the sky change rapidly, white wisps giving way to clouds black and pregnant with rain, lightning softly illuminating their underbelly, and a low, growling thunder rolling across the water. The sea was no longer blue-green, but an absolutely still slate-gray, the air silver heat.

Anne's eyes shifted to the wooden box at her feet. If all else failed, if the king's navy caught up with them, at least it would not fall into the governor's hands. Jack had said a few more weeks. When they were ready to leave Jamaican waters, they could return for the treasure and be on their way. To where? Anne did not know.

The first drops fell from the sky, large, cooling her straining arms, and the wind picked up. A blinding sheer of lightening, a great clap of thunder, and the rain began in earnest, a solid sheet of water that filled the bottom of the boat. Ahead she could see the entrance to a small harbor, and navigated the shallow reef, coral scraping her bottom. At the end of wave was a tiny beach of sand and shingle, and beyond it, a dark entrance to one of the hundreds of caves carved along the coast.

The seawater in the cave was warm, but the rain fell cold, and she found herself shivering while lightning raged outside, illuminating the walls. At her feet was a sand floor, wet, and she knew the sand would rise and fall with the coming of the tide. Behind her she found a ledge at shoulder level, and here she placed the box.

With a trembling hand, she reached to open the clasp, eyed the coin and jewelry, and then from inside her shirt, withdrew a package. In it was the lock of John's hair, the emerald cross, and the portrait she had carried from Charles

Town, her own dear treasures.

Gently she ran her fingers over the face of the girl in the portrait, one so unlike the woman who stood alone in the cave, that at first Anne struggled to remember. A long time had passed since she had been alone, for life aboard ship defied privacy. But now she stood as she had when James Bonny had gone to sea and she'd had to make decisions. Once again she recounted her life and thought to ask what it meant.

The white shirt she wore had turned grey with grime, the trousers torn through battle and fight, her feet were bare and covered with tar and dirt and sand, her only adornment a red sash to hold pistol, a belt across her chest with sword, a scarf to hide her long hair. What could Jack possibly think of her?

So here it was. A crossroads again. And she knew that surely they would all die if they continued this course. This then was her choice, to live and die with Jack, or to make a life without him, for he would never give up piracy, never. She touched her stomach and thought of the child who deserved to live . . . and the choice was made.

A half-hour passed and so did the storm. Anne closed the lid of the chest for the last time, locked it for her own peace of mind, and left it on the ledge of its sepulcher. The throaty rumbling of thunder moved away from the beach, inland to the mountains, and she had to hurry.

On the return she faced the shoreline and cliffs and eyed the landscape, marking the pines atop a bluff, noting the bays right and left of the cliff area where the cave hid beyond the obelisk of a boulder.

With the rainsquall spent, the skiff lifted and tied with Mary's help, dawn gave way to early morning. Jack came to her then, all defenses gone and his head low.

"Anne," he whispered gently, "I am sorry for yesterday. For all of it. I was wrong to let the men have their way with the woman. And I am sorry for the anger. My pride, you see . . . the fight . . ." The misery of defeat was full in his eyes. "Can ye ever forgive me?"

"It's all right, Jack," and she wrapped her arms around him, her head easy against his chest. "In a few weeks we will leave these waters, as you say. Without work there is nothing but the rum and cards and music to fill the day and night. I've a mind to sail north, to the Eastern Seaboard. I've thought I need some clothes. What must you think of me?'

He smiled and he was the Jack she knew, "Why, I think you are truly the most beautiful woman I have ever known."

"From what I've heard, I'd say that was a compliment." She smiled as well, for they were back on their footing. "The day looks to be a good one. The morning sun warms the water. The wind should pick up soon."

Indeed it did, the sails were unfurled, and the ship slid through the sea, guided by men still rum drunk, the sun hard on their eyes. Only then did Anne truly rest easy, for they were away from the place she had hidden the treasure.

At mid-afternoon the Easterlies died as they rounded the western end of the island. Here in Bloody Bay where the whalers took shelter, they called aboard the turtle fishermen for a party and rum punch, and the poor fellows, suspecting, but not truly knowing they were pirates, thought only to the taste of drink and fellowship. Again the rum flowed and by day's end all were in their cups, including the captain.

So it was, that at sunset Anne stood at the railing and saw the sail on the horizon, and called to the crew while arming, knowing at once that all she feared bore down on them. The wind was with the ship and evening shadows had turned the sails a dusky rose. Anne watched the lifting and falling of the sheets against a golden sea and sky, fullness in the canvas, every effort bent to overtake. Desperate, she waited anxiously as Jack sauntered to the foredeck, his eyes red, reeling against the wheel.

"Ahoy, the ship," a voice carried over the water. "Who is your captain?"

"That would be me," Jack shouted in return. "John

Rackham of Cuba."

"I am Captain Jonathan Barnett on the king's mission. I've a warrant for your arrest, Captain Rackham. Surrender peaceably and I will give you quarter."

The *William* rode at anchor while Mary frantically called to those below, and receiving no answer, slid down the stairs, her curses and shouts to awaken the drunkards floating up the hatch.

Suddenly, all sound aboard the *William* died, for the governor's ship let go a broadside, and as close as they were, the damage was mighty, the air filled with black gunpowder, bits of rigging cut and broken and raining slivers of wood upon them, the smoke thick enough that Anne struggled to see where Barnett's ship ran and how much time was left them.

Not until the sloop was almost upon them, did Jack's vision clear, even while his lungs burned with gunpowder and smoke. With a rude awakening he knew the desperation of the matter.

"Dear God, what am I about?" he whispered hoarsely.

A mighty fling, and the bottle was overboard, and he rushed to the swivel gun that stood on deck. The small cannon fired with a roar, the shot falling short of the governor's sloop.

Barnett was prepared and let off another round from her starboard cannon that took the mainmast of the *William,* its yardarm and halyards crashing to the deck, sending the few who had just come up, hastening back to safety below decks.

"They have us, Anne!" Jack called to her. "We haven't a chance. I must ask for quarter!"

"You can ask all you want," Anne returned fiercely, "but I'll not be surrenderin'!"

"Nor I!" cried Mary, for both women refused to give birth in a prison.

"Jack, if you give in, you'll only live a few days more. Fight, I say! Make a good end! Blackbeard knew the truth of it. When his time came he chose death on the deck to hangin'!"

"The Royal Navy hung his head in the ship's riggin', Anne. I'll not have that happen to you. If I surrender at least we have a trial and who knows what might happen?"

At that moment the ships touched, and the jolt of the meeting was hard. With a mixture of anger and sorrow, Anne turned from him and met Mary's eye. A nod, and the women were of accord.

A volley of gunfire raked the deck, and before they could stand from where they had fallen to avoid the barrage, the first of Barnett's men came aboard. Anne emptied both her pistols into the surging mass of men swinging over the side, and looked hopelessly for aid in the fight. Only Mary stood with a cutlass in each hand and Jack with dagger and sword. Then she could think no more, for the first of her attackers rushed forward. From the corner of her eye, Anne watched Jack make an attempt at his own defense, then saw his face turn toward her, a moment's thought cross his eyes, and with a smile, part resignation, part humor, part indifference, he laid down his weapon and was surrounded.

Made more desperate by Jack's surrender, Anne and Mary fought for their lives and the lives of the crew alone against crushing odds. Yet so overwhelmed was Anne at the sight of Jack with hands raised, that she slackened her grip on the sword and had it struck from her hand. Blades to her body, she could do nothing but stand, trembling and furious, a dagger still gripped tightly, while Mary soon met the same fate, completely surrounded and facing sure death for herself and her child if she did not surrender.

"'Tis not for me," Mary cried, "that I give up my sword!"

When it was over, when the surprise of Anne and Mary's sex was known and Anne had told Jack of her love with a last glance, when she had been forced over the railing with a word to Fetherston about the treasure, Anne sat in that small cabin on Barnett's ship, shackles heavy on her wrists, and took Mary's hands in her own, longing for her parents, for Jack, for the old life, and wondering just how long it would be until they were hanged.

Part 6

St. Jago de la Vega
Capitol of Jamaica
October, 1720

Philip O'Conner

Chapter Twenty-eight

The prison of St. Jago de la Vega was unlike that of Charles Town. Older, darker, encrusted with mildew and green slime, Anne knew a misery in that dungeon unlike anything before. Hopelessness weighed her down, and for the first time in her life, she saw no salvation from any quarter.

The worst of it was her separation from Jack, and she looked to Mary with such despair, that Mary turned away for fear of drowning in her desolation. The loss of Jack was shattering, for she had given up all to be with him, and now, he was taken from her.

Even the death of young John did not measure. John's demise had been innocent, and she had tended him without thinking of the future, until he had simply slipped away. The dread pain that had wracked the insides of her with his death, had all been tempered over time with Jack's touch.

But this new despair was something else, this thinking that Jack would be taken to his death. To kill in the heat of battle, for soldier or sailor or pirate, was one thing, but for the governor and his courts to plan Jack's death, deliberately and with calculation, was all the worse. The darkness weighing on her mind was endless, and she longed for him with a type of a madness, for the feel of his arms and the comfort of his strength. For many days she was unable to eat, slept in snatches, and when she did wake, it was to the horror of where she was and calling Jack's name.

"Mary, Mary, what shall I do?" she cried.

"You will live without 'im," Mary told her firmly, "and ye'll start now. Ye've but one choice t' make, Anne. You will live and give your attention to the babe that grows within, or ye'll descend into madness, for as surely as I stand 'ere, you're already half way there."

"But, I want him," she moaned, rocking back and forth, her arms hugging her body, the longing her only thought. "Dear God, I must have him! All I feel is the memory of his touch."

"And that is all ye will ever 'ave. Of course, 'e touches you in spirit, for that is the way of love."

Mary crouched down to where Anne sat on the floor, the better to speak to her face. "Listen to me. After my Edward died, I was the same as I see you now, wonderin' if a person could die of a broken heart. I took t' me bed unable t' move. Then it struck me. I 'ad t' choose whether t' live or t' die. The inn needed tending and there was nought but meself to do it. I 'ad t' get up each morning, wash, and dress. More, I 'ad t' put on a smile for the customers. If I did not, then I would lose all that Edward 'ad given me. So for 'im, in spite of the pain, I washed my face and smiled and gradually went about me business."

"One *can* die of a broken heart."

"Anne, I will be blunt, for I cannot hold us both up. The weight of it is too dear. Jack is gone from you. They will hang him soon and you must look to yourself if you expect t' survive."

"I don't know if I want to . . ."

"For God's sake, you carry a child!" Mary cried, loud enough to get her attention. "That is the only thing that is real in all of this. You've not the luxury of sorrow. Not for yourself or for Jack. We're in a mess, we are, Anne, and we must bring all we 'ave left to bear if we are not t' perish."

"And what have we?"

"We've our wits and we must think of a way out."

Anne stood and walked the length of the cell, and considered. A deep breath and she turned back, her face resolved, pain still acute, but for the first time in days, felt as if she were not drowning. Indeed, she still had her wits and could not lose them, must not lose them. For the babe, she thought. And at that moment, the child moved in her womb.

"Saints and angels, but the child has quickened! Come if you wish and feel him."

"A boy, is it?" Now Mary smiled and walked toward her to lay hands on Anne's belly. Softly, she said, "Aye, a boy, and a lusty one by the strength of 'im. Here . . ." and she took Anne's hands and placed them on her own belly. "I know not whether boy or girl, but for certes, they will be fast friends." She looked deep into Anne's eyes, "For the children, then?"

Not since John's death and the tears that fell so shamelessly, had Anne truly cried. Since that day she had hardened her heart to tears, afraid if she let them fall, they would never stop. But now she felt her eyes fill, and nodded, aghast, for Mary asked her to turn from Jack who was lost, to the babe who might live. She chose and stepped forward into the hope of a future for herself and the child, then fell in a heap into Mary's arms, crying with all her soul, finally beginning to release the hard pain that threatened to crush her heart.

Over the next days Anne began to eat again, even though it was foul and stale, but in hope to give the child some nourishment. And slowly, she began to think, to remember, to cast off dread so that she could plan. Mary reminded her frequently that she still had her background, her upbringing, and with it, wit, charm, and acquaintances. Ahead lay the trial and although Anne found she pushed against the inevitability with all the force of her will, time was merciless and dragged her forward.

Not until two weeks into their arrest did Anne and Mary learn they were something of an international sensation, the news of the capture of fighting female pirates sent all the way to London. The imagination of the world focused on the upcoming trial, and their actions were whispered behind fans as to the type of women they were. All this they learned through the unexpected arrival of a visitor—Philip O'Conner.

Four years had passed since Anne had seen Mr. O'Conner and had teased him at her ball—a lifetime ago. He unexpectedly entered the cell, decidedly more corpulent from his good life, wigged and in light blue silk breeches, white stockings and garter, a dark waistcoat and an overcoat of silver thread sewn with gold buttons, blinking and allowing his eyes to adjust to the dimness.

Anne stood and stared at him, quite surprised. Only when she watched, with some embarrassment, a perfumed handkerchief rise to his nose, did she turn to glance around the cell and see it for what it was.

The air was stifling and without ventilation, with only a wisp of breeze and light from a tiny window. The walls were streaked with mold growing on moist stone. A bucket with all the offal of their bodies was consigned to one corner, the room reeking of a cesspit. Dirty straw was piled on wooden pallets used for a bed, not even a blanket for comfort. At the door, near his feet, wooden bowls crawled with maggots from some bit of food they had found inedible. Water for washing was a luxury they did not deserve, in truth, only small amounts were given for drink, for the duty of the guards was to make their lives as miserable as possible, and this included thirst. Her feet were bare, hands and fingernails black with grime, her hair matted, mouth fetid, her skin brown, and her body unwashed and reeking of her own female odor, urine, and the smell of sweat.

Suddenly Anne laughed, and gave a courtly bow in her breeches and filthy blouse, blood from the last fight still on her sleeve.

"How kind of you to call, Mr. O'Connor. May I introduce my dear friend, Mary Read. Please forgive me if we cannot offer you tea."

"Anne, Anne," he cried horrified. "What have ye come to?"

Still laughing, Anne said, "Ah, Mr. O'Conner, 'tis your own fault, for you refused my hand in marriage."

And to her surprise and with utmost seriousness, he

exclaimed, "I do believe you're right. And that is why I have come. To make amends. I will see to this . . . this . . ." and his hand carrying the handkerchief fluttered across the room, before quickly traveling back to his nose.

Anne only shook her head, "And what is it ye think ye can do, dear Philip," she said quietly and honestly. "For you see, I am to be brought to trial as a common pirate. There is little anyone can do."

"Something will be done, for decency's sake, if nothing else."

"How did you come to know I was here?"

"You and Mistress Read are the talk of the island. Why, the governor has sent communications all the way to London and a great number of other places as well, so astounded are the justices by the fact of your sex. Well, and to be honest, Anne, by the fight you put up. Can it be true that you swore and cursed at your own men and battled like hellions to evade capture?"

"If you are asking if I can fight, Philip, why, you know that I can. If you are asking if I would fight to evade this . . ." and Anne cast an arm out to the room, "and the hangman's noose, why, yes, I fought like the devil himself. And would do so again."

"But why, Anne, why come to this?"

"How can I tell you in a sentence or two?" she answered knowing the futility of trying to explain to a man like O'Conner what had first motivated her. "Truly, can you understand injustice? Or understand why men take to the sea to make a life with their fellows? These men have established a floating country, making their own laws and abiding by them with honor."

He waved away the idea. "Democracy is an ill-conceived notion of the Greeks and one that will bring us all to ruin. I hear they actually elect their own captains. No, no, my dear, a strong monarch and class structure is the only way to maintain order. We cannot have anarchy."

"As I thought, Philip, ye cannot understand. You and

your kind create pirates by your wars and laws and greed. You take all you can for yourselves and leave precious little to the poor and weak. And when men choose piracy because nothing else is left them, you track them down and bring them to their deaths. Murder, I say."

"I . . . I do not understand. Do you say that the king's justice is murder?'

"I do. And it is little justice."

He stared at her, unable to comprehend.

"Why do we accept that the just due of those who err is prison? That torture, death, and despair are the acceptable? Does it not strike you as odd that crime is arbitrary, changing with those who hold power? Do not all men err? Yet some are caught and punished, while others support their own misdeeds with the laws they have the power to create. Oh, my dear man, is not each born, regardless of his class and skin color, a vessel holding the spirit of God? Must you demean the poor and low born . . . make slaves of the Africans . . . so that you have coin in your purse?"

As she spoke his eyes had begun to bulge. "But what you ask is impossible in the real world, Anne. There must be rich and poor, those who rule and those who work, master and slave. Only money creates beauty and the great symbols of civilization that endure. Art and architecture . . . music and literature, why, the great churches and cathedrals. Dear girl, this place has made you delusional! That pirate fellow has turned your head! Jack Rackham, is it? Please, Anne . . . and the rest of them . . . simple scum. Not your kind at all. Brutal men."

"Perhaps they are simply victims of a system forced upon them," she answered quietly.

Sighing, he glanced around one last time, gave a small bow to Mary, a deeper one to Anne. "I will see to things. And I will notify your father, you poor girl."

"My father?" Anne cried with some panic.

"Yes. He will want to know, if he already does not. I will return when I have news."

A call, the striking of his cane upon the door, and the guard opened. With great relief, O'Conner exited the cell, making quickly for the street, sunshine, and clean air.

"Well," said Mary, looking Anne over, "you should 'ave been a barrister."

"Like my father?" she grinned. "I haven't heard where they've changed the rules to admit girls to read law, have you?"

"And why should that bother the likes of us who can dress as a man?"

"Aye, like Portia who knew what she was about in *The Merchant of Venice."* Anne laughed. "But would it not be nice to be able to be oneself without costuming."

"Still, Anne, there is hope. Do ye think this man can get you out o' 'ere and away?"

Anne stopped in her pacing and looked directly at her. "I'll tell you now, Mary, and we'll not be discussin' it again. I'll not be makin' a move without you."

"'Tis kind," she answered softly, a tremor in her voice, "but if ye've the chance, ye'll take it. 'Tis the way o' the world. Those with coin and the influence it buys, 'as the edge. Why, I told you, I could 'ave been an officer in the cavalry but for lack o' money t' buy me commission. The poor will always bear the brunt of the suffering in this world."

"Aye," Anne replied firmly, "I know. And that is why I'll not be goin' anywhere unless you are with me."

For her speech, she was rewarded by the glimmer of hope in Mary's eyes.

"Anne, tell me about this Portia, for I would 'ear 'er story."

True to his word, Philip O'Conner became the lifeline between the larger world and the enclosed existence of the cell. Water and soap appeared and the women washed their bodies and each other until they rubbed the weeks and blood and dirt away and then changed into simple, clean dresses. The filth still surrounded them, for the gaoler would never carry enough water for them to clean properly, but they had a little soap left for hands and face, and it became a precious commodity. The food came and was warm and of better quality, and their bodies began to have a softer definition. The dim light turned their skin white, except for the ordinary freckles of their heritage, and their faces emitted a desperate beauty. Philip O'Conner, visiting with some regularity, was amazed by the change of Anne's appearance. At first, he had sought the relief of her trials for her father's sake, a business partner and friend, but now, as she blossomed before him, he began to take a second look.

On a day near the end of November, he came to her. "Anne, I have a proposal, if you will allow me."

Philip doffed his hat, and pointed with it to a corner of the room, where he thought to have some little privacy. Mary walked to the farthest end away from them and turned her back, already knowing what was to come, for she had seen his look. Now she prayed Anne would have her answer ready.

"Mistress Anne, I have thought of a solution that might suit all involved."

"A solution? Surely, ye've not thought of a way to extricate Mistress Mary and myself from this prison?"

For a moment Philip looked abashed. "Why, Anne, I was speaking of you . . . not . . . not Mistress Mary!"

She eyed him with a look that caused Philip pause, for he had seen that look on William Cormac's face just before delivering the trump card in court.

"What have ye to say, Philip?"

"Just this. Anne, if you will consent to a marriage and swear fidelity and reform, I may be able to have you released."

Blood rushed hot to her face, and trembling in uncertainty, asked evenly, "And who did ye have in mind for me to marry?"

"Why, Anne, can you not guess?"

"I cannot, Mr. O'Conner, for I have been locked away some weeks now."

"My dear girl, I am speaking of myself." And he placed a hand upon his chest. "I know your father would be most pleased."

"Would he now?" Anne replied quietly. "Philip, would you have me knowing that I love another? That my heart is completely bound to Jack Rackham's soul?"

"But, you cannot be serious. The man is a . . . a pirate. A complete loss. An infatuation. Some misconception about romance and the sea. Dear girl, I offer you half of all my worldly goods, my plantations and slaves, ships, my property in the Carolinas. Reconciliation with your father. And if you will permit me saying so, children."

"It is precisely this last point that makes my answer resolute, Philip. I will always hold you in high esteem, for ye've done much for Mistress Mary and myself in the last weeks. But I will never sleep in your bed. You deserve a wife who will love you and bear you the children you deserve."

"Anne, we both know you to be impetuous and you must think this through carefully. So much depends on it. I will give you some days more to consider. If I am to go to the governor, I would like to do so before trial and publicity." He turned to leave. "By the way, your father has taken ship and will be arriving soon."

Anne gasped. "Coming here? To this prison?"

"Yes," O'Conner nodded, then stopped once again just before the door, and walked back, his voice low. "I am sorry to be so inappropriate, but might I ask . . . have you . . . has Captain Rackham . . . the sleeping arrangements . . ."

"If you're asking if Jack and I have made love, then the answer is yes. Philip, Jack and I buried a child together, one we loved very much. Do you begin to see? This is not an infatuation as you would call it. Jack is the love of my life. And always will be. Now you must think again if you would have a woman to wife who loves another . . . even in death.

And one, as I said, who will never share your bed."

O'Conner did not blink. "You are yet young. These things will be forgotten and the child you lost will be replaced. Your desire will rise again, Anne, and then you will have me." He doffed his hat and rapped his cane on the door.

"Philip, if I might . . ." and Anne asked that which she dreaded to know. "When will Jack be tried?"

"Why, dear girl, I thought you knew. Tomorrow for some of them, the Captain and his staff of officers. I am sorry to be the one to tell you."

The door creaked open and the gaoler poked in a head. "Ready, sir?"

"Aye," and casting Anne a last glance, took his leave.

"You heard his proposal?" Anne asked Mary.

"I did. It's an offer, Anne. I don't know if you're in a position t' refuse it."

"I can't sleep with that man after being with Jack. Would it be fair to marry him and then refuse him my bed?"

"No. But I can see in your face, you still hope for a miracle. You think Jack may live."

"Indeed, while he lives, I have only hope."

Chapter Twenty-nine

Jack knew that things were in motion and that he had little time left when buckets of water came into the cell for the first time in a month.

"Wash up, mates," the gaoler cried as he made the delivery, "for tomorrow ye meet the judges what's to hang ye!"

When the door slammed shut, Jack turned to the men and said, "I ask all of you your forgiveness, for 'tis true, I was your captain and I led you to this end. I am sorry for it."

"Ye'll never have my pardon," Richard Corner, the quartermaster, told him bitterly, "for if ye'd a kept off the wenches, none o' this here bad luck would ever have occurred!"

"Hold your tongue!" George Fetherston bellowed. "Are ye forgettin' your own affairs? I'll not 'ave you blame Jack or the lasses for your own faults. A man takes his knocks and 'e knows when 'e's at fault and 'e doesn't cast the blame about. The ones I feel sorry for is these poor devils 'ere," and he pointed to the nine dejected turtle fisherman sitting together against one wall, "arrested with the crew. The poor blokes 'ad nothin' to do with piracy. Just came on for the rum punch and 'ere they are to share our fate unless there's justice and mercy in this world. But you, you were dead drunk when Barnett came upon us, and you're lucky you lived this long. Anne shoulda' blown your head off, not just scared you into getting' up and seein' what was comin' at us." Then he turned to Jack. "For my part, you've my pardon, Cap'n, and I ask mine of you. I was to stand at your back and I failed you. Drunk like the rest for too many days. I should've heeded Anne's warnin'. She came to me and I paid 'er no mind."

Jack put one hand on his hip, "Which reminds me, did any of you see Anne make off with the chest from my cabin?

George says she claims to have taken it. Could we have all been so drunk that we didn't see her row to shore with the dingy and the box?"

Nary a man answered.

"So, we were," Jack sighed. "Clear as sunlight, it's Anne who should've been your captain. She knew time was short and begged me to sail further north." He walked the narrow length of the cell, his hand rubbing the back of his neck. "How will we ever live it down? Can you hear the songs they will sing of us? Asleep and defended by two women! Let this be a lesson on the evils of drink."

And for there was nothing else to do, he laughed loud and long.

The courtroom was filled to bursting with people come to see the trial. At the head of the room were the tables of the judges, shaped like a horseshoe, and at the center table, Sir Nicolas Lawes himself, Governor of Jamaica. On his right, sat William Needham, Chief Justice, and to his left, Captain Vernon, Commander-in-Chief of the ships of war in Jamaica. On either side of these men were other counselors and Jack heard their titles, but he was mostly oblivious, thinking their names mattered little, indeed, that time was passing slow and unnatural, disconnected from reality. One of the commissioners took the oath of his office as ". . . directed by King William in his *Act for the More Effectual Suppression of Piracy . . .*" Jack and the men were brought before the bar and the charges against them began to be read.

As Jack half-listened, the faces gazing upon him looked in curiosity as much as in disgust, and he saw there was no hope for it. Bits of the reading made its way to him, but for the most part, he only wondered at the seated men, their clothes, what they'd had for breakfast, the bed of silk sheets for slumber, the woman waiting, the feel of sun and smile of sky and air sweet off the sea. Oh, God, Anne had been right about everything, and if he had not been so arrogant and too sure, he could be having her now.

". . . did feloniously and wickedly, consult, and agree together, to rob, plunder, and take all such persons, subjects of His Majesty, the King, which they should meet with on the high sea, and in execution of their evil designs with force and arms in a certain place and within the jurisdiction of this Court, did piratically, feloniously, and in a hostile manner, attack, engage, and take . . ."

As the court listed his crimes, Jack thought that indeed, having them all in a row was difficult to hear. Seven fishing boats he'd taken, assaulting and threatening their crews so that they were in corporal fear of their lives, carrying away fish, fishing tackle, ten pounds, goods and property. The first day of October he commandeered by force of arms two merchant sloops, taking away a thousand pounds. On the nineteenth of October shot at, set upon, and took a certain schooner commanded by Thomas Spenlow, assaulting the captain and other mariners, stealing the ship and all it contained, including twenty pounds. The *William* set upon another sloop, the *Mary,* on the twentieth of October, assaulting one Thomas Dillon and crew, carrying away apparel, tackle, and three hundred pounds. And finally, that theft and assault was made upon one Dorothy Thomas. At this last mention, Jack looked up and felt a measure of tension flow through the men, for now they were surely to meet their Maker, and what had seemed like nothing at the time, appeared like much to take to the next world.

When asked what they pled, all answered, "Not guilty," for it gave them another day to live while witnesses would be called against them.

In the evening the men stood dejected in their various parts of the cell and not much was said, heads low, shoulders slumped, eyes dark with lack of sleep and worry.

"Why, so what's it to be?" Fetherston finally said to them. "Shall we sit and moan in our cups? Or shall we stand tight as we 'ave in every battle that 'as come before us. For meself, I'll be tellin' you now, I've no regrets. Look 'ere, mates, what choice did we 'ave? Let off ship after the war, cast off, made to shift for ourselves, and those of us here lucky enough to take ship, found a master quick with the cat-o'-nine-tails, stingy with the food, nary a care to our sicknesses or wounds, and at the end, cheatin' us of our rightful wages. No, I would not change a thing I've done!"

Jack stood. "He's right. A pirate's life is the only life for a man of any spirit! God's blood! Shall we bemoan our fate, drag our heels and let them win? Or shall we make a good end of it?"

"That's all well and good," Richard Corner cried, "for you are captain and will bear the brunt of it. But there are those of us who still 'ave a chance at pardon!"

"Listen, lad," Jack told him, walking across the room to look directly in his face. "They will make you say things you do not mean so's it can be reported. The war they make against us men of the seas is not just a war of ships, but a war of words. If they can make you turn from what you know to be true, they have won your soul. Do not give it away!"

"But if I truly repent . . ."

"And what will ye repent of?" Fetherston thundered.

"Why, what they have asked of us. That we do not take the Lord's name in vain, or curse, or swear. That we regret our lust and whoring and drink. That we confess our greed . . ."

"Greed, is it?" Jack asked him. "To the women and the rum, I say life is for merriment. It's not the rum and women that's to blame. But they see our pleasure as a threat to their control of our hands and labor. By Christ's very bones, if you want to speak of greed, ask yourself where the greed really lies. They're makin' the money off the backs of the poor and won't allow us to have our share. And if we demand it, they call us pirates."

Corner stood his ground. "But have ye no fear of your immortal soul?"

"And where do ye expect your soul to be goin' if you repent as they're askin' you to do?"

"Why, to 'eaven."

"'Ave ye gone daft?" Fetherston's shout held some amusement. "'Ave ye ever 'eard of a pirate what goes to 'eaven? And good God, why would you be wantin' to go there when you could just as well go to 'ell? God's blood, we all know 'ell is a far merrier place than 'eaven!"

"Aye," Patrick Carty stood, "we knew what we was about when we made our choices. I ran from the bloody English in Ireland because I was born Catholic. But I found mates among the English and the Dutch and black men and mulatto, one nation under the black flag. I'm with ye, Captain. I've 'ad coins in me pocket and I'm not beholden' to any man. I've enjoyed me life and lived as I wished without 'avin' to slave under the lash."

"It's we who's elected you, Captain," Noah added, "and you've not used the whip or rope on any man. Nor would we allow it. Which of those who sits to judge us can say they have our sense of justice?"

James Dobbins stood then. "I sailed with Hornigold before takin' me place 'ere. I remember the day we left the king's service. The Captain 'ad just told us the war with France and Spain was over and we was expected to go to land. That we was no longer to take the ships of France or Spain. But Hornigold, 'e says to us, 'We didn't make no treaty with France or Spain and we'll continue our trade rather than join the poor'. So's we took those same needles we used to sew the sails and made a black flag and stitched on it the skull and crossbones and thought, a jolly death if need be. Proud of that flag we was, for it was a new day for all of us, equal partners in a venture of our own."

"I'm from a merchant," added Thomas Earl, "and the work of fifty men was done by fifteen so's they could make their profit. God knows the food was sparse and we was ever hungry. Why, it was ever the joke amongst us that if they chose to 'ang us, we'd not the weight to drag down the rope. Never enough water to drink, even though we still had casks aplenty when we reached port . . ."

"And the whip kept busy!"

"Aye, 'arsh discipline, to be sure," Thomas nodded. "And if ye go to any port in the Christian world ye'll see the poor blokes, them that's lost an eye or leg or arm in battle beggin' for a tuppence. Us pirates, we pays our mates what gives up a limb for the good of all. I says we've done all right by each other, and I'll not be changin' my mind about who I am. I'm with you too, Captain."

"We's 'ad plenty to eat, and good drink, and fine wenches. Life is short aboard a merchant, damned pox above-board and plague between decks, if ye know what I mean. Might as well enjoy the short of it on a pirate ship."

"A short and merry life, I say!"

"A good end, then?" Fetherston proposed.

"Aye!" the men called. "Aye!"

All but Richard Corner who still stood apart and brooded.

On the morrow the men were dragged back to court in chains to hear the line of witnesses against them. Throughout the day Jack looked into the faces of men eager to give back what once had been threatened towards them. Only when Dorothy Thomas came to the stand, did Jack blanch, for he had violated the primary rule of any captain to protect those hostages aboard ship. If not held for ransom, they were to be released, and no woman was to be touched without her consent. Here had been his failure and in this he was ashamed and he steeled himself to the fire of her words. As she began her testimony, Jack could not raise his face to hers, but then, to his amazement, she told the court of the theft but not the rape by the crew.

Poor, lass, he thought. *She cannot live with rape by a pirate crew any more than we can bear to hear it. If she tells, no man will have her. So she let's us off.*

Suddenly hope flared again, unreasonably, but still there. For they were young men and had a will to live. Perhaps they would find slavery instead of death, and in slavery, escape.

Toward late afternoon they were led from the court while those lords at the high table refreshed themselves before returning with the verdict.

"Cap'n, what say you?" called one of the men, his voice low. "We're anxious to 'ear 'ow you think it went."

"As well as can be expected . . . and I expect a bad end," Jack returned. "Say your prayers."

In an hour it was over. The crew stood before the might of the British Empire and heard the pronouncement.

"You John Rackham, and your officers, George Fetherston; Richard Corner; John Davies; John Howell; Thomas Brown, alias Bourn; Noah Harwood; James Dobbins; Patrick Carty; Thomas Earl; and John Fenwick, alias Fenis, are to go from hence to the place from whence you came, and from thence to the place of execution, where you shall be severally hang'd by the neck, 'till you are severally dead. And God in his infinite mercy be merciful to all your souls."

On the following morning the gaoler entered the hallway between the cells and called out, "Your time 'as come. I'll be back for three of you in an 'our, Jack Rackham, captain; George Fetherston, mate; and Richard Corner, quartermaster. There's a minister 'ere who will 'ear anything ye 'ave to say. Any last requests?"

"Aye," Jack called to him. "Can you make arrangements so that I can visit with Anne Bonny. Will ye do that for me, man?"

The gaoler thought for a moment, then said, "I'll see what I can do."

Within the quarter hour the man was back. "You've been granted your wish. Five minutes is all. Come with me."

Jack followed along corridors in the dungeon of the prison, the light dim, sconces on the walls. At the door of Anne and Mary's cell, the gaoler knocked hard and called out, "Visitor!"

Anne was so shocked to see him that her legs gave way

and Jack was beside her in an instant. "You're not the faintin' kind," he whispered, helping her to the ground.

"Only when I'm pregnant. Don't you remember?"

"Anne . . . pregnant? Oh, my dear wife."

"Not such good news, Jack, for what good is a babe without a mother. We shall all hang, will we not?"

"I will hang, for certes. But you, Anne, you will not. They cannot kill the unborn child and you will escape this place and live, live for our child. You will do all that you have to do, but you *will* live. Promise me you will remember me to the babe. Some day, tell him about me. Will you do that?"

"Dear God, but you break my heart!"

Then tenderly, he murmured, "You know that I love you always, even unto death."

"My love," Anne whispered.

"I've only a few seconds more, for I am on my way to the gallows this very hour. Pray for me that I make a good end."

"Jack!"

"Now separate yourself from me so that you have a chance. Cast me off so that you and the babe might live. Now! Do it! I am your captain and that is an order."

Anne swallowed and blinked her eyes, looked into his soul and touched him deeply once more. The grieving and tears would come later. Now she had a performance to give, one that would be told and retold.

She raised herself, stood tall and bold and looked at Jack with disdain, then called aloud for a great many to hear, "I am sorry to see you in such straits, but if you had fought like a man, ye need not be hanged like a dog."

A last glance and Jack turned his back on her and walked toward his death.

He was alone.

The scaffold had been placed at Plum Point at the entrance to Kingston Harbour. Master Fetherston and

Quartermaster Corner were each taken to different spots, Fetherston to Bush Key, and Corner to Gun Key, where each in his own place would be gibbeted after the hanging, their bodies left to rot in steel cages as a warning to other pirates and a source of comfort to merchants.

Brought to the gallows after a sensational trial, Captain Rackham was accompained by over one hundred armed soldiers. Although few pirates still sailed in and out of Port Royal, there were men in the town who had once been sea robbers, whose sympathies ran deep, and many were the threats and rumblings against the hanging. Only two years before, a mob had rescued one pirate from the gallows, and Governor Lawes would not have it again.

Jack was brought up to the scaffold, his hands bound in front of his body. The officer in charge asked if he would repent.

"Aye," Jack told the man's smug face. Governor Lawes stood to one side and Jack turned toward him.

"I do heartily repent. I repent I had not done more mischief to those who took from us, and who branded and enslaved and whipped. I repent that I did not fight when you came upon us, or cut the throats of them that took us. And I am extremely sorry that you shall not hang as well as we, for each of you standin' here is as much a thief and blackguard as any one of us you call pirates."

At the shocked look on the governor's face, Jack threw back his head and laughed.

A quick and angry nod from the governor, the rope was tightened, and he was cast off the platform.

Instantly the weight of his body caused him to choke, and he felt himself gagging, the pressure against his windpipe excruciating, his body instinctively gasping for air, the spittle from vomit that could not find passage, thick from his lips. His face and skin turned a purple, his eyes growing wide to bulge from his sockets, his tongue dark and protruding, his legs twitching involuntarily for many minutes, for there was no one there to lend weight, to pull at his legs to break his neck and hasten the death. He suffered for a full seven minutes before he lost consciousness and was finally still.

When Fetherston was asked if he would repent, he answered stoically, "Ye are so contemptible that ye can't even make a decent 'angman's knot as any poor sailor who knows 'is ropes can show you 'ow to do. 'Ere," and he quickly untied and retied the rope that would strangle him, much to the amazement of those onlookers.

He died soon after.

Asked if he would repent and make a clean death of it, Richard Corner, still believing he would be pardoned if he only said the right words, cried, "I do repent of my ways! I should have foresworn all works of the devil, and I do 'ere and now foreswear them ever more. A second chance, a second chance, I beg you!"

Although his words were carried in newsprint to prove to the world the effectiveness of the hangings, how it brought the poor fellows back to God, Richard Corner succumbed to the hangman's noose like every other man aboard the *William.*

Within three days all the crew had been executed, except the nine turtle fisherman who had joined the party for a few hours only for the rum, and these men were all hanged the following February, all but two, who died in the abhorrent conditions of the prison.

And every man among them, except for Fetherston, not over the age of thirty.

Chapter Thirty

The news that Jack had died reached Anne by way of a sympathetic guard within hours of the execution. Against all reason, she had been filled with hope, believing that something might happen, anything, to change his fate. Hearing that he was gone was like looking into a great dark pit, the world simply falling away, and she dropped to the floor seeking something to hold to, anything solid. For many moments the pain was like a searing wind that burned past her skin to the very core of her body, and her heart, her heart, hurt so that she wondered if she would survive the pain in her chest. Surely, surely she would vomit, and she grabbed her hair and pulled with her fingers and rocked back and forth, trying to breathe. What reason did she have to live? How could time move on, away from Jack? It was impossible.

Mary came to sit beside her, and said gently, "He's gone. We must face it. The captain's gone and with 'im John as well. Now . . . now we are truly alone and without our men. Anne, Anne, ye must not give in t' grief. We must think 'ard or we are next, t' be sure."

Anne sighed, turned to her, and said wearily, "They will not hang us as long as we are with child. We have some months left."

"But they do not know about the babes as yet."

"Nor will they, until we hear our fate. No sense in making this any more of a spectacle than it already is. Do ye really think they will hang women, Mary?"

"But if they do condemn us?"

"Then we will plead our bellies."

"And what will ye do about O'Conner's offer? Will ye take 'im up on it? Jack would 'ave wanted you t' live and marriage t' the man might be the answer."

"I've told you, I'll be goin' nowhere without you. Besides, I think I would rather die than give myself to that fat, pompous slave trader. I thought so when I was sixteen and I think so today."

"Aye. An old woman ye are," and Mary could not help but smile.

"It's not so funny. I've twenty years and I've had two husbands already. I tell you I will not make O'Conner the third."

"Then we're bound for the courts. Sooner than later, I should be thinkin'."

"I don't know if I care any more. I am disconsolate, Mary. I have never known such emptiness."

Later that same afternoon, the door of the cell swung open and Philip O'Conner entered. The Rackham fellow was gone and perhaps Anne could now understand the possibility of her own fate from his demise. Strike now, he thought, while the iron is hot.

For once Anne did not stand in greeting as she had in past weeks, for she and Mary had been hungry for the things he could give them and desperate for news from the outside. Truth be told, O'Conner could not have chosen a worse time to arrive. Anne had been stunned by the news of Jack's death, but in the last hours, she had become angry. Now she looked at him in his gold-buckled shoes, silk stockings and garter, his jacket with wide cuffs, clean silk shirt, and feathered hat, and knew him to be one of them, the elite, those who made the laws to suit their needs, enforcing them with a military based on the taxes of the people. One of those who had murdered Jack.

"Anne," he spoke in greeting, and made her a leg. "Ah, I see you have heard the news. Please, will you do me the honor of stepping this way so that I might speak with you? Come, my dear, it will not serve to pout. The man is dead and will hang to rot. You cannot have thought that any other outcome was possible, could you? Oh my dear, really . . ."

Anne stood and turned to him, eyes wide with new horror. "They . . . they will gibbet him?"

"Why, yes. And those other fellows as well. That Fetherston, and the quartermaster, Corner. Anne, I am sorry to see that you are amazed . . . that you did not understand!" he cried with some incredulity. "Rackham was a pirate and the governor had to make an example of him and his entire crew. I believe half of what's left are scheduled to die tomorrow and the rest on the day after. How else to strike terror in the hearts of other pirates if not some gruesome end?"

Anne tried to tell herself that it would not serve to attack him, and a look at Mary's stricken, white face convinced her she was right. Instead of answering, she walked past to where Mary stood and took her hands.

"I am sorry about John, Mary. I know how much you still care for him."

Then she turned to O'Conner. "As you can see we are in mourning for the men we love. Perhaps it would be best if you returned at another time."

"Anne," and he took her elbow and moved away with her. "You are widowed now, and forgive me, but Rackham's death has naught to do with me. I ask you to consider the proposal of marriage I have offered. Think carefully, for your entire future depends on it. If you give your consent I will go quietly to the governor and ask for your pardon, and you will meet with him and explain that you are reformed and that you will never take ship again. That you have learned the error of your ways."

"And what if I don't think there are any errors in my ways?" she asked too evenly.

"Preposterous! I am sorry to have to mention it, but . . . you lived with a man who was not your lawful husband. I am willing to forgive that in you, and am offering you a chance for redemption. And the thieving, killing, swearing, drinking, why, errors, my dear, errors."

"Be careful, Philip, or you will talk yourself out of love." Anne eyed him with cold anger. "Tell me, just what is it you think you will get from my father if you marry me?" No sooner had she said the words, but she knew. "Why, of course. My dowry. All my father's formidable estate, the legal practice, ships of commerce, plantation and house in Charles Town. Why, Philip, you are more ambitious than I remember! Can you tell me how that makes you any different from Jack?"

And Anne laughed, for suddenly Jack was with her, amazingly, brilliantly with her. And she knew . . . he always would be.

"Let us be honest with each other. I will never suit you, for I will always be just as you see me here. I will wear the silk dress, but never feel as if I am wearing silk. I will never care about convention, or what someone else thinks of me. I will be my own person, make my own way, and no man will ever own me. Jack loved me with a fierce desire and put his life into mine. And because he wanted me, I followed him to the ends of the earth, because I wanted him in return. He outlawed himself when I faced a flogging, took ship and sailed, and he was ever in my arms. You will never know that kind of love, Philip, because you will never be able to give of yourself the way a man like Jack can. And I could never accept less. I'm sorry, but I will take my chances with the court and with Mary. My answer is no, I will not, not now, not ever, marry you."

When he had left, Mary turned to Anne and took her in her arms. "I 'eard 'im. Not even for my life could I 'ave asked that you marry a man like that. You made the right choice."

Ten days after Jack was hanged, the trial of the women commenced on November 28th. The occasion was even more attended than that of the men. As O'Conner had said, the two were an international scandal.

The walk from the gaol was a wonder. Anne looked not

to the throngs of people lining the street, but to the blue sky with its white puffs of clouds, and reveled in the feeling of the hot sun and clean air. All she could do is breathe over and over, for this air did not contain the smell of mold and damp, rotten food and chamber pot. Trees lined the streets, many in bursts of color, and for the first time since the beginning of this nightmare, she could have wept for all the beauty in the world. Suddenly, she wanted to live, to run the earth through her fingers, to look upon sunrise and sunset, to put something on her tongue that was fresh. But then, what good was the land or sea, food or drink, without Jack? She almost fell where she walked, for again she knew that life would never be whole, and the something missing would always be Jack at her side.

O'Conner had not taken the news of her rejection well, and here he was in the courtroom, his chair in the first row. His gaze accused her, appeared to say, I could have saved you and it is your own stubbornness that has brought you to this. Now Anne bowed her head in supposed humility, but rather, to hide her smile, for she realized that O'Conner considered himself quite the catch and would never understand why any woman would reject him unless she were addled.

Because O'Conner had said her father was on his way, she looked for William Cormac, wishing for his legal expertise, but he was not present. As she stood to gaze around the room, she finally noticed the crowd, and the noise and finger pointing was great. There were as many women as men seated on benches, and they shamelessly spoke behind their fans, never taking their eyes off Mary and herself. For a brief moment Anne envied them their silk and bright colors, but then thought the better of it. Rather to have had two short years with Jack, the freedom to come and go as she pleased, live as the equal of any man, know the physical pleasure of love without guilt, than wear all the silks of the East.

Just as for the crewmen, a great table formed a horseshoe and here were seated the esquires who would hear the evidence and pronounce sentence. Within minutes Governor Lawes took his place at the center of the high table. The murmuring in the room ceased and with a collective holding of breath, the crowd waited to hear the words he would speak. There was a great leaning forward so as not to miss a thing, for the happenings of this day would be repeated over and over again for many years to come. Governor Lawes himself seemed to pause and cast a long, discerning eye over the women, and to her embarrassment, Anne found that she blushed under his scrutiny. Not so Mary, for when Anne looked to her, she stood straight as the soldier she was, her chin up and looked the governor in the eye.

"Mister Pennant," the governor finally began, "will you take the oath directed by King William."

Edward Pennant, one of the commissioners, took the oath entitling him to act as prosecutor. The prisoners were brought to the bar and William Norris, the registrar, began a reading of the charges.

"Mary Read and Anne Bonny, alias Bonn, late of the Island of Providence, Spinsters . . ."

"We're done for now," Anne whispered to Mary, leaning toward her ear.

"Why say you?" Mary murmured, startled by this pronouncement.

"They've named us spinsters. A married woman cannot be prosecuted for a crime, since it must be assumed she cannot think on her own. Instead she takes her orders from her husband. They refuse to acknowledge that both you and I have been married. We stand on our own deeds."

"As it should be," Mary concluded.

The list of charges was the same as that of the men, and indeed, much like Jack, Anne thought their deeds overwhelming when strung together. Heard at the same time, the record said much to their guilt. But rather than feel ashamed, Anne felt a certain amount of pride in her accomplishment. That she be judged by these pompous, powdered men with as many grievances on their heads as she had upon hers, was indeed absurd. When asked at the conclusion of a long list of crimes against the subjects of His Majesty what they had to say, whether or not they were guilty of said piracies, robberies, and felonies, both Anne and Mary called out loudly, "Not Guilty".

Then the court began its list of witnesses and the first among them was Dorothy Thomas, the very woman Mary had tried to defend, but who had been left to the crew. Dorothy stood and told of her ordeal, but as in the trial of the crewmen, did not mention the rape, for certainly the evidence against the women was as damning as that cruel act, and she had no wish to damn herself in the process.

"I was on the north coast fishing in a canoa," Dorothy told the court, her voice hard and determined, "and there I was set upon by a sloop commanded by one Captain Jack Rackham, his name I later learned. The two women prisoners were on board wearing men's jackets and long trousers and handkerchiefs tied about their heads. Each held a machete and pistol in her hands and cursed and swore at the men. And when I was to be let go, they argued that the men should murther me to prevent me from coming against them."

At this, a murmur arose in the courtroom, and Anne was shamed, for indeed, it was true.

"And how did you know they were women if all others believed them to be men and if they wore men's clothing?"

"From the size of their breasts."

Again a low rumbling ran through the crowd and the eyes of the entire room looked toward the women and their breasts. Because both were pregnant and their breasts full, no one could deny the truth of their largeness. Anne's impulse was to be resentful of the scrutiny, but then thought the better of it, for here was penance, a small measure of return for the indignity Dorothy had suffered.

Thomas Spenlow was sworn and gave testimony that he had seen both women aboard Rackham's ship.

Two Frenchmen from one of the captured sloops stood

and were likewise sworn, and through an interpreter, told that they had been forced to ship with the *William* for several days until release. During that time they had seen the two prisoners at the bar on board, sometimes in men's clothing, sometimes in women's skirts. Anne had given out gunpowder to the gunners, nor did they appear to be kept, but remained aboard of their own free will and consent.

Thomas Dillon stood next to swear that the *William* had come upon him while lying at anchor in Dry Harbour, sending a shot across his bow. One Master Fetherston called out that they were English pirates and that they need not be afraid, for the crew would harm no man. Dillon went aboard, and there he saw the two women. Anne Bonny had a gun in her hand, and both women cursed and swore like the rest of the crew and were willing to take on any task on board.

After the witnesses had appeared, Governor Lawes turned to the women, "Have you any questions to ask of the witnesses or do you have any witnesses of your own?"

Both women said they did not. What was there to say? Who could they produce to attest to their innocence?

"Then remove the prisoners so that this commission may consider the evidence and render judgment."

It did not take long and soon the women were brought back into the courtroom to face the tribunal and hear the verdict. Anne found that her heart beat all the faster, but taking her cue from Mary, stood straight and her eyes did not waver from the face of the governor.

"You Mary Read and Anne Bonny, alias Bonn, have unanimously been found guilty of the charges leveled against you. Have you anything to say or offer, why sentence of death should not be passed upon you?"

And here Anne and Mary touched shoulder to shoulder as they had before in other battles, still wondering what those words meant and whether the men before them would sentence women to death. Anne shook her head in answer, for she did not trust her voice.

"Then you Mary Read and you Anne Bonny, alias Bonn, are to go from hence to the place from whence you came, and from thence to the place of execution, where you shall be both hang'd by the neck, 'til you are both dead. And God in His infinite mercy be merciful to both your souls."

A great gasp went round in the courtroom for it seemed an aberration that women should hang. O'Conner gave her a pitying, knowledgeable look that proclaimed this could have been avoided.

"Have you anything to add," the governor asked the women.

"Sir," Anne called to him, through the murmurings and general astonishment, "we plead our bellies."

"I beg your pardon."

The courtroom, shocked and wondering if they had heard correctly, was immediately still, O'Conner's face no longer smug, but bewildered.

"We are pregnant, sir, and our babes have already quickened."

Now the furor in the courtroom was such, that the governor was forced to use his gavel to establish order, and when quiet filled the room once more, asked, "Do you mean to say you are both with child? And have informed no one?"

"Aye, sir, that we are."

Stupefied, Lawes replied, "This court is adjourned until tomorrow . . . after a physical examination of the condition of the women."

Taking Mary's hand, Anne walked back to the prison, her head up, grateful all the world would know she carried Jack's child.

Chapter Thirty-one

The months passed with complete monotony in that vile place. Only the growth of the babes and the appearance of William Cormac served to mark the passage of time. With O'Conner's support withdrawn, much of the accommodation had ceased, only to return with William's arrival, but still, the food and filth was beyond bearing, especially for women heavy with child.

On the day of the first meeting with her father, Anne had steeled herself against facing him, had thought to be hard and keep her composure. But her father's face was so pitying, that she dissolved into tears, not for herself, but for him, that he should see her come to such a pass and feel the pain of it.

"How is my grandchild?" he said first, and for a long while Anne could not answer, for against this she had no defenses.

"Why, growing larger by the day, as ye can plainly see."

"Aye, and taking what he needs from you. Anne, Anne, you are so thin."

"'Tis true, and my hair, like brittle straw. But no matter. The babe can have it all."

Then they had stared at each other, neither of them knowing where to start or what to say. Finally William attempted, "I am saddened that you have come to such a pass. I tried to warn ye."

"That ye did, but 'tis you who put me here."

"Me!" William cried. "And how is that!"

"Because 'twas you who taught me that the world was unfair to the poor, that human injustice was not to be tolerated."

"But that did not mean ye were to go a'pirating! Mother of God, how you must have lived!"

"It had its moments of joy and sorrow, like any other life," she retorted quickly, her temper beginning to flare.

But William would not rise to the anger. "I'm sure you are right. For my own life has been the same. I'm told ye know about Cork and how your mother and I left."

"Born on the wrong side of the sheets, only in this case, silk sheets."

"T'were not silk when we left Ireland, Anne. Your mother and I worked hard for what we had. True, I had the skills to make a new life in Charles Town, and we played as hard as we worked. Why, I'd do it all again if I could. Not a day goes by that I do not miss her. But, then, I do not have to explain your mother's virtues to you." He paused. "This fellow. Jack. Different than the Bonny lad?"

"Aye. In every way. Handsome he was. And a captain. He knew the sea and his work and in another world could have commanded any ship of His Majesty's. He held the men's respect. And my own as well."

Wistfully, then, "But more, he thought me beautiful and loved me with all the passion of his soul. 'T'was for me that he died, for he would not leave me in New Providence to Bonny, but took a ship after his pardon and me with him. There were good moments, to be sure. And bad ones. The worst was losing our first son to swamp fever. Beautiful John. John William," and here she raised her eyes to him, "named after his father . . . and mine."

"Oh, lass . . ."

"I don't think either of us ever recovered. And after that, well, Jack became a bit more reckless, as if nothing else in life would ever be so painful. Looking back, I think he knew he would meet his end sooner than later and lived every minute that was given him. I . . . I do not know how I will face the world without him."

Then she laughed, "Well, to be sure, it seems I've not much time left to worry about it. After the birth, I'm done apparently. I have a mighty thing to ask of you. Will ye take the babe and make him your own grandson?"

"Ye know that I will," William said huskily. "But we'll have no talk of dyin'."

"Have ye a plan, then?"

"Aye, and one that involves O'Conner."

Anne's face hardened. "I'll not have that man to save my soul, more less my life."

"Is it about you anymore? Or shall the babe know his mother?"

"Do not ask this of me!" she cried.

"Would ye marry O'Conner if it meant that ye would protect the child?"

And here Anne looked to Mary who sat with her back to them, but listening to every word. Anne raised a hand in her direction. "I'll be goin' nowhere without Mary."

"Ye've not answered my question. Would ye marry O'Conner if you could save the child?"

"Oh . . . aye . . . to save Jack's child, I will do it. I'll do it though it tears me in two and I will never know a moment's happiness in this world."

William sighed. "Then ye will not have to. I needed to know if ye've learned anything of value . . . besides injustice. We can know the wrongs of the world, Anne, and fight against them. But there is the reality of those closest to you that is ever important, and sacrifices need be made through life." Here he paused and studied her. "I am not here alone."

"Whatever do you mean?"

"Henry Cavanaugh has come with me."

Anne gasped. "I will not see him!"

The arrangements to have Anne and Mary released from prison and the hangman's noose moved forward slowly. The sensation of the trial had to die down and the women fall into some obscurity, then plans needed to proceed, carefully, step by step. First, William challenged the suggestion that the women were spinsters, and the entire series of crimes was placed squarely on the shoulders of Jack Rackham and John Howell. The women were merely obeying the orders of their husbands, for common law marriage was recognized. In years soon to follow, this very loophole would cause

Parliament to enact a law stating that to be recognized, a legal marriage was between a man and woman sanctioned by church ceremony. As O'Conner had suggested, Anne and Mary were to meet the governor and discuss repentance and rehabilitation. The date for the meeting was set in the first weeks of April.

Three days before the appointed time, Anne woke to feel Mary's arm on hers and she jumped at the fire of her touch. The room was black, outlines of the walls only dimly lit from some distant moon.

"Mary, good God, what is it?" Anne cried, rising immediately and tending to her where she groveled on the floor.

"Something is terribly wrong," she moaned. "I am bleeding and heavily and certainly in labor. I am so sick . . . and I am frightened. Promise me ye'll take the child if anything happens t' me."

"Here, none of that," Anne answered calmly, although she was terrified.

"Promise me!"

In a soft voice, "It goes without saying."

"Aye, but I will have it said so that I can pass on without worry."

A single candle stub was still theirs, and Anne lit it, mindful of the straw.

"I am here and nothing will happen to you or the babe. Come. Can ye lie down?" she asked, desperately moving straw into a pile and noting how much of it was blood soaked already.

Mary rested on her hands and knees, her belly huge, her face contorted with pain. Without answer she shifted to the straw, lay on her side, legs drawn up in fetal position and gasped, holding her breath, and clinching her teeth until the contraction subsided.

Anne touched her brow, her ears, her arms, all like fire. There was no water for that was not due until morning.

"I'll get someone."

At the door she pounded loudly, the sounds reverberating in that room and in the hallway outside, but no answer came. She knew the guard would not be happy about waking to answer the call of a prisoner, and was probably drunk and passed out besides.

"Anne," Mary moaned. "Stay with me, for I fear the darkness and t' die alone."

In an instant Anne was by her side, taking up her hand, "Of course, I am here. Do not fear. I will not leave you . . . ever. You and I, we are one to the end, remember?"

"Aye, and the end is nigh. So stay with me."

"Do not be so bleak!" Anne cried. "Why morning must be near and the guard will come and with him the doctor."

"We've never lied to each other and we will not do so now. You've been through childbirth before and you know what 'appens is not right. I burn up. Oh, Anne, and with me the child!"

Anne felt her tense as a great contraction seized her body and all thought of talk was gone.

"I will rub your back and we shall get through this birth. It is never easy, but we will do it together, and when my turn comes, you will help me."

And so Anne rubbed and talked soothingly, yet with each contraction she noticed the pool of blood around Mary grow. Every so often she would rush to the door to pound in desperation, furious with the guard and her own ill planning, for surely she should have realized that both she and Mary were near and have begged some accommodation. She was frantic for water, for just a cup to put drops on Mary's tongue, and a little more for washing, knowing her hands were filthy and she could not attend to Mary to see how far along she was.

At some point toward morning, Anne knew she was losing her. Mary's great belly still rippled, but she was too weak to respond to even a pain so great. Anne took her hand, and when Mary gestured for her to come closer, laid an ear near her mouth.

"'Tis over," Mary whispered. "This life is over . . . and with it all suffering. I go t' my Edward, Anne, and I go without fear. Remember your promise. My child is yours."

Afterwards, and for a long while, Anne sat with her hand on Mary's belly and felt the hardness of it through each contraction, Mary no longer feeling a thing, her heart and soul already in some other place, only her body to catch up with the rest, and cursed for a dagger to cut the unborn child from its mother. Once again she tried to pound the door to beg for a knife to save the life of the child, but again there was no response.

Just as the glow of early sunrise filled the cell with dim light, Mary's body stilled and Anne cried out, devastated that there was no way to save the babe who would die as surely as its mother. In the light of morning she saw more clearly what candlelight had not shown, Mary's pallid face, pain still etched upon it, and more blood than could be imagined pooled about her waist. Anne leaned over to blow out the candle, took Mary's hand, and began to pray. And that is where the guard found her when he came with the porridge of the day.

The story of Mary's ordeal was brought to the governor with all the gruesome details, and His Excellency agreed that Anne could leave prison to go to her father's house for the birth since her time was imminent. Even though she was technically still under arrest, those involved in the case knew Anne would never go back to prison after the soft beds and food that would be given on the outside. From this time on, Anne understood that she was to fade from view, from memory, from scandal, and that what was to come next would be quietly done.

William thought it best to schedule her meeting with the governor whilst she was still heavy with child, all the more to play upon his sympathy. He cautioned her to keep her head down and her voice demure, to put away her anger, for Anne was filled with a consuming rage, believing that neither Mary nor her child should have died. In her fury she felt capable of saying anything. Only the thought that she might give Jack's child a chance for life tempered her actions, and swallowing her pride and what she wanted to say, she went with a pretended humility to act her part, her cheeks burning at the lie of it.

Once the governor agreed to the reprieve, Anne's body relaxed, and with it, the labor of her belly began. The ordeal was shorter than the first, but more intense, yet the sheets were clean, the midwife in attendance, and true to her own feelings, she delivered a boy that she held to her breast, and looked and looked into his face for Jack's features.

When two weeks had passed and she had eaten well, when her hair had been washed and her clothing clean and worn with some style, silk stockings on her legs and feet, shoes shined, only then did her father suggest that she meet with Henry Cavanaugh.

"Anne, we are to slip you away from Jamaica, and you are to go back to the mainland. We have your reprieve in writing. But you will return with a child and no ring on your finger. Henry would speak with you. Will you do that much for me? Talk with him?"

And so she did, but insisted that the babe be present so that he would know all of it, not only of her affair with Jack and the result, but that the child would be a part of her life forever.

She stood when he entered the room, the wee one in a cradle asleep at her feet. At first they only stared at each other. Four long years had passed and both had changed. Anne wondered what he could possibly think of her, whether he thought her old at twenty-one, but knew she still had some allure, that her skin was white after months of incarceration, that for a few weeks she had eaten well, slowly at first then with greater appetite. The maids of the house had seen to her hair and dress. Henry was not much different than she remembered, a few new lines around the eyes and mouth, but still in silk, gartered with powdered wig, diamond stick pin in his lapel, surely an extraordinary voice in the negotiations. Governor Lawes would have immediately recognized Henry as one of his own.

Anne was first to break the silence. "My Lord, it is a far distance for you to come. I am glad to see you." And she was.

"No longer a lord, Anne. The title does not suit in the Virginia back country."

She cocked her head to one side. "Then you have changed, for I was sure the last time we spoke, you wished the title for your first born son."

"'Tis true. I have changed."

"And ye have not married in all that time?"

"I could find no one who enchanted me as much as another I once asked."

Anne swept her gaze to the floor, then looked again into his eyes. "Please, Henry, let us sit and you can tell me why you have come."

Instead he went to one knee, and, without warning, Anne's heart rose in her throat that this brilliant man could still want her and that he could play the courtier knowing what she was and what she had done.

"Will you have me, Anne?" he asked. "Surely you know that is the only reason I am here."

Unexpectedly, she wanted to weep. A huge gasping sob filled her breast and choked her throat and she cried out against her will, "Oh, Henry, they killed him. They killed Jack. They killed my love and my heart with him." She dropped her face in her hands and thought surely he would go.

Instead, Henry was by her side, "I know you have lost someone you love and the pain of it must be unbearable. And in such circumstances. Will you let me try to make your life easier? I know you, Anne, and I know your strength. Why," and here he smiled, "the whole world knows of your strength. There's nary a pub or inn I can enter where I do not hear songs of you and Mary Read."

Anne looked up, her eyes tear-filled, her face wet, and asked, "'Tis true?"

"To be sure."

Her gaze drifted to the cradle, and she knelt to gently rock the bed. "I have a child."

"A bonnie lad," he answered kneeling beside her.

"Jack's child."

"I know. If you will permit, we will call him William John Henry Cavanaugh, a fine mouthful, true. William after your father, John after his own, and Henry after the father who will raise him. What say you, Anne? Will you have me?"

Momentarily speechless, unable to breathe at the scope of it all, Anne finally, slowly exhaled, still crying silently, but now, for all the goodness that still existed in the world.

"What will ye say to those who see that I am not a timid woman with half a brain? For in this I will not change. I will always be an equal partner."

"I want no less. And was it not you who once told me that this brave new world expects boldness, that a man is judged by what he is, what spirit he shows? The land I have bought is on the frontier, and here, truly, no one cares about the past, for everyone has a past."

"The land near Charles Town?"

"Too many who know . . . our respective families."

Something in Anne tore, for she knew that to accept Henry was to leave Jack behind. In her acquiescence, she would have to shift her love and loyalties to Henry and their entire future. Henry saw the indecision in her eyes and knew the source.

"We will marry in name, and when you are ready, we will consummate the marriage. When you are ready, Anne, do you understand? I know your ordeal, and I will have you take me only when you are ready to love with your heart."

"You . . . you will take me on such terms?"

And the threads that bound her to Jack frayed some bit more. What else could she do if she was to live at all? Young William needed a mother and father, and by all the saints, she would give him a future. Yes, she would. She would look into his face every day and love Jack through him.

"Your father has had your marriage to Bonny annulled, although we know not whether the man lives or has died. We will marry with a priest. Soon. Before we leave the island. That is, if you will have me?"

"I will, Henry. I will. And gladly. Just . . . just give me a little time."

"Will you kiss me?"

"Indeed," and Anne smiled, and the kiss although gentle and to seal their troth, caused her to remember another kiss in a buggy under a starry sky long ago.

"May I ask your father in? To tell him the news?"

"If I know him, he listens at the door."

Henry was half surprised to see that William did indeed wait in the next room. After offering his felicitations, he told them both, "I would be away soon, three days hence. I fear it would be best to make all possible haste before any further hindrance can beset us. Anne, the authorities, they are asking after Rackham's treasure. Something to cover the cost of the trials and compensation to be paid to the robbed, but in truth, a part for the pockets of the judges and gaolers. Have you any idea where it might be? The ship has been torn apart looking for it."

"It's always about the money isn't it? It's never about morality or justice. They want to line their own pockets while they hang pirates for wanting the same." She sighed. "No, no, I've no idea what happened to it."

William looked curiously into her face, moved past what she would not say.

"The marriage is for tomorrow, if you will."

She nodded. "All right."

"And Anne, one last thing, I will say it now and not again. When we leave the harbor . . . I am sorry . . . there is no way to avoid it . . . he's there . . . your Jack . . . or what's left of him. Don't look, lass. It will do you no good."

Part 7

Virginia

1721

Henry Cavanaugh

Chapter Thirty-two

The wagon rolled up to the house and there, Anne saw the home she would live in until the end of her days. What stood was only the shell of what it would become, for over time Henry would add to it until it was as grand an estate as that which he had left in the old country. At first it would take a Georgian flat façade, but they would learn that in summer, with the sun beating against the windows, the heat would be unbearable. Gradually long porches would be added around the entire house on both stories, graceful columns to hold them, trees planted for shade, gardens built with fountains, anything to bring relief from the intense temperatures of summer. Far into the future, many would come and walk the creaking wooden floors and pay to see the architecture created along this southern river. But today, on this late summer day, Anne had yet to take the house and plans to hand.

The dress she wore spoke to her station and the staff waited at the front door. Leaving Jamaica, she had promised herself never again to wear the breeches that had taken her into the world and given her the freedom to come and go and voice her opinion. This home and marriage were part of her reprieve, the bargain that gave young William a future. Here she would stay all her days, raising her children and the horses and playing her harpsichord. She would live with Henry and be a good wife to him, and yes, she would soon go to his bed, and they would enjoy each other. About this Philip O'Conner had been right. She was twenty-one years old and her desire would rise. What better man than Henry with whom to spend her days?

Henry watched her face. "Come along," he said jumping down. "I think you might like to explore."

Anne turned to look to the trees and the green meadows, all close to the river. At water's edge they would build a dock and her father would send his boats upriver to gather the crop Henry would plant.

"It's beautiful," she told him. "We shall be happy here."

A broad smile lit Henry's face as he lifted her from the wagon. "The staff waits to greet you. Afterwards, go and wander. Your father and I will see to the unloading. Will is asleep and you'll have a moment to yourself."

"Thank you, my dear, for all your kindnesses."

"Come," he said softly, and lifted a hand to touch her face.

William watched her walk toward the line of men and women at the front door, and came to stand at Henry's side. "Do ye think she'll be all right?"

"Aye, for she does love me, and it will be a love that grows steadily over time. Perhaps not the bright flare of her pirate, but a slow steady flame, to be sure, and one day, she will know she truly wants me."

Still William was worried. The Anne who'd returned to the Virginia Colony was not any Anne he had ever known, certainly not the Anne who was the subject of tavern songs, growing into her own legend, a hero of the common people. Even in St. Jago de la Vega before meeting with the governor, she'd showed determination and backbone, some fire. No, this woman who walked toward the staff, corseted and stylish, was a shell of her former self.

Upon leaving Jamaica he had sent her below decks until they'd cleared Kingston Harbour, for on no account had he wanted her to see Rackham's body, but she had known, and the farther away they'd sailed, the quieter she had become, as if her spirit had attached itself to the corpse, and with each passing league, had grown thin and stretched. He'd watched her on deck once they were at open sea, her easy gait and roll with the ship, kin to the bit of timber that carried them. Every so often she would look up to the sails, watch the crew at work, and William thought she might make some comment, but instead, had stood silent. Perhaps she had been thinking that Jack would have done things differently, that she might have done them differently. With some consternation, he made note that her eyes seldom left the horizon, nor did those of the watch, for the waters were still pirate-infested. Good God, what would Anne do if offered the chance to sail again under the black flag?

But the journey was uneventful, and he thought with mixed emotion that the waters were quiet primarily because men like Anne's Jack had been hanged. Gone also were Charles Vane, Edward Teach, Stede Bonnet, Benjamin Hornigold, and any number of other captains and all their crews. Hundreds of men hanged in a great attempt to rid the seas of piracy, to so terrorize men that they would look elsewhere for employment.

As a merchant trader, William understood what was at stake. England's very might, her glory and wealth, was bound in her ability to keep open the shipping lanes. Commercial ventures had to go unchallenged, and chief among them, he knew, was the African slave trade, black gold. The growing importance of the sugar, rum, and molasses industry of Jamaica to the British Empire was enormous, for the profit in sugar was large. From the mainland colonies came the cotton needed to supply England's new textile mills, as well as rice and the dye indigo. To produce the products required labor, and no white man would work the cane fields of Jamaica, the work brutal, men and women dying by the scores, or strain under a scorching southern sky picking cotton with bloody fingers, or stand in water from sunup to sundown to plant rice. A matter of patriotism, O'Conner had explained, conveniently forgetting his Irish roots. The slaves that were essential to the system had to be brought across the Atlantic in huge numbers, paid for by sugar and its products. Pirates not only interrupted the flow of the slave trade by stealing the gold, guns, and cheap textiles from England meant for their purchase, even attacking the forts where captured Africans were held, but in many cases the black men were released to a berth on a pirate ship where they had an equal share in the spoils. Chief among those who had harassed the African coast with his squadron of ships was Bartholomew Roberts, but he, too, had finally fallen, two hundred and fifty of his crew captured, fifty-two executed, their bodies gibbeted at intervals along the African coastline to warn pirates off. The rest had been branded with hot irons and sold into slavery to work the gold mines or the merchant ships of the Royal Dutch Company, all to die within a few months. The mass executions were having their effect.

"She'll be all right," Henry said again. "I understand she used to ride in breeches as a girl."

"True. Much to the horror of her governess."

"She swears she will never wear them again."

"Does she now?" And William regarded Henry closely, looking to understand his point.

"Give her a month and a good horse, and she'll put them on once more."

Anne walked away from the porch steps and took the path to the river that hastened to the sea, still attracted to water, to the clean sweep of it.

The ocean, never again would she see it, not even to go to Charles Town.

Along the broad bank, the water flowed smoothly, and she pictured the place where Henry would build his dock, then paused. A new sound reached her ears, a tinkling rush of water, different from the sound of the deep flow of the river.

To one side of the house she discovered a creek emptying into the greater waterway, and this she walked along, up into the woods, until she was totally on her own. Surrounded by trees and low brush, she found herself hidden from the world for just a little while, delighting in the solitude.

At its broadest point, the stream was some ten feet wide, with granite boulders strewn about its course, speaking volumes of different tones and great reverberations. Everywhere she looked, the water was different, its color depending on its depth, on its fall over rocks of differing shapes and sizes. From the height of the debris lining the water's edge, she knew that as the seasons came and went, the course would widen and retreat, now covering the boulders, now leaving them exposed, singing on its way to the sea, its song different at each turn.

Without doubt, she knew that here she would make her journey into the past and find comfort in the present, here visit with Jack and baby John, with Mary, relive the ships and inns and stories she had shared with those she loved. Some years, and the rocks and water would see little of her, others, and she would be there with more regularity seeking solitude, comfort, and peace. One day with certainty, she and Jack would be together again, but until that time, this place would be her refuge.

Searching, she found a path where she could climb down the steepened bank to the water's edge, and there she found the perfect granite rock on which to sit, listening to the water, the roar of it drowning out all other sound. As if in answer to a prayer, Jack was there, as real a presence as the pebbles along the bank, and she called aloud his name, felt the water carry it over rocks and to the river and away to the sea he loved, closed her eyes, saw that once again she stood on deck at his side, sailing before the wind into a glittering twilight of red and gold, Jack's head thrown back in laughter, his hands on the wheel, racing into destiny.

Afterword

In actual history, Anne Bonny and Mary Read were an international sensation after their arrests. To those of society, the women were shocking, scandalous. Newspaper articles were written by those with influence decrying both their sins and their violence. Their lives were placed prominently in Captain Charles Johnson's *A General History of Pirates*, 1724.

Yet to the underprivileged, Anne and Mary became heroic figures, symbols of an underclass that struggled against poverty in a world where those with wealth and power took the majority of the resources and comfort, leaving precious little for those of 'obscure' birth. Among the common people, stories were told and retold outlining their lives and the courage with which they met the overwhelming forces of the king. Songs and ballads were sung in taverns along the waterfronts of their boldness among men and at sea. Indeed, scholars have proposed that Anne may have been the model for Daniel Defoe's *Moll Flanders*, as well as the prototype for Eugene Delacroix's painting, *Liberty Leading the People*, 1830, today hanging in the Louvre, Paris.

Anne's fate is still a matter of conjecture, for although she was not hanged, she simply, quietly, disappeared from the records of Jamaica. Recently, some evidence has emerged to suggest that perhaps she was returned to the Carolinas and married an attorney acquaintance of her father, but whether this Anne of record is the Anne Bonny of legend, has yet to be proven.

Mary did indeed die in that terrible prison, some believe in childbirth, and is buried in St. Catherine's Cemetery in Spanish Town, the old capital of Jamaica.

Today, a visitor to the island may take a small boat

from Port Royal to view the spit of sandy beach known as Rackham's Cay, the place where Jack was hanged and left to molder in a cage.

Most of the other events of this story are true to history, yet scholars and researchers differ on many details. The portrayal of Stede Bonnet's escape from jail is a piece of literary license. One legend suggests he did escape as a woman. That it was Anne who actually helped by bringing him clothing is my own fiction, but the two would have known each other in New Providence and they did have much in common.

In the nineteenth and early twentieth centuries, the image of the radical female fell out of favor, replaced by one of docile mother and wife, images representing stability and the foundation of the family. The stories and songs about Anne and Mary faded. Not until the twentieth century with its social revolutions, did their story once again come to be of interest and intrigue. Some propose that Anne was a thrill seeker, violent, a thief; others that she truly represented the strivings of the underclass, and point to the legends and ballads that suggest her strength and defiance in the face of crushing authority. Regardless, there can be little doubt that Anne was a complex figure, a source of dialogue in our quest to determine the true nature of equality and freedom for men and women of all persuasions, a touchstone in our attempts to understand issues of poverty, class, prison, and the death penalty.

Suggestions for Further Reading

Black, Clinton. *Port Royal* (Kingston, Jamaica: Institute of Jamaica Publications Limited, 1970).

Breverton, Terry. *Admiral Sir Henry Morgan, King of the Buccaneers* (Gretna: Pelican Publishing Company, 2005).

Choundas, George. *The Pirate Primer, Mastering the Language of Swashbucklers and Rogues* (Cincinnati, Ohio: Writer's Digest Books, 2007).

Cordingly, David. *Under the Black Flag, The Romance and Reality of Life Among the Pirates* (New York: Harcourt Brace and Company, 1995).

Earle, Peter. *The Pirate Wars* (New York: St. Martin's Press, 2003).

Eastman, Tamara J. and Constance Bond. *The Pirate Trial of Anne Bonny and Mary Read* (Cambria Pines by the Sea, California: Fern Canyon Press, 2000).

Johnson, Charles, Captain. *A General History of the Robberies & Murders of the Most Notorious Pirates* (Guilford, Connecticut: The Lyons Press, 1998, originally published in two volumes, 1724-1728).

Kongstram, Angus. *The History of Pirates* (Gilford, Connecticut: The Lyons Press, 1999).

_________. *Pirates, Predators of the Seas* (New York: Skyhorse Publishing, 2007).

_________. *The Pirate Ship, 1660-1730* (New York: Osprey Publishing Ltd., 2003).

Lane, Kris, E. *Blood and Silver, A History of Piracy in the Caribbean and Central America* (Oxford: Signal Books, 1999).

Little, Benerson. *The Sea Rover's Practice* (Washington, D.C.: Potomac Book, Inc., 2005).

Marine Research Society. *The Pirates Own Handbook, Authentic Narratives of the Most Celebrated Sea Robbers* (New York: Dover Publications, Inc., 1993).

Sherry, Frank. *Raiders and Rebels, The Golden Age of Piracy* (Lincoln, Nevada, iUniverse.com. Inc., 1986).

The Tryals of Captain Jack Rackham and other pirates ... who were all condem'd for Piracy, at the Town of St. Jago de la Vega, in the Island of Jamaica, on Wednesday and Thursday the 16th and 17th Day of Nov. 1720. (Robert Baldwin, printer: Jamaica, 1721)

Tryals of Mary Read and Anne Bonny ... and several others who were condem'd for Piracy (Robert Baldwin, printer: Jamaica, 1721)

Rediker, Marcus. *Between the Devil and the Deep Blue Sea, Merchant Seamen, Pirates, and the Anglo-American Maritime World, 1700-1750* (New York: Cambridge University Press, 1987).

_________. *Villains of All Nations, Atlantic Pirates in the Golden Age* (Boston: Beacon Press, 2004).

Reading Group Conversations

1. While William and Peg are walking in the snow from the waterfall, he asks, 'Why me, Peg. Why did ye come to me?' Who is William? Given the various contradictions in his character, where do you believe the real William lies?

2. Amy Cormac, Williams wife in Cork, appears devoted to William in the story. Has William a right to put his wife aside for the 'hint of distant shores he has never traveled'? Amy appears concerned for their place in 'society'. Is this wrong? Or do Peg's beliefs in a cause to bring justice for Ireland make her a more appealing partner?

3. William Cormac has taught Anne the workings of field and barn, as well as given her shooting and fencing lessons. Peg, on the other hand, has shown her a smile from behind lowered lashes, and taught her aspects of compassion. Who do you believe has a greater influence on Anne's character and development, her father or mother?

4. Why do you believe Anne is attracted to Bonny? Why does she truly choose to leave Charles Town with him when her father offers her an annulment and the opportunity to have Henry Cavanaugh call?

5. Twice, Anne insists that Jack settle down to plantation life. Twice they both return to piracy. What is the true source of Jack's indecisiveness?

6. Why do William and Peg neglect to tell Anne that they are not married? They know 'society' well enough to realize the truth will eventually follow them from Ireland to the colony. Why would they chance rumor? Is not telling Anne a betrayal of sorts?

7. Anne and William have in common a strong, unconventional sense of social justice. But William tempers his choices to meet the demands of his business in the colony. When William arranges a marriage to Philip O'Conner, a slave owner, does Anne believe him to be hypocritical, especially given the fact that William lived his life for love?

8. Anne eloquently defends democracy aboard a pirate vessel. Do you believe pirates might have to rely on shipboard democracy since they have no force of law? That their egalitarian conventions aren't out of virtue, but necessity? How can the fact that pirates kill, maim, and steal be reconciled with democratic principles?

9. Historically, Anne does utter the famous line, 'If you had fought like a man, ye need not die like a dog.' How do you believe Anne feels at the moment she utters these words? How do you believe she remembers Jack after ten years, twenty-five, at the end of her life?

10. While she is in prison, Anne understands that 'true crime . . . [is] hunger and poverty and social systems that create . . . a class destined for the gaols, a system that [feeds] upon itself by giving birth to its own prison economy, nurturing a livelihood for those who appreciate . . . dominance'. What is the relationship of poverty to crime? Is rehabilitation more effective than punishment in reaching society's goals to reduce crime? Is so, what are some alternatives to incarceration?

11. Anne abhors the idea of slavery, '[o]n this one point both [William] and Anne absolutely agreed'. Do you believe Anne has slaves working the plantation once she and Henry settle down in Virginia?

PAMELA JOHNSON was born in New Orleans, Louisiana, migrating to Berkeley, California, in 1966. A Phi Beta Kappa graduate of UC Berkeley in Anthropology, she went on to earn Master's Degrees in Education and English. Actively involved in social and environmental issues, she views her writing as an extension of her politics. She is married with three children and currently divides her time between a ranch in the Sierra foothills of California and Ocho Rios, Jamaica. Look for her next book, *A Nation of Mystics,* to be released in 2009 through Stone Harbour Press.